FAST LANE ENTERTAINMENT PRESENTS

FAST LANE

SEX MONEY DRUGS MURDER AND MAYHEM
THE DRAMA NEVER ENDS IN THE *FAST LANE*

EYONE WILLIAMS

ISBN-13: 978-0-9836279-0-6
Library of Congress Control Number:

First Edition, June, 2011
Printed in the United States

Publisher's Note

This is a work of fiction. Any names historical events, real people, living and dead, or the locales are intended only to give the fiction a setting in historic reality. Other names, characters, places, businesses and incidents are either the product of the author's imagination or are used fictiously, and their resemblance, if any, to real life counterparts is entirely coincidental.

Fast Lane Entertainment
#245 4401-A Connecticut Ave
NW, Washington, DC 20008
Facebook.com/eyone.williams

This tale of the streets is dedicated to my Mother and Brother, whom lost their lives to the things that go on in the streets...

R.I.P.

Tawana D. Lattisaw

-N-

Markelle D. Wilson

...........my love remains true ....

Chapter One: Off the Porch

The summer sun was blazing down on the D.C. streets. Mann, as they called him, was leaned back in the driver's seat of his jet black 1988 Nissan 300ZX Turbo. He was speeding up 5th Street N.W., better known as "uptown" in the city. N.W.A.'s *Fuck Tha Police* was blasting out of the speakers as he turned the air condition up in the car. Mann was in deep thought about what he had to do before the day was out. He wanted to sell his last four ounces of coke in order to buy another "half of brick" of coke from his man, Silk.

Money seemed to come from everywhere that summer, and Mann was going to make sure that his pockets stayed stacked in "89". Making a quick left turn on 5th and Rittenhouse Street, Mann pulled into the alley behind Dee-Dee's house. Everybody was outside. Mann parked his car and as he was walking down the alley toward the crap game, he saw his cousin, Black, and his partner, Dre. Passing by Dee-Dee's backyard, he saw her, Kelley, and Metra sitting on the back porch.

Dee-Dee was a light skinned girl with a well-shaped body and a behind like a black tail broad. Her house was what you could call the hang out spot around the way. Her buddy, Kelley, was the best looking out of the bunch by far. She was the one that everybody thought was going somewhere in life. She had a thing for Mann, and it was clear to see by the way she smiled at him as he walked by. Metra was the youngest out of the crew at only fifteen. Being the youngest didn't mean a thing because she had been around and knew how to survive in the streets.

"Mann!" Standing up, Dee-Dee called Mann.

"What's up!" Mann said as Dee-Dee and Kelley walked up to him. Dee-Dee hugged Mann tightly and kissed him on the cheek. Kelley did the same, but she kissed Mann in the mouth.

"What's up? I know ya'll want something," Mann said, knowing something was up.

"We tryin' to use your wagon to hit the Metro Club tonight," Dee-Dee said with a smile. Thinking about it for a minute, Black and Dre came to mind. They went on a caper in the wagon the night before and it was no telling who was looking for it. Mann knew it wasn't safe to let the girls ride around like that.

"I can't let ya'll see the wagon, but I'ma see if Dre'll let ya'll push his joint," Mann said.

"Let us know before it gets too late," Dee-Dee said as her and Kelley walked away, swinging hips and thighs like only a broad out the hood could.

Mann went on down the alley to see what the dice were hitting for. Dre was down on one knee shooting the dice, surrounded by Black, Silk, Smoke, Serge, Onion, and Quick, the young gun of the hood. Dre was picking up his money as Mann walked up on the crap game; he had just struck Onion for five hundred dollars.

"What's up!" Dre said.

"Ain't shit. What the dice hittin' for?" Mann said.

"We shootin' some small shit," Dre said.

Mann threw twenty dollars on the ground, stepped on the money, and said, "Who fadin' me?" as he grabbed the dice.

His man, Silk, threw twenty dollars on the ground and said, "Shoot, young nigga!" Smoke and Serge were side betting with Silk against Black, who was betting with his cousin. Money went from hand to hand until Silk got a beep and had to leave.

Everybody was sitting on the hood of Mann's Z passing a blunt of Skunk weed back and forth. Black passed Quick the blunt. As the younger dude took a deep pull of the smoke, Mann said, "What your lil' ass doing smokin?"

Blowing a huge cloud of weed smoke into the hot summer air, Quick said, "I'm grown, nigga! I do what I want! Suckas do what they can!" Everybody burst out laughing.

Short, brown skinned with a wild afro and not a trace of hair on his face, Quick was before his time at twelve years old. He had been in the streets for a long time now. Living with his grandmother, Quick ran the streets going and coming as he pleased. His grandmother tried to lay law, but Quick was out of control and never listened, he chose the way he was going to live his young life. Quick and Mann's little brother, Lando, were partners. The only difference between Quick and Lando was that Quick came off the porch at nine years old while Lando was just getting into the streets. Quick's grandmother didn't have the money to get him the finer things in life, so Quick hit the streets and started hustlin' for his. In the process of running the streets with the big boys, Quick grew a love for the gun play, and that made him dangerous.

Stepping away from the crowd, Mann and Dre walked down the alley to talk about their next move. It was time for them to step it up in the streets, and the first move was to get a whole brick of coke from Silk now that they had the money to do it.

Black walked up behind them and tapped Mann on the shoulder, saying, "Slim! I gotta move out Maryland. Let me use the wagon, joe!"

"Who you takin' with you?" Mann asked, always concerned. He knew Black didn't have it all. Everything was done with the trigger of a pistol in his world.

"Smoke and Serge rollin' with me on the move. They know where the joint at," Black said.

"Watch yourself, joe," Mann said as he gave Black the keys to the wagon.

Dre headed for his baby's mother's house when he was done talking to Mann. Walking back down the alley to his car, Mann asked Quick if he wanted to go find Lando with him. Like always, Quick was down for whatever. Hopping in the Z, they flew out onto Rittenhouse Street. At the end of the block, they saw a lot of pipeheads in the alley. Mann slowed down and pulled into the alley to get rid of the last of his coke.

"Let me get some of them sells, young!" Quick said.

"Come on, shorty," Mann said as they hopped out and started serving pipeheads left and right. In minutes, Quick was sold out and back in the Z counting his money. Sliding his money into the pocket of his Guess jean shorts, Quick looked over at Mann through the car window. *That nigga getting paid!* Quick thought. It wouldn't be long before he would be making money like that, Quick told himself.

Tall, slim, and dark skinned, Mann was what the young women wanted in a man. At sixteen, Mann had the street sense of a nigga that had been in the game for years. When he was twelve, Mann hit the streets looking for the dollars. Mann met Silk through his older cousin, Dez, who got shot in the head during a drug deal that went bad. After killing the nigga that killed Dez, Mann was known for being a smooth killer when it was time to put that work in, but over all, Mann was about the dollars. From ten packs of heroin to fifty dollar bags of shake coke and now crack rock,. Mann always had whatever made dollars.

Snapping Quick out of his deep thought, Mann hopped back in the car with a hand full of cash. "You finished your shit?" Mann asked.

"Yeah, I'm done, joe. I'ma call Wee and re-up."

"You fuckin' with Wee, huh? That's alright," Mann said.

Lando rode up on Quick's red and white CR-80 dirt bike and said, "What's up with
y'all niggas?"

Mann turned to his little brother and said, "Ain't shit, shorty. Where you been?"

"I was up the Ave. looking for Baby-D. We suppose to go over some broad house he know."

"I'm 'bout to go get something to eat, you trying to go?"

"Yeah, meet me down Dee-Dee's house," Lando said as he let the clutch go and took off flying down the alley.

Jumping in the hatch back of the Z when Mann pulled up, Lando told Quick to pop something in the tape deck. Quick turned it on to see what was in there, making *Fuck Tha Police* hit the speakers as Mann whipped the speeding car out onto Georgia

Avenue. Looking back at Lando through the rear view mirror, Mann said, "What you want for your birthday?"

"I'm trying to get me a dirt bike," Lando said.

"I got that, shorty!" Mann said as he pulled into the McDonald's parking lot. Cutting the car off, Mann pulled his Browning 9mm from under the dashboard and slid it in his waistband as they got out.

As they walked in the door, Mann scoped the whole spot with one quick glance. Two cops were all the way in the back drinking coffee. Across from the pigs were Marvin, Ant, and Ric. They were from 13th Street; Mann went to Jr. high school with them a few years back.

Mann stepped in line to order his food, followed by Lando and Quick. Looking back at the 13th Street niggas, Quick tapped Mann on the shoulder and said, "Check them niggas out, joe."

Mann turned to look back at Marvin and his partners. They were acting funny. Most of the time they would speak when they saw Mann, but that time they just left like something was up. Mann thought about it for a minute and brushed it off after a while.

After getting their food and sitting down, Mann's beeper went off. It was Dre's code followed by #911. It had to be important, Mann thought, he had just seen Dre no more then an hour ago. Mann got up, telling Lando and Quick that he had to use the phone. Outside on the pay phone waiting for Dre to pick up on the other end, Mann wondered what could be wrong when a worried voice answered the phone.

"Hello?" Tina said.

"What's up, Tina? This Mann. Where Dre at?"

"Yeah!" Dre said into the phone, sounding angry.

"What's up, joe?" Mann said.

"Slim! Some niggas ran up in here while Tina and my son was in here sleep."

"Is they okay?"

"Yeah, they just a lil' shook up, joe."

"So, what the fuck went down?" Mann asked.

Dre put Mann down with what had happened. Tina told him she was in the bed sleep with Lil' Dre when she heard kicking on the back door. She got up to see what was wrong and before she could get out of the room, she saw two niggas in ski masks standing in her bedroom with pistols pointed at her. She screamed, waking Lil' Dre. One of the dudes grabbed her, smacked her in the face with a pistol, and slammed her to the floor. While Lil' Dre was screaming, the other dude snatched the phone cord out of the wall and tied Tina up with it. Leaving Lil' Dre on the bed screaming, they tore the apartment up looking for coke and money. They found fifteen thousand dollars, a .357 magnum, and sixty two grams of coke. When they were done, they ran out the back door. Tina got herself free and ran to the window crying, and saw a dark brown Nova roaring down the alley with two dudes in it. She couldn't tell who they were, but one was light skinned and the other was dark skinned. Tina had seen the exact same car a day before with 14th Street Tate in it, sitting in front of the apartment. He had to have some thing to do with the caper. Mann let Dre know that he would be over Tina's house right away with Black after he dropped Lando and Quick off down 5th Street, and hung up the phone.

Mann had that look of concern on his face as he drove back down 5th Street. He knew that beefin' always led to other things. Most of the time, somebody had to die and maybe even catch a body. However it went, it got in the way of making money, and Mann didn't like that at all.

Lando and Quick could tell that something was wrong with Mann, but they said nothing on the ride back. They knew he would tell them when the time was right. As the jet black 300ZX pulled up in front of Dee-Dee's house, Mann then let Quick and his little brother know that he had to take care of some business, and he would catch up with them later on. As they got out the car, Black walked up right in time, followed by Dee-Dee.

Black hopped in the passenger seat while Dee-Dee walked around to Mann's window. "What's wrong with you, boy!" Dee-Dee asked, seeing the look on Mann's face.

"Ain't shit. What's up?"

"Did you say somethin' to Dre about the car?" Dee-Dee asked. Mann had forgotten because h. e had something else on his mind. Shaking his head no, Mann said, "Somethin' jive came up, I ain't get a chance to holla at Dre." Turning to Black, Mann said, "Let Dee-Dee use your car 'til later on tonight."

Looking at Mann like he was crazy, Black said, "What!"

Dee-Dee cut in and said, "Come on, nigga, I'ma take care of your shit!"

Handing Dee-Dee the keys to his black '88 Acura Legend, Black said, "Don't let nothin' happen to my shit, girl!" Dee-Dee took the keys and walked off smiling. Mann began to tell Black about Tina's door getting kicked in as he slammed the Z in first gear and shot up Rittenhouse Street.

Kelley and Metra were laying on Dee-Dee's bed talking about Mann, listening to Rare Essence blasting out of the speakers on the wall. Dee-Dee walked in the room and said, "I got us a ride for the night!"

"That's right, girl! I'm 'bout to go get dressed!" Metra said as she got up and headed for her house across the street.

"Who car you got?" Kelley asked Dee-Dee once Metra was gone.

Walking over to the closet, Dee-Dee said, "Mann got Black to let me push his Acura for the night." Dee-Dee began to pick her clothes out for the night when the doorbell rang.

Downstairs, Kelley let Quick and Lando in, and said, "Where ya'll comin' from?" Sitting down on the sofa with Lando, Quick said, "Mann dropped us off a lil' while ago."

"Where he at?"

"You askin' too many questions. Who you work for?" Quick said.

Frowning up her face as she stormed up the steps, Kelley said, "You lil' muthafuckas think ya'll so grown!" Lando and Quick had to laugh.

Picking up the phone to call his cousin Wee-Wee, Quick pulled out a thick knot of cash and started counting it. Wee-Wee answered the phone and Quick began talking in codes about buying some more coke. After taking care of his business, Quick hung up the phone and asked Lando what he had to do. Lando let him know that he was chilling for the day.

"You trying to go downtown with me to pick this coke up from Wee?" Quick asked.

"Yeah, I'll roll with you. You think Wee'll sell me some coke?" Lando asked. Quick gave Lando a funny look, like he didn't believe what his man had just asked him. Quick knew Lando had no reason to hustle. His Aunt Pamila gave him everything he ever wanted, and Mann gave him everything else. "What you need some coke for, joe?" Quick asked.

"I want my own shit. I ain't gon' keep depending on Pamila and Mann to look out for me. Fuck that!" Lando said. Quick thought about what Lando had said for a minute and decided to go along with his man, even though he didn't believe Lando needed to hustle.

The darkness of night fall fell upon the city streets while Mann, Black, and Dre were riding through the streets in Mann's huge green station wagon with dark black tinted windows, making them unseen to the outside world. Dressed in black, wearing bulletproof vests, and strapped for war, the plan was laid down. They were to get into 14th Street Tate's grandmother's house and find out what he knew about the brown Nova that Tina had seen him in. After that, he was a dead man one way or another. Dre checked the clip of the old AK-47 that he had laying across his lap and asked if everyone was cool with the plan. No one objected, so it was game time and somebody would pay for Tina's door getting kicked in.

Lando walked in the house at ten fifty seven p.m. with four hundred dollars in his pocket. His first day of selling drugs was one that got him paid. *It was easy*, he thought. All he had to do was hang out on the block like he did everyday, and the money would come from nowhere. It was so simple, and in just one day, Lando felt as though he had the game mastered.

Aunt Pamila was in the kitchen drinking a glass of orange juice when he came in the front door of the three bedroom house that sat in the middle of 5th Street, no more than three blocks away from the drug strip where Lando had just took his first lesson on how to get paid.

Pamila was the sister of Mann and Lando's real mother, who passed away in '83. Since that day, Pamila was the only mother or father the two brothers ever knew. The love between Pamila and her kids was a strong one and when it came to raising two young black males in the city, it was a love that would have to stand the test of time. Nowadays, Mann was a man in Pamila's eyes, even though he was only sixteen. He did for himself and never needed anything. He had always been that way. Pamila only had to focus on her daughter, Tyesha, and Lando. Tyesha was only two years old and she was no problem. The only one Pamila had to worry about was Lando now that he was showing all the same signs Mann showed her when he first hit the streets.

Coming out of the kitchen, Pamila looked down at her watch and said, "It's eleven, I ain't seen you all day, boy. Where you been?" Lando knew that Pamila did not like for him to run the streets all day with out at least checking in with her to let her know what was up with him, but once he was out the door it was a whole different world on the streets.

Looking at Pamila, Lando said, "I been riding around with Quick on his dirt bike all day."

Walking pass Lando, Pamila went up the steps asking, "Where is you brother?"

"I think he went to take Dre somewhere, he should be home soon," Lando said.

"Well, if I don't see you before you leave the house tomorrow, happy birthday!" Pamila said as she headed for her bedroom.

The cool wind of the late night summer air was hitting Quick in the face as he stood up on his red and white dirt bike flying up 14th Street on his way home with a .38 revolver in his waist band, and a pocket full of drugs and money. Bending the corner on Summer Set Place, Quick switched gears and took the bike flying onto the sidewalk. The only sound in the air was the roar of the little bike while it picked up more speed as Quick went from gear to gear fearlessly. Coming to a stop at the corner of 13th Street, Quick looked up and down the street, and then let go of the clutch again, sending the bike high into the air as he shot down 13th Street at top speed under the street lights. Pulling up at the corner of 13th and Piney Branch Road, Quick leaned over on one leg as he came to a stop with a serious look of concern on his face.

Looking Quick dead in the face from across the street was two jump outs in a brown, unmarked Ford Crown Victoria. The cops could tell that Quick was no more than twelve or thirteen years old, and by the look in the eyes of the two young white boys, Quick knew he was going to have to show his skills on the bike if he planned on making it home.

The jump outs rushed Quick, almost hitting him with the car. With ease, Quick shot around the car and went flying down Rittenhouse Street and out onto Georgia Avenue. Pissed off and embarrassed, the jump outs made a quick U-turn and the chase was on. Flying down Georgia Avenue, Quick looked back to see where the pigs were. Right on his back, less than two car lengths away and gaining every second, Quick could feel the rush of adrenalin rapidly pumping through his body, and he loved the feeling. Wasting no time, Quick made his move. Swerving hard to his left at top speed, he shot up on the sidewalk. Looking down Georgia Avenue, he saw a Yellow Cab coming up the street in the far left lane. Swerving back out into the street in front of the speeding Crown Victoria with the Yellow cab coming head on, everything came down to a split second decision between life and death. In a flash, Quick made the amazing life threatening turn and cut right in front of the cab, escaping certain death by only ten feet feet or so. The jump outs didn't make it. Smashing head on into the cab and making a huge explosion of crashing metal and flying glass, the Crown Victoria sat in a heap of twisted metal in the middle of Georgia Avenue right in front of the 4th District Police Station. Quick looked over his shoulder while he kept flying down the street, and laughed at the deadly mess that he left behind.

      Black was just popping the clip in his .45 automatic as Mann pulled up in back of Tate's grandmother's house on 14th Street. Looking around to make sure no one was outside, they all slid on ski masks and walked up to the back of the house.

      After Black slipped into an open window and let everyone in the house through the back door, they crept downstairs to Tate's room in the basement. With their burners out they walked right up on Tate, who was asleep on a sofa in the basement. Black walked over and put Tate into a deadly headlock while placing the .45 to the side of his head. Waking up to an relentless choke hold, the first words Tate heard was Black hissing through clenched teeth in a menacing voice, saying, "Wake your bitch ass up! You know what time it is, nigga!" Tate couldn't believe what he saw. At 6'4" behind a ski mask holding an AK-47 was Dre. Right beside him was Mann, five inches shorter in a ski mask, but just as deadly holding a smoke gray MAC-10.

      Tate tried to talk, but he couldn't get a word out due to the choke hold Black had around his neck. Mann walked up and knelt down in front of Dre, calmly tapping his finger on the trigger of the MAC-10. Pure fear went through Tate's body at the sight of Mann's action. Mann could tell that he had Tate's attention.

      Smoothly rolling his ski mask up on his head like a skull cap, Mann said, "I ain't gon' play no games with you. I'ma ask you one time, and one time only. Whose brown Nova was you in the other day in front of Tina's house?" Black lightened up on the choke hold in order to let Tate talk.

Taking a deep breath, Tate said, "It was Marvin and Ant, they said they was supposed to be getting some coke from Dre. I wasn't with that shit, joe! For real!"

As soon as Tate was done telling on Marvin and Ant, Mann stood up and said, "Let's go." Black let go of Tate and walked around in front of him, pointing the .45 in his face. Tate looked up at the three young killers that stood in front of him with fear in his eyes. Balling up in a knot, he looked between his arms at Black, who was still pointing his pistol at him. He could almost feel the bullets slamming into his body before the gun even went off. Without a blink of the eye, Black pulled the trigger, sending two hollow point slugs into Tate's head. BOOM! BOOM! The sound of the powerful pistol shook the whole house before the killers ran for the car.

The night was a wild one in the city streets. Through all of the madness, Lando was at home in the bed sleep. It was eleven a.m. by the time he got out of the bed. The bright sunshine hit him right in the face as he wiped the sleep out of his eyes. He was had turned twelve years old,, yet, he felt no different then he did the day before. Lando wasted no time getting in the shower and getting dressed in a fresh red, white, and blue Polo short set, white Polo socks, and a pair of New Balance 995s. Going downstairs to get himself something to eat, he stopped dead in his tracks. In the middle of the living room floor was a shiny white Yamaha YZ-80 dirt bike with little red stickers on it that read *YZ*.

"Damn!" Lando said out loud as he ran over and jumped on the bike. *That nigga Mann always come through*, Lando thought. Lando had to go downstairs to holla at Mann about getting him the bike.

Downstairs, Mann was already up and dressed. Sitting on his bed reading the Metro section of the *Washington Post*, Mann wore a look of experience. In the Crime and Justice column, there were three killings in the city streets the night before. Only one concerned Mann, and that was the one that read Donell

Johnson, eighteen years of age from the 6700 block of 14th Street was found shot in the head twice in the basement of his home at approximately twelve a.m. There were no suspects or motives in the slaying. That was all Mann really wanted to see at the time, yet, he knew that things never stayed the same when murder was a part of the game. Even so, Mann was a thinker and he was sure that he would be able to think his way through whatever came his way.

Closing the newspaper, Mann saw Lando standing at the bottom of the basement steps and said, "What's up, shorty? You like the bike?"

"Yeah! I love it, young! I'm 'bout to go find Quick right now. Thanks, joe!" Lando said. Mann had made his day once again.

Chapter Two: Gunshots rang out

As the summer moved on, the days got much longer. With his new dirt bike, Lando was always on the go. Pamila would even have to send Mann to find him some nights. With school out, Mann knew what all that free time could lead to growing up in the city. Lando was a thinker, just like he was. If Lando saw a way to make it happen, he would. Lando had met a young girl by the name of Nakia that lived just across the city line in Silver Spring, MD. Nakia was a cute young girl with a lot going for her. Her family had money and she lived in a big house with just her mother, she was an only child. Whatever she wanted, she got. Over the past few weeks, her mother, Karen, had taken a quick liking to Lando. She had only two small problems with him. She didn't like him flying down the street with her daughter on the back of "that damn bike of his" as she put it, and she didn't like the little thug that he kept with him all the time. Quick always got a bum beef when it came to grown-ups. He was always in black, his pants were always hanging off his ass, and he kept a lot of cash. Other than that, Karen thought that Lando was a sweet boy.

Lando sat on his dirt bike in front of Nakia's house for about an hour kicking it with her. He was really digging her. He always got a good laugh when they were together. She thought she knew so much about the streets. Lando, on the other hand, thought she was still wet behind the ears. He was still young himself, but had seen a lot, and he was doing a lot more as the summer grew old. Him and Quick had started buying coke together from Wee-Wee. Mann knew nothing about it at the time, so for what it was worth, Lando was making a way for himself. While Lando and Nakia stood outside, Quick pulled up on his dirt bike.

"What's up, young? I knew I would catch you out here. Let's go around the way. Bring Nakia with you!" Quick said. He didn't like being away from the hood for long; it made him feel out of place. Lando thought about what he said and decided against it.

"Na, I'm 'bout to roll out, anyway, young," Lando said as he leaned over and kissed Nakia on the lips, sending a chill down her spine. "I'll holla at you a little later, okay?" Lando said.

She hugged him tightly, and said, "Call me when you get around the way." Lando kicked his bike to life and took off behind Quick, flying down the street while Nakia looked on.

Coke was moving like hot cakes. Mann and Dre had been making a killing for the last few weeks, even with the beef still in the air. Black had seen Ant and Marvin coming out of Marvin's baby mother's house and bust shots at 'em, but they got away. Since then they hadn't seen them niggas, and Mann wasn't taking the situation light at all. He knew they would resurface. They had to, their money wasn't long enough to stay low-key too long, and when they did, it would be time to put an end to the situation once and for all.

The air condition was pumping hard in Dre's white Nissan Maxima. Blunt smoke filled the air as they cruised up 5th Street. Mann leaned back in the passenger seat nodding his head to the music. Rare Essence was blasting out of the huge speakers that surrounded the car. Black laid in the back seat puffing on the blunt with a .44 revolver on his lap. Dre was trying his best to catch up with the black Nissan Pathfinder ahead of them. It was two bad ass females in the truck, and Dre had his mind set on meeting them. As Black raised up to pass Mann the blunt, Quick and Lando went flying by on their bikes. Everybody's head turned for a second as they went by. Mann laughed as he took a deep pull on the slow burning blunt. Letting out a cloud of gray smoke, he said, "Lando think he slick. Him and Quick bad ass been buying coke from Wee."

"How you know that?" Dre said.

"I went down 7th Street yesterday to pick that shit up from Silk and Wee put me on point. I know shorty gon' do his thing, and I ain't gon' get in his way, but I ain't gon' let 'em make the mistakes we made coming up. I been meaning to pull up on 'em about that shit but he stay gone on that bike all day, plus, he in love with some little girl out Maryland, so it's been hard to catch 'em."

Black burst out laughing and said, "Shorty tryin' to get his dick wet!" Everybody else burst out laughing. Mann's beeper went off. It was Corey's code "500". Mann knew what he wanted. Corey was buying ounces from Mann damn near twice a day so that was at least a quick eight hundred dollars. Mann said, "It gotta be pumpin' around the way, joe. That nigga Corey just hit me on the box for the second time today for an O."

Black couldn't stand Corey for some reason. He didn't know why. "That nigga getting' money now, huh?" Black asked. Mann and Dre looked at each other with smiles, knowing what was on Black's mind. Only a year younger than them, Black was far more aggressive when it came to the gun play. He had always been that way. When he was twelve years old he had shot a nigga dead in broad daylight for running off with Mann's coke, and he got away clean. Since then, it was like he couldn't put his pistol down.

Mann looked back at Black and said, "Leave that man alone, joe. You gettin' more cash than he is and you ain't even out there everyday. You need to slow down and flip some of that shit you keep stickin' niggas for. You making too many niggas scared of you. That ain't good, slim. No bullshit!"

Black wasn't trying to hear none of that, he responded with a, "Yeah, whatever. You always protecting them punks!"

Finally, Dre caught up with the Pathfinder. Pulling up beside it, he rolled down his window, letting out a huge cloud of smoke, and said "Hi, how you doing, miss?"

Niggas were everywhere when Dre pulled up in the alley. They all got out the car and quickly mixed in. Onion and Corey were sitting on a small brick wall that surrounded the fence at the beginning of the alley.

"What's up, joe?" they said at the same time when they seen Mann coming out of the alley.

"Ain't shit!" he responded as he gave them five.

Onion and Corey were jive like partners. They were always together, but inside, they didn't trust each other at all. The thing that kept them close was that they trusted everybody else around the way even less. Mann and Corey stepped off together to take care of their business, and Onion spotted a pipehead coming down the alley and rushed the sale. Dre and Black had headed straight for Dee-Dee's porch. All the young niggas were in front of her house. Black stepped straight to Lil' Garvin and threw his hands up.

"What's up, sucka ass nigga!" he joked as they started slap boxing. Lil' Garvin and Quick were running neck to neck when it came down to who stayed in the most shit. Lil' Garvin had just got home from Oak Hill's Juvenile Detention Center days ago for assault with intent to kill. Him and Quick had robbed some college niggas at a Howard University football game last fall. The niggas bucked and they let 'em have it. Quick, living up to his name, got away when the Feds came. Lil' Garvin got away as well, but a hot ass bitch saw his car leaving after the shooting and ran her mouth. The Feds caught him days later in the alley hustling behind Dee-Dee's house. When questioned about the shooting and who was with him, Lil' Garvin ain't say shit, he played by the rules of the game.

"Damn, joe! You got big as shit, shortie!" Dre said as he stepped between Black and Lil' Garvin, and hugged him.

Everybody was happy to see shorty home. "Quick and Lando seen you yet?" Dre asked.

"Na, I ain't seen them niggas yet. I only been out for a week now. They got me in a group home around the corner from my house. I'm on a weekend pass, I gotta be back tomorrow night by nine," Lil' Garvin said.

"You got some money?" Black asked.

"Na, get me, joe! They say you and Mann doing ya'll thing!"

Black cut Lil' Garvin off saying, "Shit, it's more like Dre and Mann doing they thing. I'm livin' by the trigga!" Everybody burst out laughing as Black and Dre pulled knots of cash out of their pockets and hit Lil' Garvin off. Mann was coming through the cut when he heard the laughter.

"What's up, young nigga!" Mann said when he saw Lil' Garvin.

"Ain't shit, young! What's up!" Lil' Garvin said as he hugged Mann. Mann had always dug shorty's style. Now that he had gone down on a beef and kept his mouth shut, Mann dug his style even more.

"Where your brother at?" Mann said.

"He down 9th Street. He took me shopping this morning."

"Tell that nigga, Dex, I said come holla at me."

"Cool, I got that," Lil' Garvin said.

They all sat on Dee-Dee's porch and kicked it until everybody went their own way. As they left, Mann got Lil' Garvin to hang out with them.

The evening sun was setting, leaving a beautiful orange glow in the sky. Pamila and Tyesha were just coming home from the mall. She carried Tyesha up stairs and laid her in the bed. A long day of shopping always put her to sleep. Coming out of Tyesha's room, she wondered where Lando could be. It seemed like he was only in the house when he was sleep nowadays. Pamila opened the door to his room, walked in, and sat on his bed. She began to think deeply about Mann and Lando. Lando was growing up over night at twelve years old. Mann was the same age when she started finding drugs tucked in clean socks. Pamila got up and started to look through his drawers, but there was nothing. Something inside of her soul was inspiring her to keep looking. She looked under the bed, went through all his pockets, and all of his shoes. Nothing was to be found. Pamila started to walk for the door, still feeling like she was overlooking something in Lando's room that would explain why he was never around anymore. Right before she was out of the door, she looked over at Lando's stereo. She walked over and picked it up, and. looked straight in the battery compartment. Inside was a small plastic bag with a rubber band around it. Pamila pulled the rubber band off and opened the bag. There was a rack of small white rocks in tiny bags. Her fears were true. Lando was going down the same road as his father, and his brother. Pamila was going to do something fast. She took the coke and flushed it down the toilet. Pamila picked up the phone and beeped Mann,. she knew she would need his help with this, then she went and laid down. She was a very strong woman, but she didn't know where to start with this one. She had run Mann away when she went off and started throwing shit at him in the same situation just four years ago. She didn't want things to go that way with Lando, but even so, she was going to lay law one way or another.

Mann got the beep and told Dre to pull over at the gas station.

"Hello?" Pamila said in a voice of concern. Mann knew something was up. He hated being in suspense about anything.

"What's wrong?" he said. Pamila went on to tell him how she found the coke in Lando's room, and that she wanted Mann to find Lando and bring him home. Mann hung up the phone and went to find his little brother.

Dre dropped Mann off at his car. Mann was floating through the hood. He bent the corner on 5th and Rittenhouse Street, noticing it was dark. Mann knew that everyone was in the cuts since it was dark outside. Pulling up in front of Dee-Dee's house, he saw Kelley sitting on the porch with Metra. Mann rolled down his window and called Kelley. Walking up to the car in a white Polo t-shirt and a pair of tight blue Guess jeans, Kelley said, "What's up, boo?"

"Ain't shit," Mann said and continued. "You seen Lando or Quick?"

Kelley looked up and down the street, and said, "I heard them damn bikes out back a few minutes ago."

"I'm jive on a move right now, but I'ma call you later on. Okay?" Mann said before pulling off. Around back, Mann got out in the dark alley.

Baby D was the first to see him. "What's up, young?"

"Ain't shit, D. Where Lando?" Mann asked.

Lando was leaning on the fence that separated the two yards that the cut was between when he heard Mann. Coming out of the cut, he saw Mann and asked, "What's up, Mann?"

"Pamila want you. She found that shit."

"What shit?" Lando shot back. Mann wasn't about to play police, he already knew what was up.

"You know what shit I'm talkin' 'bout, joe. Let's go see what she got to say." Mann and Lando hopped in the Z and rolled out.

Marvin was sitting in Ant's green Dodge station wagon blowing the horn in back of his apartment building. Ant came to the window and said, "I'm coming, young, stop making all that noise!"

Marvin was picking Ant up from his house on 13th Street, they had a lot to talk about. Ant had been locked up ever since the day Black had shot at him and Marvin in front of Marvin's baby mother's house. Ant and Marvin went back down 5th Street, but the jump outs had got on their backs. They both got out and started running. Ant got caught in the alley leading to Georgia Avenue with a Tec-9. He had just made bond last Friday, thanks to Marvin. Marvin had been laying low waiting for Ant to get out so they could take care of their business. Now that Ant was home, it was time to see if Mann and them could stand the pain.

"What's up?" Ant said as he jumped in the wagon with a lit blunt in his mouth. Marvin pulled out of the alley and began to put Ant down with what was up as they passed the blunt back and forth on their way down 14th Street. Marvin let Ant know that he had got word that Dre and Mann knew they ran up in Tina's house. He let him know that they killed Tate for showing them where the spot was. After putting two and two together, he let Ant know that Black had bust at them for that very reason. Ant leaned back in the darkness of the tinted windows and took in all that his partner had said.

When Marvin was done talking, Ant looked over at him with his blood shot eyes, and said in a Scarface / Tony Montana voice, "They wanna play rough! Okay! We play rough!"

While Pamila was re-enforcing the law of her house, Lando's mind was somewhere else. Mann had heard what Pamila was saying far too many times. "Do you hear me talkin', boy!" Pamila yelled, and went on to say, "I'm not going to let you throw your life away with that bullshit out there! You don't have to be out there selling that shit. Do you hear me?"

"Yeah, I hear you!" Lando yelled out of frustration.

Pamila walked up and got right in his face, yelling, "Well, if you hear me, then don't bring that shit in my house no more! Do you understand!"

Lando got up from the dining room table saying, "Yeah, I understand!" and went up to his room, leaving Mann downstairs to deal with Pamila's wrath alone. Mann stood leaning on the dining room wall, looking at the floor with his arms folded. With tears in her eyes sitting at the dining room table, Pamila looked over at Mann and said in a shaky voice, "You gotta talk to him for me, Mann. He'll listen to you, Mann. Don't let him get caught up in that bullshit. Do that for me."

Knowing that Pamila was right, he agreed. Deep inside, Mann knew he was going to have to step in. He also knew that if Lando was going to hustle, the only person that could tell him anything would be his big brother. Mann thought back to when he was going through the same shit with Pamila. In the end, he still did what he wanted to do. *Shit...it even got me paid*, he thought.

Quick and Lando were flying up Georgia Avenue, dangerously swerving in and out of the evening rush hour traffic. Lil' Garvin was on the back of Quick's bike. They were on their way back uptown from taking Lil' Garvin to take his weekly piss test at the court building. Their plan was to get him down the court building and back around the way as fast as possible so that he could get some pussy before they took him back to the group home. Mann had convinced Lil' Garvin not to run from the group home since all he had left to do was a month. He would be out by the end of the summer. Lil' Garvin was cool with it. Between Mann, Dre, and Black, he always went back to the group home with at least fifteen hundred dollars tucked in his underwear.

Lando wasted no time shooting over to Nakia's house after dropping his man off over Metra's house for some quick pussy. Quick decided to hang around the way until it was time to take Lil' Garvin back to the group home. Laid out on Nakia's bed watching T.V., Lando finally slowed down for a second. He had been moving one hundred miles per hour all summer, and to him, the quick forty five hundred dollars he had hustled up was worth it. The long lecture that Pamila had given him days ago was old news, and the more Mann tried to keep the big brother watchful eye on him, the more he was determined to prove his manhood by being able to hold his own. There was no love lost between the two brothers. In fact, the whole thing seemed to bring a new understanding between them. Mann began to see, with a new light, how much Lando was like him when it came to growing up in the fast lane. Already, Lando was about the dollars, and not the name. On the other hand, Lando understood why Mann got money and kept it. Mann never played big like Dre, buying car after car, and spending Gs on women and clothes. Early on in the game, Lando was saving his cash, just like Mann. Everything he did in the game was modeled after Mann sub-consciously.

Nakia walked into the room wearing a pair of cut off Polo shorts displaying her thick, young thighs, and an oversized black Madness T-shirt tucked in. She was a cute brown-skinned girl with her features of womanhood already developed in the right places. Lando couldn't take his eyes off of her body when she came into the room. She walked over and kissed Lando on the lips as she lay down on the bed beside him.

"What's up, boo?" she said as Lando took her into his arms and rolled over on top of her. They began to kiss passionately, rolling over and over in the bed. Lando's hands were everywhere. He began to try to unbutton her shorts, but each time she would quickly grab his hand and softly say, "No don't." After a few more tries, Lando had Nakia down to just her bra and panties. He started to take his pants down when she stood up and said, "I can't." Lando rolled over and sat on the edge of the bed in front of her.

"You can't what, boo?" he gently said as he softly grabbed both of her hands and pulled her closer to him.

"I'm not ready for this, Lando." Nakia stopped and looked away from him, and went on to say, "I want to wait awhile. I don't want to be some freak you hit and forget." Her eyes were beginning to fill with tears, but she quickly wiped them dry, not wanting Lando to look at her as a little girl.

Lando flashed her a quick "take it easy" smile, and said as he stood up and hugged her tightly, "Don't cry. We can wait as long as you want to, boo. I ain't in no rush. I plan on being yours for a long time. You hear me?"

Nakia felt the realness in his words as she hugged him back, and said, "Thank you for understanding. I love you." Nakia kissed Lando and put her clothes back on.

It was just getting dark outside; everybody was chilling in front of Dee-Dee's house. She was sitting on Onion's lap talking to Kelly and Metra, who were also sitting out on the porch with them. Mann, Dre, and Black were all sitting right in front of them on the steps leading to the sidewalk. Chained to the fence that separated Dee-Dee's yard from old lady Mrs. Barns' yard was Quick's vicious black pit bull, Killa. The dog had earned the name by killing a much bigger pit when she was four months old. Along the side of the porc, in the darkness of the cut that ran to the alley behind Dee-Dee's house were Quick, Baby D, Smoke, Serge, and Corey. They stood lined up along the brick wall of the porch, passing two weed-packed Backwoods back and forth.

A dark blue Buick of some kind bent the corner and was slowly rolling up Rittenhouse Street. There were dark, black-tinted windows all the way around the car. No one could see who was in the car, or knew right off hand whose car it was that was pulling up on them in the darkness. Black, being the first to peep the bucket bend the corner, reached under his T-shirt and tightly gripped the .44 magnum he had tucked in his waist band.

"Who the fuck is this?" he said excitedly, standing up and walking out toward the sidewalk with the huge magnum in open display. Mann and Dre did the same. Dee-Dee hopped off of Onion and started walking quickly to the front door, followed by Kelly and Metra. Onion stood up and snatched a Glock from under his T-shirt, and walked down to the sidewalk with Black and them. The pit bull sensed something was wrong and began to growl. Quick and everyone else poured out of the cut and into Dee-Dee's front yard with pistols in hand. Truthfully speaking, Dee-Dee had a small army of thug niggas in black in her front yard.

About two houses away from Dee-Dee's house the car suddenly slammed on brakes, making the tires scream. The passenger side window slowly came down. Somebody yelled out of the window, "Hold! Hold! This Dex, joe!" Black recognized the voice and put his pistol up. It was Lil' Garvin's big brother. Everybody put their shit up as the car pulled up. Mann and Black walked up to the car laughing.

"You almost got this joint lit up, young!" Black said to Dex, reaching out to give him five.

"Yeah, I see ya'll on point. I like that," Dex said, and looked over at Mann continuing. "What's up, joe?" Looking up and down the street, Mann leaned against the double-parked car.

"Ain't too much going on, slim. A nigga trying to get this money, 'cause I ain't gon' be out here slangin' this shit for the rest of my life, joe. I'ma get me a store or a car lot or something," Mann said.

"I feel you, slim. If I can get my hands on enough loot, I'ma do the same thing, joe, but for right now I gotta do my thing," Dex said. They went on catching up on old times until Silk pulled up next to the car on the other side of the street. Mann told Dex that he would catch up with him, and got in the black Benz .190 with Silk. They pulled off and parked a few spaces down the street.

Silk had been around for a while, and he didn't trust a lot of people. Mann knew how to keep his mouth shut, and Silk learned that long ago. That was one of the reasons why he loved dealing with him. Knowing that Mann knew where his ass was in the streets, Silk knew to come to him when he needed a hand. Silk had a move to cop twenty bricks of raw coke from a New Yorker that he had met in Atlantic City at the Mike Tyson fight, but he was going to cop two first to see what he was dealing with. The only thing was that he didn't trust the bamma. Therefore, he wanted Mann to go along for his brains, but he also wanted Black to go, as well, for the muscle. Silk was hip to Black. He had been hearing his name in the streets for a while now. Black was just a little too wild for him to deal with on a one on one kind of time. Deep in his heart, Silk thought Black would try him and if he did, Silk would have to get his head hit. So, to avoid something like that from ever going down, he always dealt with Black through the security of Mann.

While Silk was laying the spill on Mann about the move, the street started to get a little too busy for that time of night. Cars seemed to keep going back and forth. Mann glanced back over his shoulder to see what was going on in front of Dee-Dee's house. Everything was the same. Dex and his 9th Street partners were still double parked in front of the house. Dre and Black were leaning against the car kicking it, and Quick along with everybody else was still in the cut along the side of the house. Only now, Quick had unchained Killa and was holding her by it. Mann and Silk went on talking, and suddenly, they both jumped. POW! POW! Gunshots rang out, again another POW! POW! followed by a BOOM! BOOM! Shots filled the air non-stop for a second. Silk and Mann looked back after pulling their pistols and saw a white Ford LTD right beside the Buick Dex was in with a flame of automatic gunfire jumping out of both cars. Somehow, the Buick went flying up the street with the tires smoking. Quick, Baby D, Smoke, Serge, and Corey ran out into the street busting. Off of Dee-Dee's porch, Onion did the same until his Glock stopped. The LTD was desperately trying to escape the hail of gunfire that was coming its way non-stop, from what seemed to be everywhere. Miraculously, the LTD made it to 5th Street and bent the corner in a flash of light. When the shooting was over, Silk and Mann slowly raised their heads. They were in a bad position. It was too many bullets flying in their direction for them to do anything but get low. Looking once more, they saw the street was empty. Quick and everybody else had bloomed through the cut to avoid the Feds when they came. Out of all the shooting, no one was hit that ran with Quick and the rest of the niggas around the way, but they would have to check on Dex and the niggas in the car with him. Silk was pissed off, to say the least. He looked at Mann with murder in his eyes and a .50 cal Desert Eagle in his hand, and said in a most concerned voice, "What the fuck goin' on around here!"

"I don't know who the fuck that was, slim! But, you can bet I'ma find out real quick!" Mann said as he slid his Browning 9mm between his waistband. Silk started up the Benz, and him and Mann got ghost before the strip was crawling with police.

Chapter Three: Armed & Dangerous

Dre, Black, and Quick were all sitting on the sofa in Mann's room in the basement, telling Lando what had just went down around the way. Everybody had some idea of who could have been in the white LTD, but no one knew for sure. Black swore it had to be Marvin and Ant. They were the only people he could see that would have a reason to come through busting like that. Dre thought the same, but he had doubts. Quick really could care less, he just wanted somebody to put the blame on so that he could vent his anger quickly. Mann came down the steps with Silk.

Looking at Dre, he said "What the fuck is up, young!"

Before Dre could answer, Black stood up and said, "I'ma tell you what's up! Them 13th Street niggas tried to catch a nigga slippin'!" The open conversation continued as Black went to call a number back that kept coming on his beeper back to back 911.

"Hello!" an angry voice spit into the phone from the other end.

"Yeah, this Black, who this!"

"This Dex, joe! Where you at?"

"I'm over Mann's house. You alright?"

"Yeah, I'm cool, my man Doo-Doo got grazed on the arm. We tryin' to put that work straight in. What's up? Who the fuck was that?"

"I think it was them 13th Street niggas, we jive got something going on with them niggas right now, but I ain't sure, slim." Black finished rapping to Dex and walked back over to see what everybody was trying to do. It was going down.

They were going to take a trip up to 13th Street, even though Mann insisted that if it was Marvin and Ant that they wouldn't be outside. Even so, everybody was headed for the door, even Quick. Lando stood up feeling left out and said, "I'm tryin' to go, too!"

Everyone stopped for a second and left that up to Mann. In his eyes, hustling was one thing, but killing was something all together different. Mann was going to let shorty grow up, but he wasn't about to take his little brother on a move like that with them. Besides that, Lando didn't even have a pistol yet, which meant that one of them would have to give him one, and Mann wasn't having that at all.

Mann turned to Lando with a look of seriousness never seen before, and said, "Hell no! You ain't going! You can get mad as you want, but you ain't going!"

As Mann jogged up the steps behind the crowd, Lando kicked an old pair of shoes against the basement wall. "Shit!" he exhaled. Out of all of the hustling he had been doing the summer, he never thought to buy a pistol of his own, being as though Quick kept a huge .38 revolver with him all the time. That wasn't good enough anymore, due to that very situation. It wouldn't have been so bad if he didn't see Quick roll. That alone, made Lando feel left out. After that night, he was sure that he would never be left out again.

The tail-lights of Silk's .190 were swinging around the corner at the end of the dark alley behind Mann's house as he was leaving. Black had beeped his man, Smoke, and told him to pick everybody up behind Mann's house. Smoke and Serge had pulled up in a huge, family sized Ram van with a sliding door. They were ready to roll. Being only a year younger than Black, they had met him way back in the third grade when they all went to school together down the street from Black's mother's house on Maryland Avenue N.E.. Black had stayed back that year and they clicked off the top. Smoke and Serge always had a caper, even back then. They started breaking into houses down Georgetown and in Rock Creek Park in the early eighties. As crack and gun play grew prevalent later on, they stepped it up with the times in the fast lane. Everybody hopped into the van with a small arsenal of murder metal from AK-47s, AR-15s, Mann's Mac-10, all the way down to Quick's .38. Smoke gave Mann the wheel since he was the best driver. He had never been caught by the law behind the wheel of anything, and he never crashed, either. Swiftly, yet, always on point, they made their way up 13th Street. Mann had put the plan together. He would drive through one time to see what they were working with, then pull around 14th Street, park, and creep on 'em from behind. Mann knew everyone would be beside the middle apartment building in the shadows of the cut that led to the alleys. They would come through that very cut blazing.

Carefully, Mann pulled on to Georgia Avenue, watching everything closely. They were riding too dirty for any slipping. It was too much heat on board for the police to pull them over. It would be none of that. Mann let everybody know that they were going to bust first if the Feds got on their back. Turning on to Ft. Stevens Drive, they could see flashing sirens and police cars everywhere on 13th Street. Yellow *Do Not Cross* tape was surrounding an area right in front of the cut where the niggas hustle. Two white homicide detectives were inside of the taped-off area. One was taking pictures of the body. The other one was writing down information about the shooting that had just taken place on a small note pad. An old, black woman in a nightgown and bedroom slippers was pointing in the direction that the car had went after the shooting. Mann would later find out through Black, that Dex and Doo-Doo had put the work in and killed a nigga that ran with Marvin and Ant named Dirty. He was serving a pipehead out on the sidewalk when the shooting started. He caught slugs, all in the back, running for the safety of the cut, trying to get the pistol tucked in his waistband. He never made it. Mann kept going on by after seeing that the block was hot. They would make their move at another time.

Lando was up before anyone in the house. After taking a shower and getting dressed, he was off to scoop Lil' Garvin up from the group home. The sun wasn't even all the way up yet. It was still chilly outside when he stepped out of the door into his backyard. Walking through the grass to his dirt bike, he could feel the wetness of the night's late rain coming through his K-Swiss tennis shoes. He kicked his bike to life, filling the early morning air with the loud buzzing roar of the engine. He had learned to ride the bike well during the summer. Quickly, he floated through the back streets until he pulled up in front of the group home. Every few minutes, a couple of young dudes would come out of the door on their way to summer school or summer jobs. They all gave Lando a quick look of suspicion as they walked by. Sitting on his bike with his arm-folded in a black Madness baseball cap, a black Hugo Boss T-shirt, and a pair of blue Guess Jean shorts, he looked like he was up to no good. Lil' Garvin and an older young dude came out finally.

"What's up, young?" Lil' Garvin said as he walked over to Lando and gave him five. Lando didn't like new faces and Lil' Garvin saw it in his face. "This my man, Poochie. He cool peoples, joe," Lil' Garvin said.

Poochie was a short, brown skinned nigga that had a look of a young dude that had been around for a while. Poochie met Lil' Garvin down Oak Hill Juvenile Detention Center. He had taken a liking to the younger dude when he found out how Lil' Garvin had robbed some niggas with Quick and ain't tell on his partner when he got locked up. Poochie was telling Lil' Garvin how he had some pistols for sell, some were dirty, but some were in the box. Lil' Garvin put Lando down with the move, and now all they had to do was go around Martin Luther King Avenue with Poochie and buy whatever they wanted.

At first glance, Poochie thought Lando was a Mexican or something because of his light skin and curly hair. He stepped to Lando, gave him five, and said, "What's up, shorty?! What, you a migo or something?"

"Hell no, I'm black, young!"

"So, you trying to buy a pistol, huh?"

"I'm tryin' to get two for real," Lando said.

Poochie looked him up and down. He saw that shorty was no more than twelve or thirteen. Even so, he was going to make sure shorty got something that would hold him. A shiny black Pathfinder pulled up with Rare Essence blasting out of the speakers. Poochie told Lando and Lil' Garvin that was the ride. Poochie and Lil' Garvin got in. Lando shot through the alley and parked his bike in Lil' Garvin's back yard, which was a block away from the group home. They pulled in the alley behind him and scooped him up.

Poochie had taken them to an apartment off of M.L.K. Avenue. The apartment looked like no one lived in it and Lando came to the conclusion that the joint had to be some kind of stash house. In the one bedroom apartment, there was only a bed, a T.V., and a refrigerator. Walking into the bedroom, there were three black bulletproof vests lying on the old bed. Poochie moved them and flipped the mattress over, exposing two old, beat up .44 bulldogs, a Glock that he said was dirty, and two smoke grey Tecs, one was a 9mm and the other was a .22 cal.

Lil' Garvin asked, "How much for the .44?"

Poochie picked them both up, and said, "I'll give you both of them for four hundred dollars."

"Bet!" Lil' Garvin said as he took both hammas and gave him four one hundred dollar bills. Lando had his mind set on the Tec-9. The long clip that was hanging out of it drew him to it. It was still in good shape.

"How much for this joint?" Lando said, aiming it at the wall with both hands and one eye closed.

"Gimme three for it," Poochie said.

Lando paid him three hundred dollars and said, "I thought you got some fresh shit, too?"

Poochie went into the bathroom and came back with a brand new Glock 17 in the box. "What you think about this, shorty?" Poochie said while he was pulling it out of the box.

Lando set the Tec down and got the Glock from him, and said, "This is what I'm looking for!" While Lando was checking out the pistol, Poochie pulled a thirty five shot extended clip out of his grey Polo shorts.

"This will give you thirty five shots, shorty. I'll give you everything for seven hundred and fifty. That's cool?" Without anymore talking, Lando paid him again and they were on their way back uptown.

Days later, Marvin was on his way to the Days Inn on the D.C. / Maryland line. Ant had beeped him and told him that he had a vicious freak bitch with him. Fifteen minutes later, Marvin was letting himself in the door. All he could see was Ant stretched out on the bed ass naked, blowing weed smoke into the air. A short, light brown skinned broad with short, curly hair and a fat, round ass was on her knees between his legs. Her head was going up and down with a blur of speed. Ant saw Marvin and winked his eye, saying, "She vicious, young." Not knowing who was in the room, the broad slowly pulled up off of Ant, popping her thick lips. Turning around, Marvin saw it was Metra. He knew Ant had been fucking her, he had hit her and got the head a few times himself, but since running up in Tina's house he hadn't thought about fucking a broad from down there where Mann and them be at.

Knowing full well about the beef between them and the niggas around her way, Metra slapped her ass cheeks with her hand while looking Marvin in the eye, enticing him to get with the action. She was vicious by nature, but she was a bitch in heat when high off the smoke. She motioned with her hand for Ant to slide back on the bed so she could climb up onto the bed herself, giving Marvin a better shot at her asshole. Seeing her climb up onto the bed while never coming up off of Ant turned him on. Only dropping his Nike shorts down over his Timberland boots,

Marvin crawled onto the bed behind her. Firmly grabbing her waist, he plunged deep into her tight asshole with vehement passion. Metra's head shot up off of Ant as the seductive pain generated an instant climax for her.

"Ahhh!" she moaned. She dug her nails into the mattress as Marvin pounded her asshole, in and out. Getting impatient and close to cumming, Ant reached behind her head and slammed it back down. Metra let out a quick gagging sound as her mouth was stuffed with manhood all the way to the back of her throat. She was becoming faint as she took the punishment from both ends. Her mouth was filling with pre-cum and her asshole felt like it was on fire. She began to wildly slam her ass against Marvin's every thrust, taking him all the way inside of her until she felt it in her gut. Out of nowhere, Ant exploded in her mouth, sending cum bursting out of her nose. She struggled to pull up off of him, but he kept her head pinned down, making her swallow every drop of his climax. Seconds later, Ant let her head go and it flew up in the air as she let out a scream. "Please! Please!" She tried to catch her breath. "I can't take it! You are tearin' my ass open!" Her pleas only gave Marvin more drive. "My ass is burning!" she screamed. When she thought she was about to pass out, Marvin came inside her. He kept plunging in and out until he could no longer stay hard. After Marvin pulled out, Metra rolled over on the bed beside Ant and said, "Roll some of that shit up!"

Later on, Silk, Mann, and Black were on Rockville Pike headed for the White Flint Shopping Mall to meet the New Yorker named Supreme that Silk had been talking about. Black was in the back seat of the old tan Buick 225 that Silk only drove when picking up weight or dropping it off somewhere. Gazing up at the bright, full moon, Black was already thinking of ways to rob Supreme without Silk or Mann finding out, despite the fact that Mann clearly told him not to try anything stupid. Silk was telling Mann how Supreme was going to give him the first two bricks for thirty two thousand dollars. He felt as though that was sweet for a test run.

Pulling into the parking lot behind Bloomingdale's, Silk pulled up behind a dark blue Ford Bronco. A slim, dark skinned dude smoothly jumped out of the big truck in a bright red Fila sweat suit. He walked up to the car, cautiously scoping out the whole situation. Once he felt that things were cool, he gave Silk five, flashed a gold toothed smile, and said, "Follow me, god."

They took a ten minute back road trip to a remote old house on a dark road not far away. Supreme and a chubby, brown skinned dude carrying a tan M.C.M. tote bag got out. Silk got out and waved his hand for everyone to follow. For some reason, he felt a little uneasy, but he always felt like that at times like that, even more so when dealing with out-of-towners. He pushed his thoughts aside and focused on what was going down. The chubby dude and Black had locked into an ugly staring match.

Silk leaned back on the hood of the car beside Mann, looking at Supreme saying, "Let's do this, slim."

Supreme called his man, who came over looking back at Black like, 'Fuck you, nigga!' He opened up the M.C.M. bag and handed Silk a fat zip-lock bag of white powder. Silk nodded his head for him to hand it to Mann. Supreme folded his arms, and said, "This is the best shit up top right now, son, the Fishscale gon' keep 'em comin' back. Watch what I tell you!"

Silk took the bag from Mann and tasted the coke, saying, "I'm cool with this, gimmie the other one." The chubby dude handed him the other zip-lock bag of coke as he signaled for Black to get the cash. It was good that Silk called him when he did because Black was fucked up about the way the chubby dude had looked at him and was thinking about killing the nigga. Black got the brown paper bag with the money in it out of the back of the car and gave it to Supreme. Silk told Supreme that he would be getting back at him if he liked the outcome of the coke. They shook hands and went their separate ways.

Two homicide detectives knocked on Tina's door. The loud knocks scared her; she jumped out of the bed and ran to see who was at the door.

"Who is it?" she said as she looked through the peephole, seeing a short, black man and a white man that was a little taller.

"It's the police, open up the door, please!" said the black detective in a voice of authority.

Tina opened the door only revealing her cute face. "What ya'll want?" she said in a shaky voice. The detective went on to tell her he had a warrant for Dre's arrest for first-degree murder. After finding out that he wasn't home, they told Tina to tell him that it would be best for him to turn himself in. Once they left, she ran straight to the phone to beep Dre.

Mann and Dre were sitting in Dre's new 1989 turquoise Corvette ZR1 with white leather seats, talking about how good the Fishscale coke was that Silk had given Mann a brick of after they got it from Supreme. It had pipeheads coming from way across town to get a hit. The word was out, Mann and Dre had Fishscale. While talking, Dre's beeper went off. It was Tina's "911". He got out of the car and jogged across the street to use the phone in Dee-Dee's house.

"Hello!" Tina said, clearly excited.

"What's wrong, boo?" Dre said.

"The police just left. They say you wanted for murder!"

"What?!" Dre snapped, not believing what he was hearing.

"You heard me, they looking for you. They want you to turn yourself in."

"Fuck that! Look here, don't worry yourself. I got this. Okay?" Dre said before going back to the car.

Things were not looking good. Mann and him were getting money like never before and through Silk, they had a Fishscale connect, but now he was wanted for a body and they were beefing hard. Not a day went by that they didn't go hunting for their prey. Walking back to the car, he thought about whose murder they could want him for. He knew it was no one to tell on Tate's murder because the only eyes to see it were Mann and

Black. Besides that, Black did the shooting so they would want him first, Dre thought. That left room for only one other body that he could think of, and that was the Jamaican that he smashed outside of the Black Hole in the beginning of the year. After Black hit the nigga in the middle of Georgia Avenue with the car he was driving, they got out and finished him off with twelve hollow points. Dre was sure that was what they wanted him for. He got in the car and told Mann the fucked up news while pulling off.

Lil' Garvin had been out of the group home for a few days, and all he had to do was get in school when it started in about a week. He didn't like the dirt bikes that his little partners got around on, so with twenty five hundred he bought a black Chevy Impala, and got the windows tinted dark black. Lil' Garvin was taking Lando over Nakia's house so that he could stash the Tec-9. He didn't want to take a chance with leaving it in the house anymore; he knew in his heart that Pamila would find it sooner or later. He decided to keep the Glock on him that he packed it all day; extended thirty five shot clip and all. Quick laid in the back seat playing with the Tec while he was joaning on how Lil' Garvin could hardly see over the wheel and holding it with both hands. Pulling up in front of Nakia's, Lando got the Tec from Quick and told them he would beep them when he wanted them to pick him up.

Lando crept into the house through the back door that Nakia always left open when she knew he was coming. Nakia was sitting on her bed in nothing but a T-shirt and panties, eating ice cream when Lando walked into the room with the Tec-9 in his hands.

"Boy! What you think you doin' with that!" Nakia said as she stood up, displaying her thick, brown skinned legs.

"I told you I needed you to put something up for me, boo," Lando said reassuringly.

Nakia took the Tec-9 and walked into a huge walk-in closet, swinging her hips enticingly, saying, "You gon' get me in trouble. If my mother find this gun and all these drugs, she gon' put my ass out!"

"She ain't gonna find it," Lando said as he laid across the bed. He went on to say, "If she do, I'll buy us a house." Lando had an eight of a key" bagged up in a Nike shoebox along with sixty eight hundred dollars. Wee-Wee was selling him eights for twenty eight hundred dollars, and he was seeing his little money stack by the hour hand-to-hand on the block.

Nakia came back, laid down beside Lando on the bed, and said, "How you think you gon' buy us a house, boo?"

Staring at the spinning ceiling fan, he responded in a matter of fact tone, "Pretty soon, I'ma be able to buy us whatever we want!"

Kelley walked through Takoma Park in a tan, loose fitting, linen Armani short set. She was just getting off from work, so she decided to go hang out at Dee-Dee's house for a little while, and then go in the house before it got too late. Kelley grew up with Dee-Dee and Metra; they had been girlfriends their whole lives. Now that Kelley was growing up, she felt herself being pulled away from them by her plans of going away to college the next year. She wanted something out of life, and nothing was going to get in her way if she had anything to do with it. As her mind reflected on her future, she couldn't see herself being like Dee-Dee, running the streets and living off of Onion. She damn sure couldn't see herself being like Metra, selling ass and living day for day. She promised herself that she would always love them, but she would never be like them. Her thoughts were abruptly interrupted by a loud car horn.

"Kelley! Kelley!" Metra yelled out the window of a little Toyota. With her cute, fat face behind a pair of fresh Gucci sunglasses, she said, "Come on, girl, get in!" Kelley got in the backseat and shut the door. The strong smell of weed smoke hit her nose as they pulled off.

"Where you going?" Dee-Dee said from the passenger seat.

"I was on my way down your house. What's up with ya'll?" Kelley said as she stretched her sexy legs across the back seat. Dee-Dee went on to tell her how they had been shopping all day. Metra had been dying to ask her about Mann, she swore they were fucking.

"What's up with you and that fine black muthafucka?" Metra slipped in.

"Who you talking 'bout?" Kelley said with a smile.

Cutting in, Dee-Dee said, "You know she talkin' 'bout Mann fine ass."

Kelley was digging Mann, but she wasn't going to chase him like everyone else. They had been talking a lot the past summer, but she wasn't even thinking about giving him the pussy yet.

"Is ya'll fuckin'?" Metra asked.

"Bitch, please!" Kelley said.

As they went on talking, Metra somehow started talking about how she thought Mann and them were suckas, and that Black was the only one with heart. Dee-Dee knew better, she had seen all of them work before. She told Metra that she was lunchin'. Metra went on to say that she seen them work before, too, but they were faking and if they weren't, they would have done something about Marvin and Ant coming through shooting out of the LTD. She told Dee-Dee that she heard them talking about it one night at the hotel. Dee-Dee and Kelley were fucked up that Metra knew they had done the shooting and didn't say shit. Dee-Dee was even more fucked up than Kelley, being as though bullets flew through her living room that night. Both Dee-Dee and Kelley were determined to hip Mann and the rest of the niggas around the way that they knew who did the busting that night.

Black was laying in the bed sleep with a freak bitch he had pulled the night before. Something kept telling him to wake up. He opened his eyes and saw that it was still dark outside. Rolling over, he sat on the side of his bed and grabbed his beeper off of the nightstand next to the bed. Wiping the sleep out of his eyes, he saw that it was only five forty five a.m. He ran his hand through his long hair, thinking that he would get the broad to cornrow his shit for him later on. He got up and grabbed his blue Perry Ellis jeans off of the hotel floor, pulling a half smoked fifty bag of Skunk weed out of the pocket. Black had been laying low in the Walter Reed Inn on Georgia Avenue since Dre told him that he had a warrant on him. Unlike Dre, Black was sure they were going to be looking for him next and knew why.

Dre and Black had robbed a Maryland bamma in the beginning of the summer. Dre was under the impression that they weren't going to have to kill the dude, being as though he would never know who they were behind their masks. A broad had told Black that she knew that it was fifty thousand dollars in cash in the dude's grandmother's house. Wasting no time, Black scooped Dre in Mann's old station wagon, putting him down with the move, telling him how it was sweet and that they wouldn't have to kill the bamma. They had slid in and out with ease, but they didn't put their mask on until they were at the door. While they were coming out, the dude had got strong and popped the phone cord they had tied him up with. Black grabbed him and slammed six inches of Buck knife steel into his gut. Black was sure that he died, but the only person that could be telling was the broad that gave him the lick. He was going to have to kill her.

After smoking a blunt to the head, he got back into the bed with the cute, brown skinned broad. Suddenly, the hotel door burst open. A.T.F. agents in all black with Mini-14s swarmed the room. The broad jumped out of the bed naked, titties bouncing everywhere, screaming hysterically. An agent rushed her and slammed her to the floor face first. He then pressed her face hard into the dirty carpet, smashing his knee into her back. He couldn't help but to look at the woman's fat, brown ass. Five agents rushed Black, choking him out as they wrestled him down on the bed and handcuffed him, placing him under arrest.

Mann was fucked up about Black. He knew the Feds would be charging him as an adult for the body. Black had been in and out since he was eleven years old, but that was the first murder that he had ever been boxed up for. As Mann cruised down Georgia Avenue coming back from dropping Dre off at the hotel way out Virginia, he felt his anger and frustration boiling. His cousin just went in on a murder, and his partner was on the run for it. To add to the night's problems, he saw Ant on the pay phone across the street. He was slipping. Mann glanced around to see who Ant could be with. He saw that his Dodge wagon was the only car in the mini mall parking lot. Now was the time.

Mann calmly passed by the mini mall and doubled back into the alley behind it. He quickly tied a black bandanna around his face and pulled his black Madness baseball cap down over his eyes. With the slickness and precision of a crocodile on the hunt in murky waters, Mann crept back around the corner with his 9mm in hand. Step after quiet step, he tip toed up behind Ant until he could almost reach out and touch him. Ant sensed someone was behind him, but it was too late. His senses had failed him and his slipping would cost him his life. He dropped the phone and swung around to see nothing but the eyes of a dark skinned killer with some kind of pistol in his face. He broke and ran for his car. Mann started dumping as he ran behind him. POP! POP! POP! One by one, Mann tagged him over and over, slug after slug. Ant felt his legs getting weak, yet, he put his all into making it to the car. Behind him, the sound of gunshots just wouldn't stop. He could no longer feel the pain of the hot hollow points that were murderously slamming into his body. He fell hard on his face, sliding on the black top. The gunfire stopped and he rolled over to look up into the star lit sky. He would be okay, he would make it, he thought. Mann stood right over top of him and put an end to any hopes of survival. Two shots point blank to the head left Ant blood soaked and dead, lying beside his car waiting to be found.

Chapter Four: Somebody gotta pay

The phone began to ring as Pamila sat in the living room playing with Tyesha. She picked the tall, lean child up and answered the phone. "Hello," she said as she sat down and placed Tyesha on her lap.

"You have a collect call from Black at the Central Detention Facility." Pamila accepted the call and called Black by his real name as she always did.

"Richard!" she said, not surprised at all. "What are you locked up for now, boy?"

"I ain't do nothing, Aunt Pamila, they talking about I killed somebody I never heard of."

"Killed somebody!"

"Yeah, I don't go back to court for another nine days. They got me on an eight day hold right now, but weekends don't count. I'm cool, though, it ain't nothing to worry about. I'll be out soon. I need to holla at Mann right now, is he home?"

"No, you know him and Lando are never in here. Call back later on, Mann should be in here about ten or eleven. Do you need anything?" Pamila said.

"Na, I'm cool, just tell Mann to be in there when I call. Okay? I love you," Black said and hung up the phone.

Pamila shook her head as she hung up the phone. *That boy ain't never going to learn*, she thought.

Marvin was sitting on the steps in front of Ant's apartment building surrounded by his partners Ric, Will, and Jammie, who was Ant's younger brother. They were fucked up about Ant getting smashed and they knew that them 5th Street niggas had something to do with it. Ric, the youngest one, was in a murderous rage about his man's killing. He was trying to kill everybody down 5th Street. Jammie and Will wanted to do something about the murder, but they needed Marvin or Ric to push them. Marvin began talking in a no non-sense voice, telling everybody how shit was going to get straightened, and that they were going to do it. Marvin got up and walked to Ant's car, followed by his niggas, and left.

It was two thirty p.m. Monday afternoon and Lil' Garvin was outside of Quick's grandmother house blowing the horn. His timing couldn't be better. Quick's grandmother had found a box of bullets under his bed and went off.

"You no good boy! You sell them drugs, you don't go to school, you just a bum!" she screamed as Quick slammed the door.

"I ain't tryin' to hear that shit!" Quick said as he ran down the apartment steps, and jumped in the car with Lil' Garvin and Baby D.

"What's up, young?" Baby D said, sitting in the passenger seat.

"Ain't shit, joe. My grandmother beefin' and shit, but I'm chillin'," Quick said. Lil' Garvin pulled off, headed for Paul Junior High School to pick Lando up. School started a week ago and Lando had gone everyday. He would get a ride from Lil' Garvin, drop his books off, and hit the strip to hustle until nightfall. For the meantime, it was working.

Lil' Garvin pulled up in front of the school as it was letting out. Lando was coming out of the big, green, beat up doors with a gorgeous young girl with long silky brown hair, a light honey golden complexion, and beautiful brown eyes that made her look like she was from the Philippines. Lando got her number and got into the car with his niggas.

"Who was that bad ass bitch young?" said Baby D.

"Her name is Jazmin, she cool as shit, joe. I been jive rappin' to her in class, but she on some real laid back shit," Lando said.

As they rolled around the way, everybody was asking Lando about Black. What was he in for? When was he coming home? How could they go see him? Lando let them know that he was charged with murder, but he hadn't talked to him or went to see him yet. Lil' Garvin brought up the beef between them and 13th Street, telling everybody how the dude, Ant, had got his head hit a few days ago.

"Fuck them niggas, young!" said Baby D with a mug on his face.

"No bullshit, fuck them niggas! We should ride on them niggas without Mann and them!" Quick snapped. Everybody agreed.

Lando began to think. He had never shot a nigga before and he was itching to bust his Glock dead in a nigga's ass. His wait wouldn't be long now, he was sure of it.

Dre was playing everything by ear until he heard from Black. That way, he could take care of any loose ends on the streets, and then turn himself in and beat the case along with Black. Being as though he was on the run, he only came in the city to make a drop off or to collect some of his cash. On the windy fall morning, he was going through Rittenhouse Street to serve Smoke a half a brick of Fishscale. Pulling up in his white Nissan Maxima, he parked on 3rd street, two blocks away from the heat of the strip on 5th Street. A short, stocky, black dude in a dark blue Nautica jacket with the hood pulled over his head came walking swiftly up behind Dre's car from out of the alley. Being on the run had Dre's senses on blast. He tightened up the grip on his Colt.45 and swung his head around to see who was walking up on him like that. It was clear that it was Smoke. He had been smoking an early morning blunt in the alley while he waited for Dre to come through with the coke.

"What's up, slim?" Smoke said as he flopped his heavy body down in the passenger seat of the car, sending a strong smell of weed smoke into the air.

"Ain't shit, slim. Here you go," Dre said as he passed him a folded zip-lock bag with coke in it. Knowing that Dre was on the run and that he couldn't stay in one place very long, Smoke stuffed the coke into his big jacket pocket. Smoke looked around and combed his surroundings as he pulled an overweight stack of cash out of his inside pocket.

"Here you go, slim, that's right there," Smoke said as he passed Dre the money. He went on to say, "You know I talked to Black last night!"

"Oh yeah? What's up with 'em?" Dre asked, very interestingly.

"I ain't talk to 'em that long, he said they was about to count. He told me to tell you to send Tina to see 'em, or tell Mann to come see 'em so he can holla at you. He say that they ain't give 'em no bond, and he don't go back to court until January eighteenth."

"Next year!" Dre said with disappointment in his voice.

"Yeah, slim, next year! I was fucked up, too, but we can't do shit but wait until something gives. I'm down for whatever, I'ma make sure he come home. Other than that, I just sent him a hundred dollars and told him to send me a package slip so I could get 'em some gear and shit." When they were finished, Smoke got out of the car and Dre went straight over Pamila's house to drop off two hundred dollars for her to send to Black since he knew that was who would be on top of his business for him.

D.C. Jail's visiting hall was packed with family members of all kind going to see their confined loved ones. The young females that were going to see their men had the spot looking like a small fashion show in all of the top-flight gear that was on the streets. On the other side of the scratched up old Plexiglass that separated the two very different worlds were men from all walks of life. Every face that had a phone to its ear on the other side of the glass, told a very different story of survival through their expressions. Some told stories of long nights of pipe smoking, some told stories of a hard life struggling on the streets, and some told stories of men already convicted of crimes that would have them legally fighting for their freedom for the rest of their lives.

As Black walked through the powerful sliding iron door that lead back to the cell blocks, his face told a story like no other in the room. There wasn't a trace of a worry in his face as he sat down, picked up the phone, and said, "What's up, joe?"

Picking up the phone on the other side of the glass, Mann said, "What's up with you?"

"Ain't shit, I'm just waiting to go back to court. I think they gon' throw this shit out. My lawyer say they got me on some hearsay shit, we should know more at the next status hearin', though." Black looked over Mann and saw Kelley walking toward him waving with a huge smile on her beautiful face. Black couldn't take his eyes off of Kelley's well-shaped body. Her thick thighs looked so good in her tight Gap jeans. Mann looked over his shoulder and saw that Kelley was just coming back from the bathroom. He turned back to Black with a big smile on his face as Kelley sat down beside him.

"What's up with you and Kelley, joe?!" Black said.

"We cool…" Mann said.

Before he could finish, Kelley snatched the phone and said, "What's up, Black! Don't listen to him. We more then cool nowadays." Kelley rapped to Black for a few more minutes before giving the phone back to Mann. She made sure she told him all about Metra and her knowledge of Ant and Marvin shooting at them out of the White LTD. Black never trusted Metra, but he now felt he had a reason to kill her.

Mann got back on the phone and let Black know that everything was going to be cool, and that as soon as they found out who was talking to let him know so he could take care of business. Just as Mann was about to hang up the phone, Black looked at him with a smile while Kelley was on her way to the door, and said, "You ran into Ant, didn't you?" Mann didn't even open his mouth. He smoothly hung up the phone and winked his eye as he put his hand up to the glass to give Black five as he left.

Mann was watching Kelley's hips shake all the way up the steps to her front door. Once she was in the house, he popped his 300ZX into his first gear, lighting up the dashboard as he went flying up the street. Turning on to Georgia Avenue, he saw that the Ave. was full of life. Niggas were everywhere, cars with music blasting were double-parked, and pipeheads were sadly rushing back and forth up and down the Ave. in search of a way to get a blast. Overall, it was a perfect picture of the government's "War on Drugs". Parking his car in the mini mall parking lot, he got out to holla at a few niggas he fucked with from the Ave. He saw that the Ave. was pumping, money and crack were exchanging hands with velocity. It had been a long time since he had been out on the block grinding hand to hand.

His man, Pat-Pat, stepped to him, giving him five and saying, "Let me holla at you." Mann and Pat-Pat stepped away from the crowd in front of Sam's Liquor Store. Pat-Pat was all about cash and could always relate to Mann. They had been cool since they were kids. Pat-Pat was a tall, dark dude and when he spoke, it was always with sense.

"I been hearin' about this shit between you and Marvin and them since this summer. You done let that shit ride too long. I was over there in the cut the night Ant got his head hit. I saw the whole thing go down and I peeped you double back, so I can put two and two2 together. I know how you work. My thing is this, you got to get the shit over, slim. Now that Black is in, they gon' be tryin' to catch you slippin'!" Pat-Pat said with the sound of real concern in his voice. Mann's beeper went off as he started to respond.

"You right, slim. I'm on top of that shit, joe. Believe that! I gotta call this number back, so I'ma catch up with you." Mann gave Pat-Pat five and ran across the street to use the pay phone in the mini mall parking lot with Pat-Pat's words still fresh on his mind.

Mann got on the phone and called Silk back. He turned and leaned his back against the white brick wall of the drug store so that he could see everything moving, he was in no mood to get caught slipping that night or any other night.

"What's up, Silk?" Mann said as he watched a beautiful young woman walk into the drug store.

"I just came from seeing Supreme. Come get your break down," Silk said, and quickly got off of the subject of business on the phone. Silk began asking Mann about Black and Dre.

While he was talking to him, Mann got a strange feeling in his gut and slid his hand under his thick gray Polo hoody, wrapping his fingers around the fresh Ruger 9mm tucked in his waistband. He began to think... He was on the same pay phone he had caught Ant on almost two weeks ago. He glanced over to the drug store door and saw Marvin coming out.

His first thought was to start shooting on the spot, fuck witnesses and all. Marvin was out of the door when their eyes locked for what seemed like forever. Standing right outside of the door that just swung shut, Marvin thought about running back inside, but in his heart he knew it was do or die. Mann dropped the receiver to the pay phone while Silk was still talking. That set it off. At the exact same time, they both pulled their pistols in what appeared to be slow motion. Mann got the first shot off, catching Marvin in the chest. Marvin staggered backward as he let his first shots go, knocking Mann against the wall. Pat Pat was serving a pipehead across the street when he heard the shots going off. He saw Mann and Marvin standing no further than ten feet apart with flames of gunfire between them. Mann fell to the ground, still shooting, but he was hit bad. Marvin was running. He flew across Georgia Avenue with bullets still flying by his head. Mann emptied his pistol and looked at his blood soaked shirt. He could see the huge holes Marvin's .45 had put in it. His head began to spin. He believed that what goes around comes around, but he never thought he would die on the same pay phone he killed a nigga on.

Pat- Pat ran across the street to help Mann. He knelt down beside him and grabbed him in his arms, saying, "Hold on, slim! You gon' be okay!"

Mann looked him in the eyes and said in a last breath voice, "Get rid of this pistol, I hear the bodeens comin'!" Pat- Pat took the pistol, threw it down the sewer, and came back.

Mann was looking into Pat- Pat's face as he screamed, "Hold on!" but Mann couldn't hear a word he said. Mann tried with his all to hold on, but everything went black as he slumped in Pat- Pat's arms.

Marvin sat on Ric's bed breathing like a raging bull. As Ric helped him to take off his shirt, Marvin was already telling him how he killed Mann up on the Ave. Ric was siced, he couldn't wait to finish the rest of them niggas. Pulling off his bulletproof vest, Marvin could see that his whole upper body had dark purple bruises all over it from the slugs that had slammed into his chest.

"Damn, joe! Your shit all fucked up!" Ric said as he saw the damage the Ruger did to Marvin's body through the vest.

"I'm cool, young! I just gotta lay low now. It was a rack a muthafuckas on the Ave tonight. I know somebody know me," Marvin said. He decided to stay over Ric's house for the night, and slide out of town in the morning. He knew that way he would be far enough away to see what the Feds would do without staying in a hotel where somebody might see him that knew him. All he could do was wait for the next move.

Everybody in the house was asleep when the phone rang and broke the peaceful silence of the night. Half asleep, Pamila rolled over, wondering who the fuck was calling her house at that time of the night. "Hello!" she snapped in a pissed off tone.

"Sorry to disturb you at this hour, but this is Detective Brown from 4th D. I need to know if a Mark Mills lives at this house," a deep voice said through the phone. Pamila knew what kind of life Mann was living, so she didn't want to give the Feds any information she didn't have to.

"Why do you need to know that?" she said, very concerned.

"Well, ma'am, Mr. Mills has been shot very bad and this is the phone number on his I.D. I'm trying to contact a family member," the detective said in a straight to the point way. Pamila began to feel faint. She was speechless for a moment. It was the very phone call she had dreaded for years.

"This is his mother. Is he alive?" she said, praying that she would hear him say yes.

"I really can't say, ma'am. They took him to Washington Hospital Center by Medivac. You will be able to find out how he is doing down there." Fighting tears back, Pamila quickly got dressed and rushed to the hospital, leaving Tyesha and Lando asleep.

After sitting in the emergency room waiting area for hours, she got up and called Lando on the pay phone. While the phone rang, she could see the early morning sun just beginning to shine into the lobby window.

"Hello?" Lando said, wide awake. The sound of his voice somehow put a sense of hope in Pamila's heart about Mann making it.

"Lando, look, I got a problem, so I need you to stay home and watch Tyesha 'til I get there." Lando had no problem staying home from school. He agreed and Pamila walked back into the waiting area. As soon as she sat down, an old, white man emerged through the emergency room's double doors wearing latex gloves and a long doctor's robe. Pamila felt her heart pounding rapidly as she awaited the verdict.

"Ms. Mills, your son has just come out of surgery." The doctor said, and continued. "We can't say how things will turn out at this time. Mark has slipped into a mild coma, so it's all in God's hands now. We have done our best. We have moved him up to the third floor in room 311. You may see him."

Tears ran down Pamila's face in a steady flow as she walked down the hall to Mann's room. She stepped into the room and was horrified by what she saw. Mann laid in a white robe with all kinds of tubes coming out of his body. Even one long tube was inserted into his nose pumping a thick, green fluid out of his stomach. Pamila could hardly look at Mann, he looked like he was dead already. Looking around the room, Pamila had never seen a person hooked up to so many life support machines in her life. Ever since Mann was able to walk, he always found a way to do for himself. That was how he got the nickname from Pamila years ago. Pamila slowly walked over to his bed, placing her hand softly on his forehead. Silently, she prayed. "Lord, please spare his soul. I know that this life is but play and amusement, pomp and mutual boasting. Even so, I beg You. Please, don't take him away like this." Pamila pulled up a chair beside the bed and talked to Mann until she fell asleep, knowing that he could not hear her. It was just good to know he was alive, in whatever condition he was in.

Tyesha was lying on Lando's bed in a pink pajama set watching him play *Super Mario Bros.* when Pamila walked in the front door. They both got up and went down stairs to see where she had been all day. Tyesha ran and jumped straight into Pamila's arms, not noticing the look of desperation in her face. Lando, on the other hand, quickly caught on. He knew Pamila well and it was very rare to find the strong woman perplexed about anything. The burden she carried was openly displayed in her body language, even though she tried to hide it.

"What's wrong with you?" Lando asked, becoming very concerned and uneasy. Pamila kissed Tyesha and sat her down, telling her to go play Nintendo for a minute while she spoke to Lando. The little girl ran off, leaving them alone. As Pamila sat down on the couch, she searched for the right words to say and the right way to say them. Again, Lando asked, "What's wrong?"

Pamila began to speak in a slow and serious tone. "Lando, you are growing up fast. You've seen a lot. What I have to tell you may upset you, but…"

"What's up, Pamila?" Lando cut in.

"Mann's in a coma. He got shot last night." As Pamila spoke, they echoed through Lando's ears. He couldn't believe what he was hearing. It couldn't be true. Mann was never slipping, he was always on point. Lando's thoughts of Mann's game tight mobbin' were coming from every corner of his mind.

"Shot?! Who the fu... Who did that!" Lando asked as his anger began to boil over. Reality hit Lando when Pamila spoke again.

"I don't know who shot 'em. I don't want to know. All I want is for Mann to come out of this shit alive. I don't want you out there trying to find out who shot 'em, either."

"When can I see 'em?"

"Tomorrow."

Pamila talked to Lando for awhile, trying to get him to leave the whole situation up to Mann. By no means did she want Lando out in the streets trying to straighten his big brother's beef, but some how she knew it was nothing she could do to stop him. His love for the realest nigga in his life was too deep.

Lando sat on his bed staring at the floor for a long time. The mere thought of Mann laying in a coma with bullet holes in his body was a thought that wouldn't allow him to think about anything other than pay back. "Fuck that!" Lando said out loud as he got up and went down the basement to get his Glock out of the stash spot in the ceiling. He sat on Mann's bed and took the clip out, sliding the thirty five shot extended clip in the pistol. Cocking the Glock, he swore to himself that one of them 13th Street niggas was dying that night and every other night until Mann was able to take care of his business or until all of them niggas were six feet deep. Lando needed a ride. His bike would make too much noise for what he wanted to do. He used Mann's phone to call Lil' Garvin.

"Hello?" Lil' Garvin answered the phone with NWA's *Gangsta Gangsta* playing in the background. The house was live and Lando could hear it.

"I need you to come get me, young," Lando said, sounding more serious than ever.

"What's wrong?"

"I'll tell you when you get here. I'll be on the corner at the top of my block," Lando said and hung up the phone, leaving the house.

The night was cool and windy. Lando stood on the dark corner of 5th and Tuckerman Streets in a black Eddie Bauer windbreaker, black Gap jeans, and a pair of black Timberland boots. If a person got close enough, they could see the print of the long extended clip in the Glock poking out of his waistband. In less than ten minutes, Lil' Garvin was pulling up in his black Impala with Quick and Baby D. Lando hopped in the back with Baby D and they pulled off. Lando could hardly see Quick's face in the darkness of the car when he turned around in the passenger seat and said, "What the fuck is up, young?"

Lando told everybody about Mann being shot. None of them could believe that Mann was in a coma. They all loved Mann like a brother. He had looked out for all of them as they grew up under him. Lando didn't have to ask anyone if they were rolling.

Baby D spoke for the whole car when he said, "We gotta see them bitch ass niggas tonight, young!!"

Already showing traces of the quick thinking of Mann, Lando told everybody that the 13th Street niggas would feel safe now that they thought Mann was dead Dre on the run, and Black locked up.

"Them niggas gon' be out in the open. They ain't expecting no get back yet!" Lando said, pulling the Glock out and laying it on his lap before going on. "Everybody strapped?"

"Naa, take me around the way. I gotta pump stashed in back of the crackhouse," Baby D said.

Lando looked at Quick and said, "What about you?"

"I got my .38," Quick said.

Lando looked at Lil' Garvin through the rear view mirror and said, "I know you strapped!" Lil' Garvin responded by waving his huge .44 Bull Dog in the air.

After stopping around the way to get Baby D's pump, Lando told Lil' Garvin to slide over Nakia's house to get his Tec-9 for Quick. Lando knew how blood thirsty Quick was, he always reminded him of Black. It was one time that Lando was in support of Quick's ruthlessness and to show it, he was going to arm his partner with the 32 shot Tec-9. It was murdaaaa!

13th Street was pumping. Ric had sold out twice and went in the house to bag up another sixty two. Will, Jammie, and a few younger dudes sat on the steps in front of the apartment building smoking weed while they were hustling. Boo, a six feet tall, dark skinned, heavyset nigga from 13th Street walked up. "What's up?" he said to his niggas. Everybody said what's up at the same time.

An old Cadillac Seville pulled up right in front of the crowd and stopped. Quickly, everybody turned to see who was in the car. Will squinted his eyes to make out the driver. It was a pipehead that he always served. Picking up a half way empty bottle of Cognac beside him, Will got in the passenger seat to serve the fiend, leaving the door open with one leg hanging out of the car. Two more pipeheads walked up. Jammie jumped on the sells. The rush was on. Sells were coming from every direction. Ric came jogging out of the building, coke in hand, and quickly started serving left and right. In the heat of the rush, Quick, Lando, Baby D, and Lil' Garvin exploded out of the dark cut behind them wearing black ski masks.

Boo, being the closest to the cut, never had a chance. Standing with the blunt in his mouth in a state of shock, Baby D blew him off of his feet and kept busting at the crowd. Lil' Garvin came right behind him, finishing Boo with two devastating blasts from the Bull Dog. Ric dropped his coke and money as he jumped over a car followed by Baby D's shot gun blasting. Panic set in, everybody scattered. Quick was in the middle of 13th Street waving the Tec-9 from side to side with both hands, spraying everything moving with vengeance and intensity. One of the young dudes that were running caught a slug in the back and tumbled to the ground helplessly. Never subsiding on the trigger, Quick showed no mercy to his prey.

Running up on the young dude, Quick pumped five quick rounds into him, snatching his last breath, and then turned and went after Jammie, who was fleeing down the street. Lando aggressively attacked the Cadillac Will was sitting in. 9mm slugs flew through the car, striking the pipehead in the face, instantly killing him. The car started to drift down 13th Street with Will balled up in the passenger seat while the driver laid slumped and lifeless behind the wheel. Lando jogged along side the car, firing the Glock through the window since Will had slammed the door seeking refuge. Lando filled Will with twenty or more hollow points before the car smashed into a tree at the end of the block. In seconds, the four teenage killers were gone as quickly as they came, leaving four dead and many wounded.

Chapter five: A dance with the devil...

A week later, Black was walking down the top right tier in the North 1 cell block of the D.C. Jail with the top of his pressed blue jumper tied around his waist, like 'Fuck the world two times!' He got on the phone to call Dee-Dee's house collect, turning his back to the wall so that he could face the day room that was full of young killers charged as adults, just like himself. As the phone rang, Black lit a Newport and adjusted the buck knife on his waistband that he had bought from a pipehead C.O. he knew from around the way.

"What's up, nigga?!" Dee-Dee said in an excited, high-pitched, hood rat voice.

"Ain't shit. I'm chillin', this shit ain't nothing. You seen Mann?"

"Mann?" Dee-Dee asked, sounding confused and added, "You ain't heard about Mann?"

"Heard what?" Black snapped, already becoming angry by not being informed.

Dee-Dee watched her step, picking her words very carefully, "Mann uh…"

"Mann what!" Black snapped.

"He in the hospital. He got shot last week."

Black couldn't believe his ears. He swore she had the facts mixed up. Dee-Dee went on to tell Black all that she knew about Mann being shot. She told him that Marvin did it, how he did it, and where.

"Where the fuck Dre at!" Black yelled through the phone.

"I ain't seen him in over a week. He only come through in spots. You know? But, Lando and them got the hood hot as shit! They been lighting shit up every night since Mann got shot," Dee-Dee said. Black finished talking to Dee-Dee and hung up the phone burning with anger. He had to get out and quick.

Silk was pissed off that Dre wasn't returning his beeps. He had been trying to catch up with Dre since he heard the shooting over the phone. Silk had got word from the streets that Mann was in a coma, but he wanted to know who put him in a coma. It had been years since Silk had put some work in. Since he had started getting bricks by the tens and now the twenties, he tried not to get his hands dirty. He had too many young niggas that loved the gun play. Yet and still, he had grown a love for Mann. He was going to find out who shot him and have something done about it. His first step was 5th and Rittenhouse Streets.

As soon as Silk's Benz turned on to Rittenhouse Street, he saw that the jump outs had a group of dudes against the wall in the alley searching them. Looking closer, he saw that Lando was one of the dudes that they had hemmed up. He pulled over and parked, waiting for the Feds to let everybody go so he could pull up on Lando.

Everyone went their own way as the jump outs left. Lando and Quick walked out of the alley together. Silk blew the horn to get their attention. Seeing Silk, they walked over and got in the car.

"What's up?" Lando asked from the backseat.

"I'm tryin' to find out who shot your brother," Silk said as he pulled off.

"We found out this nigga named Marvin did it. We been going through that joint every night, tearin' shit up, but the nigga don't never be around. Just some niggas he fuck with. We walked through there today, about forty minutes ago on the way home from school, that joint a ghost town," Lando said.

"Oh, yeah?" Silk responded with a smile. He had been hearing about Lando getting a little bit of money all summer, but it was like he started firing pistols overnight. Quick, on the other hand, he had been hearing about for the longest. These two young niggas would be able to hold it down until Mann was back on his feet, Silk thought. He would make sure that they needed nothing in the streets.

"Look here," Silk said, handing Quick his beeper number and continued, "I want ya'll to hit me if ya'll need anything."

"Cool," Quick said. After Silk had made his loyalty to Mann clear, and his support of Lando and Quick known, he dropped them off on 5th Street and rolled out.

Kelley had gotten tired of hearing all the rumors about how Mann was dead or how he would never walk again, so she called Pamila's house early one morning telling her who she was and how she thought she was in love with Mann. Pamila, being a sagacious judge of character, quickly dissected the girl's morals and principles, and decided to take her to the hospital with her.

Pamila stood over Mann talking to him as she had done everyday for the last week. Kelley stood behind her, fighting back tears. The one nigga that she could see herself with was hooked up to beeping life support machines with tubes coming out of his body. The sight made her somewhat understand why Lando and the rest of the young niggas around the way seemed to be shooting every night after dark. Looking at Mann, she thought about what Lando told her after him and Quick had come from seeing him the day after they sprayed 13th Street. Lando told her that he wasn't going back to that hospital until Mann came out of that coma. And, if he died, he only wanted memories of Mann at his best. He would pay his respect by busting ass every night. The knock on the thick wooden door behind her snapped her out of her daze as a doctor came in and asked to speak to Pamila in the hallway.

Pamila stepped out into the busy hallway with the tall, white doctor. As speeding nurses and doctors hurried by, the doctor gave Pamila the bad news that she had been asking him for. "Ms. Mills, we've been doing a lot of tests on your son. He's suffered five critical gunshot wounds, one of which lodged itself less than an inch from his spine, damaging the lower part of his cerebral cortex…"

"What are you telling me?" Pamila angrily snapped, cutting the doctor off.

"I'm saying that if your son comes out of his coma, he'll never walk again." Pamila didn't want to hear that and she didn't believe it either.

Walking back into the room with Mann and Kelley, Pamila saw Kelley rubbing Mann's forehead, talking to him. Pamila stood silently looking on. "You gon' make it, boo." Kelley said with tears running down her cute face. "You got too many people pullin' for you, boy." Pamila walked up beside Kelley and held Mann's hand.

That doctor don't know shit, Pamila thought. Her faith in the Creator was too firm. She knew Mann would be fine. As soon as those thoughts went through her mind, Mann showed the first signs of life. He turned his head, letting out a moan. Kelley screamed out of excitement while Pamila only smiled as her faith was strengthened.

Mann struggled to open his eyes. Immediately, the pain of the bullet wounds shot through his body, causing him to frown up his face in anguish. Kelley rushed to his aid, caressing his weak body softly. Mann rested his head, looked up at Pamila, and said in an exhausted voice, "Why ya'll look like somebody died? I know ya'll ain't count me out." Pamila and Kelley laughed. Mann's strength took a huge burden off of their shoulders.

"I'm in bad shape, huh?" Mann said as he looked at all the tubes that were running through his body.

"You're alive, that's all that matters," Pamila said. Mann thought about what she had said. He remembered the whole shooting and he began to wonder if Marvin got away or not. He remembered tagging him, but he saw him break across the street that night and that was all he remembered. Pamila was right, he thought, he was alive.

"Where Lando at?" Mann asked. Kelley looked away from Mann to Pamila, wanting her to answer the question. She knew that the 411 she had on Lando couldn't be talked about in front of Pamila. Mann read that in her actions and looked at Pamila. She, on the other hand, was already hip.

"Lando's bad ass runnin' around with Quick and them wanna be gangstas, playin' payback. I pray that you get outta here soon. You gotta do something to let 'em know that you got things under control. Every night, I stare out of my bedroom window wishing Lando was coming down the street, but with you lying here shot, I know what he's doing," Pamila said, giving up a look that showed she wasn't as green as they thought. Mann laid in pain talking to Pamila and Kelley, thinking about Lando, knowing he had to hurry up and get back on his feet.

Hand cuffed and shackled in the back of a U.S. Marshal's van being extradited to the D.C. Jail to face murder charges, Dre sat in a daze. Over and over again, he heard Mann's voice telling him how his dick was going to get him caught up one day.

Funky ass bitch! Dre thought. He had wanted some pussy so bad that he danced with the devil. After beeping Tina all morning, not knowing that she had went to see Black like he told her to, Dre called around the way for the quickest fuck he could find. Despite all of her cruddiness and snake ways, Metra had some smoking pussy, bomb head, and she could fuck for days in whatever position you were trying to hit it in. Dre paid her cab fare all the way out VA, smoked an ounce of Skunk weed with her, fucked her in the ass, came in her mouth, and paid her cab fare back to D.C. An hour after she left, VA. State Troopers and FBI Agents kicked his hotel door in. On his way to the Alexandria Jail, a cocky, red neck FBI Agent told Dre that a Metra Wilson had called him in and collected the one thousand dollar reward money for his arrest.

Black was taking a shit while smoking a Newport looking and out on to the pitch black tier when he heard 48 cell slam open, hungrily waiting for its next meal of 'Young Black Male'. Wiping his ass, Black quickly got up and looked through the side of the bars with his hands hanging out of the tray slot. Just like everybody else standing at their bars, Black was trying to see who it was that would be in the cell across from him. Black had done too much dirt to be slipping when a new nigga came on the tier. He kept his cell jammed and if the new comer was opposition, he was good as hit before the tier door slid shut.

Coming in the dark No.1 Sally port, Dre could feel butterflies in his stomach. Never showing the least sign of fear, Dre walked up to the bubble. When the lights came on, Dre saw pipehead Ronnie in his C.O. uniform. The short, big belly, dark skinned man emerged from the bubble with a smile and told the C.O. that walked Dre up from R-n-D that he had everything from there. Knowing Dre and Black from around the way, pipehead Ronnie knew that he would be smoking good as long as they were locked up because he would be their only connect to the streets.

Dre's six feet four frame stepped through the tier door into the darkness. Step by step, Dre walked passed the tiny dark cells looking into the eyes of the unfriendly faces behind the bars. "Where you from, cuz?" a husky voice called out.

Looking around the tier to see where the voice had come from, Dre responded, "You got me fucked up, slim!" Black recognized his voice off the top.

"Dre!" Black called out.

"What's up, young?" Dre said as he jogged up to Black's bars, dropping his goodie bag and bed roll on the floor.

"What's up, nigga?" Dre said as he gave his man five.

"Ain't shit, joe. How the fuck you let them peoples catch up with you?" Black said.

"That snake ass bitch Metra! I had her out the hotel with me, fuckin' her and shit. The bitch left and called the Feds on me for the cash."

"That bitch knew who was bustin' at us that night in the white LTD and she ain't say shit! I'ma hit that bitch head as soon as we hit the bricks!" Dre had no doubt that Black was serious, he ain't play that snake shit at all.

"You talked to Mann?" Dre asked, not knowing that he had been shot, being as though he got locked up a day before the shooting.

"Where the fuck you been? Mann got shot 'bout a week and a half ago," Black said.

"Damn, I been out Alexandria for 'bout ten days. Who the fuck shot Mann?" Dre asked with anger in his face. Black gave him the run down on everything around the way from who shot Mann all the way down to how Lando and his little mob put the work in about it. When Tina came to see Black, she brought Lando and Quick with her, so he had all the facts as he put his man down with what was going down.

"So, what this case look like from your end?" Dre asked, moving on.

"Shit cool, but we might gotta get somebody to hit the bitch head that put me down with the move. She the only person that know anything, even so, she ain't see shit, so whatever she say is hearsay," Black said. The cell door behind Dre began to shake as the morning shift was coming on. Dre stepped in and continued rappin' to Black until they got tired.

Mann was pissed off. He had just cursed the doctor out for telling him that he may never walk again, despite the fact that he could move his legs. He just wasn't strong enough to try to stand up yet. As Mann got better, Pamila went back to work and only visited him in the evening. Mann had a lot of time to think. He was still getting used to the idea of Lando being in the street's putting in work. There was nothing he could say, he would be doing the same thing if Lando were in the hospital shot. Mann didn't even try to tell Lando to stop doing what he was doing with his little mob. Lando had got word that they had killed Boo, Will, some young dude name Dug, and a pipehead the night they lit up 13th Street. Ric got shot in the back twice and Jammie got shot in the arm. Mann could hear Lando's words in his head as if he was still talking. "I ain't gon' stop tearin' that joint up 'til them niggas dead!" All Mann could do was put his little brother on point about the new side of the game that he was now in. Over all, what he told him summed up to, "Watch your back and leave no memories." Thinking of witnesses, Mann's mind flew to D.C. Jail. Tina had put Mann on point about Dre and Black's murder case. The Feds knew that a broad had told Black that fifty thousand dollars was in the house and they knew that Black did the stabbing. Dre's name was implicated only as being part of the robbery, nevertheless, he was charged with murder. Mann knew the case was weak from what he had heard from Pamila and Tina, yet, he still wanted the broad dead. That way, he felt sure that his cousin and partner would make it home.

Mann's thoughts were interrupted when Lando, Quick, and Nakia came strolling in his room. Mann smiled when he saw Lando with his arm around Nakia's shoulders. The young girl was cute, Mann thought.

"What's up, nigga?" Quick said as he hopped up on the bed beside Mann.

"Ain't shit, shorty. How ya'll get down here? Ya'll could'na rode yall bikes," Mann said.

"We rollin' in big boy shit!" Quick said. Mann looked at Lando with an expression of curiosity.

"Black told me where the extra keys to his AC was," Lando said, playing it cool. Every move he made had to be smooth when Nakia was around.

"Black told you that you could push his shit? You know he don't play 'bout that car," Mann asked.

"Yeah, he know, but check this out," Lando said and continued. "We just left from around the way and Tina was beatin' Metra's ass out there. I mean, fuckin' her around, young! She done busted the bitch mouth all open and everything!"

"Fuck is all that about?" Mann asked as he pressed a button to raise the back of his bed, making him sit up straight.

Quick stood up and said, "You know that bitch got Dre locked up!" Tina had failed to hip Mann to that fact when she visited him. They spent so much time talking about the case Black and Dre had, that she left without telling him.

"She did what?!" Mann asked. He knew Metra was cruddie; she had been like that since they were kids, but she had never been hot.

"Yeah, slim, she turn big boy in for a G." Lando said. Mann turned his head to the right, looking out into the clear fall afternoon, thinking how a lot of shit was going to change as soon as he was out of the hospital.

Skipping the subject, Mann looked over at the shy, young girl sitting on Lando's lap and said, "So, this is the girl you crazy about, huh?"

Lil' Garvin had just parked his car in front of Dee-Dee's house when Wee-Wee zoomed around the corner on a shiny black Ninja 900 dressed in all black with his unbuttoned leather Hugo Boss jacket blowing in the wind. He had heard that Quick was beefing with some niggas up 13th Street. Wee-Wee pulled up right beside Lil' Garvin's Impala as he and Baby D got out. Leaning on one leg still revving the loud engine of the powerful sports bike, Wee-Wee gave Lil' Garvin five, saying,

"What's up, shorty? I hear y'all beefin' with some bammas up here."

Lil' Garvin shut the door behind him and put Wee-Wee down with how Mann got shot, who did it, and who they were beefing with. Wee-Wee knew Mann and everybody down 5th street, but his main concern was Quick, who was his Aunt's son. Wee-Wee told Lil' Garvin to let Quick know that he was trying to holla at him as soon as possible. When they were done talking, Wee-Wee revved the bike aggressively, sending the RPM gauge into the red as he popped the clutch, making the Ninja fishtail straight up Rittenhouse Street. The one hundred and thirty horsepower bike flew from 0 to 60 in 3.7 seconds, propelling Wee-Wee's tall and lean body out of sight in a raging roar.

After watching Wee-Wee fly up the street, Baby D and Lil' Garvin walked up the street to pipehead Old Tima's house. That was the crackhouse on the block. Many nights, niggas would sit in Old Tima's house hustling till the sun was up or until they finished pushing all of their coke. Now that it was getting cold at night, everybody that had coke to sell could be found slanging that shit when the sun went down.

Stepping in the door, they saw Old Tima sitting in the living room hitting the pipe. The tall, gray-haired, old man saw the young dudes come through the door and said, "Where ya'll been at? It's pumpin' like shit. Karen been spending money all day. Big Busta down the basement trying to smoke all her shit up now. Ya'll better get some of that cash, just hit me off real quick and get me out the way." Baby D and Lil' Garvin both hit Old Tima off with a fat fifty rock each and began hustling.

One after another, pipeheads rushed Old Tima's house for their fifteen seconds of fame at the end of the glass dick. Two hours after Baby D and Lil' Garvin had entered the crack house, they had both made over twelve hundred dollars each. Pipehead Karen had spent one thousand dollars of her income tax return between the both of them. They had caught a good rush while nobody was around. They were on their way to get some smoke when pipehead Ronnie came through the door in his C.O. uniform.

"What's up, scrap?" Ronnie said, jeffing hard.

"Ain't shit. What's up?" Baby D said in a rush to go get some smoke. Ronnie told them that he worked in the cellblock that Dre and Black were in up the Jail. He said that they had sent him to get some weed and money. Lil' Garvin was always on point for game.

He folded his arms and said, "Don't be playing no games!" Ronnie assured him that he was serious. Lil' Garvin gave him one hundred dollars and told him to wait in the crack house until they got back so that they could send Black and Dre some smoke.

"So, what do they got on me?" Dre angrily said to the tall, white lady that sat across the table from him on his legal visit.

"They have a young woman that says she knows that you and Mr. Mills robbed Mr. Sutton and afterwards, Mr. Mills fatally stabbed him. They know that you didn't kill Mr. Sutton, but if you don't tell 'em what really went down that day, you're going down for murder with your buddy. As your lawyer, it's my job to give you the best..."

Dre quickly cut her off. "Fuck that! You got me fucked up. I think you on the wrong side of the fence already. I'm outta here." Dre got up and left the woman in the room alone. He couldn't even think of flipping the script on his man. He had made up his mind. He was going to fire the bitch and get him a paid lawyer, and if Black didn't have enough money saved, he would get him one, too.

After being in jail for the last two weeks, Dre had already gotten used to the madness. It was just like the streets, the only difference was having nowhere to take cover when the drama hit. Dre was far from a punk, but he was not as aggressive as Black on the inside. Knife, knuckle, or burner, Black was down for whatever, whenever. Dre was more like Mann when it came down to the drama, he liked to strike when least expected. Black had already had them beefing. Black stabbed a dude in the face in front of the bubble that the C.O.s sat in. Even so, Black was his man and against all odds, Dre was going to ride to the bloody end.

Walking through the sally port door, Dre saw Black on the phone with a smile on his face. Black waved his hand for Dre to come up the steps and see who was on the phone. "Hold on, shorty!" Black said into the phone as he gave it to Dre.

"Hello?" Dre said, hearing Rare Essence blasting in the background.

"What's up, young?" an excited voice said into the phone.

"Who this? Lando?"

"Yeah, joe. You know Mann walking and everything, slim. He should be home in a few days," Lando said. Dre cut his eye at Black and flashed a smile. They both knew that things would move the way that they were supposed to with Mann back in the game. Lando gave Dre the run down on what was going on around the way. Ric and Jammie were back on the move again. They had shot at Lil' Garvin's car at a red light on Georgia Avenue about two nights ago. Nobody had seen Marvin since he shot Mann.

"I heard Tina beat Metra's ass," Dre said.

"No bullshit! She fucked that bitch up. She don't even be hangin' down Dee-Dee's house no more. She got a mob of new bitches she be with. They all be sittin' on her porch. Them bitches jive like that, too!" Lando said.

Dre finished talking to Lando and walked down the tier with Black. "We gon' beat this shit, joe," Black said and added, "Mann gon' make sure shit right. But uh... anyway, what your lawyer talkin' bout?"

"That bitch full of shit. I'm 'bout to get rid of that bitch. How much cash you got saved up?" Dre asked.

"I got like fifteen stashed over my mutha's house. What's up?"

"We gotta get a real lawyer..." Dre started to say as Black cut him off.

"We ain't gotta spend no money on a lawyer. Mann 'bout to be home, we gon' get that bitch head hit and we outta here!" Black pulled a bag of weed out of his drawers and said, "Let's go smoke. joe. Shit gon' work itself out."

Chapter Six: Too much heat

While Lando and his mob were bringing major drama to 13th Street, Marvin had been laying low for the last three weeks in North Carolina. He had a cousin down there that was getting some money from selling weed. Through his cousin, Marvin met a New Yorker named Solo that had all the coke in the small town of Greensville. It didn't take long for him to cut into the hood rats and find out where Solo kept all his coke and money. Once Marvin was on point about the whereabouts of the stash house, he wasted no time. With an old book bag, a roll of duct tape, and a .45 automatic, Marvin made his move late at night. Leaving Solo duct taped and shot in the top of the head twice, Marvin left town headed for the Inner State in a used red '87 Porsche 911 Cabriolet with paper tags along with three bricks of coke and ten thousand dollars in murder money.

Marvin's first stop was over his baby's mother's house. Nicole was a short, slim, dark skinned girl with a head on her shoulders. She went to school with Kelley and knew all about the beef between her baby's father and Mann. She had always found Mann to be a good nigga and had even gone out to eat down Georgetown with him a few times. Mann had earned a spot in her heart one day after her and Marvin had a big fight. Marvin had smacked her in the face, blacking her eye, and put her out of his car downtown in the rain. Coming from paying Pamila's phone bill, Mann pulled up at the light on 16th and M streets and saw Nicole soaking wet, crying, and trying to flag a cab down. Mann took her home and told her to call him when she wanted a man that was going to treat her right. Nicole loved Marvin, but she was crushed when she found out that he shot Mann.

Nicole was sitting on the sofa in a tight pair of blue Perris Ellis jeans and a white Banana Republic T- shirt with her pretty feet propped up on the coffee table, watching cartoons with her son. Marvin came through the front door carrying the old book bag full of coke and money. His son jumped off of the sofa and ran into his arms. Nicole got up and hugged him tightly, kissing him in the mouth.

"I missed you, boy!" Nicole said with her arms wrapped around his neck.

"I missed you and my lil' man, too, but I'm back now. Let me put this up and I'll be right back," Marvin said, and then went up to Nicole's bedroom to call Ric. Once Marvin heard that Mann was alive, he told Ric that he would be on his way home, but when Ric called down to NC telling him that he had got shot along with Jammie and the rest, Marvin hit Solo and came straight home.

"Hello?" Ric said, picking up the phone.

"I'm back, joe. I'ma be over Nicole's house all night. Come holla at me," Marvin said, sitting on Nicole's bed.

"I'm on my way, young!" Ric responded. He hung up the phone and was gone.

Mann was home, still weak, but he was home and he was ready to put things back in their proper place. Mann knew that all eyes were on him, and he had no plans on doing anything while the world was waiting. Mann had to sit Lando down and tell him that since he was out of the hospital, that didn't mean he was going to go on a rampage. He told Lando that if he were to act out of his anger instead of using his mind, he would slip along the way, costing him his life or his freedom. Lando listened, never cutting him off. Lando looked up to Mann all his life. He knew Mann knew where his ass was. Yet and still, Lando was firing pistols, and he had fell in love with the superficial power of the gun play. At first, he couldn't understand why Mann wanted him to chill out on stalking anybody that was from 13th Street, but then he thought that Mann would put him down with everything when the time was right, he always did. Now, the plan was for Lando to stay strapped and on point, but not to go looking for Ric or Jammie, but if he was to catch 'em slipping it was a green light to split they wigs. Lando was with it, Mann could do no wrong in his eyes.

Mann had been out of the hospital for three days. Pamila had allowed Kelley to stay in her house after getting to know her while Mann was in the hospital. Kelley was going to Coolidge High school, which was right across the street, so she was never far away. Every time she showed her face, Mann felt himself growing closer and closer to Kelley. She was a female that a man could fall in love with. While Mann was thinking about Kelley, she came walking down the steps with her schoolbooks in hand.

"What's up, beautiful?" Mann said as he laid across his bed wearing nothing more than a pair of grey Polo boxer shorts.

"I'm okay, just tired as shit," Kelley said as she sat her books down and threw her Nautica jacket across the sofa. Walking over and laying down beside Mann on the bed, she rubbed her soft hands across Mann's chest, saying, "Sometimes, I wonder if I'm wasting my time with the school thing. So many people go off to school with all these big hopes and dreams, only to come back to the city and work at Safeway or 7-Eleven somewhere. I ain't trying to be like that, Mann."

Looking into Kelley's beautiful eyes, Mann raised up off of the bed, leaning back on his elbows. He could see that the future truly meant a lot to Kelley.

Rolling over on his side, Mann rubbed the back of his hand against Kelley's smooth cheek, saying, "Shorty, the question ain't whether or not school is worth it. The question is, are you worth it? I feel as though you are, but you gotta feel as though you worth it."

"Mann, I know I'm worth it. Shit is just so hard! I ain't got nobody helping me, then on top of that, I only got four thousand dollars saved up for college. That's only enough for like one year..." Mann sensed Kelley's frustration building.

Softly, he placed one finger over her lips, and said, "Shhhh, slow down, boo. You looking too far down the road. Deal with today for right now and plan for tomorrow. Don't worry about it. Just do what you gotta do to get into the college you trying to go to. As long as I'm around, money ain't a thing." Kelley felt every word that Mann said. She was touched by his display of care for her. She pushed on Mann's chest, slowly making him lay on his back again. Laying right beside him, she passionately kissed him in the mouth. Her hand exploringly caressed its way down into Mann's Polo boxers. As things got heated, Pamila called Kelley from the top of the basement steps.

"Kelley, Are you still going to help me make dinner?"

Mann and Kelley both smiled as Kelley responded, "Yeah, Pamila, I'm on my way." Kelley sat up on the bed fixing her clothes, thinking of what it was going to be like to make love to Mann. As she got up to go help Pamila, she looked back at Mann, saying, "We gon' finish this later."

The phone rang as Kelley ran up the steps. Mann painfully rolled over and answered it. "Hello." It was a collect call from Dre. Mann accepted the call before the recording finished.

"What's up, nigga!" Mann said.

"What's up with you, joe!" Dre said with all the noise of the D.C. Jail day room in the background.

"I'ma little weak, but I'm getting stronger everyday. I been home for three days now, why you just calling?"

"Tina just came to see me and told me you was home. We got a lot to talk about, but that can wait. I told Tina to come holla at you, so she gon' put you on point, but hold on, Black wanna holla at you." Dre put his hand over the phone and yelled out on the tier for Black. Black came pimping in the day room wearing a fresh pair of tan, double sole Timberland boots with his jail jumper on up to his waist with the sleeves hanging at his side. In his tight tank top with his blue-black arms on swole from doing push-ups and his hair picked out into a Comrade George afro, Black looked like Black Power in the flesh.

"What's up, joe?" Black said.

"Ain't shit, slim, I'm in rehab," Mann said with a laugh.

"Yeah, I'm fucked up 'bout that, but we gon' be outta here in 'bout three months. First day I'm out…"

Mann cut Black off.

"Ho! Ho! Hold! I feel ya, but we can keep that on the hush. Don't even worry about me, I got this. Trust me. We gotta worry about getting ya'll out." Mann finished talking to Black and Dre, letting them know that everything was going to be fine because he was home.

Lando was deep in the game. To Lando, he was a big nigga gangsta muthafucka and nobody could tell him anything different. He had two bodies under his belt and everybody around 5th Street knew it. At school, he was the only young nigga driving an Acura legend in the seventh grade. His money just wouldn't stop stacking. Two grand away from ten thousand dollars, Lando was making a killing in the crack house at night, along with his mob. Not realizing it, Lando was really letting his hair down, even more so that Mann was out of the hospital. He was staying out hustling all night, he was going to school only to show off his fresh gear and Black's Acura, and he was even neglecting Nakia. She would have to beep him over and over again before he would find his way to the phone, only to tell her that he was busy and he loved her, but had to call her back later.

Mann had made sure that Lando got rid of the Glock he killed Will and the pipehead with up 13th Street. Wasting no time, he shot over Martin Luther King Jr. Avenue to see Poochie, and copped a brand new Taurus .45 automatic and two eighteen shot extended clips. Lando was quickly becoming a ghetto super star. As Lando, Quick, Lil' Garvin, and Baby D all became more notorious in the neighborhood, the police became more familiar with the up and coming gun slinging, dope dealing, and murderously, violent tempered younger generation that would run the 90s and leave the late 80s with a murder rate never before seen in the District of Columbia. Mann had warned Lando of that, but now, he would see for himself and never forget it.

As the cold chill of another fall night fell upon the D.C. Streets, the dope game was in overtime and everybody from 5th and Rittenhouse all the way up to Georgia and Rittenhouse was grinding hard for most valuable player. On the 5th Street end, things had changed a little bit over the past weeks with Mann in the hospital and Dre in jail. Onion had got his hands on two bricks of coke from somewhere. The pipeheads were talking bad about the coke Onion had on the streets while Mann and Dre were gone, but it was the only thing they could buy when Lando and his little mob were not around. Corey, Smoke, and Serge were all buying coke from Onion at the time and they knew it was bullshit. That had Smoke and Serge fucked up. They had even talked about robbing Onion, but passed the idea up. Corey really didn't care about the coke being bullshit. His only beef was with Lando and the young niggas around the way. By Lando and Quick buying coke from Wee-Wee, they had much more clientele when they hit the strip. Lil' Garvin and Baby D were buying coke from Lil' Garvin's big brother, Dex, and they had good clientele also, but it was nothing like Lando's or Quick's.

All the young niggas started hanging a block over from Rittenhouse Street on Roxboro Place, which was a small one-way street with a cut between every set of row houses. After hanging out on Roxboro Place during the daytime for a few days before hitting the crackhouse at night, the young niggas had turned it into a strip almost over night.

Pulling up in the alley in Black's Acura Legend, Lando and Quick, along with his pit bull, got out and hit the block. Stepping out into the streetlight, they saw Lil' Garvin and Baby D sitting on the hood of Lil' Garvin's car. Further down the block they saw Smoke and Serge serving pipeheads. Walking up to Lil' Garvin, Lando gave him five and said, "What shit look like out here, young?"

Lil' Garvin let Lando and Quick know that the money was coming through. Hearing somebody behind them, they quickly turned and saw Corey and Onion coming up the alley. As they came out of the alley, pipehead Karen bent the corner. The first person she saw was Corey. At five feet ten and two hundred and forty pounds, Corey was a heavy weight and a knock out artist as well. He rushed Karen, knowing that she had been having money lately.

"What's up?" Corey said.

"I'm tryin' to get six for one hundred," Karen said. Corey pulled a bag of rocks out of his drawers, and began to open it. Looking across the street, Karen saw Quick and told Corey that she was going to holla at him.

"What the fuck you mean you gon' holla at him after I got my shit out!" Corey yelled as he followed behind Karen.

Becoming scared, Karen jumped behind Lando, who tried to calm the situation down by saying, "Come on, man, she tryin' to holla at Quick. What? You gon' make her spend her money with you?" The younger dude's words just added to Corey's anger.

At twenty years old, Corey had been to prison and back before any of the younger niggas started hustling around the way. They were in his way. They had the block hot and police stayed on the strip. They were shooting every time he turned around, and now they were taking money out of his pocket. He couldn't take it anymore. His anger and frustration made him feel as if the young niggas were taking him for a sucka. Knowing that he could beat all of the young dudes into a coma, Corey went off.

Putting his finger in Lando's face with his right hand balled up into a fist, Corey said with anger, "I'll knock your lil' ass the fuck out. You a lil' boy, Lando!"

Baby D and Lil' Garvin jumped off the hood of the car as Quick struggled to hold Killa back, who was trying to lock her jaws on any part of Corey that she could get her teeth into. Onion grabbed Corey to try to pull him back, but he snatched away, getting back in Lando's face. Knowing that Corey was too big for him to fight, Lando's first thought was the .45 automatic in his waistband.

"You betta pipe down, big boy!" Lando said, trying to warn Corey of the danger that waited for him if he put his hands on him. While Killa became more aggressive and angry, Corey continued to press his luck.

"I better pipe down or what?" Corey said as he got closer up on Lando, setting him up for a short, six inch hook that would no doubt put the younger dude straight to sleep. Realizing Corey was sizing him up for a knock out, Lando swiftly stepped back, whipping out the huge chrome .45 automatic with the extended clip.

Pointing the gun in Corey's face, he said, "Nigga! I'll smoke your big ass out here!" Smoke and Serge walked up on the situation as Lil' Garvin pulled Lando back, warning him it was too many people outside for him to smash Corey right in the middle of Roxboro Place.

Killa yanked away from Quick and lunged straight for Corey's thick neck. Throwing his arms in front of his face to protect himself from Killa's potentially lethal bite, Corey felt the first lock jaw bite of Killa's teeth sinking deep into his forearm as he screamed out in pain and fear. Recklessly swinging his arm to get the angry dog off of him, Corey saw blood hitting the ground. Killa let go of his arm and lunged at his chest, wasting no time. Corey kicked the dog in the mouth as he tried to run. Raging with anger, Killa caught Corey's leg and locked her teeth deep into his thigh, ripping a huge chunk of bloody flesh. Quick finally got a hold of Killa's chain and pulled her off of Corey, allowing him and Onion to run down the alley.

While Smoke and Serge were dying laughing, Lando slipped his pistol back into his waistband saying, "Fuck that nigga!" Quick gave Baby D Killa's chain so that he could go ahead and serve Karen. Smoke and Serge talked to the young niggas for a minute about what had just went down. Then, they went on their way back down the street. Lando walked down the alley fired up. His pride was hurt. With one hand on the steering wheel of the Acura Legend sitting in the car with the door open, Lando tried to calm himself down.

Lil' Garvin walked up and said, "Chill out, young. Fuck that nigga!"

"I can't stand that nigga. I'ma end up poppin' his ass!" Lando said.

"Damn, young! You came off down the country!" Ric said as he sat in the passenger seat of Marvin's Porsche, admiring the way he had went down North Carolina and came back with a Porsche 911 Cabriolet, three bricks, and ten thousand dollars. Sitting behind the wheel, Marvin let Ric know what the next move was as they flew along the belt way headed for Marvin's apartment in Bowie, Maryland.

Taking a deep pull of the blunt Ric had just passed him, Marvin said, "The nigga Mann out the hospital now, so shit gotta come to a head. I known slim since we was kids. He done always been a thinka. He gon' lay until he get better, and then he gon' strike in a way that we ain't gon' expect, but he gon' be comin' for me first..."

"But, what about them young niggas? Quick and them?" Ric asked, cutting in.

"Don't worry 'bout them!" Marvin snapped as he went on. "Mann out the hospital now. He callin' all shots. He ain't gon' have them young niggas shootin' shit up for nothing, makin' the hood hot when he know I ain't around. Them young niggas came through there and caught y'all slippin' cause they felt like that's what they 'pose to do at the time. I got a spot out here by my apartment where we gon' push this coke and get paid. You gon' pass out weight to the young niggas around the way, they can keep shit pumpin' 'til I kill this nigga Mann." Ric was down with the plan. He had trust in his man and he was down to die with him if it came down to that.

"What about Jammie?" Ric asked as he grabbed the blunt and popped NWA into the tape deck.

"I got Jammie. He gon' come out here with us," Marvin said. The plan sounded good, Marvin thought to himself, but he knew Mann was like Air Jordan down three late in the fourth. It was no telling what he would do next.

Silk was just getting out of his Benz 190 in front of Mann's house as Kelley and Tina were coming out of the door carrying two boxes.

"What's up, ladies?" Silk said, stepping to the side as he let them pass by. Always fly, Silk saw how the girls were checking out his black leather Armani jacket.

"What's up, Silk?" they said.

"Where ya'll goin' with the boxes?" Silk asked.

Tina, looking so good in her tight blue Guess jeans, said, "We on our way to the post office to mail these boxes to Dre and Black."

Pulling a knot of one hundred dollar bills out the pocket of his black Perry Ellis jeans, Silk handed Tina three hundred dollars, and said, "Send 'em a lil' cash for me." Tina let Silk know that she would make sure that they got the money as her and Kelley got in Dre's new Corvette ZR1 headed for the post office.

Walking down the basement steps after Pamila let him in the house, Silk over heard Mann talking to Lando and Quick, who were sitting on the sofa.

"I'ma see ya'll later. Take ya'll ass to school and don't forget what I said," Mann said as he ran in place on the treadmill Pamila bought for him so that he could get back in shape. Headed for school, Lando and Quick got up and left.

"What's that all about?" Silk said as he sat on the sofa.

"I jive had to pull Lando up on pullin' pistols on niggas and not using 'em. Shorty had some words with big Corey the other night and pulled a joint out on him," Mann said.

"What happened?" Silk asked.

"Corey was fucked up that some pipehead ain't want to buy his shit, so he went off and act like he was going to do something to Lando. They say shorty was 'bout to bust his big ass. Somehow, Quick let his pit bull go on the nigga. I gotta go around there and make sure Corey leave that shit alone before them young niggas kill 'em." Mann got off the treadmill and grabbed a towel. Wiping sweat off of his face, Mann asked Silk, "What's up with you?"

"The question is what's up with you!" Silk said.

After being out of the hospital just over a week, Mann was already on top of what he had to do to get things straight. Tina gave him the run down on the girl that was talking to the police on Black and Dre's case. He had to make sure that he took care of her, even though he knew he had to get himself in some better shape before he could deal with her or Marvin. He told himself that he would take everything one day at a time. The Feds had been to his house twice since he left the hospital. Before the Feds knew he was out of his coma, he was gone from the hospital already. The first time they came looking for him, Pamila told them that Mann was out. The second time, Mann let them in and got straight to the point, telling them he had no idea who shot him. They, on the other hand, told Mann they knew DeMarvin Scott shot him and that if anything was to happen to him that they were coming for Mann since he called himself being true to the game. Mann paid them no attention, knowing that when he caught Marvin, nobody would know shit.

Mann looked at Silk and said, "You know what's up with me, slim. I'm back on my feet now. It's time to get that money. They say that nigga Onion got a rack of bullshit out there. I'm trying to get back out there and lock shit down."

"What's up with this nigga that shot you?" Silk said.

"I got this nigga. He walkin' dead, I'ma push 'em in his grave when the time is right."

"I think you taking this nigga lightly," Silk said.

Mann smiled at Silk and said, "You done known me too long, joe. I got this."

Mann asked Silk about his connect with Supreme. Silk let him know that he was getting thirty bricks a week now. Supreme was charging him four hundred and eighty thousand for every drop. Paying that amount for thirty bricks rounded off to sixteen thousand a brick at a time when coke was short and a brick could go for twenty five to thirty thousand dollars, depending on your connect. Silk was dropping twenty bricks in the city at twenty five thousand a piece, and ten more out VA for thirty thousand a piece. He was killing 'em.

Mann was drunk off of all the dollar signs that were flying through his mind. Hearing Silk talk about the way he was flippin bricks had Mann ready to get down to business. "I'm ready to get that cash. What's up?" Mann said.

Giving deep thought to what Mann said, Silk responded, "How much cash you got right now?"

"I got about ninety in cash right now," Mann said as he walked over to the weight bench.

"This is what I'ma do. Gimme fifty now and I'ma give you five joints. When you finish, just hit me with thirty more. Dependin' on how you push the shit, you gon' see well over one hundred and twenty five. After that, you can do your own thing with Supreme every time I see 'em." Silk laid the cards on the table. Mann was ready and he already knew what he was going to do.

The 4th District Police Chief stormed into the office of Detective James and his partner, Detective Hall. The short, overweight, white Police Chief dropped a thick folder of paper work on Detective James' desk and hissed at him angrily. "Downtown is all over my ass about these latest shootings! These little wanna be gangstas are making my job hard! I want you and Hall on top of finding anything to lock their black asses up for!" The Chief stormed out of the office slamming the door behind him.

Detective James, an older, black man, opened up the folder that contained information about the string of shootings that had taken place on 13th Street N.W. Over the past month, there were four unsolved murders and seven assaults with intent to kill. Flipping through the papers, Detective James ran across the names DeMarvin Scott and Mark Mills.

Turning around to his partner, he said, "Hey, Hall, didn't you have that Mills shooting?"

"Yeah, he's some big dope boy down on uh... 5th Street, uh...5th anf Rittenhouse. Another young guy named uh... Scott, DeMarvin Scott got into a shoot out with Mark Mills. Why you ask, that's what that's about?" Detective Hall asked.

"Yeah, these shootings seem to occur as soon as Mr. Mills gets shot, and then they stop as soon as he gets out of the hospital. He's gotta have something to do with it," James said.

Hall had been trying to get a murder case on Black for the last three years, but no one would live to talk. He knew all about him.

Thinking about Black, Hall said, "The Mills boy gotta a cousin they call Killa Black, but he's locked up for murder right now. He's the only one I think could be responsible for some shit like that."

"It's gotta be some one else that's close to the Mills boy. These murders are related to him being shot," James said.

"Looks like we gotta hit the streets, then," Hall said.

Chapter Seven: Back on the block

It was back to business for Mann. Days after talking to Silk about the coke he was pushing, Mann was in the basement bagging up. Mann had cooked five bricks of powder into solid pies of crack rock. He decided to keep a brick for himself and break it down to ounces. That way, he would get all the cash possible when he stepped back on the strip.

Dusting his hands off, Mann stashed the bricks in the ceiling along with his money. Walking over to the bed, Mann pulled his T-shirt up to look at his healing bullet wounds. He felt blessed to be alive, but pay back was in the making, he thought as he pulled a heavy, black bullet proof vest over his head. He grabbed a thick grey Polo sweat hoody off the bed and pulled it over the vest. Sitting down on the bed, he picked up the huge, black Desert Eagle that Silk gave him and slid a clip of .44 magnum bullets in it. Sliding the pistol into his shoulder holster, Mann grabbed his big blue Eddie Bauer down coat and hit the streets

Winter was in town and only true hustlas were on the block. Bending the corner in his black Nissan 300 ZX, Mann got everyone's attention. Standing at the end of the alley in the middle of the block wearing thick black skull caps, big Eddie Bauer coats of all colors, and tan double sole Timberland boots were Smoke, Serge, Onion, Corey, and Kevin, who must have just made parole.

Slowly pulling up on the crowd with one hand on the wheel and the other on the Desert Eagle lying across his lap,

Mann could tell that his presence was making Corey nervous. Sliding the pistol under his seat, Mann rolled the passenger window down at the push of a button and spoke to everyone. From the sidewalk, everybody spoke back to Mann. Smoke and Serge pulled up on Mann and asked if he was back on. Mann let them know he had coke and told them to beep him later. After talking to Onion and Kevin, Mann called Corey over to the car. Cautiously, Corey limped to the car using a cane, still feeling the effects of Killa's vicious lock jaw attack.

Watching Corey walk over to the car, Mann reflected on his years of knowing the older dude. When Mann came off the porch, he was Lando's age and Corey was his age. Back then, Corey and Kevin had the block locked down. Mann was only getting ounces from Silk at the time. Corey had always looked out for Mann when he was just coming off the porch and still green to the streets. Mann never forgot those days. Mann could still remember when Corey caught his big drug case and went to prison. Fighting the case, Corey spent over twenty thousand dollars and still ended up taking a cop to up to thirty years, spending two years in Atlanta's Federal Penitentiary. While he was locked up, Corey's girl had a baby by a Prince George's County Police officer. She married the cop, taking the eighty thousand dollars that Corey left with her, and moved to L.A. with the money. Corey came home in 1988 broke as a bag of glass.

"Mann, I ain't got no beef with…"

Mann shook his head and waved his hand, cutting Corey off saying, "I ain't beefin' slim. I'm tryin' to make sure it ain't no beef. I already talked to Lando and Quick. I told them to leave the shit alone. You know they think they big boys now. I'm asking you to leave the shit alone for me, joe." Corey was more than happy to let the beef slide, not because he was scared, but because it was too much trouble to beef with Lando. He would have to kill Mann, Quick, Lil' Garvin, Baby-D, and then he would have to turn around and kill Black and Dre when they got home. After a little thought, Corey saw it as a no win situation. The whole thing could only get worse for him. If one of them didn't kill him first, he knew he would be back in prison before he was done beefing.

"So, how you livin' out here?" Mann asked Corey.

"Shit ain't like it used to be, but I'm making it."

"Check this out, beep me later on. I'ma do something with you," Mann said. He talked to Corey and the rest of the dudes on the strip, never once talking about the beef with him and Marvin. While they were talking, a white van rode by with Virginia tags. The flash of a camera went off and everyone turned their heads quickly. "Damn! It's hot like that out here!" Mann said as the van kept rolling down the street. Onion let Mann know that the same white van had been riding through taking pictures for the last week or so. That was all Mann needed to hear to let everybody know that it was time for him to leave.

"So, what Mann gon' do 'bout them bammas?" Quick asked Lando, laid back in the passenger seat of the Acura Legend on their way over Nakia's house.

"Mann say leave the shit alone," Lando said as they pulled up in front of Nakia's house.

"Leave the shit alone! Fuck that! I ain't gon' let a nigga shoot me and get away with it!"

"Mann ain't gon' let a nigga get away with shit! Mann gon' see all them niggas!" Lando said as he became upset about Quick doubting Mann.

Sensing the frustration in Lando's voice, Quick said, "I know Mann gon' see them niggas, but he supposed to smash them niggas off the top." Lando could see what Quick was saying. He really didn't understand why Mann was waiting to get on top of the beef, but he knew Mann knew what he was doing.

Nakia took their attention off the conversation as she came out of the house along with another cute, brown skinned girl. Dressed to impress, the two young girls got in, bringing the cold night air with them as Quick got in the back seat with the brown skinned girl, allowing Nakia to sit up front with Lando. Nakia unzipped her big grey Polo coat as the car pulled off headed for the movies. Turning back to Quick with a smile on her face, Nakia said, "Quick, this my girl, Trina. She the one I was telling you about."

"Oh yeah?" Quick said as he slid an arm around the cute girl. "So, thiss Trina, huh?" Quick moved closer to Trina and began to get very familiar with her. Before they got to the movies, Quick had his hand in Trina's pants, kissing her in the mouth while he played with her clit.

Cutting the Acura off in the White Flint Mall parking lot, Lando pulled his .45 automatic from under the seat and got out of the car along with everyone else. Looking all around the three level parking lot, Lando saw a red Porsche 911 Cabriolet with dark tented windows and said, "That joint right there like that!"

Turning to look at the car right beside theirs, Quick said, "Yeah that joint knocking, young," as he shut the car door behind him, tucking his 10mm Ruger in his waist band.

Mann pulled up in the alley between Roxboro Place and Rittenhouse Street and cut the head lights out, leaving him and Corey plunged into the darkness of the tented windows on the Z. Handing Corey a fat zip-lock bag with a half a brick in it, Mann said, "That's five hundred grams. You gon' get your money's worth with that there." Corey pulled two stacks of cash out of his blue Eddie Bauer and handed Mann the money. Sliding the rubber band off the money, Mann flipped through it and saw that it was ten thousand dollars on the nose in big bills. Mann and Corey talked for a minute, and then Corey got out the car and went to bag his coke up.

In the car alone, Mann pulled the Desert Eagle .44 from under the dash board of the Z along with a zip-lock bag full of fifty rocks and got out the car, cutting through Dee-Dee's backyard headed for the strip.

Pipeheads were commuting in and out of Pipehead Old Tima's house, in a numbed daze. As the cold winter air blew, Mann pulled his thick, black skull cap down tight on his head and quickly observed the surroundings. He didn't feel good on the strip knowing that the Feds had been coming through taking pictures. Sitting at the end of the alley in the middle of the block, Mann saw Smoke and Serge waiting for their next dollar. Seeing Mann, they waved their hands in the air. Mann responded in the same way as he looked across the street at the crack house. Seeing Lil' Garvin's car parked right in front of the crack house made Mann shake his head in disagreement. He didn't play the crack house at all. He always needed to see and know what was going on around him, and he felt that sitting in the crack house took his eyes and ears away from him, leaving him vulnerable to an unexpected attack from the Feds or some niggas trying to rob or kill him. Looking down the street, Mann saw Metra and four other bad broads in big coats standing on Metra's porch. Mann thought they must be waiting for someone.. Dre came to mind when he saw Metra. She had to get dealt with, but it wasn't the time or place. Turning to the side, Mann saw Big Busta and C.O. Ronnie.

"What's up, Mann? Boy, I done missed you. These niggas got a bunch bullshit out here," Big Busta said as he gave Mann five. Ronnie walked up and gave Mann five, too, as Mann led both pipeheads into the dark cut beside Dee-Dee's house to serve them. Once in the cut, Mann asked them what they were trying to get. Big Busta wanted four fifty rocks. Mann pulled the zip-lock bag of fifty rocks out of his pocket and gave Big Busta four huge fifty rocks for one hundred and seventy dollars. As Big Busta headed for Old Tima's house, Mann served Ronnie two fat fifties for nintety, and asked him how Black and Dre were doing up the jail.

Ronnie began to tell Mann how he was taking Black and Dre weed and money up the jail every time he went to work. Mann let him know to beep him every night before he went to work so that he could send his niggas whatever they needed. Ronnie went on to tell Mann how Dre had pulled a young C.O. broad and was fucking her every night. She would come get him before the last count of the night and take him on a medical run to the infirmary. After making sure that everyone that had to be seen was gone back to their block, the cute, young woman would make sure Dre got caught up in the count. They would go in the back of the infirmary in the empty holding cell and fuck until the count was clear while a buddy of the C.O. broad would watch their back.

Black was the same ole nigga inside and out. He was on administrative segregation again. Black had a fall out with an old timer that had come back to the jail on a writ from the Lompoc Federal Penitentiary. The old timer had been locked up for the last twenty years. He had it in his mind that the younger generation was soft because all they did was use guns. Black was the only nigga in the block with weed and the old timer had asked him for a few jays. Black sent him a few times, but the old timer wore out his welcome and ended up taking Black's kindness for weakness. Black wasted no time letting the old timer know that he wasn't about any games. Late one night, Black got Ronnie to let him down on the adult tier. Ronnie popped the old timer's cell while Black ran down the dark tier and caught the old timer taking a shit. In seconds, Black slammed the buck knife deep into the old timer's body over and over, hitting him in the neck twice, and all over his back and arms. Black would have gotten away with the whole thing, but a young dude that was scared of Black told on him and checked out of the block.

When Ronnie was done talking to Mann, he headed for Old Tima's house. Mann's beeper went off and he went in Dee-Dee's house to use the phone. Lando was beeping him *911. Something had to be up.

People flooded out of the movie theater into the crowded mall when the movie was over. Nakia was tired. She fell asleep twice during *Friday the 13th* and was half asleep on Lando's shoulder as they walked out into the mall.

"I got to use the bathroom, boo," Nakia said to Lando.

"Me too," Trina said as her and Nakia bent the corner on her way to the bathroom.

Waiting for the girls, Lando asked Quick what was up with Trina. Leaning on the pay phone as people walked up and down the huge hallway with shopping bags, Quick let Lando know that Trina was cool as shit.

"I dig shorty," Quick said. While Quick was talking, Lando began squinting his eyes, looking down by the Eddie Bauer shop.

"Ain't that Marvin and his baby mutha?" Lando asked.

Turning to look at what Lando was talking about, Quick reached for his 10mm and said, "Yeah that's that bitch ass nigga. We can smash that nigga right in the parking lot, young!"

"Naa, I got this nigga. Wait here for Nakia and them, joe," Lando said as he jogged down the hallway, following Marvin and Nicole out into the parking lot.

Hand on his .45 automatic with it hid inside his big Eddie Bauer coat, Lando cocked the hammer as he trailed behind Marvin and Nicole unnoticed. Cautiously, Lando looked all around the parking lot. No one seemed to be around. It was the perfect time to blast Marvin and his baby's mother. Stalking his prey, Lando followed the couple up a pair of dark steps that led up to the second and third levels of the parking lot. Pulling his pistol out in open display, Lando watched as the couple walked through the door on the second level.

"Damn!" Lando said as he smacked the .45 against his leg while running up the steps. Peeping through the door, Lando saw that Marvin and Nicole were walking toward the Acura Legend that he was driving. Walking up to the red Porsche beside the car he was driving, Lando saw Marvin stop and point at the Acura.

"Ain't that Black's car?!" Marvin asked Nicole as he carefully looked around the parking lot.

"Yeah, but Lando been drivin' that car since he been locked up."

"You talking 'bout Mann lil' brother?"

"Yeah."

"I thought he was a lil' boy."

"He ain't a lil' boy no more. He runnin' around with guns and shit now. Anyway, let's go. I got school tomorrow," Nicole said as they got in their car and left. After over hearing Marvin and Nicole, Lando ran back into the mall and beeped Mann.

As Lando was telling Quick why he couldn't smash Marvin in the parking lot, the pay phone rang. "Yeah!" Lando said into the phone.

"What's up, shorty? What's wrong with you?" Mann asked.

"I just saw the nigga Marvin out here at the mall with his baby mutha. I coulda smoked the nigga, but he was parked right beside Black's car."

"I told you to leave the nigga alone. Let me deal with that," Mann said as he went on to let Lando know that he had been in the streets long enough to take care of a situation like that one. Lando was pissed off about the way Mann was dealing with the whole beef and in his mind, he told himself that if he caught Marvin slipping one more time, he was going to blow his brains out no matter what Mann had to say.

Mann spent the next two days making money and checking his traps on the streets. Mann had got word that Marvin had ran across some bricks out of town and had a little spot out Bowie, MD locked down. After running into Nicole one day after school, he had also found out that Ric had been making a lot of money out Bowie along with Marvin and Jammie. Ric had bought a silver '88 Acura Legend coupe with tinted windows while Jammie had bought a light blue '89 Nissan Pathfinder with chrome B.B.S. rims. After a little thought, Mann could remember seeing the car and the truck a few times within the last two weeks. It was time to make his move.

Now that Mann was back on his feet, his money was starting to stack again. He ran into two old friends named Da-Da and LeRon that he used to sell coke to a while back. They had found a New York connection and started buying bricks from him sometime last year. Come to find out, the New Yorker had got robbed and killed about two months ago, leaving Da-Da and LeRon with no sweet connect. Mann moved right in and started selling them both a brick each for twenty five thousand dollars a whop. Onion was also buying coke from Mann now that he saw how Mann had the best deal on the streets at the time. Onion couldn't beat a brick for twenty thousand dollars. Silk couldn't believe how fast Mann had locked his block back down. Mann was coming at Silk with eight thousand dollars strong every Friday. Silk was pleased to have a for sure buy once a week for five bricks, and Mann was showing no signs of slowing down. It was back to business.

Mann felt that he was well enough to take care of the broad that was telling on Black and Dre. Picking Tina up from her house, they both slid up the jail to see Black and Dre. While Tina sat and talked to Dre, Mann got the run down on the government witness. Mann let Black know that he needed more information on the broad because she was never at the address that he had been going to. Black let Mann know that the broad could be found at the club called the Black Hole every weekend. Mann told Black that he would be on top of the situation by the end of the week for sure.

Just before the visit was over, Black began to ask Mann about the beef with Marvin. "So, what's up with the nigga Marvin? I hear he back in the streets," Black said, wondering why Mann hadn't taken care of his business.

"I got that nigga, joe. That's small shit to me," Mann said.

"How the fuck is that small shit? If I was home, all them bitch ass niggas would be dead now. You taken them suckas lightly, that's what the fuck is up!"

"Look! I know what I'm doing. I been busting ass just as long as you, but I never been locked up for murder. Not once! I know what I'm doing, so let me do this," Mann said, checking his younger cousin, who seemed to be acting more like his younger brother at the time.

Things weren't getting better at home for Lando. Pamila was at the end of her rope with him. Two days ago she had to go pick him up from the police station. He had been arrested for driving without a license and truancy. When Pamila arrived at the police station to pick him up, the police let her know that Lando had eight thousand dollars on him when he was arrested. The police let Pamila know that Lando's name was popping up a lot lately and if he didn't watch himself, he would be in a lot of trouble. Lando paid the Feds no attention at all. The only thing that got to him was that Pamila took his money, put it in the bank in his name, and it was no way for him to get it.

Standing in the kitchen cooking dinner, Pamila voiced all her frustration to Kelley. "I don't know what's wrong with that boy. I know boys will be boys, but Lando lil' ass is out of control," Pamila said. "He's out of fucking control. He comes and goes as he pleases. He don't go to school but every blue moon. Mann was nothing like this at his age."

Kelley didn't know what to say, so she said the only thing she thought that made sense. "Why don't you get Mann to talk to him?"

"I tried that. Lando still do what he wants to do, I want to put his lil' ass out of my house, but I know that my sister would turn over in her grave. Something is going to have to give. I'm not going to keep living like this!" Pamila said as her anger began to boil over.

Outside of Paul Jr. High School, Lando, Quick, Baby-D, and Lil' Garvin leaned against the brick wall in huge Eddie Bauer coats that looked twice their size. Lil' Garvin was waiting for some young girl that he was trying to pull while everybody else was talking about the fight that Baby-D had later on at the boys and girls club. Quick was telling Baby-D that he better not get knocked out in front of everybody.

Baby-D looked at Quick and said, "Nigga, is you lunchin'? I'm the quickest young nigga up town. Bet on me!"

Everybody burst out laughing. Lando walked over and

told Quick that he needed to talk to him, and they stepped off while Lil' Garvin and Baby-D pulled up on the young girl Lil' Garvin was waiting for, along with another young light skinned girl that was with her.

Lando put Quick down with how Pamila had put all of his money in the bank and he was broke. "So, what you gon' do?" Quick asked.

"I got a move for us, young!"

"A move? You ain't gotta go on no moves! Mann got bricks," Quick said.

"You right! Mann got bricks! I ain't got shit! Is you with me or not?" Lando asked. Quick was down with his man; win, lose, or draw, he was with it. Lando went on to tell Quick how it was a Jamaican that had moved in the apartments that Jazmin lived in. He was pumping weed out of his apartment by the pounds. Lando wasn't sure how much money was inside, but whatever it was, it was a quick caper. When Lando and Quick were finished talking, Jazmin walked by and flashed a smile at Lando. He told Quick that he would see him later on at the fight as he ran to catch up with Jazmin.

Jogging up behind Jazmin, Lando called her. "Jazmin! Hold up, beautiful."

Turning around smiling, Jazmin said, "Oh, you got time for me today, huh!"

"What you mean today?"

"You always on the run, you ain't never got no time for me," Jazmin said as the two began to walk toward the Acura Legend.

Putting an arm around Jazmin, Lando said, "It ain't like that with me. You always seem to be on your way some where when I see you. Where you going now?"

As they walked up on the Acura, Jazmin said, "I'm on my way home. You think you going that way?"

"Yeah, I think I am going that way," Lando said as they hopped in the car headed for Jazmin's apartment.

Inside of Jazmin's bedroom, Lando looked around the room at all of the fashion designs on her wall and asked if she drew them all herself. "Yeah, I draw those things all the time. One day, I'ma have my own fashion line," Jazmin said. Lando started laughing.

"You think my dream is a joke!" Jazmin asked, becoming dead serious.

"Naa, I just never thought you were some kinda fashion designer."

"Is something wrong with that?" Jazmin asked.

Lando stood up and grabbed Jazmin's small hands, saying in a no non-sense voice, "Look here, I ain't say nothing was wrong with that. Everybody needs a dream. I support yours. Shit! When I get one myself, I'll be cool." Lando sat and talked to Jazmin for a while, really getting to know her. For the first time in his young life, Lando had run into someone that made him think about the future, even if it was only for a minute.

Inside the boys and girls club, Baby-D was already gloved up, ready to go into the ring. Lando came in the front door in his over-sized blue Eddie Bauer. The spot was packed. Niggas from all parts of town were in the stands. Lando looked all around the gym. All the way at the top of the stands, Lando saw Mann, Kelley, Quick, and Lil' Garvin. He headed in their direction.

After showing his love to everyone, Lando sat down beside his brother. "What's up, shorty?" Mann asked.

"Ain't shit, young," Lando said.

"I heard Pamila took all your money and put it in the bank. I don't want you out there doing no wild shit, I'ma do something with you."

"Naa, I'm cool, young. I got a move I'm 'bout to go on tonight," Lando said.

"A move!" Mann said, not understanding why Lando would want to go on a move when he knew that Mann would give him anything he needed.

"Yeah! A move. I got a caper up the Ave., Lando said.

Mann and Lando got into a heated argument about the whole situation. Mann became frustrated with Lando's idea of being his own man. Lando was on some kind of tip where he didn't want anything from Mann. Mann understood where his little brother was coming from, but he couldn't see any sense in the mind set that Lando had grew into over the last few months. One thing that Mann did understand was that Lando was going to do what he wanted to do no matter what he had to say. The only thing Mann could do to keep his little brother close to him was to get him to come at him with the money when he made whatever move he had in the making. Lando agreed to that and the stage was set. Lando was calling his own shots before he was old enough to drive.

The bell rang. It was round one of three. Baby-D came out with his game face on. With his face greased up, no more then one hundred and twenty five pounds, he was still just as dangerous as his bigger opponent, who was five pounds bigger than him as well as four inches taller. The bigger fighter was from another boys and girls club. Everyone that came to support him called him Champ. Tall and very dark skinned, Champ looked like a young Zulu warrior.

Pow! The first punch of the fight was thrown, sending a loud smacking sound echoing through the whole gym. Champ caught Baby-D with a lightening jab hard on the chin. The stands went crazy, screaming, "You the man, Champ!"

Mann's voice was the only other voice you could hear that was supporting Baby-D, but he sounded like a crowd of people when he was screaming, "That nigga fakin', shorty. Knock his big ass out!"

Baby-D knew that he would have to use his speed to win the fight. Champ was packing too much power for him to go toe to toe. Champ rushed Baby-D, seeing that he was much smaller. Swinging two powerful left hooks off of his jab, Champ became angry when Baby-D slipped every punch and landed two quick stinging right hands to his face before shuffling backwards like Muhammad Ali himself. The stands went crazy once more.

Baby-D thought Mann was ring side by the sound of his voice screaming, "That's right, young nigga!"

Fish-bone, Baby-D's trainer, gave clear instructions for him to use his speed and stay away from the bigger fighter. Baby-D did just that. Using the divine speed of youth, Baby-D popped his quick jab and danced around the ring, every now and then he would stop with a little shake and dig straight to the body, and then slam a right hand down the pipe. The fight was going exactly how Fish-Bone had planned.

At the start of the third round things took a turn for the worst. Champ threw a solid over hand right, tagging Baby-D flush on the chin, ringing his bell. Dazed and off balance, Baby-D caught a thunderous upper cut that shook his brain painfully, somewhat putting him out on his feet. By the mixed sounds of the loud emotional crowd, Baby-D knew he was in deep trouble. Out of nowhere, a devastating leaping left hook took Baby-D clean off his feet, slamming him to the canvas. Fish-Bone went crazy. As Baby-D got himself together Fish-Bone got his attention and told him that the fight was his if he could survive the rest of the round. Baby-D could care less about surviving the rest of the round. All of his niggas were in the stands and they saw him hit the canvas hard. Going against everything Fish-Bone had said, Baby-D went straight at Champ. The change in his fight game so late in the last round shook Champ up and he was taken off guard. Baby-D popped two jabs and slammed two over-hand rights against the side of Champ's face. Champ shot a powerful right hand back at Baby-D as they got into a nasty clutch. Pure anger kept Baby-D safe in the clutch. His mind was made up, somebody was going out. Punch after punch was thrown and no one seemed to be slacking at all. Fish-Bone became hysterical. He couldn't believe Baby-D was throwing the fight away out of pride, he had taught him much better than that.

"Get outta there!" Fish-Bone screamed at the top of his lungs while the stands went off.

Something told Baby-D to slide out of the clutch. In a flash, he stepped back and slid out of the clutch as everything seemed to move into slow motion. Off balance, Champ ran straight into a murderous right cross that put him straight to sleep. As his big body lifelessly hit the canvas, all Baby-D could hear was Mann, Lando, Quick, and Lil' Garvin screaming, "That's right, young nigga!" The fight was over, Baby-D had taken a chance that could have gotten him hurt, but he was a gambler and that time he hit seven on the first roll.

Hours later, Lando and Quick sat in the Acura Legend in the darkness of the night on a side street a block away from Jazmin's apartment with their pistols in hand as they put the plan together on how they would get the Jamaican dude to open the door.

"This what we gon' do," Lando said. "We gon' act like we trying to buy some smoke. When the bamma open the door, we gon' go in with our joints out."

Quick thought about what Lando had said for a minute, then said, "So, we gotta pop the nigga?"

Cocking his .45 automatic, Lando said, "Yeah, you right. Let's do this, young."

Lando knocked on the door with no fear at all. Quick stood on the other side of the door, out of sight, with both hands on his huge 10mm.

A deep Jamaican voice said, "Yeah, mon! Wha yah want?"

Lando wasted no time saying, "I'm tryin to get a fifty bag."

The Jamaican said, "Hold on, mon." In seconds, the door cracked and a six feet, big, black Jamaican dude with longdreadlocks peeped through the door. Lando and Quick kicked the door open with their pistols pointed at the big man.

"Back the fuck up, nigga!" Lando ordered as he and Quick walked into the apartment.

The Jamaican dropped the fifty bag of weed on the floor with his hands in the air saying, "What ya want, mon?"

"You know what the fuck we want, nigga. Where that shit at!" Quick said as he began to look through the apartment.

Lando held the big man at gunpoint while Quick tore the place up. In less than a minute, Quick came out of the back room with a Foot Locker bag full of weed.

"I got at least two pounds in here, young!" Quick said to Lando.

"Oh yeah?" Lando said as he turned to the Jamaican and said, "Where the money at, nigga?"

"Me ain't got no money in here, shorty!" the Jamaican said.

"Watch this nigga," Lando said as he went to take a look in the bedroom. Seconds later, he came back out with a shoe box of cash. The Jamaican dude gave in to his anger. He tried to rush Quick and take his pistol. Dropping the Foot Locker bag of weed, Quick popped three quick 10mm slugs straight into his chest, sending the big man flying back against the wall with his arms swinging in the air.

Wasting no time, Lando let the .45 auto go, sending six .45 slugs flying into the dude's chest as well. The slugs went straight through the dude and hit the wall. The Jamaican dude fell dead to the floor. Quick picked up the Foot Locker bag of weed and ran behind Lando out the door. Running down the hallway with their pistols still in hand, they didn't even see that Jazmin was looking out of her apartment door.

Once in the car, Lando got him and Quick out of there in seconds. Pulling up in the alley behind his house and out of breath, Lando said, "That nigga was lunchin'! What made that nigga think he was gon' get away with some shit like that?"

"Man, I don't know what was up with that nigga, but he dead as E-muthafucka now!" Quick said with a murderous laugh.

Opening the shoe box full of money, Lando said, "Let's go break dis shit down, young."

Chapter Eight: New Yorker

The Black Hole was packed. Mann walked through the door without a search because he knew the dude that was patting everyone down. He walked in the go-go with his Desert Eagle tucked in his waist band. The small dance floor was packed with people and through the darkness, Mann couldn't tell who was who, so he kept his hand inside his Hugo Boss jacket with his finger on the trigger of the .44 he was carrying. Mann saw a few old friends in the spot. All they wanted to know was who had shot him and if he had put that work in yet. Others asked about Dre and Black, and when they would be coming home. Mann told no one more then they needed to know, and then he began to pull up on the females.

Leaning against the wall sipping a cup of Hennessy was a beautiful, dark skinned girl in a tight pair of blue Gap jeans and a soft leather Armani coat on. Mann pulled up on her smoothly and got her phone number. Moving to the back of the dance floor, Mann ran into a small cute light skinned girl with long, black hair. She looked as if she could be from an island somewhere in the Caribbean.

"How you doin'?" Mann asked as he flashed a smile.

Turning to look at Mann, the cute girl responded, "I'm chillin'."

"So, what can I call you? You gotta have a name."

"You can call me Mika if I can call you something."

Rubbing his hand seductively through the girl's hair, Mann said, "You can call me New Yorker."

"What? You from New York or somethin'?"

"Yeah, why? You don't like out of towners?" Mann asked the cute girl.

Smiling up at Mann, she said, "Naa, they cool. I just never messed with one before."

"Well, look here, it's a first time for everything in this world. So, check this out, can we leave here, maybe go get something to eat, and then you show me a good time?" Mann asked.

"Sure, that sounds good to me, let's go," the cute girl said as they left the Black Hole.

Days after Lando and Quick had killed the Jamaican dude in Jazmin's apartment building, they were walking down the hallway of Paul Jr. High School about to sneak out for lunch. They had came off with a nice little bit of cash on the caper. It turned out to be ten thousand dollars in the shoe box and three pounds of weed in the Foot Locker bag. The two of them broke the money and weed down 50/50. They decided to keep the weed for smoking and to buy some coke from Mann with the money. They hadn't gotten around to buying the coke yet, and they seemed to be in no rush, either. Waiting for their chance to run across the school yard to the Acura that they were riding in, Jazmin walked by. Lando saw that she wasn't trying to speak, so he told Quick to hold up and ran up behind her.

"Jazmin, what's up with you? You act like you beefin' with me or something," Lando said.

Turning to face Lando with her books in hand, Jazmin snapped, "You ain't no different than Quick and them. I was a fool to think you were different than them wanna be gangsta ass niggas you be with…"

"Hold up! What you talkin' 'bout?"

"You know what I'm talking 'bout, Lando. I saw you and Quick runnin' down my hallway the other day! I know what ya'll did!" Jazmin said. Looking around to see who could hear, Lando saw no one. He was shocked by the information Jazmin had just given him. He didn't know what to do.

Looking Jazmin in the eyes, he said, "So, now what's up? You saw us and what?" Jazmin was still very upset. She had feelings for Lando but she didn't want to get involved with a dude that was living like he was living.

Looking Lando in the eyes, Jazmin said, "I can't fuck with you, Lando. When you make up your mind what it is you want to do with yourself, then we can be more than friends. Until then, we just cool." After letting Lando know how she felt, Jazmin walked down the hall on her way to the lunchroom.

"So, what was Jazmin talkin' 'bout?" Quick asked Lando as they were riding down 9th Street.

"She saw us smash that nigga the other night," Lando answered.

"So, what you tryin' to do about it?"

"I ain't tryin to do nothing, she ain't gon' say shit about it. Her beef with me, young," Lando said as he turned down Rittenhouse Street.

At the top of the block, Lando stopped the car and quickly tapped Quick on the arm, saying, "Look down there, young!" Rittenhouse Street was packed with FBI, DEA, and Metropolitan Police. Cars and vans were parked all on the sidewalk and in front yards, up and down the street. It was a full scale raid, DEA agents were bringing Corey, Onion, Smoke, Serge, Lil' Garvin, Baby-D, and Kevin out of Old Tima's house in handcuffs. DEA and FBI agents were bringing Dee-Dee's mother out of her house in her bed robe and slippers, hand cuffed as well. "Let's get the fuck outta here, young!" Quick said as Lando backed out of Rittenhouse Street and shot down 9th Street.

Mann was just getting off the phone with Black when Lando and Quick came down the basement steps with the news of the raid.

"So, the Feds had everybody, huh?" Mann asked.

"Slim, they even locked Dee-Dee's motha up! They ain't playin' down there, young!" Lando said. Mann knew a raid was in the making and had been laying low for that reason. Catching cases wasn't his thing. He knew that out of all the people that had just got locked up, somebody would give a few names. He didn't want Lando and Quick hanging out until he could find out what was what around the way. Lil' Garvin and Baby-D would most likely be the first to get cut lose being as though they were under age and the Feds always wanted someone they could build a good case on.

Rubbing his hand on his chin like he always did when he was in deep thought, Mann said to Lando and Quick, "Look here, I want ya'll to stay away from the strip until we find out what the fuck is going down around the way. Ya'll got that?" Lando and Quick were both in accord with that. They both knew the strip was too hot at the time.

"So, what happened the other night on the move y'all went on?" Mann asked.

Quick looked at Lando, not wanting to say too much about the killing. Lando gave up a deadly smile and told Mann all about how the caper went down. Mann shook his head. He didn't agree with how they went about the whole thing and he would have been even more upset if he knew that Jazmin had seen them kill the Jamaican dude that night.

"If ya'll wanna be big boys, ya'll gotta think more than ya'll thinkin'!" Mann said as he gave the two young killers the game. "In these streets, the man that think the best on his feet gon' live the longest. Everything ain't what it seems to be. Ya'll coulda ran in that joint and lost your life. Y'all ain't case the spot or nothin'! Ya'll ran in there with y'all little pistols and just so happen, a nigga like Black was in there. Some niggas don't care about life or death. It coulda been four or five niggas in the joint! Y'all ain't know! Y'all can't just think y'all gon' shoot ya way out of everything. The game don't go like that!" Lando and Quick paid close attention to every word that Mann said. It was the first time he had ever spoken to them as if they were on his level and by him doing so, they took the whole lesson to heart.

Black came back from his legal visit smiling like he had just been found not guilty on the murder case that he was facing. Once locked back in his cell, the cell doors on the tier opened, allowing the general population out. Dre came over to Black's bars and said, "What the fuck you so happy about?" Black's lawyer had just told him that the government's only witness had been found dead with her neck slit from ear to ear. The government was in a no win situation. It was no way they would be able to indict Black and Dre with no one to testify at the Grand Jury.

"Yeah?" Dre said, full of excitement. "So, we out of this joint for sure when we go back to court?"

Black pulled out some paper work that he brought back from his legal visit and showed it to Dre, saying, "See this? This says found dead! That means no witness to testify!"

Dre smiled and said, "That nigga Mann done took care of business already!"

Taking off his fresh jail jumper and sitting down on his bunk, Black said, "Yeah, my cuz must have put that work in. I can't wait to get back out there. I'ma murda that nigga Marvin and all the rest of them bitch ass niggas!"

Ric had started putting his guards down a lot lately. He was even hanging out on the Ave., knowing that Mann was out and about. It had been awhile since anyone had run into each other, so Ric had began to take Mann lightly. Mann, on the other hand, was on top of his game. Watching every move Ric made when he was in the city, Mann knew exactly how to catch him slipping. That made Marvin much harder to catch than Mann had planned, so he went after Ric first.

Laying in the bushes besides Ric's mother's house late at night dressed in all black, Mann put his first move in effect. The front door was open and Mann could see Ric coming out of the house with a brown shopping bag in his hand. As Ric walked down the walk way to his car, Mann waited for the door to close, and then quietly crept up behind Ric, putting his huge Desert Eagle to his back.

Ric's first words were, "Damn!" he thought he was being robbed. Putting his hands in the air, he dropped the shopping bag and said, "I ain't got no cash on me, slim!"

Putting a tight grip around the collar of Ric's leather jacket, Mann leaned over, pressing the .44 deep into Ric's back, and whispered into his ear, "I don't want no money, nigga." Then, with a little laugh of revenge, he said, "You ain't think them yesterdays was gon' come back and get you. Did you?" Ric tried to snatch away when he realized Mann caught him slipping, but it did no good. Mann had him and he wasn't letting him go.

Marvin and Nicole were in the bed cuddled up under the sheets. Nicole hadn't felt so close to him in a long time. They had just made love for hours. With Nicole in his arms, Marvin looked her in the eyes, and said, "I'm tired of the streets, boo."

Not believing what she was hearing, Nicole raised up, and said, "Are you serious?"

"Yeah, I'm sick of this shit, boo."

"So, what you gon' do?"

"I'm thinking 'bout moving down Virginia Beach. I got the cash to do it now, but you and my son gotta come. What you think about that?" Rubbing her soft hands up and down Marvin's chest, Nicole thought about what he was saying. It sounded good, very good the more she thought about it.

"I like it. I like the thought of us moving down there together. I'm with it," Nicole said.

In the middle of their deep conversation about the future, the phone rang. Nicole reached across the bed and answered the phone. Turning to Marvin, she said, "Here, it's for you."

"Hello!" Marvin said, wondering who was calling him that late at night, and at Nicole's house at that.

"Marvin! Dis Ric, young!" Ric said, sounding very nervous, "Mann just shot at me right in front of my mother's house!"

"You okay?"

"Yeah, I'm cool, slim, but I'm tryin' to go get this nigga! I'm 'bout to come get you. Be ready!"

"Where the nigga at right now?"

"He over his mother house right now! I saw his car in the alley."

"You sure!"

"Yeah, man!"

"Okay then, come get me! I'ma be out front!" Marvin said as he hung up the phone.

Marvin stood out front waiting for Ric to come get him so he could put an end to Mann once and for all. Everything would work out fine. He would kill Mann, and then take his money and move down Virginia with Nicole and his son, leaving the streets to Ric and Jammie. Mann was slipping Marvin thought. It wasn't like him to just be shooting at a nigga and letting him get away. Marvin thought that Mann must be acting out of his anger and that would be exactly what would allow him to kill him with ease. *Even the best has to die some day,* Marvin thought as Ric's silver Acura Legend bent the corner at the top of the block. It was time to put all the beefing behind him Marvin thought as he walked up to the car looking at his reflection in the dark tinted windows of the Acura.

Looking back over his shoulder as he opened the door, Marvin hopped in the car and shut the door. Rubbing his hands together to heat them up, Marvin turned to ask Ric how he wanted to go about getting into Mann's mother's house and almost shitted on himself. Smiling at him with a huge Desert Eagle .44 pointed right in his face, Mann said, "Pay back's E-muthafucka!" Pulling the trigger of the .44 one time as he pulled off in Ric's car, Mann blew Marvin's brains all over the passenger side window. The rest of Marvin's body lifelessly slumped against the dash board, bleeding all over the place. Mann carefully drove up to the Fort Totten woods and set the car on fire, leaving Marvin shot dead in the passenger seat and Ric shot dead in the trunk. Mann walked back to the main street after wiping all finger prints off of the .44, and tossed it down the sewer hole before catching a cab home. The killing was over for Mann. If Jammie wanted to find him some heart over night, Mann decided that he would let Lando and Quick deal with him since they were firing pistols now, or Black would be more then happy to kill him now that him and Dre would be coming home thanks to Mann slicing the throat of the only government witness.

Inside the 4th District police station, Officer James came into his office very upset and slammed a bunch of paper work on his desk. Seeing something wrong with his partner, Officer Hall walked over and asked him what the problem was.

Flipping through the paperwork, Officer James said, "What's not wrong! First of all, everyone that got busted with that big raid on Rittenhouse Street has made bail and were now right back down there pushing more drugs in the neighborhood. On top of that, the DEA has no real case on any of them. The only scum bag that was caught with any drugs on him was the one they call Onion or something like that!" The younger officer knew Onion well, he had arrested him once before.

"So, what did they find on Onion?" Hall asked.

"He had at least sixty two grams of crack on him when the Feds ran up in that crack house," James responded.

Thinking back to the time when he had arrested Onion, Hall said, "That guy Onion owes me a favor. We can cash in on it if you need to."

James looked up at Hall with a look of relief. That was what he needed to hear. The Chief was all over him about finding out who had all the coke down 5th and Rittenhouse Street, as well as who was doing the killing. Downtown was making a big fuss about the Rittenhouse raid being a big fluke. The Feds wanted no more to do with the case unless 4th District could produce a bust of a kilo or better. That meant that the whole case load of the last raid, as well as all other investigations on Rittenhouse Street, had to be done by James and Hall.

Pamila's house was packed. Upstairs in the living room, Pamila, Kelley, Dee-Dee, and young Tyesha sat around the T.V. while Pamila talked to the younger girls about life and how she used to run the streets just like them when she was young, but she realized that life had more to offer as she got older.

Downstairs in the basement, Mann had music blasting while him, Lando, Quick, and Lil' Garvin played Nintendo on Mann's sixty inch inch T.V. Mann asked Lil' Garvin what the Feds had locked him and everybody else up for. Lil' Garvin let him know that Onion was the only one dirty that day, everybody else went downtown for petty stuff like no identification or in the case of him and Baby-D, they had well over one thousand dollars in loose cash on them with no way to prove how they made it at a work place.

"So, what they catch that nigga Onion with?" Mann asked.

"They caught that nigga dirty as shit! He just cut up a fresh sixty two before the Feds hit the joint. I don't know how that nigga got out when everybody else did," Lil' Garvin said. The first thing that came to Mann's mind was that Onion was talking to the Feds. Mann didn't trust him as it was, but now he told himself that he wouldn't sell Onion a dime rock.

Jammie was scared to death when Nicole called him crying, and told him that Marvin and Ric had been found shot in Ric's burnt up Acura Legend. Jammie first thought was to take all the money and coke they had stashed over Marvin's house and leave town, but he knew he couldn't stay away from the city for long, so he did the next thing that came to mind. He made a phone call to the 4th District police department and told Officer

Hall everything he knew about the beef Mann had with Marvin, and how Lando and Quick were the ones doing all of the shooting in retaliation for Mann's shooting. With no real evidence, Officer Hall got a warrant for Mann and Lando's arrest since he knew their whole names off hand. All Jammie knew Quick by was Quick, therefore, Hall would have to catch up with him after questioning the other two, if he could get any information out of them.

Waking up in the bed next to Mann was something that Kelley had grown very used to over the past weeks. It was not only something that she had grown used to, she was in love with it. She was in love with everything about Mann. She had seen none of the horrible things that people had told her about Mann being a killer and even though she knew he sold drugs, she never saw him with any or even heard him talk about selling any. The Mann she knew was the smooth, dark skinned man of her dreams that made love to her every night, and then held her in his arms and listened to all of her worries, giving the solution to everyone as if he was always divinely inspired with Universal Laws about living life.

Mann was wide awake when Kelley opened her eyes that morning. He had seen Nicole walking down Georgia Avenue Lil' Marvin. As Mann passed by in his Z, they caught eye contact. Mann had never seen so much hurt and pain in a person's eyes in all of his life. For a second, he felt bad that Marvin had forced him into a situation where he had to take his life. Nicole flashed Mann a look of more than a thousand words, and Mann read each of them in one way or another. He knew Nicole knew that he was behind the murder of her baby's father, yet, she some what had a look of understanding that what goes around comes around and that time around, Marvin got the short end of the coming around. Mann really couldn't find the balls to over play his hand and speak to Nicole, so he waited for her reaction to seeing him. Sadly, she understood that Mann wasn't trying to add any more pain to a painful event and she waved at him as if to say, "Why..." Mann could not get that haunting look that Nicole gave him out of his mind and for the first time in his life, he understood why Black went through life saying fuck the world, it made times like those much easier. Even so, Mann had a heart and it was one move that he had to make in life that he would never forget.

Rolling over on to Mann's chest looking beautiful as always, Kelley saw something was on Mann's mind.

Rubbing her soft hands on his arms, she looked up into his eyes, and said, "What's wrong, boo?" Mann was quickly turned on by the feeling of Kelley's soft body against his. Sliding his hand down under the covers, Mann softly caressed Kelley's soft ass.

"Ain't nothin' wrong with me. I was just thinkin' 'bout what we was talking about last night. I'ma get into that G.E.D. class I was telling you about." Kelley was pleased to hear that, it made her feel like she really had a say so in Mann's life since she had been pressing him about getting back into school.

Smiling at him, Kelley said, "You ain't nothing like everybody be sayin' you is," as she threw her thick thighs over Mann's body and climbed on top of him.

Pushing her hands down on Mann's chest, Kelley raised her sexy body up into a sitting position on top of Mann with her well shaped breast sitting enticingly in his face. Mann grew full of sexual excitement instantly.

Rubbing his hands slowly up and down Kelley's smooth back, Mann said, "What do everybody be sayin' I'm like?"

Raising up off of Mann, sliding him slowly inside of her with her hand, Kelley let out a tiny sigh of pleasure as she said, "It don't even matter right now."

Placing both of her hands back down on Mann's chest, she began to wiggle her body up and down. Opening her mouth as she threw her head back in the air, Kelley started to move faster and faster on top of Mann.

As her ass started to slap against Mann's thighs, she began to moan and scratch his chest, saying, "Ohh... I love you so much. I love what you are doing to my body. Ahhh... don't stop, Mann, I love you so much." Mann slid his hands down around her hips and locked an unrelenting grip around them as he began to push himself deeper and deeper into Kelley's accepting body. Kelley couldn't take the act of Mann's aggressive desire to push her off the cliffs of ecstasy. She came in seconds. Mann continued at the same pace, making Kelley come over and over again. Grabbing Kelley tightly as he could, Mann pulled her down to him as he reached his climax. Looking into Mann's eyes as she felt him exploding inside of her, Kelley smiled and said, "I love you so much!"

Officer Hall was out riding around with the jump outs. Since Officer James was in charge of all affairs that had anything to do with Rittenhouse Street, Hall had the authority to carry things however he chose to. Being as though he was much younger than James and closer to the streets, James put his trust in him when it came to finding out who was who. On top of that, Officer Hall was glad to work the Rittenhouse investigation because it gave him another shot at making a case stick to Black when he got out of jail this time around.

Hidden behind the tinted windows of Black's Acura Legend, Lando, Quick, Baby-D, and Lil' Garvin sat on the corner of 5th and Rittenhouse Street smoking weed and talking about how the Feds had to have somebody telling them something. Baby-D was telling everybody that when they took him back into the interrogation room, the only people they wanted to know about was Mann and Dre.

Lando turned back to Baby-D, and said, "What they was saying 'bout Mann and Dre?"

Baby-D blew a cloud of weed smoke out of his mouth as he said, "They was talking bout they know Mann got all the coke around the way and they trying to get somebody to tell them that they buyin' coke from him or Dre. I told them crackers that I ain't know Mann or Dre, but somebody done told them muthafuckers something."

While Baby-D was talking, Quick peeped the jump outs bending the corner, and said, "Jump outs!" Even though the four of them were hidden behind the tinted windows, they all slid down in their seats.

Across the street standing in front of Dee-Dee's house was Corey, Onion, Smoke, Serge, and Kevin. Corey was serving pipehead Big Busta when the jump outs bent the corner in the black four door Cadillac Seville. "Jump outs!" Kevin yelled as everybody broke through Dee-Dee's yard, running through the cut and into the alley going their separate ways. The jump outs made a quick turn into the alley and jumped out, each one of them picking one person to run down. In a black Polo sweat shirt, blue jeans, and high top Air Jordan's, Officer Hall ran after Onion.

Onion hopped the fence across the alley from Dee-Dee's house and ran across Roxboro Place and into another yard that led to another alley. Hall was right on his back, no less than three or four steps behind him.

Pointing his Glock at Onion, Hall screamed, "Freeze! Motherfucker!" Onion kept running and cut into a yard full of bushes. Throwing a zip lock bag full of fifty rocks, Onion hopped the fence that led to the street in front of the house. Hall came running through the yard seconds later, never seeing Onion throw his coke. Running out into the front yard of the house, Hall saw Onion running down the sidewalk. Hall took off after him, showing no signs of fatigue. Onion was slowly but surely running out of gas. Hall ran up on him and tackled him to the ground like an All Pro free safety.

"Where you think you going!" Hall said as he wrestled Onion down to the ground.

"Get the fuck off me!" Onion yelled as he tried to get Hall off of him. Choking Onion out until he calmed down, Hall stood him up and slammed him against a car while pulling a ready made bag of dime rocks from under his black Polo shirt.

Seeing Hall pull the coke from under his shirt, Onion said, "That shit ain't mine!"

Throwing the coke on the hood of the car, Hall said, "Oh, yes it is. Now, I could get rid of these nice little rocks if you let me know something."

"Let you know what!"

"You know Marvin and Ric from 13th Street?"

"Yeah, I know 'em. Why?"

"Who smoked 'em?"

"I don't know who smoked them niggas!" Onion said.

Hall became angry and smashed Onion's face into the cold hood of the car, saying, "Don't play dumb with me, you piece of shit!"

"I don't know who smoked them niggas!"

"Look here! I know Marvin shot your homeboy, Mann. I also know that Black is the only one of you little wanna be gang bangers that got the balls to murder a motherfucker in cold blood, but he's locked up now so who the fuck is the next in line to be the trigger man around here!" Hall said. Onion really didn't know who had killed Marvin and Ric, but he had a feeling that Mann did it. Hall got fed up with Onion telling him that he didn't know who shot Marvin and Ric. By the time the rest of the jump outs pulled up, Hall had his mind set on taking Onion in for the bag of dime rocks that he had planted on him. Asking Onion one last time about Mann, Hall told him that if he didn't tell him something, he was going back to jail. Onion knew that he had just been caught with sixty two grams of coke just over a week ago. He wasn't going back in. Onion gave Hall the only information that he had, telling Hall that Lando and the young niggas around the way were the ones doing all of the shooting and killing around the way. Hall questioned Onion for a while, getting everything he needed to know about Lando, Quick, Baby-D, and Lil' Garvin, and then he let Onion go, telling him that if he was to ever act like he didn't know what was going on around the way, that he would let everyone know that he was dropping dimes.

Later on, Mann sat at the kitchen table eating pizza while Lando told him everything that Baby-D had told him in the car just before the jump outs came through.

"So, the Feds askin' 'bout me, huh?" Mann asked.

"Yeah, slim. Baby-D say they askin' 'bout you and Dre."

"Do they know anything?"

"I don't think so. Baby-D say they tryin' to get a nigga to say they buyin' they shit from you," Lando said.

Mann began to think about what his little brother was telling him. Mann knew that things were going to be hot around the way ever since he saw the Feds come through taking pictures in the van a while back. Mann knew what he had to do and it wasn't hard at all. Mann told himself that he would get all of his coke, money, and guns out of Pamila's house just in case the Feds wanted to play dirty and kick the door in.

Officer Hall had decided to take a ride down to the Homicide department. He knew the detective that had the case that Black and Dre were about to come home, on and wanted to find out how in the world did the system let Black slip through the cracks once again. Hall walked into the office of his old high school buddy, Detective Walt Brown. Brown had gained a lot of weight since Hall had seen him last, but he still had the look of a young man.

Sitting down in front of the desk of the short, black man, Hall said, "I see you been living good."

Brown leaned back in his chair, lighting a Newport Long, laughing as he said, "Yeah, I've gained a little weight now that I'm not running down those thugs anymore. So, what brings you to see me?" Hall got straight to the point and asked Brown how did he let Black get away from him.

"Well," Brown said, "it's like this. No witness, no case. In fact, I never really had a case. All I had was some young girl saying that she told Black that there was like fifty thousand dollars in the guy's house that he killed. I thought that maybe Black would get scared of being charged as an adult and take a cop, or even act like a big boy and go to trial where anything goes. But, he done got somebody to kill my witness, so I'm back at the drawing board."

When Brown was done talking, Hall gave him the run down on all the information that he had picked up from Jammie and Onion. He let him know that there was an arrest warrant out for Mann and his little brother, Lando. Brown was very interested in the information. He had the Marvin and Ric double murder case.

"So, what's up with the guys, Mann and Lando?" Brown asked. Mixing opinion with the truth, Hall told Brown that Mann was the big dope boy around his way and just so happens to be the cousin of Black, not to mention that he was shot by DeMarvin Scott about two months ago. He went on to tell Brown that Mann's little brother, Lando, was an up and coming killer with a gang of side kicks. He believed that Lando and his gang of juvenile delinquents were behind the murder of the government witness as well as Marvin and Ric. He also let Brown know that he didn't believe Mann was behind the murders because he was a pretty boy that was used to telling someone else to kill for him.

"So, why do you have a warrant out for his arrest? Why not just his little brother?" Brown asked.

"Because if I'm right and the youngsters are behind it, then Mann is putting them up to it. He has all the brains in the family," Hall said.

"Let me ask you this," Brown said, "if we bring these brothers in, what can we charge them with?" Hall was stuck, he had nothing on them but hearsay, and Brown let him know flat out that his boss would not support another hearsay case right after the bad gamble they had taken with Black and Dre.

"Get something that will stick to these brothers and then I'll pull some strings for you since you seem to be taking this whole thing with the Mills boys so personal," Brown said. Hall rolled with the punches and let his buddy know that he would nail this one for sure. Hall got up and shook Brown's hand as he headed back up to the 4th District Police station.

Mann had been taking GED classes for a week now. He was into the little work that he was getting, besides that, going to school for a few hours a day, three days a week gave him a break from the madness of the streets. Silk had found it very pleasing that Mann was taking GED classes. He had been telling Mann all year how easy the GED was for him and that Mann should take the test so that he could get into the Business Management class that he was taking. Silk always told Mann that he was going to have to put the dope game to the side sooner or later and go legit. Mann and Silk came to an agreement that when they both got a million dollars out of the game, they would go legit. Silk was to start a chain of restaurants called Silky's, and Mann told him that when he hit the million mark he was going to open a night club in the city that would have local bands performing in it, and he would also rent it out for parties and cabarets. Thinking of all that the future would hold when they both hit the million mark, Silk decided to pay Mann a visit at school.

Mann had to smile coming out the door of the Armstrong Vocational Center. Smooth as always, Silk was leaning against a cherry red Ferrari 355 Spyder, in a thick black Hugo Boss leather coat and a pair of black Polo jeans that were hanging down over his black Timberland double sole boots. Mann walked over to Silk, hugged him, and said, "What you doing up here?"

"I came to check on you. I went by your house and Kelley told me you were down here. I see you gon' go ahead and take that test," Silk said. Mann talked to Silk for a while about how he had been talking to Kelley about school and it made him think about his night club and the agreement they had made about the million mark. Silk was pleased to hear that. Mann was like a little brother to him. Mann switched the subject to the raid on Rittenhouse Street and how the Feds were trying to get somebody to say that they were buying coke from him. Silk knew that once the Feds were on your trail, they wouldn't leave you alone until that got you for something if you were the type that was never caught dirty, like him and Mann. Silk asked Mann what he planned to do about the situation, and also let him know that he couldn't pass out weight around the way being as though anybody could be working with the law. Mann let Silk know that he was going to lay low and only serve coke to his old buddies, Da-Da and Leron, out Maryland. Silk was in accord with that, he told Mann to do whatever it took to duck an indictment. Before leaving, Silk asked about Black and Dre.

Mann smiled at him and said, "They gon' be home soon."

Silk understood exactly what Mann meant by the smile. Opening the door to his Ferrari, Silk said, "Let Dre and Black know that it's a rack of money out here to get. I'm sure you can show 'em how to get it."

Mann turned the head lights to his Z on as the night grew dark. On his way home, he was thinking about what Lando had told him. The Feds were on his back. He knew they had nothing on him, but he didn't like the heat on him. He was all about the money, not the fame.

Looking into the rear view mirror, Mann saw a patrol car pulling up behind him. He wasn't dirty, so he played things cool even though he could tell that the pigs were running his plates. The pigs hit their lights as a white uniformed officer got out of the car and walked up to Mann's window.

"Shit!" Mann said out loud. Tapping on the window of Mann's car, the officer pulled his radio out again. Mann rolled the window down and said, "What's up?" The officer asked for his ID and told him that there had just been a shooting a few blocks away and his car matched the description of the car that fled the scene. After Mann gave the officer his ID, the officer on the passenger side of the car got out and walked up beside his partner.

"Would you mind stepping out of the car, sir!" the other white officer said. Mann got out while the officer with the radio was running his name. "Mr. Mills," the officer with the radio said, "you're under arrest."

Downtown inside of the Homicide Department, Mann waited for Detective Brown to come into the interrogation room.

Handcuffed to the floor, looking around the tiny room, Mann had never been questioned for a murder before. Even so, he knew that the best answer to a question from the Feds was no answer, and that was exactly how he played it when Detective Brown walked into the room with him.

"So, Mister Bad-ass," Detective Brown said as he sat down in front of Mann, "what do you know about ah...a mister DeMarvin Scott and Ric Jones?"

Mann smiled, it would be easier then he thought. "I don't know nobody by those names, slim!" Mann said with no sign of fear.

"Well, here's the deal, smart ass! You and your little brother, uh...Lando, ya'll are suspects in three murders, so if I were you, I wouldn't be acting so damn tough."

"Yeah? Well I guess that't why I'm cuffed to the floor and you ain't! That shit you talkin' don't scare me at all, if you ain't gon' charge me with something you gotta let me go, and if you is... you gotta call my mother so I can get a lawyer because I ain't nothing but seventeen! You dig!" Mann said with a very no nonsense look on his face.

Detective Brown was stung by Mann's aggressiveness, not to mention shocked by his age. Officer Hall never once told him that Mann had just turned seventeen years old. By the way, Hall talked about Mann he assumed that he was in his twenties. Mann had Brown in a do or die situation. He was a juvenile, therefore, he was right, his mother had to be notified that her child was under arrest, meaning that Brown had to charge Mann or let him go. Brown wanted so bad to charge Mann and take him through the procedures because of his slick ass mouth, but he had nothing on him and he knew that Mann knew it. Uncuffing Mann, Brown let him know that he had the double murder case that he was a suspect in and that he was going to be on his back until he could place the beef on him. Mann knew he had played his cards right once again. Walking out of the interrogation room, Mann did something that he had never done before. He played big, saying, "You can do what you want to do. You'll never place a beef on me. Believe that, playboy."

Chapter Nine: Not so fast

The rest of the year seemed to fly by at the speed of light. Mann stuck to his plan and cleaned all of his coke, money, and guns out of Pamila's house. He made sure that he didn't sell a crumb of coke on Rittenhouse Street. Every brick he sold went for thirty thousand dollars now, and they were all sold through Da-Da and LeRon. They had their White Oak apartment complex locked down. Mann was never dirty. The only thing the Feds could catch him with was a GED book. All his coke, guns, and money were in a one bedroom apartment right around the corner from where Da-Da and LeRon lived, and they didn't even know it. The only people that had ever been to the apartment were Silk and Lando. All was going well for Mann. Dre and Black went to court in days, the Feds hadn't bothered questioning him again about the double murder, and life was what it should be in his eyes.

Lando, on the other hand, was a different story. He brought the new year in with a murder. Him and Quick got into a fight with some older Maryland dudes inside of a party they went to for New Year's Eve. One of the dudes had bumped Lando coming into the party. Lando turned around and punched the bigger dude in the face. The Maryland dudes tried to jump Lando and Quick, but they ran outside. Once in the parking lot, they ran for the Acura Legend and got their pistols. By the time the older dudes got into the parking lot there was no way out. Lando and Quick unloaded they pistols at the group of five. As they tried to run, Lando ran the dude down that had bumped him in the party, shooting him in the back until he fell between two cars. Walking up and standing over top of the older dude, Lando shot him in the head twice and ran back to the car where Quick was waiting behind the wheel.

Pamila had grown very close to Kelley over the past few months. She believed that the young girl was going to do something with her life and Pamila loved to see a young person go after their dreams. Mann had inspired Kelley to go to school to be a lawyer, and Pamila was in support of the idea. Pamila told Kelley that as long as there were little bad asses like Lando running the streets that she would always find work if she knew the law.

Pamila was fed up with Lando. She hadn't spoken to him in at least two weeks. His school was calling her at work every other day. Lando would go to school when he wanted to, and Pamila didn't understand how he could go from a regular kid to and out of control young thug over night. Pamila had to get Mann to help her understand Lando these days. She truly believed he had lost his mind and wanted to get him some psychiatric help. Mann assured Pamila that Lando would slow down once he became sure of his manhood. Pamila had decided to go with Mann's theory and she prayed that if he was right, Lando would live long enough to see true manhood.

The District of Columbia Superior Court was busy on the morning of January 18th, 1990. Pamila, Mann, and Kelley walked into the court room of the Honorable Judge John H. Suda. Black and Dre were already in the court room sitting down beside their lawyer, a tall white lady named Mary Armstrong. Black turned to look back at his Aunt Pamila, Mann, and Kelley as the judge began to speak.

"Does the government have an indictment for the two defendants?" Judge Suda asked the DA. Fumbling through her papers, the slim white DA tried to beat around the bush.

"Either you do or you don't!" the judge said, becoming very angered. "I'm throwing this case out if there is no indictment!"

"Your Honor, all I need is two weeks and I will have the …"

"No! Ms. Miller, this case is dismissed as of today. The defendants are to be released from the D.C. Jail. Good day, Ms. Miller. Next case!" Judge Suda said as the Marshals took Black and Dre back into the bullpen.

"I told you we was outta here, nigga!" Black said to Dre once they were in the holding cells downstairs in the court building, waiting for the bus ride back to the D.C. Jail.

Smiling, Dre hugged Black and said, "We outta this muthafucka. I can't wait to hit them bricks. Mann say the money comin' like shit out there."

Sitting down on the hard metal bench inside the holding cell, Black and Dre talked about what they were going to do when they were back on the streets. Black had his mind set on killing Metra for turning Dre in to the Feds for the money. Dre let Black know that it was too much money out in the streets to be thinking about Metra. He told Black to leave the hot bitch alone. Skipping that subject, Black started talking about Lando and all of the young dudes around the way. Black couldn't wait to see what was up with his cousin. Lando's name was kicking all over the streets for the five months that Black and Dre had been up the jail. While Black was talking about Lando and his little mob, Dre stood up at the bars and looked over to the bubble where all the Marshals were.

"Ain't that the homicide nigga that had our case?" Dre asked Black, sounding concerned.

Standing up to take a look himself, Black said, "Yeah, that's that nigga."

The Marshals opened the gate and let Detective Brown into the bullpen. Behind him was Officer Hall. They both walked over to the holding cell that Black and Dre were in alone, being as though they were still juveniles. Hall leaned against the bars smiling while Brown began to speak. Black and Dre stood on the other side of the bars with their arms folded, anxiously waiting to see what the pigs had to say now that the murder case had been thrown out.

"Well, Dre," Brown said, "looks like you were the lucky one this time around, kiddo."

Confused, Dre said, "What the fuck do that supposed to mean?" The door to the bubble where the Marshals were opened and a big, blond haired, young white Marshal came walking up to the cell with a pair of hand cuffs and shackles dangling from his hand.

"Who's going?" the Marshal asked Brown as he opened the holding cell.

Unable to pass up the pleasure of breaking the news, Hall let out a little laugh and said, "Mr. Mills." The Marshall told Black to step out of the cell. Coming out of the cell, Black asked the Marshall what was going on. Pointing at Brown, the Marshal started handcuffing Black.

"Mr. Mills," Brown said, "you are under arrest for murder."

Looking back at Dre with a look of defeat, Black said, "Ya'll fucked up that the judge threw that weak shit out so ya'll come at me with some fake shit like this, huh?" Dre watched as the Marshal walked Black out of the bullpen with Brown and Hall, who was reading him his rights.

Dre walked out of the gates of the D.C. Jail happy to be free, but fucked up that Brown and Hall had played dirty with Black, hitting him with another body right after the case they were on was dismissed. Mann, Lando, and Quick were sitting outside the gates in Quick's big, brown Cadillac Fleetwood. Hidden behind the dark tinted windows of the old bucket that Quick had paid twenty five hundred dollars for, Mann watched Dre walk out into the parking lot, not knowing where he was being as though he had never seen the car Quick had just bought a week ago.

Rolling down the window, Quick said, "You lost or something?" Looking over to the car, Dre smiled as he ran over and got in the back seat. Weed smoke filled the car as Rare Essence blasted through the speakers.

"What's up, nigga!" Mann said, full of genuine love for his partner as he reached over and hugged him.

"Ain't shit," Dre said. Quick and Lando turned around in the big front seat showing nothing but love. Quick passed Dre a fat blunt full of weed.

"Where the fuck Black at?" Lando asked Dre as he took a deep pull of the weed smoke. Dre let out a long sigh of disappointment.

"What the fuck is up, joe?" Mann asked, sensing that something was wrong. Dre broke the news, letting everybody know how Brown and Hall had came and rearrested Black downstairs in the court building right after the case was dismissed.

"What the fuck they arrest him for in the court building?" Lando asked, not understanding how a person could be arrested for a crime inside the court building.

"They playin' dirty with slim. They done charged him with another body." Dre let everybody know that he had just seen Black in R-N-D when he was leaving. Black let him know that he had already been arraigned and that he went back to court in a week for his preliminary hearing.

"Who the fuck they say he smashed?" Mann asked.

Black had told Dre that he knew the dude they were saying he killed, but couldn't remember his name. He knew he had shot a nigga down S.W. on Half Street at the weed spot in the middle of the summer sometime the year before. Black assured Dre that there would be no witnesses at all on the case because the only person that was out there that night was one of the dude's partners, and Black said that he had ran into him at the Black Hole two days later and dumped seventeen hollow points in his body while he sat in his car lighting a blunt. Mann remembered the whole situation and was sure that Black would come home on his first court date.

Kelley walked into Dee-Dee's house and hung Mann's huge Eddie Bauer coat up on the back of Dee-Dee's chair.

"What's up, girl?" Dee-Dee asked as she turned around, blowing weed smoke into the air.

"I see ya'll getting ya'll smoke on," Kelley said as she sat down at the dining room table with Dee-Dee and Tina.

"I hear Dre came home yesterday," Dee-Dee said, looking at Kelley. "You ain't even tell me that."

"I ain't seen you since he been home, Mann and them ain't go get him 'til last night some time."

"So, why Black ain't come home? You know that's my boo," Dee-Dee asked with a smile. She always ran to get Black when a nigga got out of line with her, she had been like that since her and Black were kids. Kelley gave her a funny look. Kelley knew that Dee-Dee wanted to fuck Black, but Onion always seemed to watch her when Black came around.

Smiling at Dee-Dee, Kelley said, "They charged Black with another murder."

Tina shook her head. Black was trouble in her eyes. She had always told Dre to stop hanging with him. The three young girls went on talking about Black until the conversation some how moved on to who fucked the best around the way.

The jump outs had just hit the block, causing Smoke, Serge, and Onion to take cover inside Dee-Dee's house. Coming through the door, they smelled the weed smoke in the air. Onion ran over to Dee-Dee and grabbed her.

"Get off me, boy! You cold as shit!" Dee-Dee said. Everyone laughed. Smoke and Serge sat down on the floor in the living room watching HBO. Tina and Kelley were sitting on the sofa watching T.V. as well. Onion picked Dee-Dee up out of her chair and carried her into the living room with everyone else.

"What bring ya'll niggas inside?" Tina asked.

Wrestling Dee-Dee while kissing her all over, Onion said, "The jump outs out there." Smoke pulled a big zip-lock bag of Skunk weed out the pocket of his big blue Eddie Bauer.

"Ya'll tryin' to smoke?" he asked. Everybody let it be known that they were trying to put something in the air.

"Where them Backwoods at?" Smoke asked Serge.

"Here they go," Serge said as he tossed Smoke the box. In seconds, four fat Backwoods were floating around the room. Smoke was feeling the effects of the strong weed in no time. Kelley began to look more attractive than usual. Smoke had always had a thing for Kelley, whose attention had always been on Mann.

Smoke looked up at Kelley from the floor, and said, "What's up with you?"

Not knowing if Smoke was coming on to her or not, Kelley said, "What you mean what's up with me?"

"You know what I'm saying," Smoke said. While everyone seemed to be waiting for her reaction, Kelley quickly set things straight.

"Look here!" Kelley said as she began to check Smoke, "It ain't thatt type of party with me, nigga. You ain't just gon' come in here and blaze a lil' bag of bud and think you gon' get some pussy from me. You got your people mixed up." The room went silent as reality seemed to smack Smoke in the face, it was not Metra he was talking to, it was Kelley, and male or female, she would stand firm if she felt disrespected or taken for granted.

Onion broke the tension by looking out the window and saying, "The Feds gone, let's hit the block."

Once outside in the cold night air, Onion, Smoke, and Serge got right back to business. No longer playing Old Tima's house since the Feds had raided it, they hustled out of the cut beside the house now. Pipeheads came from every direction as soon as they stepped back on the strip. Now that Mann was no longer passing coke out on the block or hustling on the block, Onion was somewhat the man. He had everyone buying coke from him once again, just like he had done while Mann was in the hospital. Onion walked down the alley with pipehead Karen, leaving Smoke and Serge alone in the dark cut beside Old Tima's house.

"What's up with that nigga, Corey?" Smoke asked.

"I don't know, but Onion was talking to 'em the other day 'bout some money he owed 'em. It was like fifteen thousand dollars," Serge said.

Smoke had wanted to rob Corey for the last month. Money wasn't coming like him and Serge wanted it to. Mann was to blame for some of their problems being as though he kept telling them that he was laying low until the Feds let up off of the strip, and Onion was the other part of their problem being as though he always found a way to lock shit down when Mann and Dre weren't around. Onion would've been their first choice for a quick robbery, but seemed to give them whatever they wanted due to the fact that he was scared of them turning on him. That meant that Corey was the one person, other than Mann, that they could rob and would be worth robbing around the way. Smoke had even said something about robbing Mann and Dre, but Serge wanted nothing to do with that move. Serge couldn't see himself crossing Black like that, and not crossing Black was a safe thing to do.

Corey and Kevin, who had become very close again since Kevin had come home from prison, both walked up on Smoke and Serge in the dark cut behind Old Tima's house. Showing no signs of the snake shit that they were just talking about, Smoke and Serge showed Corey and Kevin much love.

"Ya'll know Dre home?" Corey said. Smoke let him know that he heard, then asked if they knew about Black.

"What's up with Black? Why the fuck he ain't come home if him and Dre was on the body together?" Kevin asked. They all began talking about how the Feds had hit Black with another body the day him and Dre got their case dismissed. Onion walked back into the cut a few minutes later with a lit blunt of weed. Passing the smoke around, the five of them started slipping as the smoke took effect.

At the end of the block on 5th Street, two young dudes in ski masks were getting out of an old silver Nissan 280 ZX with paper tags. They walked straight over to the cut beside Dee-Dee's house.

"I thought you said the niggas be out here," the short stick up boy with the Tec-9 said.

His partner, a fat dude, just a little taller than him, said, "They might be up their by Metra's house. It's a crack house 'bout two houses from her house. I saw some niggas in the cut up there last time I dropped her off. She say they be hustling up there at night." Creeping up the street to Old Tima's house, the two stick up boys over heard the group of dudes talking, they could even smell the weed smoke strong in the cold air.

"Let's go!" the short dude said. They ran up in the cut catching everybody off guard.

"Lay the fuck on the ground!" the fat dude said.

Smoke acted as if he wanted to buck, but the Colt .45 automatic that the dude behind the ski mask held quickly talked him out of it. Laying everybody down in the ice cold, dirty grass, the two stick up boys checked everyone. They took pistols from everyone but Onion. The short dude was so upset that Smoke had a Glock .40 on him that he smacked him in the back of the head with his Tec-9.

Lando and Quick were just coming back around the way from dropping Lil' Garvin off down Crittenden Street where he had been hustling with Dex since the Feds had brought so much heat down on Rittenhouse Street the last few months. Getting out of the Acura Legend, Lando and Quick headed for Old Tima's house. Pipehead Sheila was coming down the street. She had watched the stick up boys run up in the cut with ski masks on.

Walking up to Lando and Quick, she grabbed Quick's hand and said, "Baby, you and Lando be careful going up there. Some boys got Corey and them up there in the cut beside Old Tima's house robbin' them." Lando pulled a brand new Mac-10 from inside his Eddie Bauer. Quick pulled a 10mm from out the pocket of his Eddie Bauer. They both crossed to the other side of the street so they could walk in the shadows of the tall trees while looking across the street where Old Tima's house was. Lando had never fired the Mac-10 or any other fully automatic weapon at the time, and he was dying to spray it, all thirty six shots of it. Seconds later, the two stick up boys came running out of Old Tima's yard. As soon as they stepped foot on the sidewalk, Quick and Lando ran side by side into the middle of the street firing their joints with both hands. The short dude with the Tec-9 started firing back. His partner never had a chance. As soon as Quick let his first couple of shots off, the fat dude caught a slug in the side of the head and fell to the ground with his pistol sliding out of his hand. Gun fire filled the night. As the stick up boy ran down the sidewalk sideways shooting at Lando and Quick, they ran down the street shooting back at him while shooting car windows out and everything. Running and gunning for his life, the stick up boy cut through a yard and disappeared into the darkness of the alley. Lando and Quick began to follow him, but a police car came roaring around the corner with no lights or sirens on.

Two young, black officers jumped out of the car and started shooting at the two little gunmen. Running right in front of the pigs as they crossed the street shooting at them and their police car, Lando and Quick ran through the cut beside Dee-Dee's house and were gone in the night. The officers called for back up and in no time, the whole block was covered with Feds.

At ten a.m. the next morning, the National Guards came rolling in dressed in army fatigue carrying M-16s. Twenty deep in four Hummers, they shut the block down. Two Hummers pulled up at the 5th Street corner and placed 60 cal. machine guns on stands in back of the Hummer. The other two Hummers did the same thing. Not a rock was sold on Rittenhouse Street all day, they made sure of that.

At about noon, Officer Hall and Detective Brown were on the murder scene. Yellow tape was all in front of Metra's house where the body of the stick up boy turned murder victim was found. Hall was walking around with Brown trying to get him to see that who ever was doing the killing now was different than all the killings before. Hall told Brown that Black was the known killer around Rittenhouse Street and that he had never left so many shells at a scene.

"So, what are you trying to say?" Brown asked. Hall told him that this meant that there was a new breed of killers and it had to be Lando and his buddies Quick, Baby-D, And Lil' Garvin.

Looking at the back of the shell casings that he had picked up around the murder scene, Brown said, "We are going to have to do something about these little motherfuckers. They are running around here with fully automatic weapons. That poor son of a bitch that they took to the morgue last night had two pistols on his waistline and a .45 no more then three feet away from his body, and he still had twenty .45 slugs in his ass when he got to the morgue."

Lando and Quick were no longer little boys around the way. Smoke, Serge, Onion, Corey, and Kevin watched the whole shooting up until the cops came. It was the first time they had seen the young dudes in action alone, and they held their own. They were all pissed off at them for shooting at the police and bringing the National Guard around, but it was nothing they could say.

The whole shooting was all over the news for the next four days. That scared Lando and Quick. They were staying in a hotel just across the Maryland line until things cooled off, whenever that would be. Lando sent a cab to pick Nakia and Trina up from Nakia's house, and drop them off at the hotel. The girls stayed there with them the whole time.

Mann could no longer stand by and watch Lando and Quick run wild. They were both family as far as Mann was concerned. Before going to the court building to see if Black was going to get his murder case dismissed, Mann and Dre stopped by the Days Inn Hotel to check on the two younger dudes. Mann knocked on the door as he blew hot air on to his hands to heat them up in the cold winter air. Quick answered the door in his boxers with his 10mm in hand.

"What's up with ya'll niggas?" Quick asked as he stepped back and let the two older dudes in.

Inside the hotel room, Trina was lying in one bed asleep with the covers pulled over her head. Lando was in the next bed rolling a blunt with his Mac-10 laying out in the open on the nightstand. Nakia was in the bed next to Lando knocked out sleep. Lando and Quick smoked too much for the young girls, they had passed out late last night and hadn't come back around. Dre couldn't believe how much Lando and Quick had grew up in the short five months that him and Black had been up the jail. The last thing he remembered about Lando was when he wanted to roll on the 13th Street niggas and Mann wouldn't let him, now the same little dude that he had watched grow up was running around killing niggas and busting at the Feds, things seemed to change over night in the fast lane.

Mann got Lando and Quick to step in the bathroom with him and Dre so that he could talk to the young dudes about what was going on.

"Look here," Mann said to his little brother and Quick. "Ya'll gotta slow the fuck down. I understand thatt ya'll caught some niggas robbin' niggas around the way. Ya'll was right 'bout putting thatt work in and no matter what ya'll lil' muthafuckas get into, I'm with it but ya'll gotta stop runnin' around here like this the wild west or something. Shit all over the news. Pamila worried as shit."

Mann went on to tell the two young dudes that they had to lay low. He felt that somebody that was on the strip that night was going to tell the Feds something. Mann made it clear that he didn't want Lando and Quick to do anything wild if the Feds were to start looking for them. He told them that if they were to get locked up for the murder and assault on two police officers, that they would only go down Oak Hill for two years being as though they were only twelve years old. Everything Mann said to them eased their worries, because despite how much Lando and Quick acted like they ain't care about what was going down, they were a little shook by seeing the shooting on the news and hearing things like "manhunt" and "wanted for murder." When Mann was done talking, he made them give their word that they would lay low and only leave the hotel when the girls left so that no one would know where they were except him and Dre. Whenever they left, Mann told them to go to his apartment out White Oak Maryland and hang out until they heard from him. Lando and Quick agreed to the plan that Mann had laid down.

Pamila couldn't sleep for the past week; all she did was toss and turn. Even at work, all she could do was worry about Lando. The Rittenhouse shooting was all over the news. Pamila knew that Lando had to have something to do with it because he hadn't been home since the night of the shooting. Then, Quick's grandmother called her looking for him and told Pamila that she hadn't seen Quick in a week as well. Pamila knew that the two sweet little boys that she had known for the last twelve years were the two gunmen that the police were looking for. The mere thought brought tears to her eyes.

Kelley had picked Tyesha up from school and was just walking in the house when Pamila got off the phone with Quick's grandmother. Wiping the tears from her eyes, Pamila told Kelley to take Tyesha upstairs. Kelley did just that, and then she came right back to see what was wrong with the loving woman that she had grown to look at as a mother over the past few months.

"What's wrong, Pamila?" Kelley asked. Pamila told her everything, even though Kelley already knew without a doubt that Lando and Quick were the ones that did the shooting that drew so much heat to the neighborhood. Kelley gave Pamila a firm hug and told her that everything would be fine.

Pulling herself together, Pamila looked at Kelley in the eyes, and said, "No, Kelley, everything won't be fine. I done lost my baby to the streets and I don't know if I will ever get him back." Kelley had never seen the strong woman so shook up. As strong as Pamila was, Lando filled her soul with pain and didn't even know it.

Killa Black was back on the loose and dying to get into something. On the way to Mann's apartment to go see Lando and Quick, Mann let Black know that shit was too hot at the time for him to come home with that trigger happy shit. In the back seat of Dre's Nissan Maxima, Black let Mann know that he was trying to stay out in the streets this time around.

"It ain't easy to get two bodies dismissed in two weeks, slim. I ain't tryin' to be in front of no judges for a while, joe," Black said.

Dre looked back at Black through the rear view mirror, and said, "I damn sure hope you mean that shit cause shit hot as E-muthafucka out here. I ain't made a dime, yet."

Mann began to tell Black about everything that was going on in hopes of making him understand why he needed for him to chill out. Black told Mann and Dre that he was going to chill, but he was going to blow the bitch Metra's brains out as soon as he got a chance. Mann and Dre tried to talk him out of it, telling him that it wasn't the time and that he could take care of it as soon as everything cooled down. Black wasn't trying to hear any of that. His mind was made up, and Mann and Dre both knew that when he got like that it was no stopping him.

Mann, Dre, and Black walked into Mann's apartment and saw Lando and Quick laying on the floor smoking weed and playing Tecmo Bowl on Mann's huge T.V. They were surprised to see Black. Walking up to Black, they both gave him five and showed their love.

"What's up, nigga?" Quick asked.

"Ain't shit, young nigga," Black said as he went on to tell the young dudes what he had been up to over the jail.

"I thought you was goin' to have to wait to go to trial?" Lando said.

"Na, they dropped the shit," Black said. Mann and Dre walked back into the bedroom, and left Black in the living room with Lando and Quick.

"So, what the fuck is up with ya'll? I hear ya'll got the National Guards and shit round the way," Black said as he flopped down on the sofa behind the two younger dudes. Quick got up to get a light for the blunt while Lando began to tell Black how things were going around the way. Where Mann would always give him the rules of the game, Black would sometimes encourage him to use the "fuck the world" outlook without knowing. Quick came back with a fat blunt of Skunk weed and passed it to Black while Lando was proudly telling Black how him, Quick, Baby-D, and Lil' Garvin had slaughtered shit when Mann got shot.

"No bullshit!" Quick said as he sat down on the floor with Lando. "We went up that joint and sprayed shit."

Black let out a cloud of weed smoke as he laughed a little bit, saying, "Oh yeah, ya'll put that work in, huh? That's right, fuck them niggas. They better be glad I wasn't home."

Back in the bedroom, Mann and Dre were talking about how Dre was going to get some money with the Feds being all over the place now. Opening a safe and pulling four zip lock bags out, Mann laid the bricks of coke down on the dresser, and said, "This what I'ma do. I'ma give you two and a half of these joints and we gon' go half on ten of 'em when you done. Silk only want eighty thousand for five, so when you done we can both put up eighty and we'll be set. The only thing is that you can't push this shit around the way."

Confused, Dre said, "Where you think I'm supposed to push two and a half joints at if I don't push 'em around the way?" Mann let Dre know that right outside of his apartment was a strip that was pumping from sun up to sun down, and that he would put him down with the two dudes that had shit locked out there, which was Da-Da and LeRon.

"Cool," Dre said. "I'm with that, but what we gon' do 'bout Black?"

Mann knew he had to find something for Black to do that would stop him from robbing when he didn't have to, but that was so hard to do. Many, many times before, Mann had tried to get Black to slow down and just make some money, but Black loved to run the streets and live from caper to caper. It was something that he did well.

"I'ma see if I can give 'em a brick of this shit, he might be ready to slow down," Mann said. He also told Dre that he knew Black couldn't hustle out Maryland because he would try to take the dudes that he was dealing with bad, therefore, he would have to find a spot for him, but until then he would make sure he was taken care of. At the present time, Lando and Quick was his biggest worries.

It was snowing very hard in the city. Mann had given Black a brick of coke and talked him in to trying to hustle for a while, and Black was doing just that since he gave Mann his word that he would chill for awhile. Slowly riding down Rittenhouse Street in the snow, Black saw Dee-Dee walking up the street to her mother's car. Blowing the horn, Black got Dee-Dee's attention. Looking over at the tinted window car that Lando had been driving, Dee-Dee thought it was Lando blowing the horn as she walked over to the car. The driver side window came down slowly and Dee-Dee screamed when she saw that Black was home.

"Shh," Black said as he put one finger over his lips. "Stop making all that noise." Dee-Dee ran around the car and jumped in the passenger seat.

Shutting the door as Black pulled off, Dee-Dee said, "When did you get out, boy!"

Black was amused by Dee-Dee's excitement to see that he was home. Smiling at Dee-Dee as he turned up 5th Street, Black said, "I been home for 'bout a week."

Smacking Black on the arm, Dee-Dee said, "You been home a week and I'm just seeing you?" Black let Dee-Dee know that things were too hot around the way for him to come through. He told her that the detective that had the case that he just came home on was the same one that had been riding around the neighborhood with the hot dude Hall, whom everybody in the neighborhood knew.

"So, you ain't got to go back to court or nothing? You out to stay?" Dee-Dee asked.

"Yeah," Black said as he went on to ask her about Onion. "So, what's up with your sucka ass boyfriend?"

"Ain't nothing up with him. Don't even start that shit, Black!" Dee-Dee said. Dee-Dee wanted to give Black the pussy bad, but she felt that he would tell somebody. Black some what sensed that in her and came right out with it.

Reaching over and rubbing Dee-Dee's thick thigh, Black said, "You know I done wanted you for a long ass time, why you keep actin' like you ain't tryin' to fuck with a nigga?" Looking down at Black's hand that was creeping up her leg, Dee-Dee was forced to say something.

"You talk too much, Black. If I give you some pussy you gon' let everybody know and it's gon' get back to Onion." Black assured Dee-Dee that he would say nothing if she let him hit the pussy. Dee-Dee thought about it for a minute. She had wanted to fuck Black for a long time and it was her chance.

Smiling at Black, Dee-Dee said, "Fuck it, let's do it." Black took her straight to the hotel and Dee-Dee welcomed him home in a way that he could get used to.

Chapter Ten: Man down

Onion picked a fine time to get locked up for carrying a pistol without a license. Hall was the first officer to talk to him after he got booked at the 4th District Police Station. Hall knew that Onion had a drug case pending in court and if he was to go back in front of the judge with a gun beef, he was sure to lay down for awhile. Onion couldn't see himself going back over the jail when he had information that he knew would set him free. He told Hall and the homicide detective Brown all about the shooting that they were trying to solve. Lando and Quick were now officially wanted for murder and assault with intent to kill.

It had been three weeks since Lando and Quick had killed the stick up boy and shot at the police. They were feeling a bit more comfortable. Being as though Black was home, he was driving his car and they were rolling in Quick's huge Cadillac. Even though they weren't hiding out at Mann's apartment anymore, they still didn't feel safe going around Rittenhouse Street. The National Guards still had the spot under siege, so Lando and Quick were basically living off of Mann at the time. They felt as though things were too hot for them to be riding around robbing niggas, so they just laid back and waited for things to cool off, even though it seemed like they were only getting hotter.

Kelley was sitting at the dining room table studying for a big test that she had to take at school the next day when she heard a loud knock at the door that scared her.

"Open up, it's the police!" a loud voice said from the other side.

Pamila ran down the steps when she heard that it was the police. Opening the front door and looking outside from behind the thick steel door, Pamila saw at least ten police standing on her porch, five of which were in all black with helmets on. Taking a closer look, Pamila saw that they were ATF agents. The sight of force that the police presented, standing on her porch with their guns out, put fear in Pamila's heart.

"What do you want and why do you have those damn guns out on my fuckin' porch!" Pamila yelled.

"Sorry, miss," a small, white ATF agent said to Pamila as he let her know that they had a warrant for the arrest of a Mr. Orlando Mills. Pamila's heart dropped. She knew the day was coming, and she knew that it was because of the shooting that she had been hearing about on the news a few weeks ago.

"Do you have a search warrant?" Pamila asked, knowing that just because they had a warrant for Lando's arrest didn't mean that they had a warrant to search her house for him.

"No, ma'am, we don't, but it would be best for you to help us take Mr. Mills into custody safely so that nothing happens to him. If he's caught on the streets, he might be shot. He's wanted for murder and assault with intent to kill a police officer," the small, white man said. Pamila let him know that Lando wasn't in her house and that he hadn't been there in the last three weeks, and then she shut the door on the Feds and went to beep Mann.

"Hold up, hold up. What you just say?" Mann said into the phone as he sat on the sofa in the living room of his apartment with Black and Dre. Pamila was hysterical and talking one hundred miles a minute.

"Find Lando, damnit!" she screamed at Mann. "Find him and take his lil' ass somewhere safe until I can send him to Ohio with Grandma Doris. You gotta find him before the cops do. They are going to shoot 'em!" Mann tried to calm Pamila down, but she snapped at him. "Don't try to calm me down, damnit! Find that boy!" she said as she hung up the phone.

Turning to Black and Dre, Mann said, "We gotta find Lando and Quick before the Feds do!"

Lando and Quick were watching Nakia and Trina walk into Nakia's house when Lando's beeper went off. Mann was beeping him *911.

"Who that, young?" Quick asked.

"Mann hittin' me 911," Lando said. "It's too hot out here, I'ma hit him back soon as we cross the line." Quick pulled off and headed for the D.C. line.

Carefully driving down Georgia Avenue, they pulled up at a gas station right across the D.C. line. Lando hopped out and jogged to the pay phone, leaving Quick in the car. Still very paranoid to be out in the open, Quick watched his back vigorously. From behind the tinted windows of the huge Cadillac Fleetwood, Quick looked up and down Georgia Avenue with a queasy feeling in his gut. Quick didn't like when he got that way. He became very impatient and started looking over at Lando to see what was taking so long. Lando stood over at the pay phone with a numb look on his face. Quick could tell something was wrong.

The jump outs were riding around looking for a group of young black males to jump out on, but the still, cold weather had everybody inside. Jump out Speedie, a short, slim, white dude with outstanding speed, sat in the passenger seat of the 1990 Nissan Pathfinder that the jump outs were using. He was with his three road dogs Big Al, who was driving, along with Pac-Man and Officer Hall, who had been reassigned to the vice cop squad. The four door Pathfinder that the jump outs were rolling in had just been seized on a drug bust downtown, therefore, no one knew who was behind the tinted windows of the truck as it prowled the city streets.

Speeding down Blair Road, Big Al made a left turn onto Georgia Avenue.

"Don't anybody seem to be outside today," Hall said from the back of the truck.

The three other jump outs laughed as Speedie said, "You gotta take it easy, Hall. This shit is just like fishing, something's gonna bite in a minute." He couldn't have spoken sooner. Riding by the gas station on Georgia Avenue, Hall saw Lando jogging back to Quick's Cadillac. Hall couldn't control his excitement.

"There he is!" Hall yelled. "That's that little motherfucker right there!" Everyone turned to see what Hall was so excited about and saw Lando hopping into the huge car. Wasting no time, Big Al made a quick U-Turn as the Cadillac pulled off.

"What the fuck did Mann want?" Quick asked as he watched the black tinted window Nissan Pathfinder buck a quick U-turn and get behind him.

"Slim!" Lando said with a no non-sense tone. "We on the run for real now, young! Mann say the ATF and shit been over my house looking for me. Mann want us to go out his apartment until he get there."

Making a right turn down Blair Road to see if the black Pathfinder would follow, Quick said, "That ain't no problem, but this black Pathfinder behind us made a U-turn on the Ave. and been on our back since."

Lando pulled a small black .380 out the pocket of his over-sized Eddie Bauer, and said, "You seen that joint before?"

Turning off into an alley, Quick said, "Na, I ain't never seen that joint before, but let's see if the joint follow us through this alley." Slamming his foot down on the gas, the huge Cadillac picked up speed as it flew through the alley. The Pathfinder was right behind them, picking up speed as well.

"These niggas on our back, young!" Quick said as he swung the big car out of the alley and fish tailing into the traffic on Georgia Avenue. Looking over his shoulder, Lando saw the Pathfinder swing out onto Georgia Avenue right behind them.

Police sirens hit the air somewhere close as Quick whipped the big Cadillac in and out of traffic.

"That's the muthafuckin' Bodeans!" Lando said, sounding worried.

Quick dangerously swung the big car down a side street with the Pathfinder close behind. Flying through a stop sign at the end of the block, Quick looked back at the Pathfinder through the rear view mirror and saw police car after police car swinging out onto the side street behind the Pathfinder. A helicopter grew close in the air. Police sirens became louder and louder. Quick and Lando could both feel their blood pressure rising. Flying through stop sign after stop sign, they kept looking back at all of the police cars behind them. A police helicopter was now hovered right above them. Quick bent the corner and took the huge car flying and fish tailing out into 5th Street with a trail of police following. Smashing into a passing van, the huge Cadillac pushed it across the street into the parked cars as Quick took it full speed ahead like a raging war tank. The police cars and helicopter had Quick and Lando on the run with nowhere to go, yet, they kept pushing. Flying up 5th Street and pass Pamila's house, the Cadillac went into the air at the top of the hill and came slamming back down hard, sending flaming sparks flying from under the car. Coming down the street, Quick rolled down his window and threw his 10mm out into the street while he tried to control the big car. Lando rolled down his window and threw his .380 as well. Slamming on the brakes, Quick tried to slow the car down as a police paddy wagon shot out in front of them, but it did no good. The huge Cadillac smashed straight into the paddy wagon and spun out of control as it flipped over and slid onto the sidewalk, knocking Quick and Lando unconscious.

Hours later, Quick woke up chained to a bed in D.C. General Hospital. Rubbing his head, Quick tried to shake off the pain. Amazingly, him and Lando only suffered a few scratches in the terrible crash. Painfully, Quick looked over at Lando, who was chained to the bed beside him.

Slowly Lando opened his eyes as well. "Lando," Quick called out in a low voice. Lando slowly looked over at Quick as if he was lost somewhere.

"What's up, young?" Lando said in a low and weak voice.

"You okay, young?" Quick asked.

Lando slowly raised up and said, "Yeah."

Looking at the cuffs on his hand, Lando said, "We gotta find away to get the fuck outta here!"

"How the fuck we gon' do that?" Quick said, not seeing any sense in what Lando was saying. They both looked over at the door to the room as it slowly opened.

Smiling, Hall and Detective Brown came into the room. "Well, well, well," Hall said, "That was some real brave driving that you boys did. You almost killed yourself. Even so, the party is over. We know that you two little bad motherfuckers killed that guy on Rittenhouse Street. Ya'll going down for it, too! The only thing about it is that we can't charge you little motherfuckers as adults."

Brown cut in and began to tell the two co-defendants that they were under arrest for murder and that they would be in court in the morning.

The next morning, Pamila, Mann, and Black sat in the courtroom of the Honorable Judge Queen. Pamila was still shook up about not being able to see Lando and Quick the night before. Judge Queen was not playing with the juveniles that were coming in front of her that morning. She was sending each one of them down to Oak Hill's Juvenile Detention Center. Pamila knew that Lando and Quick were not coming home, they had no chance. She only came down to support them and to see when they would go back to court again.

The side door to the court room opened, and a big, white Marshal came out behind Quick and Lando. They walked up to the thick wooden table where their public defender stood. The crazy looking white man told them to sit down while the prosecutor began to talk.

"Your Honor, these two juveniles are charged with murder and assault with intent to kill. I asked that they be detained until their next court date." Judge Queen, an older, brown skinned woman with gray hair looked down from her high seat at the two little juveniles.

Raising her glasses to get an up close look at the two murderers, Judge Queen said, "These two little babies are charged with murder?"

"Yes, ma'am, Your Honor," the white female prosecutor said.

Looking over to the crazy looking white man that Quick and Lando had for a lawyer, Judge Queen said, "What do you have to say, Mr. Shwortz?"

"Your Honor, I ask that my clients be released to the custody of Ms. Mills," Mr. Shwortz said.

Judge Queen laughed and said, "You can't be serious. I don't think so. The two juveniles will be detained at Oak Hill until their trial date. Ms. Prosecutor, what is a good date for the city?"

Looking through a folder in front of her the prosecutor said, "Your Honor, May 11th will be great."

"May 11th it is. Next case," Judge Queen said. As the Marshal walked Quick and Lando back to the bullpen, Lando looked back at Pamila, who was crying. They caught eye contact as Lando walked through the door, Lando felt her pain for the first time, but there was nothing he could do to stop it now. He was in something Pamila could not get him out of no matter what she did. Lando and Quick were on their own for the next three months.

All the lights were out when Lando and Quick walked into Unit 10A. A big, black counselor took them to their cells after letting them take a shower. Standing at the door of his cell in a dark red institution shirt and blue institution jeans, Lando looked through the small glass window over at Quick, who was right across from him, and said, "We gon' be down, young!"

Quick flashed a smile, and said, "No bullshit! We ain't gon' beat this shit, joe. Everybody on the block probably saw us kill that nigga, plus, the police gon' come in there and swear that he remember us."

Lando looked around his small cell, letting out a sigh as he said, "Fuck it, young, we gotta go with the flow!"

"You right, fuck that shit. I'm 'bout to go to sleep. I'ma see you in the morning, joe," Quick said as he stepped away from his window. Lando did the same.

Lando laid in the bed with all of his clothes on for hours thinking about the way Pamila had looked at him when he was leaving out of the courtroom. He couldn't get it off of his mind. He knew that he had fucked up big this time. He didn't really care about the little two years that he could get at the time, he had Quick with him and he knew that whatever he needed, Mann would get to him. What had him so upset was that he knew how Pamila felt this time around. He saw the pain in her eyes as he walked away and no matter what happened with the case, he knew that he had to slow down. Even though he had no plans to stop running the streets, he promised himself that he would stop all the wild shit.

A week had passed. Lando and Quick had both been transferred to Unit 7A where all the juveniles that were waiting to go to trial were. They were in cells that were side by side. Quick had met a little brown skinned dude named Freeway, who had all of the Newports in the unit. Freeway had shown Quick how to knock the wall out between him and Lando's cell, so that him and Lando could talk all night while they passed Newports back and forth.

Freeway was from S.E., and he was cool. Quick had become close to him almost over night. Lando had taken a liking to him as well, but he stayed into so much shit that Lando would only play him close when Quick was with him. Freeway had all the dudes in Unit 7A scared of him before Quick and Lando got there. He had tried Quick the first day he came in the unit, but he quickly saw that Quick was ready to go all the way with whatever so he began to like Quick himself, which brought Lando into the picture.

Quick and Freeway were robbing everybody for their canteen and even taking their shoes when neither one of them needed shoes. That had Quick into some kind of beef everyday.

A big, black dude named Big Youngin' had a fresh pair of Air Jordan's that were Quick's size. Quick and Freeway had taken the shoes, and now Big Youngin' had worked up the heart to do something about it.

Lando was sitting in back of the T.V. room playing cards with Short Dogg, a short, brown skinned dude that Lando had taken a liking to. Lando looked up at the T.V. and saw Big Youngin' with a pool stick in his hand about to smack Quick in the back of the head. Lando jumped up and ran over to Big Youngin' with the hard wooden chair that he was sitting in, in his hands and smacked Big Youngin' to the floor. Quick and Freeway turned around and saw what was going on and got with it, stomping Big Youngin' out on the ground. Short Dogg came running over with another wooden chair and broke it across Big Youngin's head. Blood was everywhere. Counselors flooded the T.V. Room, causing everyone to scatter. Big Youngin' was knocked out on the floor when the crowd was gone.

After locking the unit down and taking Big Youngin' to the infirmary, the counselors came back to get Freeway and Short Dogg, being as though they were the only faces that they recognized. Quick and Lando got away with everything and it was known that they were going to roll together with whatever.

Early the next morning, Unit 7A was walking to the chow hall dressed in their light blue institution sweat shirts and blue institution jeans. With his Oak Hill hat cocked to the back, Quick was at the front of the line with Lando right beside him. Walking across the compound, they heard somebody calling them from 10A's window. Looking to see where the counselors were, Quick and Lando ran over to see who was calling them from the lock down unit.

"What's up with ya'll niggas, young?" Freeway said with a smile. Quick and Lando let him know that everything was cool, even though Big Youngin's older homies that were in Unit 8B were acting like they wanted to do something about the situation.

"So, where Short Dogg at?" Lando asked. Freeway let him know that he was down the hall.

"When ya'll get out?" Quick asked. Freeway let him know that him and Short Dogg would be out in ten days.

"Check this out, joe," Lando said. "My brother supposed to come down here today. He gon' bring some smoke. When we come out later on, I'ma get you." Freeway was cool with that and let Lando and Quick know that he would make sure that Short Dogg got some. Lando and Quick then caught up with the rest of the unit and went into the chow hall.

Pamila and Mann pulled up outside of Oak Hill's Juvenile Detention Center just as the compound was clearing. Pamila watched as the basketball court full of young kids emptied. She shook her head. Lando was actually locked up for murder and that was a fact that she just could not come to grips with. Sitting behind the wheel of her Volkswagon Rabbit, Pamila stared at the tall, razor wire fence. To Pamila, Oak Hill reminded her of going to see Mann and Lando's father down Lorton's Maximum Security Prison. The sight itself filled Pamila's heart with sorrow for the bad situation that Lando and Quick had put themselves into this time.

Lando came into the small visiting area with his Oak Hill hat cocked to the side. Pamila sat at a table with her arms folded. Mann was leaning back in a chair playing with an ink pen; he was the first to see Lando.

"What's up, shorty?" Mann said. Pamila looked up when she heard Mann speak. Before Lando even said anything to Mann he looked at Pamila, wondering how she would act. It was the first time that she had been to see him since he had been down Oak Hill.

Slowly walking over to the table still watching Pamila's every expression, Lando said, "What's up, Mann?" Sitting down across from Pamila beside Mann, Lando looked at Pamila and tried to break the ice. "What's up, Pamila?" Lando said very cautiously.

Unfolding her arms and putting her hands together in front of her face with her elbows placed on the wooden table in a serious thinking posture, Pamila said, "What's up?" and looked around the room as if to say how can you ask me something like that. "This is what's up," Pamila said. "I shouldn't be here, that's what's up, Lando. You don't have no business being locked up. What is on your mind these days?" Lando knew that Pamila wasn't going to just accept the present situation without trying to understand what was on his mind.

For the next thirty minutes, Pamila scolded, and even tried to reason with Lando about the way him and Quick were living. Lando looked over at Mann like, "Damn do something, joe." Mann knew it was nothing that he could do or say that would make Pamila lighten up on Lando, besides that, Mann knew that everything Pamila was saying were things that she had deep within her heart that she had to get out of her system.

After Pamila felt as though she had chastised Lando long enough, she said, "Come here, boy." Lando got up and walked around the table. Pamila stood up and hugged him tightly, full of emotions of love, care, and concern. "Boy, I love you so much," Pamila said as she held Lando in her arms. "I'll always be here for you, but I just want you to wake up and see that the streets ain't got no love for you. The system is just waiting to take you away from me. I can't lose you to the streets!" Lando felt every word that Pamila said.

"I know, I'ma slow down. I promise," Lando said. Pamila let him go and he sat back down.

"Where is the restroom?" Pamila asked. Lando walked her to the door and pointed her to the bathroom.

Walking back into the room with Mann, Lando smiled and said, "What's up, joe?" as he sat back down beside his brother.

Mann reached over and rubbed his little brother on the top of the head as he said, "Ain't shit, shorty. How you doing down here?"

"I'm chillin'. This shit ain't shit."

"What's up with Quick lil' ass?"

"Slim chillin'. He down here takin' these niggas bad," Lando said as Mann laughed. He had a feeling that was how Quick would be down Oak Hill. Mann always thought that Quick would be another Black when he got older, and it sure looked like he was going in that direction.

"So, What's up?" Lando said. "You bring that?" Mann looked around and pulled a sandwich bag of weed out of his black Polo jacket.

"How you gon' get dis shit back to your unit?" Mann asked. Lando let Mann know that he knew what he was doing, and then they began talking about the case that Lando and Quick had.

"So, what your lawyer talking 'bout, shorty?" Mann asked. Lando looked away as if to say that he wasn't even thinking about what his lawyer had to say, he knew in his heart that he wasn't going to come home. Lando and Quick both knew they would be gone for at least the next two years of their young lives, which to them seemed like a lifetime.

Looking back at Mann, Lando said, "It really ain't shit that he can say, joe. Me and Quick smashed that nigga right on the sidewalk, joe. It ain't no telling who seen us. Besides that, we shot at the bodeans that night and I know they gon' swear they remember us." Mann shook his head.

He had never did any time before. He felt sorry for his little brother. Mann had a feeling that Lando and Quick were going to do some time himself, but he was going to do whatever he could to get them off on the beef.

Rubbing his hand on his chin, Mann said, "Just take it easy down here. I'ma make sure you and Quick stay tight while ya'll down here and I'ma do all I can to get ya'll out as soon as possible. These juvenile peoples play a lot different than the adult system." Lando knew Mann was right. Pamila walked in the room while they were still talking.

"They say it's time for us to go, Lando," Pamila said as she walked over and hugged him. "You take care of yourself down here. Don't trust nobody but Quick. These boys down here know more about doing time then ya'll, so ya'll stick together. I'ma pray that the Lord looks over ya'll." Lando looked over at Mann as he hugged Pamila, and smiled at him. He knew Mann knew that him and Quick would be able to hold their own, but to

Pamila, they would always be babies. Lando kissed Pamila and let her know that he would be fine.

Walking back to his unit with Counselor Mr. Roy, Lando thought more and more about all that Pamila had said to him about slowing down. She was right. He began to think about all of the money that him and Quick had been making in the streets at their age. He felt that they could have been much smoother with what they were doing. He began to think about his brother and how Mann had been making money in the streets for the longest and never went to jail for anything. No matter what the outcome of his stay down Oak Hill, Lando swore that he was going to get back to the streets and get money just like Mann, even if he had to murder for it.

Mr. Roy, a big, light skinned man that stood at least six feet, let Lando in the unit and said, "Stay out of trouble, shorty. Your lil' name is kickin' round here and you ain't even been down here a whole month yet."

Lando looked at Mr. Roy, waving his statement off with his hand as he said, "Whatever, nigga." Lando walked on down the hall to Quick's cell, never looking back at the counselor as the door shut behind him.

Quick had a full house when Lando walked in the small cell. Mann had taught him about crowds long ago and Lando didn't trust a lot of new faces, which could be seen by the look on his face. Laying on his bed surrounded by Demo, Hub, and Monkey-D, Quick saw that Lando wanted to say something to him about all the niggas he had in the cell. Before Quick could say anything, Lando said, "Let me holla at you, slim." Quick got up and walked next door to Lando's cell.

Lando sat on the bed, told Quick to shut the door, and put some paper over the window. Quick took care of that and turned around asking Lando why he was acting like he had a problem with the dudes in his cell.

"You know I don't fuck with a rack of new niggas, young. I don't know them niggas!" Lando said as he pulled the weed out of his drawers.

Looking down at the weed with a smile on his face, Quick said, "Look, joe, I dig them niggas. They cool as shit, you ain't gotta fuck with them, slim." Walking over and sitting down beside Lando, Quick went on to tell him that he was smoking with the new dudes that were in his cell.

"You put them niggas in our business, young?" Lando asked.

"Yeah, I told them we were getting some bud, stop trippin' nigga," Quick said.

Lando looked at Quick for a minute, thinking about the whole situation, and then said, "If you say them niggas cool like that, then I'ma go with that, joe. Let's go put this shit in the air."

On the bricks, days seemed to go slow for Mann. His money was still coming like he wanted it to. Black was laid back for a minute. Dre was moving coke like it was legal out Maryland. Kelley was beginning to mean more and more to Mann by her display of trust, love, and loyalty. Silk was giving Mann deal after deal now that him and Supreme were getting to know each other better. Things were smooth, but without Lando running around getting into shit, life was not the same and would not be the same until shorty was back on the streets. Mann knew that Lando would be down for awhile, and he could tell that he would miss his little brother everyday that he was gone.

Mann stood in front of the oven in his small apartment out Maryland cooking up a brick of coke for Da-Da, who had beeped him thirty minutes ago saying that he had twenty five thousand dollars and needed to cop a brick quick because he had sold out early that week.

Dre walked in the kitchen with the cordless phone in his hand, and said, "Lando on the phone, slim." Mann told Dre to watch over the coke while he went to talk to Lando in the living room.

"What's up, shorty?" Mann said as he sat down on the sofa in the living room, turning the T.V. on with the remote control.

"Ain't shit, joe. What's up with you, slim?"

"Some lil' girl called the house for you 'bout two days ago," Mann said as he tried to recall her name.

"Was it Nakia?." Lando asked. He had told her to call Pamila and ask her if she could bring her to see Lando the next time she went.

"Na, it began with a J... That's it! Jazmin, she called asking for your address. Lil' Garvin told her you were locked up. I gave her your address and all that good shit. She act like she want to come see you..."

"You tell her you gon' bring her to see me?" Lando said. Mann laughed at the excitement in his little brother's voice. He could tell that shorty had feelings for Jazmin.

"I thought you was in love with the young girl Nakia?" Mann said.

"Yeah, Nakia my folks, she s'pose to be comin' down to see me this weekend with Pamila. Jazmin my lil' buddy, I digsher and everything, but she got me on big brother shit," Lando said. As the conversation went on, Mann asked Lando about Quick.

"Quick chillin'," Lando said. "Hold on, I'ma call him for you, joe." Lando ran down the hall and got Quick, who was in Freeway's cell shooting dice with him, Short Dogg, Demo, Hub, and Monkey D.

Quick ran back to the little room where the phone was, and picked it up as he sat down on the wooden chair looking out into the hallway.

"What's up, nigga!" Quick said. Mann laughed out loud. Quick sounded like he had grew years in just a few weeks.

"What's up with you, shorty?" Mann responded.

"I'm chillin'. This Oak Hill shit ain't shit, joe. I'm down here takin' these suckas bad, young."

"Shorty, you can't keep thinking everybody a sucka, joe. You gon' sleep on the wrong nigga."

"Yeah, yeah, I know you right, but these niggas punks. Anyway, you seen Baby-D and Lil' Garvin?"

"Yeah, I saw them young niggas down 14th Street 'bout two days ago. They jive getting a lil' money, too. Lil' Garvin want me to do something with 'em."

"Oh yeah?" Quick said, sounding happy that his niggas was doing something for themselves on the streets.

"Check this out, Mann, tell them me and Lando tryin' to catch up with them and we need a number where they be at so we can holla at them."

"I got that, shorty, I'ma do that for you when I go back around the way."

"Cool, I'ma put Lando back on the phone," Quick said. Lando got back on the phone and let Mann know that it was time for him to roll, and that he would call back later on in the week.

"Take care of yourself, shorty, I'ma see if I can get Pamila to bring the lil' girl Jazmin down to see you," Mann said. Lando hung up the phone and went back down the hall to shoot dice with everybody else.

Metra had been hanging across town with a few of her buddies for the last few months. She knew she wasn't welcomed around the way, being as though she had turned Dre into the Feds. Now that nothing had happened to her since Dre and Black had been home, she began to feel too comfortable.

Black was sitting in his Acura Legend with the driver side door wide open. Now that Mann and Dre were doing their thing out Maryland, Rittenhouse Street was his. Smoke and Serge were sitting in the back of the car counting money while Black rolled a blunt of weed up front.

"Ya'll ready to roll out?" Black asked as he shut the door of the Acura.

"Yeah, lets' get the fuck out of here," Smoke said. He really didn't like being around the way longer than he had to be these days. Things were just too hot. The Feds were coming through in every kind of way that you could think of. Black, Smoke, and Serge had cut themselves off from everybody else.

They were doing their own thing and didn't care who didn't like it.

As Black started the car, he saw a black BMW 325i bend the corner and pull up in front of Metra's house. Black watched as Metra ran out of her house and jumped in the BMW.

"I thought that bitch lived over S.E. somewhere now?" Black said as he pulled off behind the BMW, headed up Rittenhouse Street.

Smoke raised up and saw the car that Metra had just got in, and said, "I been seein' that joint right there around a lot lately, joe." As Black drove up the street behind the car, he thought about how Metra had turned Dre in. All of his anger came back.

"I'ma smash this hot bitch!" Black said as he pulled out onto Georgia Avenue behind the BMW. His two partners in crime were always ready for drama, so they didn't object at all. As far as they were concerned, it was Blacks' call.

The BMW pulled over in the McDonald's parking lot and a slim, brown skinned dude got out and jogged inside. Black pulled up at the end of the parking lot and told Serge to stay behind the wheel while he took care of business. Smoke wanted to roll with Black even though Black wanted to put the work in solo. Black agreed to let his man roll. They slid on ski masks that Black had on stand-by in the glove compartment and whipped out their pistols.

Creeping through the parking lot unseen on the cool spring night, Black and Smoke slid up on the side of the BMW with the speed of professional hitmen. Metra turned to look out of the window and screamed when she saw the two killers in black pointing pistols right at her face. She covered up her head and jumped over into the driver seat. Her actions were of no use. Smoke and Black pumped the whole car full of hollow point slugs from their .45 automatics. Gunfire exploded into the air. Metra laid in the driver seat lifeless, but is wasn't enough for Black. Pulling his sweat shirt sleeve over his hand, he opened the passenger side door, stuck his pistol inside, and hit Metra in the head two more times. In seconds, Black and Smoke were back in the Acura Legend with Serge flying down 14th Street smoking weed. Once they were downtown, Black told Serge to pull the car into an alley where him and Smoke wiped their fingers prints off of their pistols and threw them down a sewer hole.

It was noon the next day when Kelley came home for lunch. She walked downstairs to the basement and saw Mann laying on the bed. She walked over and laid down beside him, asking, "Why you ain't in school?"

"I ain't gotta go 'til two today."

"Oh yeah, well guess what happened yesterday," Kelley said in a way that got Mann's attention quickly.

"What's up?" Mann asked, sounding very concerned. Kelley had just seen Dee-Dee, who had gotten back in school and she had told her about Metra getting shot in the McDonald's parking lot. Kelley gave Mann the whole run down just as Dee-Dee had given it to her, and she had the facts as far as the killing went. Metra had been shot nineteen times and never had a chance.

"Who killed her?" Mann asked.

"Don't nobody know. Some nigga she was with told the police that two dudes in ski masks ran up on his car while he was ordering food and started shooting," Kelley said. She told Mann a little more of what Dee-Dee had told her about the shooting, and then she had to go pick Pamila's work clothes up from the cleaners.

Mann got up and got ready for school himself. All he could think about was Black, it was no doubt in his mind that Black killed Metra. Mann hoped that Black left no loose ends. He would have to check on Black as soon as he got a chance. Grabbing his car keys, Mann hit the streets.

Chapter Eleven: Surprise

Mann never got the chance to check up on Black. Officer Hall and the jump outs caught up with him first.

Black was high as a kite standing in the alley slanging rocks like it was legal. Hall and the jump outs sat in a new Chevy Blazer with dark tinted windows, watching him. Black had sold just over an ounce when somebody beeped him. As he began to walk through Dee-Dee's yard, Hall and the rest of the jump outs ran up to Black and slammed him to the ground. Black was caught and he knew it. Hall pulled a bag of fifty rocks out of Black's Polo jacket and placed him under arrest. On the way to the police station, Black thought he was going down for Metra's murder. He couldn't believe he was out there on the strip slipping just two days after killing the hot bitch.

Hall made Black's day when he came to the holding cell and told Black he was going down to Central Cell Block for distribution of crack.

Black smiled at Hall, and said, "You happy as shit that you done locked me up for something."

Hall put Black against the wall placing the handcuffs on him while he said, "Yeah, I'm happy, motherfucker."

"I ain't nothin' but sixteen. I ain't goin' nowhere but down Oak Hill for a few months. That ain't shit!"

"Yeah, well tell your lil' cousin Lando I said hi and I'll be at his upcoming trial," Hall said with a laugh as he walked Black to the police car.

Down Oak Hill two days later, every unit was out on the compound for their outside recreation. Lando, Quick, Freeway, Short Dogg, and Demo were sitting behind the gym smoking weed when Monkey D ran over, and said, "Lando, some new nigga up 10A say he want you to come to his window." Lando passed the jay of weed to Demo and walked across the compound like he had a .44 magnum tucked in his waistband, wondering who could want him that was up 10A. Maybe Lil' Garvin or Baby-D could have caught a case or something.

"Lando!" an excited voice called from the same window that Freeway was in a few weeks ago. Lando recognized the voice off the top and ran over to the window to see what Black was doing locked up.

"What's up, young?" Lando said in an excited voice. "What the fuck you doing locked up, joe?"

"I let that hot nigga Hall catch me slippin' around the way. I jive got caught with 'bout an ounce in back of Dee-Dee's house."

"Yeah, when you go back to court?"

"I gotta status hearing in 'bout a month."

"You think they gon' let you go?"

"I ain't sure, if they don't, it ain't shit. Where the fuck Quick at?"

"He over there smoking behind the gym."

"Ya'll got bud?!"

"Yeah, I'ma run over to the unit and get some for you. I got this nigga holding it for me, I'ma tell Quick you over here, too," Lando said before he ran across the compound to get Quick and some weed for Black.

In less then five minutes, Lando and Quick were back at Black's window with three fat jays already rolled up. Lando slid them through a hole in Black's window. Black got the jays and told Lando that he needed a light.

"You think I'ma forget the cow?" Lando asked as if Black had said something stupid. They all started laughing as Lando slid a lighter through the window.

"So, what's up with ya'll niggas?" Black asked.

"Ain't shit," Quick said. "We chillin' like shit, just waitin' to go to trial."

"Y'all know who telling on y'all?" Black asked.

"We don't know, slim," Lando said. "Mann asked me the same thing last week. It was a rack-a-niggas outside that night, young."

"No bullshit," Quick said. "Pipeheads and all. We won't know who tellin' on us 'til we get to trial, joe."

"So, what's goin' on 'round the way?" Lando asked.

Black let them know that he had the block locked down now that Mann and Dre were both doing their thing out Maryland. He told them how he ain't fuck with Onion and Corey no more because they had been acting funny since that Mann and Dre weren't around. Black was getting the feeling that they really didn't want him around the way since that he was hustling and not just robbing niggas.

"What you mean they actin' funny?" Lando asked.

"They be rollin' out when me, Smoke, and Serge be comin' around. Fuck them niggas for real, Smoke and Serge tryin' to rob them niggas, anyway."

"I heard the bitch Metra got her head hit up the Ave. bout three or four days ago," Lando said.

Black smiled and said, "Me and Smoke caught that hot ass bitch up the Ave. in some nigga's BMW and aired the joint out."

"Damn, young! Ya'll put that work in right in front of the police station?" Quick said, sounding surprised.

Black went on to tell them how him and Smoke killed Metra and before they knew it, it was time for the compound to clear. Black told Quick and Lando to call Mann and tell him to send him some money. They told him that they would get right on top of that and they were waiting for him to get out of 10A so that he could get in the same unit with them. When they were done talking, they ran across the compound and into Unit 7A for the night.

Mann, Dre, and Silk were in Pamila's basement watching UNLV play Duke. Dre had bet Silk five hundred dollars that UNLV would pull the game off. Dre was a die-hard fan. While Silk and Dre sat on the sofa, Mann sat on his bed with a cup of soda in his hand.

"You know Baby-D fight out Maryland University this weekend," Dre said to Mann.

"Oh yeah, shorty stickin' with that shit, huh?" Mann said.

Dre let him know that he saw Baby-D when he was on his way home earlier and that he asked him if he was coming to see him fight. Dre let him know that he would be there. Silk was a big fight fan himself, he knew Baby-D but he didn't know he could box. Asking Dre about Baby-D, Silk and him got into a conversation about his fight game. Pamila called Mann from the top of the steps and told him to pick up the phone.

Rolling over on his bed, Mann picked up the phone and said, "Hello?"

"What's up, joe?" Lando said into the phone.

"What's up, young nigga?" Mann said.

Lando began to talk and let Mann know that Black was down Oak Hill with him, which took a load off of Mann's back because he was worried that Black might have gotten charged with killing Metra. He could deal with him being down Oak Hill. One thing was for sure, he wouldn't have to worry about Lando and Quick with Black down there with them.

"So, what Black locked up for?" Mann asked.

"Slim gotta punk ass coke beef," Lando said as he went on to tell Mann that Black wanted him to send him some money. Mann told Lando that he was going to send all of them some money in the morning and that he would be to see him sometime within the next two weeks. After talking to his little brother for a few more minutes, Mann got off the phone and told Silk and Dre that Black was cool and he was only down Oak Hill on a coke beef.

With Lando, Quick, and Black down Oak Hill, Mann only had two dudes on the street that he had any trust in, and that was Dre and Silk. That made Mann begin to think more and more about getting out of the game. His money was growing like never before with him and Dre going half on ten bricks of coke every week. As the weeks turned into months, Mann had been riding by an old Subway fast food joint that was for sale. Everyday that he rode by it, he kept thinking of what him and Silk had always talked about. Suddenly, he made his mind up one day as he passed by the Subway and it was no longer for sale. He was going to buy a small store of some kind and he knew where he was going to do it. All he needed to do was find out whose name he was going to get it in. The place was no problem, there was an old corner store owned by an old black couple that sat on Georgia Avenue right by the Maryland line. Mann told himself that it was going to be his as soon as he saw the for-sale sign go up. His next move was to pull up on Silk, he knew Silk would help him get the store the right way because his sister named Pam had good credit. His goal was set.

Oak Hill wasn't the same for the last three months with Black on the compound. As soon as he was moved from Unit 10A to Unit 7A with Lando and Quick, the corruption started. Black had the Oak Hill counselors bringing in weed, pizza, beer, and just about everything else you could think of that wasn't supposed to be on the compound. Freeway, Demo, and Short Dogg had been found guilty of their charges and were in Unit 8B, but they still ran the compound with Quick and Lando during school and at rec. time. Monkey-D and Hub went home two weeks ago, both of them had juvenile murder charges. By being found not guilty, Quick and Lando began to believe that they could actually beat their murder case when they went to trial in two days.

Quick had grown a love for basketball over the past three months and played everyday after school, no questions asked. He was running late and was in a rush to get his rec. shoes before they locked the door to the compound. Running down the hall to his cell, he saw that his door was locked. "Damn!" he said out loud as he ran up the hall to Black's cell to get his Air Jordan's.

Black was lying on his bed reading Sun Tzu's *The Art of War*, a book that Mann had sent him in the mail, and Black had read it every day like a Bible since. Seeing Quick at his door in a rush, Black thought that something was wrong.

"What the fuck is up, shorty?" Black asked, rising up off the bed with his war face on.

"Ain't shit, joe. Let me see your shoes, I'm 'bout to go shoot some ball," Quick said. Black got the shoes from under the bed and gave them to Quick, asking him if the mail had been passed out yet. Quick kicked his Oak Hill boots off and slid into the Jordan's, telling Black that the mail hadn't come yet as he took off running down the hall.

Almost out the door, Quick ran by the back room where the phone was.

"Quick!" a voice yelled out. Quick knew it was Lando and if it was anyone else, he would have kept on going because he knew that the teams would already be picked by the time he got outside.

"What's up, young?" Quick said in a voice that displayed his hurry as he stepped in the phone room where Lando was.

Lando covered the phone so that Nakia could not hear what he was talking about, and said, "Our lawyer supposed to come see us at six tonight, so don't get wrapped up out there." Quick let Lando know that he would be ready for their legal visit, and ran out the door and onto the basketball court where Freeway, Short Dogg, and Demo were waiting to run a whole court.

"Yeah, I'm back, boo," Lando said in his smooth 'I'm like that with the ladies' voice that had grown a little deeper over the last three months.

"So, are you coming home or not, Lando?" Nakia asked. She had been growing very impatient with Lando's stay down Oak Hill. Lando kept telling her that he would be home in May, and now May had arrived and Nakia wanted Lando home. He was her first love and the only person she had ever been with sexually. The things Lando did with her and showed her made her love him, at least that's what she thought at her young age.

"Look, I can't tell you what the future holds. All I can tell you is that I should be home after my trial."

"You gotta come home, Lando. You ain't kill that boy, so they gotta let you and Quick go, right?"

"Nakia, I told you, they gon' do what they want to do. Somebody telling them that they saw me and Quick kill the nigga, so they gonna try to make us do some time."

"Why, Lando!" Nakia said as she began to cry like she did very often, "Why they won't just let ya'll go?" Lando hated when Nakia cried about the situation and he spent the rest of his time on the phone trying to make her believe that things would be fine.

The court bus was packed leaving Oak Hill that bright spring morning. Shackled and handcuffed on their way to court were thirty of D.C's most out of control youths. Seven of which were some of the most vicious teenage killers of the 90s. Quick, Lando, and Short Dogg were an outstanding three in the bunch due to their names floating around the streets at such a young age.

Chained together at the waist, Lando and Quick sat behind Short Dogg, who was going to court for his disposition hearing for a murder that he had been found guilty of. Short Dogg was telling Quick and Lando how the Feds were going to have someone that they least expected to pop up at court and say that they saw everything go down. Short Dogg wasn't guessing either, his partner in crime on the murder, who was an old childhood friend, came to court and told everything, so Short Dogg knew what he was talking about.

"Yeah, your man told on you huh, young?" Quick asked. He was disgusted at how Short Dogg told him and Lando about his man telling on him. Quick couldn't think of telling on Lando about anything, he was going to go all the way with him.

"Yeah, slim," Short Dogg said. "They gon' play real dirty in there." Lando sat back listening to everything that Short Dogg was saying. He tried to come up with the person that the Feds could have telling on him, besides the police, that him and Quick shot at that night and the only person he could come up with was pipehead Sheila, being as though she put him and Quick on point about the robbery that was taking place. Other than that, Lando couldn't think of anyone else. He sat on the court bus kicking it with Short Dogg and Quick for the rest of the ride to the Receiving Home where the U.S. Marshals would later pick all of the juveniles up and take them to the Superior Court of the District of Columbia.

Sitting in a holding cell behind the courtroom of the Honorable Judge Queen, Lando and Quick talked about their feelings toward the case as well as their feelings toward their weird ass lawyer. Quick didn't like Mr. Shwortz at all and had cursed him out every time he went on a legal visit. Quick's whole outlook on the case was one that he had got from Black, and that was to let nature take its course. Quick felt that whatever was going to go down, was going to go down and that he would deal with whatever came his way. Lando, on the other hand, felt that if his lawyer could just do a half way decent job at defending them, that all they would have to worry about was the statement that the two police would give. As they sat and talked a Marshal came back into the bullpen to get them for trial.

"It's time to go," a tall white man said as he opened up the door to the holding cell and escorted the two young killers into the courtroom.

Walking into the court and seeing his grandmother sitting in the back of the courtroom next to Pamila and Mann, Quick waved at them as if there was nothing wrong at all. You would've never guessed that the young dude was on trial for murder. He showed no signs of worry at all as he sat down beside Mr. Shwortz and folded his hands on the long wooden table. Lando was a little more concerned than Quick, and you could see it in his face as he looked back at Pamila and Mann. Lando slowly walked over to the table where Quick had already taken a seat beside their lawyer. Lando paid attention to everything in the courtroom as he sat down. Sitting across the aisle from Pamila, Mann, and Quick's grandmother, there was a cute, light skinned young girl with a baby in her arms. Lando kept looking back at her to see if he could recognize her face from somewhere. The young girl had a very angry look on her face, which led Lando to believe that she had to be some kin to the dude that got killed that night on Rittenhouse Street. Judge Queen came out of her chambers and snapped Lando out of his thoughts by calling the court to attention.

With no jury in juvenile trials, all arguments were directed to Judge Queen. The government marched in witness after witness into the courtroom and onto the witness stand to report their professional opinion of the way the victim was slain. A doctor reported how the victim was brought to the hospital already dead, then a coroner got on the witness stand to report to Judge Queen how many wounds the victim sustained on the night of the murder. Mr. Shwortz put up minimal fight against these witnesses because they could not point the finger of guilt at his two clients.

The slim, white lady that was the prosecutor for the government called one of the officers that Lando and Quick had shot at on the night of the murder to the stand. Officer Wilson, a short, brown skinned young man was the officer driving the police car that came flying around the corner on the night of the murder. After being sworn in under oath, Officer Wilson was directed by Prosecutor Jamerson to tell Judge Queen what he witnessed as he and his fellow partner ran across the shooting. Officer Wilson told the judge everything that he had seen that night, and he told the whole truth. Lando cracked a slight smile as the officer wrapped up his story by saying that it was no way that he could say for sure that the two juveniles that were on trial were the same two that shot at him and his partner.

"No further questions!" Ms. Jamerson snapped with anger in her voice. Mr. Shwortz stood up and began to reinforce the fact that Officer Wilson could not identify Quick nor Lando as the shooters. Making sure he didn't go overboard, he wrapped up his cross-examination with speed and allowed the government to try their hand again.

"I call Officer Halkins to the stand, Your Honor," Prosecutor Jamerson said. The double doors that led out of the courtroom opened and Officer Halkins walked in, causing everyone to turn their heads his way. A sick feeling went through Lando's body as he caught eye contact with the officer. Lando remembered looking him right in the face as he shot at him that night, and by the way the officer looked at him, Lando knew that he remembered as well.

"So, tell us what happened on the night of January 19th," Ms. Jamerson said to the officer. He told the story exactly how he remembered it up until where his partner had said that he couldn't identify the shooters.

When he got to that point, he looked over at Lando and said, "I know for certain that the little light skinned kid right there was one of the kids doing the shooting that night."

Prosecutor Jamerson stood up smiling as she walked over to the table where Lando was sitting and while pointing right at him, she said, "You are sure that this is the child that you saw shooting at you and your partner?"

"I'm sure. He looked me right in the face while he was shooting at us that night. I can't believe he's just a child."

"Well what about this one?" Prosecutor Jamerson asked as she pointed at Quick.

"I can't say. The other shooter was further away and it was very dark that night," Officer Halkins said. Ms. Jamerson led him on for awhile trying to make him say more than he wanted to say about the shooting, but Judge Queen put an end to the legal games that she was trying to play and allowed Mr. Shwortz a chance to defend his clients.

As it stood, Lando was the only client in danger as far as Mr. Shwortz was concerned. Quick couldn't be identified by either officer that had been on the stand. Therefore, Mr. Shwortz tried to save Lando as best as he could by bringing everybody back around to the matter at hand, which was murder.

"So, Officer Hawkins," the crazy looking white lawyer said, "you say you know that one of my clients shot at you, but Ms. Prosecutor so conveniently forgot that these two kids are charged with first degree murder. Did you or your partner see them kill this guy uh…Ramen Biggs?" The officer told the judge that he had seen no such thing that night.

Mr. Shwortz had done what he intended to do, he made sure that everybody in the courtroom still felt that there was a chance that Lando and Quick might be innocent of murder. Officer Hawkins was dismissed and Judge Queen asked Ms. Jamerson if she had any other witness before she passed her judgment. Looking through her folder, the prosecutor said, "As a matter of fact, I do, Your Honor."

As it stood now, the government had only succeeded in proving that Lando had shot at a police officer that was far from the attempted murder of a police officer that the government was saying took place. Lando was cool with that; he would take assault with a deadly weapon any day over a murder.

Leaning over and whispering into Quick's ear, Lando said, "Looks like you gone beat this shit, young."

Quick turned to Lando and said, "This shit ain't over yet."

"I call Mr. Kareen Swan to the stand," Ms. Jamerson said.

Looking at Lando, Quick said, "Who the fuck is that, joe?"

"I don't know, young." Lando said as he looked back at the double doors that led out of the courtroom.

Slowly, the doors opened and a U.S. Marshal came through. Mann looked at the look on Lando's face as he looked back at the doors and turned to see what had his little brother looking so confused. As Mann turned to look at the double doors himself, he was fucked up to see Onion coming through the doors behind the Marshal.

"You bitch ass nigga!" Mann said out loud as Onion walked by him on his way to the witness stand. Pamila saw the anger in Mann's dark face and tried to calm him down.

She grabbed his arm and said, "You can't be mad. I've always told you and Lando that y'all can't trust them boys around there, they ain't no good."

"You right," Mann said as he got himself together and made up his mind that Onion was a dead man.

Dressed in all black with a black bandanna around his neck, Onion looked like a model thug nigga straight out of a 'how to be a gangsta' handbook. His face showed no sign of shame about what he was doing. He looked over at Lando and Quick, and then back at Mann as the prosecutor walked up to the stand and asked her first question.

"Mr. Swan," she said, "would you tell the judge what you witnessed on the night of January 19th?" Onion turned and looked at Judge Queen with a look of a man that had no regard for the side of the game that he came from.

"Yeah, I'll tell her what I saw that night," he said in a smooth voice. "Me and my niggas Smoke, Serge, Corey, and Kevin were hustlin' and smokin' weed up by the crack house when some niggas tried to rob us…"

"Your Honor, I object." Mr. Shwortz said, cutting Onion off. "This man is a street thug and a confessed drug dealer. Ms. Jamerson can't truly expect this honorable court to allow him to come in here and tell the truth."

"Objection overruled. You may go on, Mr. Swan," Judge Queen said. Onion went on to tell her how the stick up boys had robbed him and everyone else outside that night. He said that when they were done, they ran out onto Rittenhouse Street.

"Is that when the shooting started?" Ms. Jamerson asked.

"Yeah them young niggas put that work in that night," Onion said. "They shot one of the dudes as soon as he came outta the yard where we was."

"Who shot the dude?" Ms. Jamerson asked.

"Lando and Quick. Them two young niggas right there," Onion said as he pointed the finger at them.

"No further questions, Your Honor," Ms. Jamerson said as she sat down.

"Your witness, Mr. Shwortz," Judge Queen said.

Nothing seemed to surprise Mann these days, but seeing Onion get up on that witness stand truly puzzled him. He didn't understand how Onion thought he was going to get away with something like that. Mann looked up at Lando, who had turned to look at him as Mr. Shwortz got up to question Onion. Looking in his little brother's eyes, all Mann could do was shake his head. He knew Lando and Quick were gone for the next two or more years of their life.

Mr. Shwortz's cross-examination didn't last long. The case was over when Onion got on the stand. All of Mr. Shwortz's efforts to discredit Onion fell on deaf ears. Judge Queen passed her judgment. Lando and Quick were guilty of murder in the first degree. They were to come back to court for disposition in one month.

Lando and Quick looked back at Pamila, Quick's grandmother, and Mann as they walked back into the bullpen with the Marshal. They saw the way their loved ones looked at Onion as he walked by, but Mann caught their attention the most. They knew Mann was going to do something about Onion getting on the witness stand.

"I'ma kill that bitch ass nigga when we get out, young!" Quick said to Short Dogg on the court bus on their way back down Oak Hill.

"You ain't gon; get a chance, young," Lando said as he looked out the window into the night in a daze. "That nigga gon' be dead long before we hit the bricks again, joe."

Short Dogg had heard a lot about Mann over the past few months that he had been locked up with Quick and Lando, he felt like he knew him.

In fact, he felt so strong about the way he thought of Lando's older brother that made sure they all always had weed to smoke, that he said, "Your brother gon' smash that nigga, joe. He ain't gon' let 'em get away with no shit like that." They all agreed that Short Dogg was right, they knew Mann was going to do something about the hot nigga, Onion.

Black was in front of the T.V. watching the Chicago Bulls go after a win against the Detroit Pistons. Air Jordan himself had just hit a big three pointer late in the third to put the

Bulls on top. The T.V. room went off. Quick and Lando bent the corner and walked to the back of the room and sat at the card table by themselves. Black knew that things didn't go well at court, but he would never guess what they would have to tell him. Black got up and walked to the back of the T.V. room where they were.

"What's up with y'all?" he said as he rubbed Lando on the top of the head.

Lando looked at Quick and said, "Tell 'em, young."

Looking up at Black with a look of defeat on his face, Quick said, "That bitch ass nigga Onion came to court and told them peoples that he seen everything, young."

"What!" Black said, his anger already boiling. Lando and Quick could see the all too familiar look of murder in Black's eyes as they told him how things went at court. When they were done, Black said, "Oh that nigga dying first thing in the morning!" Black walked off headed for the phone room.

"Hello, can I speak to Smoke?" Black said into the phone. Smoke's mother knew Black's voice well and she knew when he was upset.

"What's wrong with you, boy?" she said in a motherly tone. Black told her that he had just got some bad news and that he was okay. Smoke's mother, then, went and got him.

"What's up, nigga?" Smoke said into the phone. It was clear that he was glad to hear from his man. "Me and Serge just sent you some money, young. You should get it in a few days."

"That's a bet, but check this out. That nigga Onion…"

"Yeah?"

"He came to court on my lil' cousin and Quick today. He got 'em found guilty on that body."

"He did what!" Smoke said, not believing Black had said what he thought he said.

"Yeah, that's right. That nigga told like the bitch he is. I want you to smash that nigga!"

"I got that for you, joe. Believe that. That nigga good as got!" Smoke said. His word was good as gold to Black. Black knew Onion was a dead man. Black hung up the phone and called Mann to see what he had to say as well as to let him know that he didn't have to kill Onion because Smoke was already on top of it.

The next afternoon, Smoke and his cousin, Serge, sat in a dark blue Thunderbird on Rittenhouse Street waiting for Onion to come out of his house. They had already got word that he had been on the block earlier that morning. It was just a matter of time and the beautiful day was sure to bring their prey out.

Sitting in the tinted window Thunderbird smoking weed, Smoke and Serge were somewhat unseen. The car was new with paper tags on it, and no one would know who got out of it shooting when Onion walked out of his front door at the end of the block. The loud sound of a powerful motorcycle hit the air, and Smoke and Serge turned to look back up the street to see where the loud bike was coming from.

Dressed in all black on a 900 Ninja, Wee-Wee pulled up and parked his bike right in front of Dee-Dee's house. He had got the news that Onion had told on Quick and was coming up Rittenhouse Street to take care of the situation. Getting off of his bike, on point, he looked up and down the street noticing the dark blue-tinted window Thunderbird on the other side of the street. He gave the car a quick second look, and then went into Dee-Dee's house to find out where Onion was since he knew that Dee-Dee was fucking with him and she would not play games with him being as though she had known him since she used to live down V Street where he was from.

"Ain't that Wee?" Smoke asked as he took a deep pull of weed into his lungs.

"Yeah, that's him. He must have heard about Onion, too, he don't pop up unless something wrong," Serge said. Tapping Serge on the leg to get his attention while pulling his .40 cal pistol from under the seat, Smoke pointed down the street towards Onion's house. He was coming out of his front door with a brown paper bag in his hand.

"Let's get this nigga and jump right out on 'em,"Smoke said as he began to pull off.

Seconds after Smoke and Serge pulled off in the Thunderbird, Wee-Wee came out of Dee-Dee's house. Standing on her porch, he adjusted his Glock 17 on his waistband. Putting his hand over his eyes to block the sun, he looked down the street toward Onion's house and saw him walking down the steps. "Shit!" he said out loud.

Slowly crossing 5th Street in the Thunderbird, Smoke and Serge could taste death. Coming to a stop, Smoke grabbed the handle to the door and was about to jump out when he stopped suddenly and watched.

As Onion walked down the long steps that led from his porch to the sidewalk on Rittenhouse Street, two little dudes in ski masks popped from out of the bushes beside his house. Gunshots hit the air. Bullets slammed into Onion's back, knocking him down the rest of the steps and flat onto the sidewalk. Smoke slammed his door back shut and smashed the gas. Him and Serge didn't know what was going on. Flying down the street, they looked over their shoulders and saw the two little dudes in ski masks standing over top of Onion with gunfire jumping out of their hands.

Later on as the sun started to go down, Mann was just coming back in the house from taking his GED test. For eight hours he sat behind a desk, taking test after test, and it was worth it because he felt that he had passed it. Walking down the basement steps, Mann heard the sobs of a female crying. He thought that Kelley was downstairs crying, so he hurried down his steps to see what was up. When he got to the bottom of the steps, he saw Dee-Dee sitting on his bed crying her heart out into her hands with Kelley hugging her telling her to be strong. Mann knew what was up with out asking, but he thought that Smoke was the reason.

"What's wrong?" Mann said as he walked over to Dee-Dee and showed his concern.

Looking up at Mann, Dee-Dee managed to say through her sobs, "They killed my baby!"

Grabbing Mann with her tear soaked hands, Dee-Dee said, "Why, Mann? Why?"

Looking at Kelley as he sat down beside Dee-Dee rubbing her head Mann said, "They killed who?" as if he knew nothing. Dee-Dee got herself together enough to tell Mann that two young dudes had shot Onion to death on his front steps, and that nobody knew who did it. Mann was puzzled, he couldn't think of who would have killed Onion before Smoke. He sat and talked to Dee-Dee for a while to calm her down, and then he left her and Kelley alone so that Dee-Dee could get the rest of her hurt and pain out.

Mann had to meet Silk at a night club called Takoma Station so that they could put the plan together for Mann to buy the store that he wanted because Silk's sister had already agreed to put it in her name.

Pulling up outside of the nightclub in his 300ZX, Mann parked and dug into his pocket to get his beeper that was going off. A set of headlights hit Mann in the eyes as a car pulled up behind him. Not being able to see who was behind him due to the bright lights, Mann got a little uncomfortable and pulled a 10mm from under his seat. The car door of the car behind him opened and a short dude got out of the car and began walking toward Mann's car. The passenger side door of the car opened and another little dude got out of the car and started walking up to Mann's car on the other side.

"What's up, nigga?" Baby-D said as he tapped on Mann's window.

Rolling his window down and sliding his pistol between his waistband, Mann said, "What's up, shorty?" as Lil' Garvin walked up and stood beside Baby-D.

"What y'all niggas been up to?" Mann asked.

"We chillin' out here, you know how we do it, slim," Baby-D said.

"We heard about Onion telling on Lando and Quick yesterday," Lil' Garvin said.

"Yeah, somebody smashed the nigga earlier today," Mann said.

"We smashed thatt bitch ass nigga. Young! Fuck that nigga. Lando told us what happened on the phone last night," Baby-D said. Mann looked at the two younger dudes standing outside of his car and smiled, he couldn't believe how fast all of them had grown up.

"Oh yeah," Mann said. "Yall put that work in, huh?"

Baby-D and Lil' Garvin went on to tell Mann how they had hid in the bushes beside Onion's house for thirty minutes waiting for him to come outside. They told Mann how they were fucked up about him getting Lando and Quick found guilty, so they killed him. As they told Mann about the whole situation, he knew in his heart that the two young dudes knew what loyalty was all about. Their partners from childhood were locked up for murder and somebody around their way told on them, and that was all that needed to be said for them to fill Onion with hollow point slugs. After they were finished telling Mann about the killing, Mann told them not to tell anybody about what they had done hours ago. He told them that he wanted them to come over Pamila's house tomorrow so that he could talk to them about something important, and then they got back in their car and left.

Sitting in his car thinking about what Lil' Garvin and Baby-D had just told him, Mann decided that he was going to make sure that he did something big with the two young dudes so that they would be set for awhile. He felt that they deserved a shot at some bigger money than they were making, and he was going to give it to them for what they did for his little brother and Quick. Looking out of his window, Mann saw Silk pulling up across the street in his Ferrari. Mann turned his car off and got out to go talk to Silk.

A week later, Lando was coming back off of a visit with a big smile on his face. Pamila brought Nakia down Oak Hill to see him, and Mann brought him a fifty bag of weed, along with the news of how Baby-D and Lil' Garvin had killed Onion the very next day after he had testified against him and Quick.

Black and Quick were playing a game of chess in the T.V. room when Lando came walking down the hall and passed them with a smile on his face. They knew what time it was and they both got up and walked down the hall to Lando's cell together.

"What up, joe?" Black asked as he walked in Lando's cell and sat on the bed.

"Y'all ain't gon believe this shit here, joe," Lando said as Quick walked by him and sat in a chair in the corner of the cell. "Y'all know Lil' Garvin and the Baby smashed the nigga, Onion," Lando said as he began to tell Black and Quick how they had killed him while dumping the weed that Mann had brought him on a piece of paper on the bed beside Black.

Grabbing a big bud of weed and putting it into a split blunt, Black said, "Them young niggas ain't playin' out there, joe." Quick shut the door of the cell and put a piece of paper over the window while Lando lit an incense, hanging it by the door while Black lit the blunt of weed that he had just rolled.

Blowing a cloud of weed smoke out of his mouth and passing the blunt to Lando, Black said, "That's how shit s'pose to be done. Them young niggas ain't do no fakin'!" Black was impressed, to say the least. He didn't know who could have killed Onion. Smoke told him how he was in the car with Serge and they were about to smash Onion when two little dudes jumped out of the bushes and gunned Onion down right in front of his house. Black's first thought was that Onion had tried to take some young niggas bad and they killed him. Now that he knew that Onion got killed for telling on Lando and Quick, he felt a lot better.

After smoking another blunt with Quick and Black, Lando went to get on the phone. He called a pay phone number that Lil' Garvin had given to Mann for him to reach him. Without saying the wrong thing on the phone, Lando let Lil' Garvin know that he knew what was up and that he respected the move.

"You know how we roll, slim, that ain't shit, joe," Lil' Garvin said.

"Where Baby–D at?" Lando asked, sounding high as ever.

"Hold on. He in the alley," Lil' Garvin said as he called up the alley for Baby-D.

"Hello?" Baby-D said as he got on the phone, breathing hard from running down the block.

"Yeah, slim, I was telling Lil' Garvin that y'all real as shit. Y'all keep it in the famil,y you know," Lando said.

Baby-D knew exactly what he was talking about and said, "You my nigga from jump street, you know that, slim. But, check this out, the jump outs at the top of the block, joe, I gotta roll. I got a joint on me. Call me over Lil' Garvin's house later on," Baby-D said as he hung up the phone. Lando missed Baby-D and Lil' Garvin, but he knew that no matter how long he was locked up, they would be there for him and Quick, and that was all that he could ask of a partner.

High as a kite and thinking about Jazmin, Lando called her house. "Hello?" a young dude said into the phone.

Surprised, Lando put some bass in his voice and said, "Jazmin there?"

"Who this?" the dude asked as if he had a problem with a dude calling Jazmin's house.

Lando laughed a little, and said, "Can I speak to Jazmin or not, slim?"

"Who the fuck is this?" the dude said as he got angry. Lando could hear that Jazmin must have just walked in the room because the dude was saying that somebody was on the phone and wouldn't say who it was.

"Hello?" Jazmin said, sounding sexy as always.

"What's up, joe?" Lando said.

"What's up, boy!" Jazmin said, sounding excited when she heard that it was Lando on the phone. He hadn't called her in about three weeks, but he could hear in her voice that things hadn't changed between them except for the dude answering the phone.

"So, you gotta a man now?" Lando said without the least bit of jealousy in his voice.

"Yeah, that's my boyfriend," Jazmin said. Lando could hear him complaining in the background about him calling her house. "Look, this is my friend and he can call here anytime he want, this is my house!" Jazmin snapped at her boyfriend.

"You want me to call you later?" Lando asked, feeling like he was causing a problem between her and her man.

"No, you don't gotta call me later. We always gon' be tight and anybody that's in my life gon' have to accept that or they really don't want to be in my life."

Lando respected what Jazmin said and took it to heart. If there were a way to finalize a bond, it would have been that very statement. Lando began to tell Jazmin that him and Quick had been found guilty on their case and that they would most likely be down Oak Hill for the next two years.

"That's a long time." Jazmin said.

"Yeah, you right. It feel like it's the rest of my life, but I gotta do it the best way that I can."

"You strong, boo. I know you can make it. I asked your brother could I come see you, he told me that I gotta holla at your mother," Jazmin said. Lando explained to her that Pamila was cool and that she would dig her. Jazmin agreed to call her and ask if she could go see him with her. Lando let Jazmin know that he would be writing her a letter and sending her some pictures soon, and then got off of the phone.

Lando walked back down the hall to his cell where Black and Quick were talking about different ways to make money when they were back on the streets. Lando thought that it was cool for Black to be thinking like that, he might be out within the next month or so, but Lando knew that him and Quick would be spending the next two years down Oak Hill. That was enough to make him think of other things at the time, he would deal with the streets when he got there again.

Chapter Twelve: Mann's World

With the summer arriving and his GED behind him, Mann had two goals for the summer. The first one was to get his store, which he had decided would be called Mann's World, and his second goal was to pay the rest of Kelley's way through college. His money was right and his mind was set, it was all about putting his plan into effect. Silk's sister had already gotten a loan from the bank and spoken to the old couple that owned the store that Mann was going to buy. To make Pam feel a little safer about her decision to put the store in her name, Mann gave her the whole loan of one hundred and fifty thousand dollars up front so that she was already out of the hole. On top of that, he gave her an extra five thousand dollars just for her trouble. After Mann spoke to a friend of Silk's named Rick, who had a degree in business management, Mann's World would be open for business.

After Kelley graduated from Coolidge High School, Mann took her on the best trip of her young life. They spent seven long and beautiful days and nights in Barbados, along with Dre, Tina, and their son. The trip did a lot for them all, but moreso for Dre and Mann because it showed them that the world was bigger than the small city of Washington, D.C. and its money, drugs, and murder.

Kelley woke up early in the morning and began rubbing on Mann's chest to wake him up. She knew that he had plenty of reason to be dead tired after the love making that they did the night before, but she knew that Mann had to meet Pam downtown at the law office of Mr. Larry A. Williams, Sr., who was the father of Rick.

Rolling over on his side to face Kelley, Mann began to rub his hand through her hair, and said, "I dreamed about last night all night."

"Is that right?" Kelley said, clearly turned on by Mann's straightforward approach. Mann began to get closer and closer to Kelley until she had to remind him of his meeting with Pam and Rick.

"You know you gotta make sure everything is right so you can get the store this week," Kelley said.

Thinking of the store and how it would be his way out of the game, Mann began to tell Kelley how it was the beginning of something that may become as big as Bloomingdale's or a store of that nature. Mann explained to Kelley that all big things start out small and that as long as he was alive, he would always think big. Kelley was amazed by Mann's belief in himself. That was one of the reasons that she wanted to be his woman for the rest of her life.

Pulling up behind Pam's silver BMW 850i, Mann parked right in front of the law office of Mr. Williams. Getting out of his car, Mann walked up to Pam's window and tapped it with his car keys.

"You ready, beautiful?" Mann said with a smile. Pam found Mann very attractive since the first time she laid eyes on the dark skinned young man. Stepping out of her car into the hot summer sun, Pam drew all the attention of the busy downtown street and 16th Street was very busy during the working hours of the day.

Short and brown skinned with long, jet black hair, not to mention a body that could cause a car crash, Pam hugged Mann after shutting her car door. Mann had to take in the sight of such a beautiful woman. In her tight Guess jean shorts with her hairy legs shining in the summer sun, Mann thought about shooting his shot at Pam, being as though he knew that she had a thing for him for the longest, but that would take away from what they came downtown to do. Mann and Pam talked for a minute, and then went inside to get down to business.

Eight days before his thirteenth birthday, Lando and Quick, were committed to two years at the Oak Hill Juvenile Detention Center. Now that they had time, they were transferred from Unit 7A to Unit 8b where Freeway, Demo, and Short Dogg were doing their two year commitments as well.

The sun was in full blast and while everybody was out for rec, Lando stayed inside to use the phone. Nakia was starting to grow further and further away from him as the days started to turn into weeks now that Lando had two years to do. Pamila had told him that the girl was too young to stay put for two years, and Lando had accepted the fact that Pamila was right as always. Out of the feelings that he had for Nakia, Lando talked her into being his friend because he felt that she would somehow cross him if they played any kind of love games while he was locked up. After awhile and a lot of protest, Nakia agreed with Lando's plan when she began to see how hard it was for her not to deal with other dudes that were after her now that she was becoming more and more of a young lady every day. Lando made sure that he stayed in touch with her and Jazmin, but did his time playing sports and lifting iron, not to mention, using the phone, which was exactly where he was when Short Dogg came running inside the unit looking for him.

"Lando," Short Dogg said as he stepped into the small phone room. Lando put Nakia on hold to find out what he wanted. Black had sent Short Dogg to get Lando so that he could see him before he went to the group home. Black had pleaded guilty to his drug charge in order to get out on probation for the summer. They had just called him for the group home about fifteen minutes ago and Short Dogg told Lando that he had to hurry up. Lando told Nakia that he had to call her back and then hung up the phone to run over to Unit 7A to see Black before he hit the streets, again.

Short Dogg and Lando walked into Black's cell while he was throwing away all of his mail. Quick was already in the cell along with Freeway, who Black had taken a liking to.

"What's up, joe? You know I'm outta here, young!" Black said as he walked over and hugged his little cousin.

"I know, take care of yourself out there, young," Lando said as he walked over and sat on the bed along with Quick and Freeway. Lando was happy to see Black leave, but at the same time, Black was taking a part of Lando to the streets with him, and Lando felt it. Black started giving away his name brand shorts and T-shirts as well as his fleet of one hundred dollar tennis shoes.

"I'ma miss y'all niggas, young," Black said as he began to tell everybody how he was about to hit the streets and take shit bad.

"You betta get you some money," Quick said.

Everybody started laughing, they all knew Black well enough to know that he didn't care about anything but trouble. Black went under his bed and pulled out a plastic bag. Opening it, he pulled out a knot of cash, two thousand dollars exactly. Black gave all of the younger dudes five hundred dollars each. A counselor came to the door and told Black that if he wanted to stay he could, but his ride was leaving with or without him. Black hugged everybody and hit the road, leaving only his love behind.

Mann wasn't the only one making plans for the legit world. Silk had already bought a barbershop on Minnesota Avenue. He had kept it from Mann until it was open, and today he picked him up and took him to Silky's Barber Shop for its grand opening, which was a get together of old buddies and the three barbers that he had given jobs to. There was music, weed, and drinks in the back, there were free hair cuts going on for all who wanted one. The whole place was live, but most of all, Silk's plan to inspire Mann worked well.

"Yeah, that was big shit, joe," Mann said as he sat in the passenger seat of Silk's car while they flew through the 9th Street tunnel on their way back uptown. Mann was impressed by the way Silk had kept everything to himself about the barbershop.

"Yeah, that was just somethin' I wanted to try before I try this other move out Maryland with a car lot," Silk said as he slid a Sade CD in his disk player, "Pam signed the papers for the store today, so Mann's World is on the move now. I talked to this dude that work with my uncle, he gon' do all of the remodlin' for me. The place in good shape."

"After your man, Rick, give me all the paperwork, I'm in business, joe."

"How long you think that's gon' take?"

"I give it 'bout three weeks at the most. I got the legal shit and the insurance shit done already, thanks to Pam," Mannsaid.

Silk looked over at Mann with a brotherly love in his eyes, and said, "You know how to get that cash, young nigga, that's one thing I respect about you. So, what the fuck Dre gon' do?"

"Dre ain't made up his mind yet. He say he gon' put some of his money into my store and see what he get back. On the real, he think this shit ain't gon' work, but I know it is, so I'ma kick him a little extra cash back like money coming from everywhere so he'll think it's something to take serious. He'll get the idea and try the same thing, he been like that since wewas kids." Silk really respected the fact that Mann always took Dre along for the ride. Silk could remember when Dre was wild and running the streets, gunning everything down with Black. It was Silk that encouraged Mann to get Dre to get some money that would last.

When they pulled up in front of Pamila's house it was like a block party. Pamila had the front door open with two big stereo speakers out on the porch. The front yard was packed with neighbors and their little kids. Pamila was on the grill. Kelley,

Dee-Dee, and Tina were sitting on the front steps while Lil' Garvin, Baby-D, and Dre were sitting on the hood of Dre's ZR1. Tyesha was playing catch with Dre's son and two other little kids on the side of the house. You could feel the summer time spirit in the hot evening air.

Everybody paid close attention to Mann and Silk as they got out of the Ferrari, it drew a lot of attention, and Mann could see that it may have drawn a little too much attention by the way Pamila looked at it.

Silk stepped to Dre and the two younger dudes that sat on the hood of his car with him. They all showed much love to Silk, he was somewhat a ghetto icon, to say the least. Mann walked by and said what's up to everybody, but Pamila had given him an eye like she wanted to speak to him, so he told everyone that he would be right back. Walking by Kelley, Dee-Dee and Tina, Mann hugged and kissed Kelley, asking all the ladies how they were doing, and then walked over to the grill where Pamila was standing over the food talking to an old lady from her church named Mrs. Gather.

Tyesha was very excited to see Mann. As he spoke to Mrs. Gather, Tyesha ran and jumped into his arms.

Catching his balance, Mann said, "You gettin' big, shorty." Tyesha smiled and kissed Mann on the cheek as she broke loose from his hug and ran back over to the crowd of kids to play catch.

"What's up, Pamila?" Mann said. Pamila closed the grill and led Mann away from Mrs. Gather so that she couldn't over hear the conversation and take it back to church and put it on the grapevine.

"Mann, you know I don't like you bringing your friends over here showing off all that drug money. It ain't right. You do what you want to with your life, but don't bring it around here," Pamila said, and it was nothing Mann could tell her about Silk not being involved with drug money, Pamila was too bright for that. Mann just agreed and went on with the program. "You know your bad ass cousin is out of jail. He called here looking for you."

"Where is he?"

"He's in some group home. He said he gets to come out on the weekend. Ask Kelley where he is," Pamila said. "While you at it, try to keep that boy out of trouble!" Mann hugged Pamila and told her that he would do just that, and then walked back over to Dre's car.

"Y'all know that nigga, Black, home?" Mann said to the group of dudes standing in front of Dre's car.

"Yeah, Kelley was telling me," Dre said. It was news to Baby-D, Lil' Garvin, and Silk. They were all happy to hear that Black was home.

"Where he at?" Baby-D asked.

Mann let everybody know that he was in a group home and that he would be out for a home visit on the weekend. They all sat and talked, just kicking it about what was going on around the way, how Lando and Quick were doing, and about Mann's store. Mann enjoyed times like those, times where everybody was just laid back, yet, even at times like those, he was always thinking, and Black was who he was thinking about. Mann wondered if Black would chill this time. Only time would tell.

Black was awakened by the loud sound of the group home counselor screaming, "Wake up! It's breakfast time!" Black rolled over in his bed still wearing Oak Hill drawers and saw the small, dark skinned man coming into the room that he shared with two other juveniles that he knew from down Oak Hill. The counselor kicked the bed of one of the young men to wake him up. The whole sight reminded Black of being locked up. He sat up on his bed trying to rub the sleep out of his eyes so that he could get up before the counselor came at him with the same bullshit. Trouble was truly the last thing Black wanted for once in his life.

"Mr. Mills. Do you think the rules don't apply to you?" the counselor asked as he kicked the bed and snapped Black out of his sleep. In a flash, Black shot to his feet and knocked the counselor onto the floor. The counselor was out cold. Black looked around the room as if he was unsure of what he had just did.

"Shit!" Black said out loud as he reached for his clothes. He had fucked up. His anger had gotten him into another bad situation and he had only two choices to make. One was wait until the head counselor came upstairs to see what was going on, which would surely lead Black right back down Oak Hill not even twenty four hours after he left, or he could go on the run.

Black decided to run. Throwing his clothes on with lightning speed while the other two juveniles watched in amazement, Black shot down the steps, knocking the head counselor down as he hit the door and ran down Harvard Street.

Pamila sat at the dining room table opening bills after a long day at work. She came across a letter with Kelley's name on it from the University of Ohio. Pamila called Kelley downstairs to open her mail. Kelley came downstairs with Tyesha in her arms. Walking over to the table, Kelley began to smile, she knew what was in the envelope. As Kelley began to open her mail, the phone began to ring.

"Hello?" Pamila said as she answered the phone.

"What's up, girl?" her sister said.

"What's up, V?"

"You seen my bad ass son?"

"No, he called here yesterday looking for Mann. Why?"

"Girl, the police is looking for him. He done beat up a counselor at his group home and ran away from the place. He just won't do right," Black's mother said. Pamila wasn't surprised at all. Black was always into trouble. Pamila talked to her sister for a few more minutes and let her know that she would get Mann to find Black, and then they hung up the phone.

After getting off of the phone, Pamila said a short prayer for her sister and her son, and then asked Kelley what kind of news she got. Kelley let her know that she had been accepted to the University of Ohio on a partial scholarship.

"That's still good, girl. It's so good that you will have the chance to go away to school. The city ain't no good for you," Pamila said. Kelley felt as though she was right and she knew that going away to school was what she wanted to do. All that was left to do was to get Mann to pay the rest of the way through school, which was nearly a given.

Mann had got a beep from Da-Da on his way home from doing the last of the paperwork for his store. Da-Da wanted a brick and he needed it that night, so Mann shot out White Oak to get the coke for him. That was an easy twenty five thousand dollars, and Mann knew he had to grind up some money now that he had put so much cash into Mann's World. Things were going to be okay, Mann thought to himself during the ride to his apartment. With Pam on paper as the owner and himself on paper as a supervisor, Mann still called all the shots. Legally, he would run the store for Pam, but they knew who was in charge.

Mann pulled up in front of his building, parked his car, and got out into the cool summer night wearing an all black Polo short set with a .40 magnum thirteen shot strapped under his shirt. Walking up to his door, Mann noticed that someone had been inside of his apartment due to the top lock not being on when he stuck his key in to unlock it. Looking over his shoulder to see if anyone was looking, Mann pulled his pistol from under his shirt and let himself in the door with it pointed in front of him, ready to blast the first thing moving.

Once inside, Mann hit the lights and saw Black lying on the sofa sleep. "Black!" Mann yelled. "Wake the fuck up!" Mann put his pistol up, walked over to the sofa, and started shaking Black, who was dead sleep, still wearing his Oak Hill clothes and smelling like a pound of weed. Black opened his eyes and sat straight up when he saw Mann.

"What's up, young?" Black asked as he sat back on the sofa.

"What the fuck is up with you? Why you ain't in the group home, it ain't Friday yet?" Mann asked.

"I fucked up, joe. I knocked a counselor out this morning and had to roll out the joint, slim."

"You did what?"

"Yeah, joe, I'm on the run," Black said as he shook his head, truly not pleased with his own situation. Mann sat down beside his younger cousin and began to scratch his head. He didn't understand how Black always put himself in such fucked up positions.

"So, what you gon' do now, Black?" Mann asked, knowing that Black had some extra go hard plan of how he was going to stay on the run for the rest of his life.

"Slim, I don't even know this time. I ain't gon' turn myself in, that's out, joe. I'ma lay low here for a few days until I come up with something."

"I'm cool with that, just don't let nobody know where this spot at," Mann said as he got up to get the brick of coke that he had came to get. Once back in the room with Black, Mann began to get on him about how he was still doing the same dumb shit that he was doing when he was Lando's age, and that now was a new day in time, he was older now and couldn't make those same mistakes. Mann gave Black the little bit of money that he had in his pocket, which was close to three hundred dollars, and then left to go serve Da-Da the brick of coke that he wanted.

Days later, it was sweep time in the neighborhood. Hall and the rest of the jump outs were floating through all drug spots uptown just waiting to catch somebody in the wrong, but nobody was dumb enough to be on the block until later on.

Riding through Rittenhouse Street in a new Isuzu Trooper, Hall turned to one of the four vice cops in the truck with him, and said, "Al, did you hear anything about the killing of the guy, Onion?"

"Who is that?" Big Al asked, not remembering the rat off hand.

Speedie cut in from the back seat, and said, "You know the guy he's talking about, the snitch that got wacked about a month or two ago."

"Oh, yeah, I remember the dirt bag. Two little gangsters gunned him down like a day or two after he told on the two little guys that shot at Wilson and his partner," Big Al said. Hall went on to ask if anyone had heard anything about the situation. No one had any information about that, but Speedie told Hall that his favorite thug was home and on the run.

"Who is that?" Hall asked.

"Black!" Big Al said with a little laugh behind it, knowing that Hall took every case that he put on Black to heart. Hall had anger written across his face.

"They let that motherfucker get away with murder. We'll catch his ass wrong. It's summer time, he'll pop up and kill somebody before September," Hall said as he turned up 5th Street with his mind set on sending Black to jail before the summer was out.

Pamila decided to pop up and surprise Lando and Quick by bringing Jazmin and Quick's grandmother down Oak Hill to see them. They all walked into the chow hall where the rest of the visits were, and waited for Lando and Quick to come out. Pamila could tell that the place made Quick's grandmother very uncomfortable, she was like that the last few times that she brought her down to see him. Pamila also saw how all the boys in the visiting area were looking at Jazmin. She was a very cute young girl. After bringing her to see Lando a few times, she had learned that the child had something on her mind. Pamila was really impressed by the fact that Jazmin had plans for the future at such a young age. She could really get used to dealing with Jazmin.

Lando and Quick walked into the visiting area only expecting to see Pamila and Quick's grandmother. They were both surprised to see Jazmin.

Quick looked at Lando and said, "Damn, joe, your folks lookin' good as shit." Lando responded with only a head shake as they both walked over to their visits.

Quick hugged his grandmother as Lando did the same to Pamila. Jazmin watched as Quick and Lando embraced their loved ones. Quick turned to hug Pamila as Lando hugged and kissed his grandmother. Lando turned to Jazmin and just looked at her for a second. She was growing more and more attractive as the year went on.

Quick's grandmother, Mrs. Jones, said, "Go ahead and hug the young lady, she ain't gon' bite you, boy." Pamila and Quick laughed at the old woman's statement. Jazmin stood up with her hair pulled back into a beautiful ponytail, and opened her arms to hug Lando.

As they hugged, Lando said, "I'm glad you came to see me. I been thinkin' 'bout you a lot."

"I been thinking bout you, too, boy," Jazmin said before they sat back down and began to talk with Pamila and Quick's grandmother for the rest of the visit.

Slapping a ninety shot clip into an AK-47, Black sat on the sofa in Smoke's apartment and aimed it at the wall. "That ah work!" Black said to Smoke and Serge, who sat at the dining room table loading clips to their Mac-11. Black had been on the run for a week and was ready to hit a quick caper. Smoke and Serge, who were not doing too good moneywise, were both more than willing to go on the move. They both knew what to do to get money and had the balls to carry it out, but for some reason they needed the quick aggressiveness of Black to push them into bigger caper situations, and Black came up with just the caper that they were looking for.

It was a jewelry store ran by two Chinese dudes right across the Maryland line in Silver Spring. Black had been inside already and he had put the plan together for them to hit the joint. He knew how much money was in there, and he knew when and how they moved the money. He began to tell his crime partners that they would hit the store from the back as the Chinese dudes tried to move their money at seven p.m.

"So, what y'all think?" Black asked. Smoke and Serge were ready for the move. "Let's roll, then," Black said as he led the way to the car they were going to use for the move.

Mann was sitting on a bucket of paint watching the remodelers put the last touches on the wall. They had transformed the old store into an up-to-date urban version in only two weeks. Mann had been making calls to big wholesale stores in New York all week and his first shipment of Polo, Nautica, and Eddie Bauer clothes would be in Mann's World and on the racks no later than the end of the week. The word was out on the street that the store would be making its grand opening on the 4th of July. Pam had gotten a radio commercial on the top radio station in the D.C. area to promote the grand opening. Mann couldn't wait. He had food, drinks, live music, fireworks and he was giving away a free Polo short set along with a pair of new Air Jordan's to the first ten people to show up in front of Mann's World where everything was to go down.

Pam was on the phone behind the computer making phone calls to a few wholesale companies when Dre and Tina eased their way through the fleet of working men. As they both spoke to Pam, Tina stopped to talk for a minute while Dre walked over to talk to Mann.

"What's up, joe?" Mann said to Dre as he waved at Tina. Tina smiled and waved back at Mann, while Mann responded by throwing his hands up in the air and looking around the almost complete store like 'look at what I got here'. Dre laughed at Mann's gesture. He knew Mann had the right to play big for a second, he put his plan into effect from scratch and it was ready for take off.

"So, what's up with you, joe?" Mann said to Dre, noticing a slight worry in the face of his partner.

Dre let out a small sigh and said, "Joe, the Feds raided the White Oak spot."

Mann rubbed his chin as he stood up and told Dre to follow him into the back office that he had made strictly for himself. Mann sat on a new sofa as they walked through the door. Dre sat across from him in a padded leather office chair and looked at Mann, who was still thinking about what Dre had just told him.

"So, what went down?" Mann asked. Dre began to tell him that some young dude that was buying coke from Da-Da and LeRon had been selling coke to an undercover. They raided the strip early in the morning and locked the young dude up, along with his little crew. "Did they get Da-Da and them?" Mann asked. Dre let him know that the Feds only locked the young dude up and that everybody else was okay.

"What can the young dude tell 'em?" Mann asked, wanting to know whose names could be given up.

"He only knew Da-Da and some other lil' dude that be hustlin' for 'em," Dre said.

"So we jive cool then," Mann began to say. "We gotta lay low for awhile, that's all."

"I'm cool with that, slim. I'ma go back around the way for a minute while shit cool down out Maryland," Dre said. Mann didn't agree with him going back around Rittenhouse Street because things stayed so hot around there, but he knew Dre lived for the cash of the fast lane.

Sitting in his black Impala outside of the Coolidge High School Gym, Lil' Garvin smoked a blunt of weed with a cute young girl named Imani that he had met downtown. As people came out of the gym and went their own ways, Lil' Garvin waited patiently for Baby-D to come out of the doors. As Imani leaned over to pass Lil' Garvin the blunt of weed, Baby-D crept up on the side of the car and jumped at the window, scaring the two of them. Lil' Garvin jumped out of shock, dropping the lit blunt of weed on his black Polo shorts as he quickly reached for his Glock .40. Baby-D burst out laughing as he hopped in the backseat. Lil' Garvin saw nothing funny as he smacked the burning blunt on to the car floor to stop it from burning his leg. Leaning over to pick it up, he said, "Ain't shit funny, nigga! That's a good way to get shot!" Imani began to laugh at the scene.

Lil' Garvin looked over at her, and said, "What the fuck is so funny?"

Still giggling, Imani said, "You was scared as shit!"

"You was scared as shit, bitch! Matter of fact, get the fuck out my car," Lil' Garvin said, becoming dead serious.

Imani gave up a sad face, and said, "I'm sorry…"

"Fuck that. Get the fuck out, bitch!" Lil' Garvin said as he started up the car. Imani began to cry as she got out of the car into the dark summer night while Lil' Garvin pulled off with Baby-D in the backseat laughing at the top of his lungs.

Corey, Keith, and a few younger dudes from the neighborhood were in front of Dee-Dee's house pushing rocks when Lil' Garvin and Baby-D pulled up and parked. The two younger dudes got out and spread their love as they walked up and leaned on the fence with everyone else that was out for the dollars. Lil' Garvin, still upset at Baby-D for making him burn his leg with the blunt, was in no mood for anybody's funny style ways, and he noticed Corey looking at him and Baby-D in a strange way. Lil' Garvin had been picking up vibes from Corey ever since Onion got killed. Lil' Garvin decided to say something about it.

With his hand inside his shorts on the pistol that he had tucked between his waistband, Lil' Garvin said to Corey, "What the fuck you keep starin' at me for, nigga!" Tension hit the air as things were about to come to a head, and everybody outside waited to see the explosion.

"Who the fuck you think you talkin' to, young nigga?" Corey snapped.

"You know what the fuck is up, bitch nigga. You think I had something to do with your hot ass man gettin' smashed? If you fuck with 'em so much, do somethin' 'bout it!" Lil' Garvin said, full of anger. He knew that Corey thought that him and Baby-D had killed Onion, and he was tired of him acting like he wanted to do something about it. As Corey began to walk up on Lil' Garvin, Black bent the corner in the red Oldsmobile that him, Smoke, and Serge had just robbed the jewelry store in no more than thirty minutes ago.

Seeing the conflict, Black slammed on brakes and got out of the car, leaving it in the middle of the street with Smoke and Serge still inside while he walked over to the sidewalk.

"What the fuck is up!" Black said with a murderous frown on his face as he looked Corey's way. Keith began to take the whole situation much more serious now that Black was on the scene. He walked up beside Corey in clear support of his man.

"You ain't got shit to do with this, Black!" Corey said, appearing a little worried now that Black had popped up.

Stepping between Corey and Lil' Garvin, Black got up in Corey's face and began to tap his finger on Corey's forehead while he said, "Bitch nigga! Anything that got something to do with these young niggas got somethin' to do with me!"

Keith began to step around Corey as he said, "Black, man, you need to mind your..." BOOM! Two gunshots rang out and Keith's words were cut short as he fell to the ground holding his chest. The gunshots scared everybody. They all turned to see who had fired the shots, and saw Baby-D with a smoking .45 automatic in his hand.

Baby-D began to walk toward Keith to finish him off as Corey ran through the cut beside Dee-Dee's house. Two more gunshots put Keith to rest.

"What the fuck you do that for?" Black said as he looked down at the body.

"That nigga was reaching for a joint!" Baby-D said as he began to run toward Lil' Garvin's car followed by Lil' Garvin.

The few other younger dudes that had just watched their first murder all ran as Black leaned over to see if Keith was really reaching for a pistol. With Smoke and Serge screaming for Black to hurry up and get in the car, Black bent over and pulled a

9mm from Keith's waistband. With the pistol in his hand, Black ran to his car, leaving the dead body on the sidewalk as he jumped in and pulled off, followed by Lil' Garvin's Impala.

Keith's murder changed Rittenhouse Street for good. In the weeks that followed, a new breed of young dudes seem to come out of nowhere and take over the abandoned drug strip. Corey hadn't been seen since and Baby-D and Lil' Garvin had shot to the status of shot callers on the block now that they had the most years in the fast lane out of the new young dudes on the block and they loved the ghetto fame.

Things didn't look as good for Black. Whoever witnessed Keith's murder had the facts mixed up. They told Homicide Detective Brown that Black was the person that they saw shoot Keith that day. Now, Black was no longer on the run from the juvenile system alone, he was now wanted for a murder that he would be charged as an adult for. Once again, Black would be facing life in prison if the police caught him, and Officer Hall was so happy to be on the hunt for Black.

Mann was not happy with the events that had turned the whole neighborhood upside down, but he had learned a long time ago that some things were just meant to be and that had to be one of those things as far as he was concerned. Even so, he stuck by Black and made sure that he always had a place to lay his head and anything else that he needed. Mann had got Tina to get an apartment outside of D.C. in her name for Black to stay in while he was on the run. While Black turned the apartment to a headquarters for his nightly capers, Mann went on with his plan of getting out of the drug game.

The local sounds of Rare Essence, a D.C. go-go band, filled the air at noon on the 4th of July. The crowd already filled the whole block of Georgia Avenue between Eastern Avenue and Fern Place. Little kids ran up and down the block. Mann stood at the front door of Mann's World passing out free shoes and short sets. Silk, Dre, Pam, Tina, and Kelley enjoyed the music in the hot summer sun as well. Mann felt a sense of pride for himself looking at the huge crowd of people that he had brought together for his grand opening. It was a sight to see.

Pamila and Tyesha decided to drop through to see what Mann had going on. Pamila had said that she wanted nothing to do with the store since she knew Mann had put it together with drug money, but the more she thought about what Mann was trying to do, she had to show her face in the place.

Mann was standing beside a rack of T-shirts that he was giving away when he saw Pamila. He couldn't believe his eyes. He told Dre to pass out the rest of the shirts while he walked over to Pamila and Tyesha, and wrapped his arms around them both.

"I'm glad to see you, you know this means a lot to me. I'm tryin' to leave the streets alone. This is bigger than me. This for me, this is for Lando, Dre, and everybody else, Pamila! If I can just get this store off the ground, the streets will be history. By the time Lando come home, everything should be up and rollin', and he will see that he can make it without the streets. Feel me?" Pamila smiled as Mann talked. As much as she hated how he started his store, she knew that his intentions were good and for that, she had to agree with his dream of getting out of a life of drug selling.

"You right, Mann. Do what you have to do to make this thing work, maybe you will wake Lando and Black up," Pamila said. Mann was pleased with Pamila's slight approval. He told her to enjoy herself as he got back to making sure that things were running smoothly with the festivities. Pamila walked around for a while, spoke to Kelley about her SATs, and then went back home.

Inside of Mann's World hidden away from the public in the office hideout, Black, Lil' Garvin, and Baby-D sat in front of the huge sixty inch color T.V. playing John Madden's Football on Sega while they smoked blunt after blunt. Mann walked inside of the office and smelled nothing but weed smoke in the air. "Damn!" He said out loud as he sat down and got on the phone. Lil' Garvin, who was not playing the video game at the time, walked over and sat down beside Mann, who was just hanging up the phone with a New York retailer that he was trying to do some business with.

"What's up, shorty?" Mann asked Lil' Garvin.

"Ain't shit, slim, I just wanted to tell you that I digs this shit here, joe. You be thinkin' big as shit, young," Lil' Garvin said. Mann smiled at the younger dude. He knew that Lil' Garvin could see what he was putting together, and he liked the fact that he called himself commending him on his actions.

"You gon' have all this shit, too, shorty. All you gotta do is want it, joe," Mann said.

Silk walked into the office, and said, "Y'all niggas 'bout to miss the fireworks."

Everybody hit the door and followed Silk out front.

Mann and Black were side-by-side when they walked out into the crowd of people. Black had been inside all day and didn't know how many people had shown up to support Mann's World.

"Damn, slim, everybody and they momma out here, this big shit, joe," Black said as the first rocket exploded into the night air. Mann smiled as the five TNT rockets hit the air right behind the first one.

"I just want this shit to work out, joe. If all goes well, this is just the beginning," Mann said as he looked down at his beeper.

Silk had overheard Mann's statement as he was walking over, placed his arm around Mann's shoulder, and said, "All is going to work out, slim. This is just the beginning. Ain't that right?"

Looking over at Silk with a smile, Mann said, "Yeah, that's right. This is just the beginning." Things would never be the same, and there was no looking back for Mann. He had his mind set on making Mann's World a success, and that is just what he set out to do as he put all of his energy into it.

Chapter Thirteen: Home for a minute

By early 1992, Mann was already an eighteen year old entrepreneur that had his business in order. Mann's World was in his name and paid for legally. He also owned a recording studio in Silver Spring, Maryland that he was in the process of putting together for business. His goal was to have it up and running by the summer so that he could start renting out studio time. Mann had hired Dre as the manager of Mann's World just to put him on the payroll. Dee-Dee worked as a cashier, along with a cute light skinned girl that she had introduced to Dre by the name of Naomi. Mann's World was up and running, not to mention producing enough revenue weekly for Mann and Dre to live off of, but they still flipped bricks of coke on the side to keep their money stacking until they were sure that they could hang with the big dogs in the corporate world.

Kelley was in her second year of college at the University of Ohio studying criminal law, thanks to the deep pockets of her true love, Mann. She called D.C. every night of the week to talk to Mann, who never missed a call from her no matter what he was doing, and Kelley wanted for nothing while she was away at school. Mann made her feel as if he was around the corner by popping up out of the blue to visit her and bring her small gifts every now and then. As long as Mann had something to do with Kelley's future, it would be a success as far as he was concerned and she felt the support by the minute.

Black's constant run-ins with the law never stopped. By late 1990, he was spotted by Officer Hall and his gang of vice cops. Black took the cops on a wild car chase that extended all the way into Fort Washington, Maryland. He was caught with a ..50 Caliber Desert Eagle and sent to D.C. jail to await trial for Keith's murder, which Baby-D committed. Black played by the rules of the game and told the Feds nothing about Baby-D. Mann got Black a top notch lawyer and Black beat the murder charge, but was found guilty of an armed robbery that he committed in late 1990. He was sentenced to a three year youth act in the adult system, and was now waiting to see the parole board at Lorton's Youth Center.

It had been two years since Lando and Quick went down Oak Hill for murder. Despite how long two years seemed to them in 1990, by now it only seemed like weeks. They were eligible for weekend home visits and would probably be coming home on an after care program by the summer time if they did good on their home visits. They were a lot bigger and eager to hit the streets after all that they had been hearing about Lil' Garvin and Baby-D running things around the way. Quick was much more aggressive at fifteen. Lando began to see more and more of Black in Quick everyday. Lando, on the other hand, was still a little wild, but at fifteen, he was more focused than he had ever been, which had a lot to do with the many visits Mann had paid him over the last two years. As Mann spit the game to his little brother, Lando listened to every word and was ready for the streets now that they were so close that he could taste them.

Pamila stuck by Lando and Quick every step of the way while they were locked up. Pamila had even gotten legal custody of Quick since his grandmother had passed away. Quick loved Pamila for that and he truly looked at her as his mother. The only guidance that he got was from her. Pamila couldn't wait for her two boys to come home on their first home visit.

At five years old, Tyesha was growing by the hour. The cute little girl was almost four feet tall already. She had grown very close to Lando while he was locked up, being as though she saw him more. She had been talking about seeing Lando ever since Pamila had told her that he would be coming home for the weekend, she couldn't wait to see him.

Mann walked in the front door and saw Tyesha sitting at the dining room table drawing on a big drawing pad. Seeing Mann, she jumped down from the table and ran into his open arms.

"What's up, shorty?" Mann asked as he laughed at the child's joy of seeing him. Tyesha kissed Mann and led him over to the table to show him her picture.

Pointing at the colorful drawing, Tyesha said, "Look, that's Lando when he come home this weekend." Mann smiled at Tyesha as he picked her up and looked at the picture she had drew of her, Pamila, Mann, and Lando. Mann could tell that the love that the little girl felt for Lando was more than just a love from cousin to cousin, it was a love from sister to brother and Mann was pleased by the whole situation.

Pamila came down stairs to see who had come in the house and saw Mann holding Tyesha in his arms.

"Black called here for you a few minutes ago. He wants to know if you gave something to his girl for him," Pamila said.

"Yeah, I did that already," Mann said. Walking over to the table to look at the picture that Tyesha had been working on since she had been home from school, Pamila told her that it was lovely and that Lando was going to love it.

Looking at Mann, Pamila said, "You know Lando and Quick are coming home for a weekend visit this Friday. I won't be home from work by the time they are supposed to be picked up from the Receiving Homem so you gotta do it." Mann had no problem with that. In fact, he couldn't wait to see his brother and Quick himself. Pamila told Mann to talk to the two younger boys and to encourage them to do right. Mann told her that he would do just that and then went downstairs to call Black's girlfriend.

Black had met a beautiful young lady named Mia while he was locked up. Mia was a nineteen year old law student at Georgetown University. Black had been trying to get legal advice about an issue on his armed robbery case and had written a letter to the legal department at the school. Mia saw legal errors in Black's case and decided to help him. She began to go see him on legal visits in order to get a better understanding of the case and quickly became infatuated with Black's style. After Black's appeal for a new trial was denied, Mia was already in love with Black and began to come see him every visiting day down Youth Center, and was now talking about marriage.

"Hello?" Mia said into the phone in her tiny voice.

"What's up, Mia? This Mann."

"Hi, Mann."

"What's up, did Black see the board today?"

"Yeah, he did. He said he should know what they gonna do in about a month or so. I pray that they let him go, I want him here with me," Mia said full of warmth. Mann thought of how he knew Black would act when he hit the streets and wondered if Mia would be able to deal with his madness. Even so, Mann knew that Black thought that he was in love as well, so however things went would be up to him.

"Check this out, Mia," Mann said. "Tell Black I'll be down there to see 'em first thing next week."

"I'm supposed to go down there next week," Mia said, feeling like Mann was taking her time away from seeing her man.

Mann laughed. He understood what was up with Mia so he told her that they could go together, he just wanted her to tell Black that he had the new shoes that he wanted and that he would wear them down Youth Center when he came. Mia was cool with that arrangement and told Mann that she would tell Black what he said later that evening when she went to see him. Mann got off the phone thinking about the sweet girl that Black had in his corner as he went to pick some coke up from Silk.

Sitting around the conference table in the back office of Mann's World, Silk, Rick, Mann, and Dre worked on the taxes for Mann's World and Silky's Barber Shop. Rick was a financial genius, he made sure that Mann and Silk had the revenue books straight while showing them how to pull all of their drug money into play with their business money.

After they had taken care of all business, Mann leaned back in his chair and stretched, saying, "Another day at the office." Everybody laughed.

"I see you like the business world, huh?" Silk said to Mann.

"It's more like I like working for myself," Mann said.

Dre looked at his watch, and said, "It's almost time to go get Lando and Quick, ain't it?"

Mann slid his chair back and told everybody that he had to leave to go get Lando. Silk asked Mann to bring Lando and Quick to see him before they went back down Oak Hill. Mann told him that he would try, but he didn't think that Pamila would let them out of her sight. Silk understood. Mann and Dre shook Rick's hand, and hit the streets to go get Lando and Quick.

Impatiently waiting for Mann to show up with Lando and Quick, Pamila stood at the living room window talking to Kelley on the cordless phone.

"I know you can't wait to see them two little rough necks."

"I'm standing here looking out of the window right now waiting for them to pull up. I just pray that they stay out of trouble this time," Pamila said. It was nothing more she wanted than for Lando and Quick to just live their young lives outside of a detention center. She stressed that over and over in many conversations with Kelley, and Kelley could feel her pain every step of the way. As they talked for a few more minutes, Pamila saw Mann's gold Range Rover pulling up with Lando and Quick in the backseat.

"They outside right now!" Pamila said, full of excitement.

Pamila passed Mann the phone as she stepped around Dre and opened up her arms to hug Lando and Quick. She couldn't believe that they were standing inside the living room.

"I don't want no shit outta y'all, you hear me?" Pamila said.

"You ain't gon have no problems out of us," Lando said as he smiled at Pamila.

"That goes for your little behind, too!" Pamila said as she looked at Quick.

"You ain't gotta worry about me, Pamila, I'm chillin'," Quick said.

Tyesha heard all of the excitement going on downstairs and came running down the steps to see if Lando was home. At the bottom of the steps, she saw Lando and Quick standing in front of Pamila.

With her drawing, she ran over to Lando, and said, "I made this for you." Lando picked Tyesha up in his arms and began to look at the picture, asking Tyesha who was who. She told Lando who was in the picture and Lando began to tell her that Quick would be living with them from now on. The loving child told Lando put her down so she could go and put Quick into her drawing. As Tyesha ran up the steps to fix her family picture, Lando and Quick sat down on the sofa beside Dre and Mann and listened to Pamila talk about how they didn't have to sell drugs and run the streets anymore. They assured Pamila that she didn't have to worry about them at all.

By eleven a.m. the next day, Mann had taken Lando and Quick shopping, and they were now fresh again. They had grown a lot while they were locked up. Quick had gotten tall and slim while Lando had gotten just a little taller and very thick from weight lifting. They both had let their hair grow long and they kept it in cornrows. Over all, they were no longer little boys anymore, they were now young men.

After talking Dre into letting him keep his Corvette for the night, Lando was flying down Georgia Avenue with Quick in the passenger seat on their way over Jazmin's house. Quick leaned over and picked up a Geto Boys CD and slapped it into the CD player. Lando rolled down the window to let the cool night air into the car as the music began to blast through the speeding car.

"It feel good as shit to be back on the streets, young," Lando said to Quick as he pulled up in front of Jazmin's apartment building.

"No bullshit!" Quick said as Lando cut the car off and got out.

Lando kept his home visit a secret from Jazmin in order to catch her off guard. Standing at her door in a grey Polo sweatshirt, Lando couldn't wait for her to open the door. He wanted her to see how serious he was about her being the first female to see him when he hit the streets. Even though he still had deep feelings for Nakia being as though she played fair with him while he was locked up, Jazmin still lived inside of his heart one way or another.

"Lando!" Jazmin screamed as she hugged him tightly after opening her door. "When did you get out?" Taking a step back from Jazmin while still holding her in his arms, Lando took in the beautiful sight of the young woman.

"I'm on a home visit. I gotta go back down Oak Hill Sunday night," Lando said as he smiled uncontrollably.

Hugging Lando again, Jazmin said, "I can't believe you home, boy!" Lando was pleased that Jazmin was so happy to see him. They stood out in the hallway and talked for about fifteen minutes before Quick popped up.

Walking up on Lando and Jazmin, Quick couldn't believe how much of a woman Jazmin had grown into while he and Lando were gone. In a pair of tight blue jeans and a Madness T-shirt standing in the hallway with no shoes on, Jazmin looked beautiful.

"What's up, Jazmin?" Quick said.

Jazmin looked at him and said, "Hi, Quick." She walked over and hugged him, saying, "Are you two going to stay out of trouble now that y'all coming home on home visits?" Quick laughed and let Jazmin know that he planned on staying home, but that he was going to be himself, which worried her a little, but she knew that Quick was always going to be himself. She then asked Lando the same question.

Thinking about what the truth was and what Jazmin wanted to hear, Lando said, "I'ma do my best to stay out. I ain't as wild as I was two years ago. You ain't gotta worry about me." Jazmin was pleased with the way Lando had responded to her. She could tell that he had grown up a lot while he was gone. Jazmin stayed in the hallway talking to Lando and Quick for about an hour before telling them that she had to go out of town for the weekend with her mother, but she would be able to hang out with them next time they came home on the weekend. Lando hugged Jazmin and kissed her on the cheek before he headed back to the Corvette with Quick.

Their next stop was Rittenhouse Street. They had to roll through the hood to see how Lil' Garvin and Baby-D were doing since they had been hearing so much about them.

Pulling up in front of Old Tima's house in Dre's turquoise tinted window convertible ZR1, Lando and Quick were taken off guard by the crew of new young dudes that were pushing coke on the block, but they were even more bothered by the way they ran up to the car thinking Dre was in it. A tall, new young dude walked up and tapped on the passenger side window.

Quick rolled the window down and said, "The fuck is up, shorty?" The young dude was a little shook when he saw Quick because he didn't know his face.

"Where Dre at!" The young dude asked, becoming very uneasy. The rest of his little crew began to walk up to stand beside him. Lando had flashbacks of when he and Quick were just like them.

One of the young dudes that had walked up with the crowd said to the taller one who had tapped on the window, "Ah, Tank, who the fuck is them niggas?"

Tank said over his shoulder without taking his eyes off of the car, "I don't know, young." As the scene became more and more heated, Lando tried to take control of the situation by telling the young dudes who he was and that he was looking for Lil' Garvin and Baby-D.

"Oh, you Lando?" Tank said. "So, you must be Quick then?" he said as he looked at Quick. Rubbed the wrong way and feeling a little forgotten, Quick shook his head yeah. Tank reached out to give Quick five as he told everyone to back up. Quick gave him five as Tank told them that Lil' Garvin and Baby-D were up Georgia Avenue.

On their way up Georgia Avenue, Quick expressed his displeasure with the whole situation that had just took place. "You can't be fucked up at them young niggas, joe. We was just like that when we was they age," Lando said as he laughed at the whole situation.

"Fuck that! You see how them young, punk ass niggas walked up on us when we was talkin' to the young dude, Tank?" Quick said. Lando saw the anger in Quick's face and knew where his mind was already. Lando began to remind Quick of all the wild shit that they had done coming up and what they would have done if some niggas had pulled up on them like that.

"Look, joe!" Lando said. "Them young niggas most likely hustle for Dre or Lil' Garvin and them. Don't trip off that shit, joe. We just hit the streets." Quick thought about what Lando had said and took it to heart. He knew that Lando was starting to become more of a thinker.

Georgia Avenue was packed. People were everywhere and doing everything from shooting dice to pushing crack rock. Quick spotted Baby-D standing by a group of young females and told Lando to pull up and park in the parking lot.

Baby-D spotted Dre's Corvette pulling into the parking lot and began walking over to it as it parked. The driver side door flew open and he saw Lando step out looking like a running back for a N.F.L Team. Baby-D couldn't believe his eyes. Quick added to his excitement by getting out of the car on the other side.

"I can't believe y'all niggas out, joe," Baby-D said as he sat on the hood of Dre's car with Lando and Quick after showing his love.

"Yeah, we only out for the weekend," Lando said as he began to explain how he and Quick had to do a few home visits before they were done with their juvenile commitments.

"Damn, young, y'all 'bout to come home, Black 'bout to come home. Everybody gon' be out by the summer," Baby-D said, full of excitement.

"So, where Lil' Garvin at?" Lando asked as he looked over at the young females that were sitting on the black BMW 850i that Baby D was standing by.

"He went to get some Backwoods so we can smoke weed with these bitches we met earlier," Baby-D said.

"Them bitches right there?" Quick said as he pointed to the crowd of females. Baby-D told them they were all trying to go to the hotel, and that he and Lil' Garvin were going to take Tank and some of his little men with them, but now that they were on the scene it was only right that they go.

Dressed in an all black Versace sweat suit, Lil' Garvin walked up on the three of them talking. "What the fuck is going on out here!" Lil' Garvin said out loud as he smacked hands with Lando and Quick. They got up off the hood of the car and hugged him, they could tell that Lil' Garvin and Baby-D missed them. After talking for a little while Lil' Garvin asked his two partners if they had been high since they had been out. They told him that they were trying to do that now. Lil' Garvin told them to follow him down 5th Street where his van was and that they would hit the hotel from there.

Starting up the Corvette, Lando saw Lil' Garvin, Baby-D, and three of the young females get into the BMW.

"Damn, I know that ain't slim's joint," Lando said as he pulled off behind it.

"Shit!" Quick said. "They say him and the Baby gettin' that cash. It might be his." Shaking his head in approval, Lando said, "We gotta get out here and get this cash, joe."

"You right," Quick said as they followed behind the BMW down Rittenhouse Street.

Once inside Lil' Garvin's huge family sized van with Baby-D and the three females, Baby-D began to light Backwoods and pass them around while Lil' Garvin began to put Lando and Quick down with the way things were going around the way.

"Shit ain't the same no more, young," Lil' Garvin said as he took a deep pull on the Backwood and told the females to go sit in the back of the van for a minute.

"Me and the Baby got shit locked out here. We getting six to seven bricks a week from Dre. Shit is pumpin' around the way. We got the young dude, Tank, and his lil' crew flippin' the shit like hotcakes left and right."

"Yeah, joe, that ain't shit, Baby-D got the twin turbo joint, we doing the muthafucka out here. We just waitin' for y'all and Black to come home," Lil' Garvin said as they pulled up in front of the Super 8 Motel.

As they all got out and went into the hotel, all Lando could think about was coming home to get him some cash. He was ready and had his mind right, but right now he was trying to get him some pussy.

At noon the next day, the phone rang in the hotel room and woke Lando up. Lil' Garvin woke up and answered it. Looking over at Lando after a long night of fucking, Lil' Garvin said, "It's check out time, joe." Lando looked around at the room of sexy, naked, young females and all he could think about was how Pamila was going to be beefin' about how he and Quick didn't call home last night. He decided that he would deal with it when he got home. Meanwhile, he woke Quick and Baby-D up so they could smoke an early mid-day Backwood of weed before they dropped the females off.

Pamila was flaming with anger when Lando and Quick walked in the house at four p.m. that afternoon. She wasn't really upset that they had been running the streets all night, she was more upset that they didn't call and let her know that they wouldn't be coming home. She hated worrying and that was just what she had been doing all night. She began scolding them as soon as they walked in the door.

"What kind of camp do you muthafuckas think I'm running here? I'ma let you little muthafuckas know this right now. If y'all think y'all gonna come back out here with that same wild shit y'all were doing two years ago, y'all asses won't be staying in my house!" Lando and Quick sat on the sofa and listened to Pamila vent her anger without saying word. After about twenty minutes, Pamila cooled down a little bit. She told them that she knew that they were older now, but as long as they lived in her house they would have to play by her rules and there were no exceptions to that at all. When she was done talking, she told them to go take a shower so that she could take them out to eat with her and Tyesha.

Later on that night, Lando decided that he had to go see Nakia. That time, he got Mann's Z. After dropping Quick off downtown atWee-Wee's house, Lando shot out Silver Spring, Maryland to see what was up with Nakia.

Stepping out of the shiny silver car, Lando not only felt like a big boy, but he felt free. Waiting for Nakia to open the door, all he could think about was how he was going to get rich as soon as he was done with his juvenile commitment.

Nakia opened the door as her mouth fell to the ground when she saw Lando in a slick Hugo Boss leather jacket with his hair in fresh cornrows that he had gotten one of the females to do the night before. Rubbing her hand over Lando's silky hair, still in shock, Nakia said, "Boy, you look so good. Come in."

Upstairs in Nakia's bedroom, they talked for a while about how things could, should, and would be now that he was going to be home in a few weeks. The more Lando looked at Nakia in her nightgown, he could see how much he had been missing while he was locked up. Even though she came to see him at least two or three times a month, it was always with Pamila. He hadn't been that close to her alone since he was on the run two years ago. He was still in love with her after all of that time. Lando's mind was made up; he wanted his childhood love back.

"Lando," Nakia said, "I still want you. I prayed that you would come home every night while you were gone and you're here. I want you all to myself." Lando thought about where Nakia wanted to take their relationship and he had no problem with it, but he learned to leave a little up to the imagination while he was away.

Grabbing her into his arms while not playing too big, Lando said, "Let's see where things take us. You know how much I love you, boo." Lando leaned over and kissed Nakia in the mouth while laying her back on her bed. Nakia could feel her whole body heat up as she thought of what was about to take place.

"I waited for this for so long," she said as she began to let Lando pull her nightgown up. In seconds, they were deeply intertwined in a heap of love making that neither one would ever be able to forget.

Just after two a.m., Lando was back in Mann's Twin Turbo on his car phone with Pamila, telling her that he was going to be in the house late because he was going to the Black Hole with Quick. She told him to make sure that he and Quick didn't get into any trouble and that she would see them in the morning. It felt good to be on good terms with Pamila for once, Lando thought as he began to dial Wee-Wee's car phone number to see if he and Quick were going to meet him at the go-go.

"Hello?" Wee-Wee said in his little kid voice with Rare Essence blasting out of his car speakers. Lando could tell by his voice that he was smoking weed.

"What's up, joe? I'm on my way down the Hole. Y'all gon' meet me there?" Lando said as he flew down Georgia Avenue at sixty miles per hour.

"Yeah, shorty, we on our way up there now, joe," Wee-Wee said. Lando told Wee-Wee that he would see him down there and told him to put Quick on the phone.

"What's up, nigga!" Quick said, sounding like he was having the time of his life hanging out with his big cousin while he was on his home visit. Lando told him that he talked to Pamila and that she was cool with them hanging out for the night, and that he would talk to him when he got down the Black Hole. Lando hung up the phone and began thinking about Nakia as he continued racing down the Avenue.

Coming through the door of the Black Hole dressed to impress, Lando saw people from all over town, some he knew from down Oak Hill and some from the streets. Making his way through the crowd, he was already feeling the loud music of the Back Yard Band and you could see it in his step. Looking over to his right, Lando saw Mann, Dre, Silk, and the New York dude, Supreme, that he had heard about a few times. Lando made his way over to the group of older dudes as they all embraced him as if he was a movie star of some kind.

"You stayin' outta trouble, shorty?" Silk asked as he pulled out a knot of one hundred dollar bills and gave Lando a few. Lando told him that he was just having a little fun for the weekend and that he didn't plan on getting into any shit while he was out. Everybody laughed at how much he had grown up while he was gone. Dre pulled out a knot of cash and handed it to Lando as he hugged him and told him to stay cool. Mann told everybody that he would be right back as he walked away from the table with his little brother.

Standing by the restroom, Mann told Lando that he was fucked up that he had been home all weekend and that they ain't even hang out together yet.

"It ain't like that, joe. You my nigga, slim. I just been gettin' some fresh air, Mann. We gon' hang out all day tomorrow. Okay?" Lando asked as he smiled at Mann.

"I'ma hold you to that," Mann said, "Go ahead and have some fun, shorty. I saw Lil' Garvin and them young niggas come in a while ago, they in here somewhere."

"You seen Quick and them?."

"Yeah, he came in with Wee-Wee and them a while ago, too," Mann said.

Giving Mann five, Lando said, "I'ma see you in the morning, pick me up over Pamila's house."

"Cool, I'll call you before I come, and don't let nothin' happen to my car," Mann said.

Lando made his way to the dance floor, bobbing his head to the thumping music. All the way up front by the stage, he saw Wee-Wee, Quick, and about thirty V Street niggas, Quick was right in the mix with them. Spotting Lil' Garvin and Baby-D leaning against the wall with Tank and his crew of young niggas, Lando walked over.

"What's up, nigga?" Baby-D said as he puffed on a blunt.

Looking around at all of the young dudes that they had with them, Lando said, "Ain't shit, joe. Let me hit that smoke." As Lando began to hit the blunt, Lil' Garvin introduced a few of the young dudes to him, Tank being the first.

"These my niggas right here, Lando," Lil' Garvin said as he pointed at the crew of five.

"I met shorty right there already, I like 'em," Lando said as he looked at the tall, brown skinned one they called Tank. Not getting too friendly with the young dudes, Lando got to know them and then made his way up front.

A group of healthy body, young women caught Lando's eye as he made his way up front to where Quick and Wee-Wee were. "Hey, boo!" a female voice said as someone hugged Lando from behind. Not knowing whom it was, Lando snatched away and quickly turned around to see Dee-Dee and a group of new broads.

"I heard you was home, why you ain't let me know?" Dee-Dee said. Seeing Dee-Dee's face made Lando think about Onion, and he had to hide his feelings.

"I jive been on the move," he said as he looked at how good Dee-Dee was looking.

"Well, go ahead and do your thing," Dee-Dee said as she licked her thick, shiny lips. "I might have a welcome home present for you." Lando smiled as he continued on his way up front.

"What's up, joe!" Lando said to Quick once he made it up front. The music of the go-go band was so loud now that Quick really couldn't hear him.

"I said what's up?" Lando screamed. Quick told him that he was chillin' and that he was high as shit. "Me too," Lando said as he smiled at his partner.

"Check this out," Quick said as he told Lando that he had ran into Ant's brother, Jammie, while he was downtown.

"Oh, yeah!" Lando said. Quick said that he was hanging down by 7th and N Street, and that when he saw him he started acting scared as shit.

"Fuck that nigga!" Lando said, not even thinking about the punk. While they were talking, Lando noticed Wee-Wee and a big fat dude in each other's face. "What's up with Wee?" Lando asked. By the time Quick turned around, there was a circle forming around the two dudes. Everybody that was with Wee-Wee was getting behind him and everybody that was with the fat dude was getting behind him. Suddenly, the music stopped playing and Big G from the Back Yard Band was calling for security to clear the floor.

Wee-Wee whipped a long, shiny butterfly knife out and started swinging at the fat dude, stabbing him in the neck. The two different crowds of dudes charged each other. Lando and Quick went with the flow and started swinging punches. In seconds, the floor was covered with blood and everyone was running for the doors.

Outside, it was complete pandemonium; people running and screaming, police everywhere, car tires screaming. Lando made sure that he ran to Mann's car with his head low, he knew gunfire was about to hit the late night air. Unlocking the car door, Lando quickly looked around for anybody he knew, but with people running every which way, he couldn't make anyone out. Starting up the car and shooting out on to Georgia Avenue, Lando heard the inevitable. Automatic gunfire hit the air in three quick successions followed by the sound of breaking glass and a loud car crash. Somebody was dead for sure, and Lando knew it as he went flying uptown in a flash of light.

Rolling over on the sofa in Pamila's basement the next morning, Lando saw Quick stretched out on the floor knocked out. He was glad to see him. Walking over to Quick, Lando began to shake him.

Wiping the sleep out of his eyes, Quick said, "What's up, joe?" Lando asked him when did he get in the house. Quick told him that Wee-Wee dropped him off about four forty five a.m. Lando then asked if anybody they knew got shot last night. Rolling over to sit straight up, Quick told Lando that Wee-Wee and two other dudes that were in the truck with them had pulled up beside the dudes car that they were beefing with and unloaded on it with an AK-47.

"Them niggas smashed right into the wall of the Black!" Quick said. Quick finished telling Lando about the shooting and who got shot.

While they were talking, Tyesha came downstairs with her drawing and ran over to Quick, saying, "I got you in the picture now." Quick smiled and hugged Tyesha, asking her if he could have the picture. She told him yes as she laughed.

Turning to Lando, Tyesha said, "Mann called here a few minutes ago. He said he on his way to get you and Quick." As Tyesha went back upstairs with Pamila, Lando and Quick got themselves together.

"Shit gon' be sweet for y'all, joe," Mann said as he talked to Lando and Quick while they sat in the back of his Range Rover on their way out Silver Spring to see his recording studio. "I'ma make sure y'all be okay as long as I live, joe, y'all know what's mines is yours," Mann said as he pulled up in front of what looked like a garage.

After walking around to the back, they went inside and things looked much different. Lando and Quick saw that Mann wasn't bullshitting at all. The studio was more put together than they thought. Mann had four different recording studios full of equipment and padded walls.

Taking them upstairs into an already furnished office that over looked all four studios, Mann said, "This shit here gon' make money and y'all gon' be a part of it." Lando and Quick listened as Mann gave them the run down on his plan for the recording studio. He told them how he had gotten the idea from Supreme and ran with it and that the studio would be open by the summer. He already had two white boys that knew how to work all of the equipment that would be running things when the spot first opened for business. Quick and Lando were amazed, once again, by Mann's ability to think his way through the streets.

After Mann gave them a tour of the studio, he took them shopping again and then they went to the movies. The whole time Mann had them with him, he was telling them how things would be as long as they stayed out of trouble when they came home. He knew they were not going to stop running the streets, but he wanted them to at least think for the future. They seemed to take everything to heart.

When the movie ended, Mann took them way out Maryland over Silk's house. They had never been there before, and the sight of the huge gate that they had to go through to get to the main house was something they had only seen on T.V.

"You see this shit here?" Mann said as he drove up to the house. "All this kinda shit gon' be y'alls when the time is right, joe, but you gotta want it and the only way to get it is with clean money." Quick was really feeling Mann's big money talk, but he couldn't see how he and Lando were going to do it.

"How we supposed to get money like this, joe?" Quick asked. Mann laughed and told him that he was going to show him.

A maid opened the door and led them back to the entertainment room where Silk was playing video games with his son. "Well, well, look what we have here," he said as he offered them a seat. Mann, Lando, and Quick sat down while the maid brought them all something to drink. Silk began to talk to Lando and Quick about what they planned to do when they were out. They really had no plan. They just wanted to get out first. Silk could feel where they were coming from. They all sat down and listened to Silk talk for a while before leaving. It was the first time Lando and Quick had ever felt close to Silk, being as though he always played things by ear and never on the scene.

As the time grew near for Lando and Quick to go back down Oak Hill, they sat in Mann's Range Rover laughing and joking in front of Pamila's house. Everybody seemed to be out front as the nightfall grew over the D.C. Streets. Dre, his son, Mann, Tina, Dee-Dee, Lil' Garvin, and Baby-D all stood around the truck spending the last little bit of time with Lando and Quick before they had to leave. A gray Volvo pulled up beside Mann's truck. Lando looked over to see who it was. A huge smile grew across his face when he saw Jazmin in the passenger seat of her mother's car.

As Lando walked down the street alone with Jazmin, leaving the crowd of people behind, they spent his last few free minutes talking about how their friendship was something that was very important. Jazmin expressed her feelings for Lando. She was attracted to him, but she felt that if they took their friendship to another level that it may hurt it if their relationship didn't work out. Lando grabbed Jazmin's hand and looked her in the eyes as they stopped walking. Lando felt nothing but love as he said, "Your friendship means more to me than anything, boo. I love what we have just as it is, and I'm cool with us being friends." Lando's words hit Jazmin in the heart and she knew that she would always have a friend in Lando. She kissed him on the lips and told him that she wanted to hang out with him when he came home the next weekend. Lando hugged her and let her go as she ran back up the street and got in her mother's car.

By the time Lando walked back up the street, Pamila was outside running everybody away for making too much noise. "It's time to go," Pamila said, standing on the porch beside Tyesha. Lando and Quick spread their love as they told everybody that they would see them the next week. Dre passed Quick a sandwich bag of weed, making sure Pamila didn't see him, while Baby-D passed Lando one as well. Their first home visit had come to an end safely.

Chapter Fourteen: Road Trip

Black was in the 1010 halfway house downtown. Mann had him on paper as having a job at Mann's World so that he could get out from eight a.m. until eight p.m. Monday through Friday. Black actually did a little bit of work while he was in the store. All he had to do was keep a job for thirty days and he was good to go as long as he checked in with his parole officer once a week. Black felt as though he could deal with that.

Lando and Quick were home as well. They were trying their best to get back on their feet. Mann gave Lando and Quick a brick each when they first hit the streets for good a month ago after weeks of successful home visits. They were now buying two bricks each and stacking cash like they had never been gone. Mann gave Lando his Z. Quick hustled up a 1992 red Chevy Suburban and put shiny chrome Hammer rims on it along with huge tires. They were right back in the fast lane with no problem and living in Pamila's basement on good terms with her. Things were smooth for them by far.

Kelley was home for the summer and staying with Mann at his new apartment in Landover, Maryland. Mann gave her a job working with Dee-Dee and Naomi. She didn't need to work, but she felt better about herself by doing so.

Smoke and Serge were starting to come back around the way now that Black was back on the streets, but they were still up to their same old ways, just looking for a caper here and there, but not making any real cash. Lando was selling them quarter bricks for five thousand dollars. They were trying their best, but it just wasn't in the script for them to be paid unless they robbed for it, so that's what they did.

The bright summer sun was shining off of Lando's car as he slowed down in front of Old Tima's house to talk to Tank for a second. Lando was trying to find a little dude that ran with Tank that owed him some money. Because Lando had taken a liking to all of the younger dudes, he dealt with them more. Quick, on the other hand, still had a hard time dealing with them, though he was getting better.

"What's up, joe?" Tank said as he walked up on Lando's car while keeping his eye on everything moving since he and the rest of the younger dudes were beefing with some young dudes from across town.

Smoking a fat blunt of weed, Lando turned down his blasting Geto Boys CD and said, "Where Lil' Mo at?"

"I ain't seen him since last night," Tank told Lando as he began to tell him that the little dude had lost all of the coke Lando had gave him running from the police about a week ago.

"Tell shorty, I ain't fucked up at him. Tell 'em I said holla at me, he ain't gotta duck me," Lando said.

Mann and Dre pulled up beside Lando in Dre's Corvette ZR1. "What's up, shorty?" Mann said, sitting in the passenger seat.

Lando reached over and gave his brother five as he said, "Where y'all on y'all way to?" Mann told Lando that he and Dre were on their way out to the studio to see how a female singing group sounded.

"I'ma be out there later," Lando said. Dre told Lando to stay out of trouble as he pulled off.

"You tryin' to roll with me?" Lando asked Tank.

Tank got in the car, and said, "Where we going, joe?"

As Lando passed the young dude the blunt that he was smoking, he said, "We going horseback riding." Lando pulled off and headed for Nakia's house to pick her and Trina up.

Mann's World was busy. Young people came in and out buying clothes and tennis shoes all day while they shook their heads to the music that played throughout the store. Black sat in the back office on the phone with Mia, who was fussing about him not coming to see her the day before, before he went back to the halfway house.

"I told you I got caught up, boo. Why we gotta keep going through the same ole shit?" Black said into the phone while he watched *Rap City* on BET.

"I love you, that's why, Black. Why can't you understand that?" Mia said in her sweet voice. She always got Black with it. He couldn't see himself taking her for bad after she had done time with him.

"I'll be over your house before I go back to the halfway house," Black said. Mia was happy, she didn't ask for much. Hanging up the phone with her, Black leaned back in his chair. Dee-Dee came into the office, and said, "Quick and them out front waiting for you." Black got up and went outside.

Jumping into the huge Suburban with Quick, Baby-D, and Lil' Garvin, Black felt at home as they pulled off.

"You still ain't smoking no weed?" Quick said from behind the wheel of the big truck. Black let them know that he wasn't smoking until he was out of the halfway house. Baby-D laughed as he took a deep pull of the weed and blew it into the air.

"We 'bout to go shoot some ball, joe," Quick said as he flew down Georgia Avenue.

"I need y'all to take me down Mia's house, joe," Black said. Quick headed in that direction.

Black knocked on Mia's door as Quick took his huge truck roaring down the street. Mia opened the door and jumped into Black's arms.

"What's up, boo?" Black said as he carried her into the house, kicking the door shut behind him. Sitting down on the sofa with Mia, Black asked her where her father was. Black couldn't stand him and Black knew the feelings were mutual. Mia's father always tried to come between the two of them, he swore Black was a street thug and would never be anything. Mia didn't give a damn what he thought and her actions showed it.

"My father ain't here, boo. Let's go upstairs," she said as she took Black's hand and led the way to her bedroom.

Black watched as Mia slowly and seductively undressed in front of him. "Good girl gone bad!" Black said as he licked his lips and rubbed his hands up and down Mia's smooth body.

"Who said I was ever a good girl?" the dark skinned girl said as she pushed Black down on the bed and jumped on top of him with no clothes on.

Undressing her man, Mia said, "I got you all to myself now, boo. I'ma enjoy myself today, I deserve it." Throwing Black's clothes to the floor, Mia raised up and sat right on top of Black as she slid him inside of her thin, but sexy, body. She began to slowly slide up and down while scratching Black's chest with her nails, and swinging her long hair into the air like a wild woman.

Mann, Dre, and Silk sat in the office of Mann's studio that over looked the four studios. Through the tinted window, they looked down on the three young girls that were paying eighty dollars an hour for studio time. The girls called themselves PASSION, which ess just what they filled anyone with that listened to them sing their songs of love and heart break. Cherry, the lead singer of the group, had been putting up the money for their studio time. Mann took a liking to anyone who followed their dreams, so he gave her the eighty dollar deal while everyone else paid one hundred to one hundred and twenty dollars for studio time. The other two girls, Chocolate and Caramel, were both committed to one day finding a record deal somewhere. All of their talks about a big record deal made Mann think of bigger and better things as he faithfully came to hear their studio sessions.

"Them girls sound good as shit, slim," Mann said as he shook his head to the sound of one of PASSION's better songs. Silk was feeling the song as well. He began to tell Mann how Supreme kept telling him how he had a record label in New York that he was trying to get started. Right now, he had a few rap groups that he was trying to put out, but so many people thought that they could rap these days that it made it hard to put them out.

"These broads can get a deal from one of them big labels if somebody get behind them," Dre said. Mann had an idea.

Cherry took off her headphones and told the recording engineer to kill the beat when she saw Mann waving at her through the door. Dressed in a black Versace body suit that showed off every inch of her thick body, Cherry walked out into the hallway to see what Mann wanted. Mann smiled at the cute light skinned, almost pink young woman as she shut the studio door behind her.

"What's up, Mann?" Cherry asked. She knew it had to be important because Mann never came down to the studio while people were recording on their own money.

"What kind of moves are y'all making with your music?" Mann asked, sounding inspired. Cherry let him know that her and the other girls were just making tapes and sending them out to big record labels, but none of them had got back at them yet, and lately they were just doing it because they loved it.

"What would you think about me managing your group?" Mann asked. Cherry smiled, she loved the idea but she had no idea what kind of money Mann had and what he could do when he put his mind to it. Everybody that had ever heard her group sing had stepped to her with the same idea, but nothing had ever happened and her and the girls really didn't believe in the manager thing anymore.

"I gotta ask the others and see what they have to say," Cherry said.

"Well, let's call them out here and see what they have to say," Mann said. His mind was made up and it was no way that a person could turn him down when he got that way.

Cherry called Chocolate and Caramel out into the hallway, and gave them the run down on the deal Mann had just offered. Caramel, a light brown skinned, young woman who was tall and thick in the thighs was all for the idea, in fact, she was for just about anything that Mann had to offer. Chocolate, on the other hand, respected Mann a lot and would have even given him some play if he would have ever tried his hand, but she was no non-sense when it came to her music.

She crossed her arms and said, "I'm cool with that Mann, but what's in it for us? Everybody always step to us with these great ideas, but we always end up right where we started, right here in the city singing to ourselves." Mann respected where she was coming from and was ready for her reaction, he knew she was the only one that would have any real questions. Mann let her know that he would set aside a studio just for them that they would use for free everyday of the week, he would also begin working on getting them a few shows somewhere. The girls were pleased with the sound of things, but Chocolate thought that things sounded a little too good.

"What's in it for you?" she asked, sounding very suspicious.

Mann rubbed his hand on her shoulder and smiled while letting her know that all he wanted was a little money on the side, which he would put in writing for them later. Right now, everything would be free and if they didn't like the way things played out in the end, then they would owe nothing because they wouldn't have to sign anything until they saw some kind of money. In the end, if it were all a waste of time they would have had their chance to show the music world that they could sing. The young women agreed and went back into the studio very excited.

Days later in the alley behind Old Tima's house, Smoke and Serge were in the shadows of darkness wearing ski masks with their pistols in their hands creeping through the cut. Looking out onto Rittenhouse Street, they could see all of the younger dudes standing on the sidewalk. They were easy prey as long as they never saw what was coming.

In a flash, Smoke and Serge shot out of the shadows and laid everybody down. Tank acted like he wanted to buck, but Smoke put his .357 magnum to the back of his head and said, "Act like you want it!" Taking money, drugs, jewelry, and four pistols, Smoke and Serge ran off into the night. They were too slick for the younger dudes. Even though they had gotten away with the robbery, Smoke and Serge knew that they couldn't let anyone know about it, not even Black. They would have to keep that one under their hat.

Lando and Quick pulled up in Quick's big red Suburban blasting NWA's *Niggaz 4 Life* just a few minutes after the robbery. They could tell something was wrong, so they got out and walked over where the younger dudes were. They were talking about who could have robbed them when Lando and Quick walked up.

"What the fuck is up?" Lando said to Tank, who looked like his face was on fire. Tank told him that they had just been robbed.

Lando looked around as if to see if there was any trace of the recent stick up boys as he said, "Y'all don't know who it was?" Tank shook his head no. All he could think about was the five thousand dollars that he lost in the robbery, his mind was set on getting it back one way or another.

"I ain't gon' sit around here and look stupid, fuck that. Let's roll out," Tank said to his little crew as they all got up.

"What you 'bout to do?" Lando asked with a little smirk on his face.

"We going on a caper," Tank said as he and the rest of the young dudes jumped into Lil' Garvin's huge van that Tank was driving.

Standing in front of the drugstore on Georgia Avenue along with Lil' Garvin, Baby-D, Quick, and a few other dudes that all slung coke on the Ave., Lando carefully served a pipehead four fifty rocks for one hundred and fifty dollars.

Walking back over to the phone booth where everybody was, Lando said to Quick, "Light some of that shit up." Quick took a fat blunt from behind his ear and lit it while Lando began talking to Lil' Garvin about the robbery that had just taken place down 5th Street.

"Them young niggas gon' kill some shit if they find out who did that shit," Baby-D said as he opened the door to his red 1992 Twin Turbo that was parked right in front of them. Sliding his pistol and his bag of fifty rocks under the seat, he shut the door just in time.

Hall and his gang of vice cops came flying around the corner and into the mini mall parking lot. Quick threw the blunt that he had in his mouth and took off running. He was too fast. The jump outs didn't even bother to chase him. They jumped out and put Lando, Baby-D, Lil' Garvin, and the rest of the dudes against the wall.

While the other vice cops were searching everybody else, Hall took pleasure in harassing Lando.

"Well, I guess you are the big boy on the block," Hall said. Lando knew Hall had only gotten hotter with time. He didn't even respond to his statement, Lando knew that his coke was stashed away in his car. He just waited for Hall to finish doing his thing so that he could go ahead and finish pushing the rest of his coke for the night.

When Hall and the jump outs were done shaking them down, Hall leaned over and whispered in Lando's ear, "I'm watchin' you. Let me catch you wrong and it's no more Oak Hill for you. No more two years. Kill somebody now and your lil' ass is going to the big house."

As Hall and his gang of vice cops left, Lando thought about what he had said to him. Lando hadn't shot a pistol in over two years. He wasn't even thinking about killing anything. It was all about the money now. Lando had no plans of running wild anymore. If he was to blast a nigga nowadays, it would be because somebody jumped way out of bounds.

A pipehead walked up on Lando while he was still in a daze of thought, and said, "I got a ball, let me get two of tehm fifties." Lando walked him to his car and served him. Dollars made sense now.

Quick had a .44 magnum on him along with a half of brick of coke that he was about to serve when the jump outs came through. With his Olympic speed, he ran all the way down 5th Street to Pamila's house in less than five minutes. Walking in the house out of breath, he saw Tyesha and Kelley sitting in the living room watching T.V.

"Who you running from, boy?" Kelley said as Quick walked by her and Tyesha on his way to his room in the basement, which he shared with Lando.

"The bodeans just jumped out, up the Ave., I had to get ghost," Quick said on his way down the steps to the basement.

Pamila was in the back room washing clothes when Quick came downstairs.

"Where is Lando?" she asked.

"He still up the Ave. chillin'," Quick said. Pamila had been getting on them about hanging out on Georgia Avenue. She didn't like it because she knew that it was only a matter of time before they got in trouble with the law again.

"I keep telling you about hangin' out on Georgia Avenue, find somewhere else to spend your time," Pamila said as she walked by Quick and headed up the steps.

As Quick began to lie back on his bed, Lando, Black, and Lil' Garvin came through the basement door bringing the smell of weed smoke with them. Lil' Garvin and Black went over and sat on the bed with Quick while Lando ran upstairs for a minute. Black started wrestling with Quick while Lil' Garvin grabbed the remote and turned the huge color T.V. on that sat in the corner.

Rap videos were on. Black stopped playing for a minute to see what video of NWA's was coming on next.

"I fucks with them niggas, joe," Black said. "Them niggas puttin' they lil' city on the map. You got niggas that don't even know where Compton is, screaming Compton. That's how niggas supposed to be screaming D.C., joe." Lando came back downstairs with a rack of money in his hand and cut into the conversation.

"Mann 'bout to try to put some singing broads out on that New York nigga's record label."

"We need some street niggas outta D.C. to come through," Black said.

Lil' Garvin was feeling him, he said, "You know Lil' Tank and them young niggas think they can rap and shit, joe. You wanna take them young niggas out to the studio and see what they sound like?"

"Yeah, let's do that. I'll pay for the time, 'cause Mann ain't gon' let us go in there for free," Black said. The idea was a good one and worth a try as far as they were concerned.

Flying down the beltway on their way to Wild World's water park was damn near the whole neighborhood. Racing through the beltway traffic and leading the fleet of vehicles, Lando and Baby-D put their Twin Turbos to the test. Lando had Nakia in his passenger seat scared to death while he flew from left to right at top speed. Baby-D wouldn't be out done. With Tank in his passenger seat, he made move for move right with Lando. Mann, Kelley, Dee-Dee, and Naomi moved at a much safer speed in Mann's Range Rover while they watched the two sports cars put on a show in front of them.

"Lando shouldn't be drivin' like that without no license," Kelley said as she saw Lando dangerously swerve across the beltway followed by Baby-D, Quick, Black, Lil' Garvin, and Lil' Dee-Dee, who were in Quick's big Suburban smoking weed and playing Sega on the T.V. that Quick had a pipehead put in his truck for him. Dre, Tina, and their son were in Dre's Corvette

ZR1 right behind Quick's truck. It was going to be one of those good ole summer days.

Once inside the water park, the females split up from the dudes and went on their own way, they were all supposed to meet back up at the Wild Wave sight at two p.m. Dre took his son with him as the dudes went to have a little fun. Dressed in all top flight swim wear from Polo to Madness, the dudes roamed the park in the blazing hot sun as if they owned it. Dre's little son had the time of his life watching Black almost drown at the bottom of a water slide. Walking around to get back in line for the water slide, Lil' Garvin saw a beautiful, brown skinned girl in a two-piece Gucci bikini. In his black Polo swimming trunks and colorful Nike aqua shoes, Lil' Garvin tightened his stomach muscles to flex his six pack and stepped up to bat.

"How you doin'?" Lil' Garvin asked the beautiful girl that was standing alone, licking on an ice cream cone.

Lil' Garvin saw the girl's eyes drop down to look at his stomach as she said, "I'm doin' okay, it's just hot as shit out here."

"You out here by yourself?"

"Me and a few of my girl friends," the girl said as she began to play with her licks on the ice cream.

"What's your name, beautiful?" Lil' Garvin asked as he stepped closer to her.

"Yummie," she said. Lil' Garvin smiled when he heard her name, it fit her.

"Yummie says a lot," Lil' Garvin said as he began to shoot his spill at Yummie. She was all smiles before Lil' Garvin left with her number.

Across the park by the eating area, the girls were getting their fair share of play, too, but all of them had a man and were not giving up any rhythm. Kelley had her hands full with a dude that just wouldn't take no nicely.

"Look, nigga! I told you I gotta man!" Kelley snapped as she walked away in her pink two-piece. The dude and all of his buddies couldn't help watching Kelley's behind shake every which way as she walked over to the water fountain. The dude walked up behind Kelley, who was bending over getting a drink of water. Pointing at Kelley's ass and smiling back at his men, the dude squeezed Kelley's ass. Kelley turned around in a flash and smacked the taste out of his mouth. His friends burst out laughing as he pushed Kelley against the water fountain and raised his hand to smack her. Dee-Dee, Tina, Naomi, and Nakia walked up just in time, they all got up in the dude's face and caused a big scene. The dude's friends came over to cool the situation off before it got out of hand, but it was too late. The girls went looking for Mann and everybody else.

Why on Earth did they run into Black before Mann? After they told Black what had went down and how the dudes looked, he went looking for them by himself, not thinking about Mann, the halfway house, or the law. After Black stepped off to run the dudes down alone, Dee-Dee realized that they had made a mistake by telling Black before they saw Mann. Worried about what Black might do out of his anger, they began to frantically look for Mann.

About ten minutes later, Kelley and the rest of the girls ran into Mann and everybody else. Mann almost lost his cool when he found out what had happened, but when he thought about Black running around the park in a rage, he got himself together as everybody began looking for Black. As they walked back toward the eating area, Mann knew that he was too late. Ten park security guards came running by them on their way toward the eating area. Mann, followed by everyone else, ran behind the guards.

Once at the eating area the guards rushed a crowd of people. Dre, being a little over six feet tall, could see over the crowd. Black had the dude that had felt Kelley's ass on the ground punching him in the face thunderously. As the guards broke up the fight, the dude got off of the ground and ran for the parking lot with his men. Black and everybody else ran, too.

Black ran straight for Lando's Twin Turbo, knowing that he kept some kind of pistol under the dashboard just like Mann. Mann ran up behind Black, followed by Lando.

Grabbing Black, who was flaming with rage, Mann said, "Hold on, joe! You can't smash these niggas right out here in the parking lot."

Holding Lando's .45 automatic in his hand, Black tried to think about what his older cousin was telling him. The sound of screaming car tires hit the air as a black Nissan Pathfinder went flying out of the parking lot. Standing up with the pistol in his hand, Black could see the dudes in the truck. Mann felt relieved that they had gotten away because he knew what state of mind Black had slid into.

Mann was back to his old tricks. He had pulled a few strings and got PASSION a spot on Amateur Night at the Apollo. Chocolate was won over by the move and couldn't stop thinking of how things might turn out if they won. They were all over Cherry's house packing their things for the trip to New York. Mann let them know that he would be to get them at nine p.m.

Trying on different clothes to see what she would wear, Caramel stood in the mirror talking about how excited she was to have a chance to sing on live T.V., she couldn't get over it.

"Who knows, I might even have a shot at Mann when this is over," she said.

Chocolate, being the backbone of the group, checked her quick, calling her by her real name, "Look, Tracy, we got other shit to think about right now. Worry about Mann later." The girls went on preparing for their big night while waiting for Mann.

Meanwhile, Mann had rented two huge mobile homes to ride everybody to New York in. He wanted it to be fun for the whole neighborhood. He would drive one and let Dre drive the other. Everybody seemed excited about the trip, which made Mann feel as if he was really doing something that everybody could get something out of.

Pulling up outside of Caramel's apartment in a huge mobile home with Dre right behind him, Mann blew the horn for PASSION to come out. It was already a full house in the mobile home that Mann was driving with Kelley, Tyesha, Lando, Black,

Quick, Baby-D, and Lil' Garvin inside. The three young singers would have to ride with Dre.

Coming downstairs quickly with their luggage, Cherry, Chocolate, and Caramel jumped in the mobile home that Dre was driving along with Tina, Lil' Dre, Dee-Dee, and Naomi. Once inside, Dre pulled off behind Mann and headed for the interstate.

The trip to New York was fun from the start. In Mann's mobile home, Baby-D and Black had everybody laughing as they tried to sing and began joaning on one another's voice.

Laughing at Black, Baby-D said, "Your black ass sound like you just got shot in the neck and you talkin' 'bout you gon' get on stage at the Apollo. Sandman gon' run down on you with dogs and beat your ass!" Everybody burst out laughing, even Black himself. Mann almost spit his soda out when he heard what Baby-D said. Their whole ride was live.

PASSION entertained everybody in Dre's mobile home. They even made Tina a believer in them and that was hard because if you weren't some big singer with a record deal already, she wouldn't even hear you out.

"Y'all really sound good," Tina said.

Dee-Dee cut in and said, "Yeah, y'all think I could do a song with y'all?"

Dre laughed when he heard Dee-Dee trying to cut into the girls' deal, and said, "Don't fuck up they program, you know you can't sing." Dee-Dee began singing an old Anita Baker song and made everybody laugh as they rolled along up the highway.

While Mann had everybody on their way to New York, it was business as usual for the young dudes around Rittenhouse Street. Tank and the rest of the young dudes had the strip pumping with fifty rocks left and right. Smoke, a snake in the grass, was out on the strip with them and the sad thing about it was that the young dudes not only knew nothing about him and his cousin Serge robbing them a while ago, but they really fucked with the two cruddy niggas.

Walking down Rittenhouse Street on his way down 5th Street to push a little coke, Serge thought deeply about his status in the game. He had been in the streets just as long as Mann and Dre, and he remembered when he was on the same level with them. They seemed to blow up, and he wondered why his luck wasn't as good as theirs. He was tired of nickel and dime capers. He wanted a big fish now.

Walking up on the group of dudes that were pushing coke in front of Old Tima's house, Serge gave them all five and didn't think twice about how he had laid them down at gunpoint and took all of their money and coke not too long ago.

"You tryin' to smoke with us, joe?" a little dude named Lil' Dee-Dee said to Serge as he and rest of the young dudes began walking into the dark cut beside Old Tima's house.

"I'm on my way, shorty," Serge said as he pulled Smoke to the side.

"What's up, slim?" Smoke asked, knowing Serge had something up his sleeve. Serge knew Smoke wouldn't go for his snake ass plan up front, so he beat around the bush and appealed to Smoke's pockets by telling him how this caper would put them on for good.

In the cafeteria of the Marriot Hotel in New York, Mann and everyone else acted as if they were right at home. Black always acted straight ghetto, and Quick, Lando, Baby-D, and Lil' Garvin went right along with it. They ran all of the white people out of the cafeteria when Black started throwing food and getting loud.

Shaking his head at the foolishness, Mann looked over at the table where they were making a mess, and said, "Black!" Black looked over at Mann with the look of a child caught in the wrong and smiled. "Stop actin' like a bamma, nigga," Mann said as he finished eating.

When they were done eating, they all went upstairs to the hotel rooms that Mann and Dre had paid for. Lando, Quick, Black, Lil' Garvin, and Baby-D shared a room together. They had the room lit up with weed smoke in no time. Stretched out on the bed, Black blew weed smoke into the air as Lando stepped over Quick to get on the phone. After calling Nakia to let her know that he was already in New York, Lando called Jazmin to see if she had finished a design that she had shown Lando that he thought would be slick for a T-shirt.

"Yeah, I finished it. I don't know why you like that one so much, it's just like some Madness shit. I only finished it because you was talkin' 'bout you liked it," Jazmin said, talking about a design of what looked like a solar system of all the things you could think of in the streets revolving around a dollar sign instead of the sun. Lando thought that it was a big statement for those that could understand that the design was saying that all of the things revolving around the dollar came with money in the streets. He wanted to show it to Mann when it was done and see if he would get the design put on a T-shirt and manufactured so that he could sell them out of Mann's World.

"I told you I'ma get my brother to get some shirts made with that design on it and sell 'em out his store," Lando said. Jazmin knew Lando always did what he said he would, but she didn't think Mann would like the design, so she really didn't have her hopes up about what Lando was telling her.

"Yeah, whatever you say," she said.

"I'm tellin' you, that joint like that. Niggas gon' dig some shirts like that. Watch, my brother gon' give you some money for that joint," Lando said. Lando and Jazmin talked for a while, but the room started to get loud now that everybody was high and playing around. Lando told Jazmin that he would see her when he was back in town and hung up the phone.

Noon the next day, Dee-Dee was helping Cherry pick out an outfit from the many that she had brought with her.

"Un unh, that's some plain Jane shit. Let me see how you look in this," Dee-Dee said as she pulled out a DKNY skirt out of Cherry's suitcase. As Cherry slid her thick body into the outfit, Dee-Dee gave her the much needed approval that she needed to kill the butterflies in her gut. Chocolate and Caramel came into the hotel room dressed to impress as well, but Caramel stole the show with Baby-D walking with her resting his arm around her shoulder. Dee-Dee's mouth dropped to the floor. Caramel was twenty years old with Baby-D looking as if he had played his cards right at sixteen years old.

Kissing Caramel on the lips, Baby-D said, "I'll see you at the Apollo," as he left out of the door.

"Oooooh, what's that all about?" Cherry asked Caramel with a sly smile on her face. Dee-Dee couldn't even get her words out of her mouth.

Caramel smiled as she pulled a white Prada body suit out of her suitcase and walked to the bathroom, saying, "I like shorty, he got style."

Chocolate, being no nonsense, shook her head and grabbed her suitcase, saying, "She don't know what she want to do. First she want a man and now she want a boy."

Later on, everybody was walking down the crowded street that led to the Apollo as if they were from New York and everybody else were out-of-towners. Holding Kelley's hand with Tyesha riding on his shoulders, Mann gave PASSION some comforting advice.

"Just be yourself. Take it easy, act like y'all act when y'all in the studio. We gon' support y'all no matter what nobody say," Mann said. Cherry felt better already, she smiled at Mann brightly.

Chocolate was a little over confident. "We gon' do fine, Mann, watch. You gon' be glad you put your time into us," she said.

Mann laughed, and said, "We gon' see," as he looked over at Caramel, who was walking hand and hand with Baby-D.

"What you want me to say?" Caramel asked Mann.

"I don't want you to say nothin', I just want you to do your best. That's all," Mann said as they all walked into the

Apollo behind the huge crowd that had shown up for the taping of the live event.

Inside of the world famous Apollo Theater, Mann and everyone else made their way to the front where their seats were. Black immediately got his face on camera. The crowd began to applaud as Sinbad came out on stage and welcomed them to the Apollo.

"We have a wonderful show for you tonight. Special guests BBD will be with us tonight," he said. The crowd went off again. Sinbad cracked a few jokes and let the show begin.

BBD came on stage and performed their hit single *Poison*. The crowd went off, the women went extra crazy. Dee-Dee ran up front along with Naomi and Kelley. As BBD took control of the crowd, they began throwing roses out into the crowd. Dee-Dee caught one and started yelling and screaming as if she had just hit the lotto. As BBD brought their song and super star performances to an end, everybody went back to their seats.

Sinbad came out again, and said, "I wish I could make the ladies yell and scream like that. I might have a lil' more fun in the bed." The crowd exploded with laughter as Sinbad called out the first amateur guest. A tall, white man came out talking about he was going to play his guitar and sing a country song he wrote. He was on stage no longer than thirty seconds before the crowd ate him up and forced Sandman to run down on him.

Sinbad quickly snatched the attention of the crowd by saying, "Ole Uncle Sam need to take his tired behind back down Texas where he from." The crowd burst into laughter once more as the next guest came out for amateur night. A slim, sexy, brown skinned young sister came out saying that she was from Arizona and that she would be singing an old Teena Marie song called *Cassanova Brown*. The sister had a beautiful voice and sang the song as well as Teena herself. The crowd applauded her great performance as she left the stage.

"Mary Williams from Arizona. I guess they ain't got no lotion out there cause that's sister's arms were ashy as beat up knuckles!" The crowd began to boo loudly as Sinbad called for the next guest.

"Okay, okay, I take it back, but it's gonna be your fault for her going through life ashy as hell," Sinbad said with a laugh. "Our next guest is all the way from Dodge city. Give up a big round of applause for PASSION!" Sinbad said as he dragged their name out adding a little essence to it. Cherry, Chocolate, and Caramel walked out looking like runway models. Sinbad asked them all their names and what they did for a living. Cherry told him that they all worked at Bloomingdale's and that she wanted to thank the person that made it possible for them to be at the Apollo.

"Thank you, Mann, I knew you would make something happen for us. I love you, D.C.," she said.

"What about you, you pretty thing you?" Sinbad said as he looked at the thick tall, sexy, brown skinned Caramel. She was a little shy. All she said was that she wanted to win and that the song that they were going to sing was one that she had wrote for the group, called *Destiny*. Sinbad said a few lasts words and sent them on stage.

Cherry walked up to her microphone in her tight white DKNY skirt and kicked the show off. The first note to the song, which began with the pleasant sound of Cherry's beautiful voice singing "Destiny!" Chocolate and Caramel quickly came in backing her up as the song went into telling the world how much of a role destiny played in a relationship. The ladies in the crowd went off. The dudes had to bob their heads as well as Chocolate walked to the edge of the stage in her black Fendi outfit singing a part of the song that was all hers.

"That's right!" Black yelled, supporting PASSION. The whole section where Mann and everybody else was sitting made sure that everybody in the building knew that they were there to support PASSION. Lando was so high that all he could do was bob his head to the music. He felt if he was to get up and clap his hands like everybody else that he would fall out.

As PASSION finished their song, they walked off stage feeling the love of the crowd. They just knew that they had won. They could feel it in the air.

Sinbad felt PASSION's song so much that he just watched the bodies of the healthy young women as they walked by, saying, "That's a whole lot of lovin' there. Too much for one man." Moving right along, Sinbad called the next guest out. Two brown skinned dudes came out on stage and said that they were from Brooklyn. The crowd automatically went off and accepted them as their own.

"So, what y'all gone do for us tonight?" Sinbad asked.

"We gon' represent for BK with some hip hop. Big up, Brooklyn!" the taller of the two dudes said. The crowd went off again, barking and screaming BK. The two dudes walked for the microphones and did their thing, sending the Apollo into an uproar. Black, Lando, and everybody else from D.C. had to bob their heads to the New York dudes that called themselves Double Barrell. They electrified the Apollo and walked off stage like "What!"

Sinbad watched them leave off of the stage and didn't dare to say anything about them.

"I ain't gon' get on your homeboys 'cause I might not be able to come back next week if I do," he said to the crowd of mostly New Yorkers. Sinbad then called out two more guests that were quickly booed and ran off stage by Sandman.

The moment of truth was at hand. All amateur guests were called back out onto the stage. The lovely Kee-Kee Shepard marched out onto the stage showing off one of her many beautiful gowns and the decision-making began. Kee-Kee walked behind Mary Williams of Arizona and placed her hand over her head and waited for the crowd's response. They showed a little love, but everyone knew that it wasn't enough to win. She then did the same to PASSION. The crowd went crazy, sending chills through the bodies of the three young women. They couldn't control their smiles as they heard Mann and everybody else supporting them. Kee-Kee then went over to Double Barrel. The Apollo was on its feet yelling and screaming for the New York rap group.

"Looks like we have a winner," Sinbad said. "Double Barrel!" PASSION and Mary Williams walked off of the stage in defeat.

Chocolate showed no signs of anger, she felt that life always went the way that it was supposed to go, she took the defeat in stride. Cherry walked away with her head down, she couldn't believe that they didn't win. Caramel's eyes began to water as she followed her two buddies off of the stage. She thought they had lost because their song wasn't good enough, however, Chocolate later assured her that her song was great and that it just wasn't meant for them to win.

"Fuck that!" Black said as he stood up and looked at Mann in disbelief.

Mann shook his head, and said, "That's how shit go, slim. We in New York, they gon' support they own, joe."

"Fuck that! I'm gone, slim. I'll see you back at the hotel," Black said as he headed for the door with Lando, Quick, Baby-D, and Lil' Garvin.

"Fuck these New York niggas!" Black said out loud as he walked to the exit. A group of New York dudes sitting right behind him overheard what he said.

They gave Black a funny look, and Black snapped, "You don't like what I saidn , bitch ass nigga!" Black asked the dudes out of his disappointment.

Mann sat through the rest of the show not upset in the least bit. He knew in his heart that the three young women had done their best and that someone else would see the same thing he saw soon enough.

Chapter Fifteen: Let's Chill

A week after the trip to the Apollo, Mann and Silk were walking in the door of Mann's studio talking about how Mann thought the girls were a little discouraged with their singing after not winning. Silk was listening carefully and saw that Mann had really taken a liking to PASSION.

While they walked up the steps to the office, Jimmy, one of the white boys that ran the studio for Mann, walked up, and said, "Mann, I need to talk to you when you get a chance." Mann told Silk to go ahead upstairs while he talked to Jimmy.

"What's up?" Mann said as he leaned against the wall in a grey Hugo Boss sweat suit. Jimmy began to tell him that the studio was getting a lot of business lately and that with him and Todd running all of the recording equipment, he felt that Mann needed to hire someone to keep up with all of the paperwork being that the studio was actually serving its purpose. Mann thought about what Jimmy was saying and told him that he would get right on top of the situation.

Walking into the office, Mann saw Silk looking down on a group of young white boys that had been renting studio time for the last few days.

Looking over at Mann, who was sitting down behind the desk full of paperwork, Silk said, "What the fuck is up with these white boys?"

Mann laughed while putting all of the paperwork into one stack, and said, "You know they do that heavy metal shit, joe." Silk had his face balled up as he looked and listened to what the white boys were playing down in the studio.

"They look like they playing some Satanic shit!" Silk said before walking over and sitting down on the other side of Mann's desk.

"So, when was the last time the girls were in here?" Silk asked Mann.

Typing some financial figures into his computer, Mann said, "They only been out here once since we been back from New York. I talked to Cherry yesterday and asked her what was up, she didn't sound interested in coming. She talkin' 'bout she got bills to pay and that she was on her way to work."

"So, what you gon' do? You gon' let them give up on themselves?" Silk asked. Mann let him know that he had no plans on letting them give up on themselves. Mann was going to go over Chocolate's house himself, and see where her heart was and what would be next for PASSION.

Mann was getting out of his Range Rover outside of Chocolate's apartment at eleven p.m. Walking up to her building's door, Mann kept his eyes on the group of young dudes at the end of the parking lot. He knew he was an outsider in their neighborhood after dark and he wasn't about to sleep on the locals deep in the heart of S.E. Washington, D.C..

Chocolate heard a knock at the door as she sat on the sofa in her living room looking through the paper for a better job. Putting down the paper, she walked over to the door and opened it with the chain on it. Looking through the crack of the door, she saw Mann and quickly let him in.

"Have a seat," Chocolate said as she moved the newspaper out of Mann's way so that he could sit down. "What you doing out dis part of town dis late at night?" Chocolate asked as she sat down beside Mann.

"I'm out here to talk to you," Mann said as he got straight to the point as he always did. He let Chocolate know that he could tell that her and the other girls were discouraged after not winning at the Apollo, and that he wanted them to put their hearts back into their music.

"Mann," Chocolate said, "I got a son I gotta look out for. I can't keep pretending that I'ma be a big super star. I gotta think about bills and shit like that." Mann could feel her pain and it was only one thing he could think of to restore their drive. "Check thiss out. I'ma turn my studio business into a record label myself," Mann said.

Chocolate smiled, and said, "I love the way you believe in yourself and I love the way you believe in us, but that kinda shit will take forever. What am I supposed to do until all of this stuff come through?"

Quick on his feet, Mann said, "How much do you make an hour at Bloomingdale's?"

"I make six fifty an hour."

"Check this out. I'll pay you, Cherry, and Caramel, ten dollars an hour to work at the studio."

"Doing what?"

"Paperwork, answering phones, and scheduling people for studio time. If everyone else likes the offer, y'all all show up Monday morning and y'all gotta job," Mann said. He knew he had victory in his hands once more in life. By the way Chocolate's face lit up, he knew he had put the drive and desire back into her heart to sing.

Standing up and walking for the door, Mann said, "Part of y'all job is to work on y'all music, so make sure you let the other girls know." Chocolate understood what Mann had just done. She wished all men could be as much a man as Mann was. Walking toward Mann, she passionately hugged and kissed him on the cheek before he stepped out into the nightfall.

The next morning, Mann walked into Mann's World just to see how things were running. As the glass door shut behind him, he could hear the music of Anita Baker in the air.

"What's up, Mann?" Dee-Dee said from behind the counter as Mann walked up.

"Ain't shit, what's up? Shit don't look busy in this joint today," Mann said. Dee-Dee let him know that it was too early and that in another hour or so a rack of young people would be in the store buying the latest outfits, tennis shoes, or tapes. Mann liked the sound of that.

"Keep up the good work," Mann said as he began to walk toward the back office, laughing at his businessman like statement.

"Whatever, nigga!" Dee-Dee said, catching on quick.

"What's up, Mann?" Naomi said as she walked by Mann with an arm full of brand new Polo shirts. Mann spoke to her and went into the office where Dre was standing in front of a pile of boxes writing down what was there on a pad.

"I see you hard at work, joe," Mann said to his partner.

Dre turned around, and said, "Ain't shit, joe. Just makin' sure all this shit here."

"Where that nigga Black at?" Mann said.

Dre walked over to the desk and sat on top of it as he said, "Black took the day off so he could move in with Mia."

As Mann began to think of what the future would hold now that Black didn't have to check in with the halfway house people anymore, he asked Dre what he had planned for the day. Pulling out a box of price tags for Naomi to put on the new clothes, Dre told Mann that he was going to take Tina and his son out to the Baltimore Harbor for the day after he served Da-Da two bricks of coke. Mann told Dre to come by his apartment later on as they headed out into the store area.

Walking up to the counter where Naomi was ringing up a pair of Jordan's and a few CDs for a young dude in a Fila short set, Mann looked out of the glass door onto Georgia Avenue and saw Lando pulling up with his long hair out and a black bandanna around his head. Mann smiled and began to think of how much his little brother had grown up over the last two years as Lando came pimping into Mann's World with a folder in his hand.

"What's up, joe?" Lando said as he walked up on Mann and gave him five.

"Ain't shit, shorty. What's up?" Mann said as he looked down at his beeper. Lando told him that he had the design that

Jazmin made and that he wanted Mann to look at it to see if he could do something with it for him. Mann told him to come back into the office so that he could look at it. They both started walking toward the back as Lando spoke to Dre and Dee-Dee, who were going over what needed to be put on the store floor.

Once in the back office, Mann jumped on the phone real quick as he sat on top of his desk. Naomi was pulling Hugo Boss T-shirts out of a well-taped box from New York.

"What's up, cute thing?" Lando said as he smiled at her and flopped down on the leather sofa while turning on the T.V.. Naomi found Lando smooth for his age and came over to enjoy a quick conversation with him while Mann was on the phone.

Mann hung up the phone and walked over to sit down beside Lando, who was laying his lick to take Naomi out to eat. Naomi, being about four years older than Lando, was trying to play big, but walked away telling the young dude to call her. Mann laughed a little bit as he asked Lando for the folder with the design in it. As Mann laid eyes on the creative design, he was all for it.

Lando's face lit up as he said, "So, you can get some shirts made like that for the summer?"

Mann smiled, and said, "Slow down, young nigga, shit don't happen overnight."

Mann began to explain to his little brother how he had to do all of the paperwork and get the design sent to a company that he worked with that made Mann's World T-shirts for him. It would be early September before the shirts would be on the rack in Mann's World, which meant that they would have to be sweatshirts instead of T-shirts. Lando was cool with that. He had accomplished his goal and he felt good about being able to tell Jazmin that her design would be on a sweatshirt by the fall. Lando gave his brother five and told him that he would catch him later, and walked out of the office on his way up Rittenhouse to serve a nigga a half a brick.

Walking out into the store area, Lando saw Short Dogg trying on a pair of new Air Jordan's. Lando hadn't seen Short Dogg since he had gotten sent out of town to a residential program from down Oak Hill. Lando walked up behind Short Dogg, put his hand against his back like a gun, and said, "You slippin', nigga." Short Dogg spun around and saw Lando.

Standing up to hug Lando, Short Dogg said, "What's up, nigga?" Short Dogg was excited to run into Lando.

"What you doing up this part of town?" Lando asked. Short Dogg told him that he was staying uptown with an aunt of his. Now that he was home, he was trying to buy himself a little gear for the summer.

"You gettin' you some money?" Lando asked as he sat down beside Short Dogg. Short Dogg began telling Lando that he had only been home for a week and that he hadn't even tried to get himself any money yet. Being well off in the fast lane, Lando gave Short Dogg his beeper number and told him to beep him later on so that he could do something with him to welcome him home. Short Dogg was happy to see that Lando was real as he claimed to be when they were locked up.

"You know this my brother's store?" Lando said as he began telling Short Dogg about how he and Quick were getting money now days. "You gon' see, joe. Hit me," Lando said as he stood up to leave. Short Dogg told Lando that he would beep him later on. Lando gave him five, and then ran outside. Short Dogg watched as Lando jumped into his car and took off flying down Georgia Avenue.

Across town in Silky's Barbershop, Lil' Garvin and Tank just finished getting their hair cut while Quick stood in the side door talking to Silk about how all the young dudes were going to go to Mann's studio and make a tape.

"Yeah, y'all should do that, shorty. Y'all livin' that for real, while them bammas niggas rappin' 'bout it. You know Mann bout to get the rights to the name of a record label for PASSION, he might be able to do something with y'all," Silk said. The words inspired Quick to really try to rap. Quick gave Silk five and told him that he would see him later.

Hopping into Quick's huge Chevy Suburban, Tank and Lil' Garvin started playing Sega in the backseat on the color T.V. that hung from the ceiling. Quick lit a fat blunt of weed as he pulled off into the thick Minnesota Avenue traffic.

"Can y'all young niggas rap for real or what?" Quick asked Tank as he passed the blunt back to him. Tank grabbed the blunt and began free styling for Quick.

"Nine millimeter, nickel plated..." Tank started to rap. Quick and Lil' Garvin felt him off the top.

"Shorty, like that!" Lil' Garvin said as he began to hit the blunt. Quick turned onto 37th Street behind a black Nissan Pathfinder.

Tank rose up, and said, "That's them bitch ass niggas Black was beefin' with down Wild World, joe." Quick and Lil' Garvin leaned up to look at the truck full of niggas. Sure enough, it was them.

"What you trying to do, young?" Tank said as he pulled a .45 automatic out of his waistband that looked bigger than he did.

"Hold up, shorty," Lil' Garvin said as he pushed Tank's hand down.

"Let's follow these niggas and see where they go," Quick said as he began to follow the Pathfinder.

Unnoticed and creeping behind the Pathfinder, Quick followed it all the way to East Gate Gardens. The Pathfinder pulled over and parked on Drake Place. Passing by and stopping at a stop sign at the end of the block, Quick, Lil' Garvin, and Tank looked back and saw the dudes get out and start mixing with the dudes out on the drug strip.

"Let's hit them niggas up, joe!" Tank said, ready for whatever.

Quick, now older and wiser, said, "Naa, we gon' holla at Black and Lando first. If they still tryin' to see these niggas, we'll come back at night and light this muthafucka up!" Lil' Garvin agreed as Quick pulled off and headed back uptown.

In the dark, broken glass littered and trash-filled alley behind Sam's Liquor Store on Georgia Avenue, Quick stood to the side telling Lando how he, Tank, and Lil' Garvin had ran into the niggas that were driving the black Pathfinder down Wild World.

Watching Short Dogg shoot the dice in the crap game that was going on in front of them, Lando said, "Fuck them niggas, joe that's old news now."

Quick shook his head in agreement with Lando as he said, "What you think Black gon' have to say about it?"

Pulling some cash out of the pocket of his Guess jean shorts, Lando said, "Don't tell 'em 'bout them niggas." Quick felt it was best to leave the situation alone as well. Walking up behind Baby-D and Lil' Garvin, Lando and Quick got right into the crap game along with the crowd of young niggas that were letting the dice roll to see who would walk away a winner.

By Monday, Chocolate, Cherry, and Caramel had quit their jobs at Bloomingdale's to work at Mann's studio. The girls naturally found their places. Chocolate took on the responsibility of booking who would get studio time and when, along with filing the fees for the studio time. Cherry had a thing for computers and went into the File Manager of Mann's computer and reorganized everything in a very easy to use way. Caramel got the easy end of the deal. When there was nothing more to really do, Mann told her to answer the phones at the front desk, which turned out to be good for her, anyway, because she was the songwriter of the group. In only her first two hours at work, she had written a beautiful song called *Sun Rise* and was already humming a beat for it.

Mann and Rick sat on the black leather sofa inside the office of the studio while Cherry sat at the computer working on different ways to name files. Filling out the paperwork that would turn the studio into a record label, Mann sat back with his hand on his chin thinking of what the name should be when Pamila walked in the door.

Mann got up and introduced Pamila to Cherry and Rick as he pulled a chair out for her to sit in. Pamila shook hands with them and began to tell Mann how professional the studio seemed as she came through the front door.

"You got somebody at the door answering the phone, all the studios downstairs have people in them, you're up here working. This looks like a real place of business," Pamila said as she looked over Cherry's shoulder to see what she was doing.

Sitting back down on the sofa with Rick, Mann said to Pamila, "What you think the name of my record label should be?" Pamila laughed, not knowing where to begin.

"Give me anything," Mann said. Pamila thought for a minute.

She began to think of how Mann got the money to do all of the things that he was now doing and she said, "You should call it Fast Lane Records, 'cause you got everything in the fast lane." Mann liked the sound of that.

Looking at Rick with a smile, he said, "Look like it's Fast Lane Records."

Back around 5th and Rittenhouse Street, Black was jumping out of a cab in front of Dee-Dee's house where Smoke, Serge, and a few young dudes were leaning on the fence smoking weed in the early morning summer sun. Walking up on the small crowd, Black showed his love and grabbed the blunt from Lil' Moe.

"What's up with y'all niggas?" Black said to Smoke and Serge. Breaking away from the younger dudes, they began to walk up the street as Serge told Black about a caper that he had his eyes on for the last two weeks.

"Who is the nigga?" Black asked as he blew a cloud of smoke into the air. Serge began telling Black about the move and that it was at least two bricks and about sixty thousand dollars in the house. "Who is it, joe?" Black asked again.

Serge said, "Lil' Tim."

Looking at Smoke to see if he agreed with the move Serge was talking about, Black said, "Fuck naa!" Smoke already knew Black wasn't going to be with the move due to the fact that they all went to school with Lil' Tim when they were younger. Black had no picks in the game, but he did have principles and never went against the grain.

"The money got you fucked up like that, joe!" Black asked Serge, looking at him in a way that showed his disgust.

Looking over at Smoke, Black said, "I know you ain't with no shit like that!" Smoke knew in his heart that the move was a snake move, but he felt as though Serge would find a way to get Lil' Tim one way or another. Black was against the move whole- heartedly and let it be known.

"I ain't with the shit. If y'all hit slim, I ain't got nothin' to do with it," Black said.

While Black was still venting his disgust about Lil' Tim, the jump outs bent the corner at top speed, slammed on brakes, and jumped out. All of the young dudes broke through the cut beside Dee-Dee's house. Smoke threw the blunt he was smoking as he, Black, and Serge just waited for the jump outs to put them against the fence.

Two jump outs ran after the young dudes while Hall and Big Al walked up on Black.

"You know what the deal is, Black. Get against the fence," Hall said. Black smiled and sighed as he turned around and got on the fence. Big Al made Smoke and Serge do the same while Hall began to harass Black.

It was the first time that Hall had the pleasure of running into Black in almost two years and he was happy to catch him on the drug strip, even though he knew Black wasn't dirty, but he knew it would only be a minute before he would be.

"So, you finally worked your way out of the system again," Hall said as he patted Black down.

"Well, I want you to know that I'm still around. I ain't gon' no where. I know all about your little cousin, Lando, being the big dope boy now. I guess crime runs in the family," Hall said as he went on and on about how he was going to find a way to bring their whole neighborhood down.

"Are you finished?" Black asked, becoming fed up with the bullshit.

"Yeah, I'm finished for right now," Hall said. "But, don't let me catch you slippin'."

Sitting in Quick's big Suburban outside of what was now FAST LANE RECORDS, Quick, Lando, Lil' Garvin, Short Dogg, Tank, and Lil' Moe smoked a bag of weed before going into the studio to see how the two younger dudes would sound. Short Dogg let everybody know that he could play all instruments and that he would make a hittin' beat for the young dudes to rap to.

"Don't be bullshittin'," Quick said with a little laugh. Short Dogg assured him that he was good at making real tracks.

"Let's see then," Lando said as they all got out and headed for the studio.

Lando was the last to walk in the door when he heard a car pulling up behind him. Looking over his shoulder, he saw Baby-D parking his red Twin Turbo behind Quick's Suburban with Caramel in the passenger seat. Lando smiled and went on into the studio.

At the front desk, Chocolate had the whole mob on hold giving them instructions that Mann had left.

"Ain't gon' be no playing and all that shit in the studio. Mann said he don't want no shit!" she said as she led the mob into studio B.

Once inside the studio, Chocolate called white boy Jimmy into the studio to show Lando how to work everything. While everybody touched and turned this and that in the studio, Lando listened to everything Jimmy had to say. Like magic, Lando caught on in seconds, and knew how to load the disk into the digital mixer and make it a record.

"I got it from here," Lando said as he grabbed a pair of headphones. Getting everybody's attention, Lando took control like a real producer. Jimmy sat back and watched as Short Dogg went from the drums, to the keyboard, to the bass guitar. In less than thirty minutes, Short Dogg had a deep bass track blasting in everyone's headphones.

Looking around at all of the nodding heads in the room, Short Dogg said, "Y'all like this?"

Standing up and walking over to an open mic, Quick said into everybody's headphones, "Let's light some smoke up and see what these young niggas sound like." Lando knew Mann wasn't going for weed smoking in the studio, so he quickly killed the idea telling everybody that they had to see what Mann thought about it. Out of respect for Mann, they all agreed. Tank and Lil' Moe jumped on the mic and put the tales of the bloody D.C. streets into rhymes like it was nothing.

Baby-D walked up to the studio door and looked through the window. Seeing everybody nodding their heads back and forth, he could tell that Tank and Lil' Moe had the spot rocking. Walking in and grabbing a pair of headphones, Baby-D listened to Tank and Lil' Moe go back and forth free styling.

"Damn! These young niggas like That!" he said, looking at Lil' Garvin, who was smiling as he shook his head to the beat.

Mann and Dre were just coming to the studio this morning after buying some more recording equipment for PASSION. Walking upstairs into the office, Mann looked down through the window over top of the studio that Lando and everybody else was in and could tell that something was going on that had to be worth listening to.

Calling Dre over to the window, Mann said, "Look at this, joe."

Dre walked over to the window and saw everybody into what was going on, and said, "Ain't no way we can hear what's going on down there?" Mann looked over at Cherry, who was doing some work on the computer and told her to get the headphones out the desk drawer. Cherry brought the headphones over to Mann and hit a switch on the wall that allowed him to hear what was going on downstairs in any studio from A to D.

"These young niggas sound good as shit, joe," Mann said as he shook his head to the beat.

Handing Dre the headphones, Mann said, "Listen to the beat, too." Dre agreed, Tank and Lil' Moe sounded like they could be on a tape in the record store somewhere.

"Who made this beat?" Dre asked.

Mann threw his hands up in the air as if to say he didn't know as he looked at Cherry, and said, "You know who made this beat?" Cherry got up from the computer and walked over to the window.

Looking down into the studio, she pointed at Short Dogg, and said, "See the short one with the black bandanna on his head?" Mann shook his head yeah. "He made it," Cherry said.

Mann and Dre went downstairs to see what was up with Lando and everybody else, and to see who the young dude was that had made the beat that they were rapping to. Lando introduced Mann and Dre to Short Dogg, and told them that Short Dogg was a good nigga that he and Quick had met down Oak Hill.

Mann looked at Short Dogg, thinking about what Lando had just told him. Lando didn't call everybody a good nigga, so it must be something good in Short Dogg. "Let me holla at you real quick, shorty," Mann said to Short Dogg as he walked for the door.

Outside in the hallway, Mann gave Short Dogg the run down on how he had just started a record label and that he had a female group on the label already. He also let him know that he was looking for someone that could make R & B tracks.

"I can do it all, slim," Short Dogg said, looking up at Mann.

"Good then, I need to see what you can do for thissong that they workin' on now," Mann said. "I'ma pay you for it, too." Short Dogg smiled, Mann was talking his kind of talk.

"So, when you want me to do this?" Short Dogg asked. Mann told him to come back up to the studio about nine p.m. and then they could talk some more. Short Dogg was all for the plan and was waiting to see what would manifest.

Later on as the night began to grow dark, Quick, Black, Lando, and Short Dogg were on their way back to the studio. Quick had the tape of Tank and Lil' Moe free styling in the tape deck blasting.

"I ain't know you knew how to make beats, joe," Black said to Short Dogg, "When we was down Oak Hill, all you wanted to do was smoke weed and shit." Short Dogg began to tell Black how he used to play drums and stuff when he was small at his grandmother's church.

"I can't see you in church with a ski mask on, shorty," Black said.

Pulling up in front of the studio, Quick said, "Well, we gon' be up the Ave., joe. Beep me when you done, slim." Short Dogg showed his love and jumped out of the truck into the darkness of the Silver Spring side street.

Flying down Wisconsin Avenue early in the morning on his way to pick Black up from his apartment down Georgetown, Quick spotted a group of young girls in catholic school uniforms. Something about the uniforms told Quick that he wasn't supposed to be able to pull one of the girls, which made him want to try his hand even more. Riding by the young girls, who had to be on their way to some kind of summer camp, Quick looked over his shoulder with a blunt hanging out of his mouth and saw a cute, brown skinned girl in the group of white girls. Quick put the blunt in the ashtray and pulled over at the end of the block waiting for the girls to walk by.

Dressed in all black with his hair in cornrows, Quick leaned against his truck as the girls walked by smiling in their green and yellow uniforms. Looking at the black girl, Quick noticed the white girls smiling his way, too.

Walking up on the side of the girls, Quick went straight to work. Addressing all of the girls, Quick said, "Do y'all mind if I have a word with ya friend?"

The white girls laughed as the one who seemed to be the oldest said, "No, go ahead."

Looking at the brown skinned girl with pretty eyes, Quick said, "Can I have a minute of your time?"

A little scared of Quick's thugged out look, the girl said in a real soft voice, "Yeah."

Stepping off to the side by his truck, Quick asked her what her name was. Not able to look Quick in the eyes, the girl said, "Amber."

Smiling at the girl, Quick stepped closer to her, grabbing her hand, and said, "Well, Amber, they call me Quick." Amber felt a sudden ease when Quick grabbed her hand and worked up enough courage to look him in the face.

"Why do they call you Quick?" she asked. Quick told her that he has always been quick to go after what he wanted, and that was how he got the name. Amber giggled a little bit and Quick knew he had the little catholic schoolgirl. In less than two minutes, Quick had her deeply interested in him and the side of the world he was from. After getting Amber's phone number, Quick let her know that he would be calling her later. She was so excited. Quick gave her and her friends a ride down the street to St. Albins Catholic School and went down Georgetown to pick Black up.

As Quick blew the horn outside, Mia was beefing with Black about how he had been running the streets all night now that he was out of the halfway house.

"You don't never be in the house!" Mia said. Black turned and put his hands on Mia's shoulders as he comforted her, knowing that was all she ever wanted.

"Look, boo, you know I love you, but you also know that I'ma street nigga. I'ma run the streets, yet and still, you gon' wake up beside me every morning. Okay?" Black said as he kissed Mia. She wanted to melt in his arms. Black knew what made her tick and he gave her what she wanted every time, being as though he could never forget the loyalty that she showed him out of nowhere when he was locked up. Mia hugged Black, smiling brightly as Black walked out of the door.

On the way uptown, Quick put Black on point about the news that he had heard last night.

"You know a nigga robbed and killed Lil' Tim 'bout two nights ago, slim," Quick said as he slid a Spice 1 CD in the disc player. Black shook his head. He knew Smoke and Serge had to have been the ones behind the caper. Some niggas just had no cut cards in the game. Black thought that Smoke and Serge would leave the situation alone after the way he reacted a couple of days ago, but now Black began to think that the keep it real shit didn't apply to them at all.

Standing in the bedroom doorway in his two-bedroom apartment, Mann watched Kelley put her clothes on as he asked her what she wanted to do for the day. Looking out of the bedroom window in the bright, beautiful sunlight of the late summer day, Kelley thought that it would be good to just go downtown and go pedal boat riding. Having only one day left with Mann before going back to school for the fall, she wanted to go somewhere that none of his friends or partners from the hood would be able to steal her time.

"I was thinking of pedal boating or something, I don't care. I just want to be with you alone, boo," Kelley said as she got up and hugged Mann. Thinking of what he could do to bring her wish to life, Mann's mind quickly went to work.

"I got an idea," Mann said, "Get a change of clothes and some swim gear." Kelley backed away from Mann smiling, she knew Mann could come up with anything at the drop of a dime and she wanted to know what he was thinking.

"Where we going, boo?" Kelley asked full of excitement. Walking out into the living room to use the phone, Mann told her she would see when they got there.

"What's up, CEO?" Silk said in a joking way. Mann laughed, even though it was a true statement. Mann wasn't used to the realness of it at only eighteen years old. Getting straight to the point, Mann told Silk that he was trying to use his beach house along with the yacht that he had down Virginia Beach to show Kelley a good time before she went back to school.

"I like your style, young nigga," Silk said with the sound of admiration in his voice, "Come get the keys and shit. I'ma be here till 'bout noon." Mann told Silk that he was on his way and hung up the phone.

Mann wasted no time getting to Silk's huge house out Maryland. Pulling through the huge gates upfront, Mann looked at his watch. It was only ten fifteen a.m. He had good time, from there it would only take about three hours, at the most, to get to the beach house. Looking over at Kelley, who was still intrigued about their secret destination, Mann kissed her and told her that he would take her inside, but he was on a clock.

Once inside, Silk's beautiful baby mother led Mann back to the pool where Silk and his son were playing out in the sun. Seeing Mann, Silk got out of the pool with his son and walked over to Mann dripping wet.

Giving Mann five with his son in his arms, Silk said, "Have fun," as he handed Mann the keys to everything he needed.

Putting the keys into his pocket while giving Silk's son some candy, Mann said, "I hate to stick and move, but I'm trying to catch a lot of day light." Silk laughed, he understood. Walking back toward the pool, Silk told Mann to call him later as he jumped into the water with his son in his arms.

Mann had to do everything but lie to Kelley about where they were going. Just when it seemed that she was going to guess where they were going, Mann pulled in front of Silk's beach house.

Pointing to the house as he turned his Range Rover off, Mann said, "We staying here for the night, boo."

Kelley's face lit up with joy as she said, "Come on, let's go in."

Silk had the place decked out as if he really lived in the house. As soon as they walked in the door, Mann noticed all of the new furniture that wasn't there the last time. Mann, himself, was impressed. Dropping her bags to the floor, Kelley dived on a big, black leather sofa in the living room.

"You really know how to treat a woman," Kelley said to Mann, who was walking around the huge house, looking around himself.

"I gotta get us one of these joints, boo. Maybe next summer the record label thing will make enough cash for some shit like this," Mann said as he dove on top of Kelley.

"I don't put nothing pass you, boo," she said as she kissed Mann passionately in the mouth. "Let's see what upstairs looks like," Kelly said.

Walking into the main bedroom, things only got bigger and better. Silk had a king sized waterbed already made up with silk Versace sheets. Right in front of the bed was a mini movie screen that hung from the ceiling. Kelley looked around, amazed at the show of class along with money. Looking to her right, Kelley could see the ocean through the balcony window. Walking over and pulling back the curtains, Kelley opened the door, letting the cool air and the smell of the ocean water breeze into the house. As Kelley took a deep breath of luxury, Mann walked up behind her and wrapped his arms around her.

Rubbing his dark arms, Kelley said, "This is much more than I could think of."

Leading Kelley to the bed, Mann said, "The day is just beginning." They both sunk down into the waterbed and began to make love.

Hours later, they were just getting out of the shower. Getting dressed in the bedroom, Kelley told Mann how good he made her feel and that she wanted to make love to him again. Grabbing the keys to his truck, Mann told her that they would do everything that she wanted to do before the sun came up.

"I'm bout to go get us something to eat down the street. I'll be right back. Be out front in fifteen minutes," Mann said as he walked out of the room.

Kelley laid back on the bed and gazed out at the ocean. Mann had made her dreams come true once again. He was all that she had ever wanted. She loved him with all of her heart. Rolling over on the waterbed, she felt as if she was floating as she grabbed one of the fluffy pillows and closed her eyes, thinking of the beautiful love making that she and Mann had just enjoyed. She couldn't keep it to herself. She grabbed the phone and called Dee-Dee to tell her all about her day at the beach.

Kelley was standing out front with a beach towel around her, hiding her bikini. Mann pulled up with a bushel of crabs in the back of his truck.

As Kelley jumped in, Mann said, "I got one more surprise for you," as he pulled off.

"You got us some crabs?" Kelley asked as soon as she jumped in. Mann knew she loved them and he had his mind set on making it her day.

"Today is your day, boo," Mann said.

About a mile down the road, Mann pulled up and parked across the road from a small port of anchored boats. Some of which were just small fishing boats, but two beautiful yachts sat at the end of the pier. As Mann and Kelley walked across the road, Kelley couldn't take her eyes off of the huge, white yacht with the two jet-skis on the back.

"I know we ain't 'bout to get on one of these boats," Kelley said as she and Mann walked up to the gate of the port.

Flashing a members-only card to the young, white dude at the gate, Mann grabbed Kelley's hand, leading her down to the yacht that she had been looking at while saying, "We 'bout to get on this one right here." Kelley hugged Mann tightly before they stepped over onto the yacht.

Walking around the deck behind Mann, Kelley asked if he knew how to drive the yacht. Mann let her know that Silk had shown him how to drive a long time ago. Walking up behind the wheel, Mann cranked the beautiful boat up and slowly pulled out into the setting sun.

Thirty minutes later, Mann and Kelley were so far out into the Atlantic Ocean that it seemed as if they were the only two people in the world. The sun had just set, leaving a beautiful bluish orange haze in the sky. Looking out at the horizon, Kelley sat on Mann's lap, telling him how much the day meant to her. Mann was pleased to hear that Kelley was enjoying herself, but he wanted to add more to the day.

"Come on," Mann said as he jogged to the back of the boat.

"Where we goin', boy?" Kelley asked as she jogged behind him. At the back of the boat, Mann hit a switch that lowered one of the jet-skis into the ocean.

"I ain't getting on that thing," Kelley said, standing behind Mann in her bikini.

"Yes, you is!" Mann said as he grabbed Kelley and jumped into the water beside the jet-ski.

Soaking wet, they both climbed on the jet-ski as Mann started it up. As they took off flying, water shot way up into the air behind them. Kelley yelled and screamed for Mann to slow down as she held on for her life. Looking over her shoulder, Kelley saw that the yacht was growing further and further out of sight.

"Let's turn around before we get lost out here, Mann!" Kelley said. Spinning the jet-ski around like some kind of dirt bike, Mann looked back at the yacht, which now looked like a white dot on the horizon.

"We cool. We got 'bout ten or fifteen more minutes of light left," Mann said as he took off flying through the water again. As the jet-ski soared through the waves, the sound of a racing boat began to grow near. Slowing down, Mann looked over his shoulder and saw a Coast Guard boat speeding their way. About one hundred yards from where they were, a uniformed Coast Guard officer came out onto the deck of the boat, and said into the bullhorn, "You are in international waters. Please, turn around!" Mann wanted no problems with the law, and quickly turned around and headed for the yacht as the Coast Guard went on their way.

Back on the yacht, Mann and Kelley went downstairs and laid out on the bed.

"I'm tired as shit, joe," Mann said as he grabbed the remote and turned the T.V. on.

Lying beside Mann in only a towel, Kelley rolled over on top of him, and said, "You ain't going to sleep on me." Wrapping his arms around Kelley, Mann looked her in the eyes and thought of how bad he used to want her years ago. Now, he had her and so many other things that he had set out to get. As Kelley sat straight up on top of Mann and threw her towel to the floor, all he could think of was making love to her.

After taking a shower and getting dressed all over again, Mann and Kelley went up on deck and sat at the edge of the yacht looking up into the sky.

Pointing at the stars, Mann said, "It's gotta be a Creator out there somewhere. No one can put something together like that." Kelley looked up into the dark sky and listened as Mann began telling her that someone or something was in control of everything that goes on in the world and that whoever that someone was knew what they were doing because all things in life worked itself out if a person just played by the rules of the game of life.

"I did a little wrong, but I don' always played by the rules," Mann said as he went off into deep thought about what the future would and could hold. "We gon' be alright, me, you, Lando, and everybody else. Watch," Mann said as he laid down on the deck beside Kelley. Kelley cuddled up tightly beside Mann and they both fell asleep.

As the early morning sun began to cross the horizon, Mann opened his eyes and looked over at Kelley, who was still fast asleep on his chest. He had out done himself. Life wasn't as bad as people made it out to be, Mann thought.

Waking Kelley up, Mann said, "Well, was this what you call havin' me all to yourself?" Kelley sat up and looked out at the endless water. She got all that she wanted and had more fun in one night than she had all summer.

Looking back over at Mann, she said, "It was more than I could have dreamed of, boo."

Chapter Sixteen: Over before it even started

September opened up a lot of doors for Mann and Fast Lane Records. Mann decided to manufacture PASSION's first album himself, and then find a distribution deal with the final product in hand when the time was right. Spending over ten thousand dollars on duplicating equipment along with bulk boxes of over five hundred thousand blank tapes, Mann was set to put PASSION out. No one could tell him that his plan of having PASSION's debut album out by the first months of 1993 was a fluke.

Mann had paid Short Dogg three hundred dollars a track for every track that he had made for PASSION. Mann thought they all had what it took to be a hit. Mann's next move was to launch an all out promotion campaign to prepare the world for PASSION by putting out their first single that would drop at the end of the month if all went well. A small distribution company by the name of Cross Country Distribution had agreed to distribute the single for Fast Lane Records for fifteen percent of all sales generated. Mann had worked hard using everything the streets had taught him to secure the distribution deal and PASSION was very pleased with the turn of events in only a couple of months.

The start of school in the city was right around the corner and Lando decided to spread some love by taking Nakia and Tyesha shopping. They had spent the day out White Flint Mall buying everything from book bags to boots. Lando enjoyed being able to buy Nakia and little Tyesha anything they wanted.

On their way back to town, Lando thought that it would only be right for him to spend some money in Mann's World. Besides that, Nakia wanted a Mann's World sweatshirt to go with the rest of the fresh gear that she had to wear to school.

Walking into Mann's World with Nakia and Tyesha, Lando walked over to talk to Dee-Dee for a minute while Nakia and Tyesha looked around for what they wanted.

"What's up, bad ass?" Dee-Dee said as she sat behind the counter eating some fried chicken.

"Ain't shit," Lando said as he hopped up on the counter, telling Dee-Dee how he had heard the single that PASSION was about to put out. Dee-Dee was still impressed by the fact that Mann actually had a record label. She began talking of videos and concerts around the country. Lando laughed as he watched Tyesha run around the store, dancing to the music that was coming through the speakers.

Looking at Dee-Dee, Lando said, "Yeah, Mann 'bout to put D.C. on the map, joe. Slim ain't bullshittin'." Naomi walked out of the back office with some Polo sweat shirts thrown over her shoulders and saw Nakia and Tyesha picking out clothes. She knew Tyesha through Mann. She also knew Nakia, but she thought Nakia was just some young girl Lando was having sex with. She had no idea how serious the two were.

Walking up behind the counter where Dee-Dee was sitting, Naomi looked at Lando with a crazy look on her face and asked if Nakia was his girl now or just another broad he was fucking. Firmly, yet, still smooth, Lando told her that Nakia was his folks. He gave her a look that told her that she better not start no shit. Naomi was very jealous of the younger girl, but it had only begun to show the last few times that she had saw Lando and Nakia together. Naomi's feelings for Lando were starting to show in her actions. She had slept with Lando a few times during the past summer and she was on him harder than she even knew. Annoyed and hurt, Naomi walked off and went into the back office so she could get away from everyone and get her emotions together. Older and much smoother than he used to be, Lando noticed that Naomi's feelings were hurt, so he went into the back to make her feel better without letting Nakia see what was going on.

Lando walked into the office and saw Naomi sitting on the sofa pouting like a child. He walked over to the sofa and sat down beside her, putting his arm around her neck ,saying, "I know you ain't fucked up 'bout me bringin' my folks to the store."

Looking over at Lando, the older girl said, "You know how I feel about you." Lando thought back to the first night he had sex with Naomi, and how she told him how she hoped he knew what he was doing and that she didn't want him to get hooked. Now, it seemed as if she was the one hooked on Lando. Even so, he didn't rub that in.

Instead, he played his cards right, saying, "Naomi," as he put his hand on her chin, turning her face toward him, "I ain't did nothin' to hurt you. I done played everythin' like you asked. You said you ain't want me actin' like you my woman, so that's how I been carryin' shit. You know we still tight." Naomi's face lit up with a bright smile, and no matter how much she tried to make herself believe that Lando was a little boy, he always showed her that he was very much a young man.

After making Naomi feel better, Lando stood up and walked over to some boxes sitting over in the back of Mann's office.

"What's this?" Lando asked. Walking over to the boxes, Naomi told Lando that they were some sweatshirts that Mann had been waiting for. Against Naomi's protest, Lando ripped one of the boxes open, thinking that the shirts with Jazmin's design on them were inside. Lando was right. Pulling out one of the thick cotton sweatshirts with the heavy sewed design, Lando said, "This joint like that!" Naomi was still upset that Lando had went inside the boxes without Mann being around, but she still had to agree that Mann had the shirt made as a top quality shirt. To Lando, the shirt looked like a Hugo Boss sweatshirt, only with a hood. He had to take one to Jazmin's house. Lando kissed Naomi on the cheek and left out of the office to pay for the clothes that Tyesha and Nakia wanted before dropping them off for the day.

Lando wasted no time dropping Nakia and Tyesha off. In less than thirty minutes, he was knocking on Jazmin's door wearing the sweatshirt with her design on it. Opening the door, Jazmin didn't even look at the shirt, instead, she invited Lando in and led him back to her room where she was drawing another design.

Lando walked over and sat on Jazmin's bed while she sat down at the little desk she was working at in her room. After adding a few lines to a sketch that she had been working on, she turned around to Lando and laid eyes on the design that was sewed into the thick grey shirt. "Ohmi God!" she screamed as she jumped out of her chair. She couldn't believe that one of her designs was actually on a shirt that looked so good. Lando stood up to calm her down.

As he hugged her, she said, "I don't believe you pulled it off." Lando laughed a little as he told her how it was boxes of the shirts in Mann's store. "When is he going to start sellin' 'em?" Jazmin asked.

"He gotta put 'em on the rack before school start cause that's when the most business gon' come through the store," Lando said as he began to explain that the shirts were in all colors and that Mann would be in to check them out the next day.

"How much they gon' cost?" Jazmin asked as she stepped back and began rubbing her hands over the thick stitching in the shirt. Lando didn't know how much the shirt would go for, but he knew that Mann would give Jazmin some of the money he made off of them; he was that kind of nigga.

Crime paid and Black had been on leave for too long. Two nights later in the darkness of an alley behind an apartment across town, Black, Smoke, and Serge ran back to an old Chevy Impala dressed in black. Black had four bricks of coke and eighty thousand dollars in a book bag on his back as he led the pack. Once again, Black had led Smoke and Serge on a caper that produced more than thirty thousand dollars, which was all they got when they robbed and killed Lil' Tim.

As Smoke jumped behind the wheel of the car, Black and Serge ran around to the other side. Serge blatantly by-passed the front seat and jumped in the back seat as Smoke started the car. Black's danger alarms quickly went off. He had seen Serge trick niggas into the front seat after capers and blown their brains all over the windshield. As Black hesitated to get in the car, Smoke became impatient, knowing that someone had heard the shots that had just went off inside the building. Black put his paranoia to the side and jumped in the car as Smoke took them flying down the alley.

Black had been robbing niggas and going on capers with Smoke and Serge since he was twelve years old and had never felt like he needed to watch them, but for the first time he began to doubt Serge. Even though he didn't respect that Smoke and Serge had robbed and killed Lil' Tim, a nigga that they all grew up with, Black never thought that they would try him in the least, but now he believed that Lil' Tim's murder affected him more than he had first thought.

Downstairs in the basement, Lando and Quick broke bricks of coke down to ounces like they had been doing all summer. Together, they were moving five bricks a week. What Lil' Garvin and Baby-D didn't have locked down, Lando and Quick quickly snatched up and were moving coke from the city all the way out to Maryland. Slowly but surely, they were learning what it took to be money makers.

"Weigh that shit right there," Lando said to Quick as he ran across the room to answer the phone. "Hello?" Lando said as he sat down on his bed and turned the T.V. down. All he could hear on the other end were soft sobs. "Who the fuck is this!" Lando said as he listened closely. It sounded like someone was outside in the rain crying.

"Who is this!" Lando asked again, soundingconcerned.

"Lando…" a female voice said through small sobs. "I'm pregnant."

Lando thought it was Nakia for a minute, and then thought otherwise, and said, "Who is this?"

Nakia cleared her voice, and said, "It's me."

"Why you cryin'?" Lando asked.

Nakia began to tell him that she told her mother that she was pregnant, and that her mother went off and put her out. She was at the gas station down the street from her house standing out in the rain. Lando cut her off and told her he was on his way to get her and that she could tell him the rest when he got there. Hanging up the phone with Nakia, Lando told Quick to bag all the coke up for him because he had to roll out and that he would be right back.

Flying through the evening rain, Lando began to think of the situation at hand. He knew that he had been making love to Nakia all summer without a rubber, but he thought that he always was on time when it was time to release his load. He didn't doubt that the baby was his for a second and he knew that no matter what came about in the end that he would be there for his child and his child's mother.

Slowly, Lando pulled into the gas station and saw Nakia sitting on top of her suitcase beside the pay phone in the rain. Despite her tear stained face, Nakia managed to smile when she saw Lando getting out of the car.

Walking over to Nakia as she stood up, Lando hugged her and kissed her.

"You okay?" he asked as he picked up her suitcase and led her to the car.

"Yeah, I am now that you here," Nakia said.

Walking around to the driver's seat, Lando said, "I'm always here for you, boo." Pulling out of the gas station onto Georgia Avenue, Lando said, "Tell me what's up," as he rubbed Nakia's thick thighs.

Nakia began telling Lando that she had been pregnant by him since his first home visit from Oak Hill. She didn't know how or when to tell him, but her mother had found out about her pregnancy a month ago. Her mother told her to get Lando to pay for an abortion or get out. Nakia had stalled for awhile, but her mother finally drew the line and told her to pack her bags and leave. She could only come back home if she was to get rid of the child, which she was not going to do, even if it killed her.

Lando listened to her every word and felt her pain. He was doing well enough in the streets to take care of him, her, and a child. He took her home with him and put her to bed in Tyesha's room so that she could calm down. They would talk to Pamila in the morning.

Outside of Fast Lane Records, Baby-D sat in his red Twin Turbo waiting for Caramel to finish her studio session. As the sound of Tank and Lil' Moe's free stylin' tape blasted through the JVC system that Baby-D had just put in the car, he lit a blunt of weed as he looked up and down the dark side street. Baby-D looked over at the bright lights that read *Fast Lane Records*. Mann had done it again. To see Mann go from neighborhood street hustler to C.E.O. of a record label gave Baby-D the hope and inspiration he needed to look passed the street life of the fast lane. The sound of talking and laughter hit the air and snapped Baby-D out of his moment of thought as he saw Mann, PASSION, and Silk's sister, Pam, coming out of the double doors.

Caramel told everyone that she would see them at the studio in the morning as she jumped in the car with Baby-D and kissed him on the cheek, saying, "What's up, boo?" Starting up his car, Baby-D looked over at Mann and waved as he pulled off. Shooting by Mann, Baby-D saw Mann giving him a look that said, 'That's right, shorty'. Baby-D knew Mann was impressed by the way he had pulled Caramel, being as though she was much older than him.

Flying across town through the empty D.C. streets, Baby-D asked Caramel what was going on with the PASSION single. Turning the loud music down, Caramel said, "We finished with the single. We workin' on the album now." Pulling out a CD, Caramel cut the tape deck off and threw a copy of PASSION's single in the disc player. "Listen to this," Caramel said as the booming sound of the song *Destiny* filled the car.

"Short Dogg made that beat?" Baby-D asked. Caramel told him that Short Dogg had made all the beats that they were going to use on the tape. Feeling the R&B song more than he thought he would, Baby-D turned it up and said, "Y'all ain't bullshitin', huh?" Caramel began telling him how Mann made moves so quick and so precisely that she couldn't believe that he hadn't ran a record label before.

In what seemed to be overnight to Caramel, Mann had turned the studio into a record label. He had gotten a distribution deal for the single and was working on another one for the album. Through Rick, Mann had secured a publishing deal that would get PASSION paid years after their single was old news, if it did well. Within the upcoming week, Mann had two interviews set up for PASSION. One was with BET and another on WPGC 95.5, the local D.C. radio station. A week after that, Mann had a crew of Howard University filming students coming in to shoot a video to promote the upcoming single.

"Damn, Mann ain't bullshitin'," Baby-D said as he pulled up outside of Caramel's apartment on Martin Luther King Avenue.

"You done known Mann longer than me. You know how he carry shit," Caramel said as she and Baby-D got out of the car and headed for her house.

After parking his truck around the corner, Quick walked around to the drug strip on Georgia Avenue and ran into Lil' Garvin, Short Dogg, and a few older dudes that used Georgia Avenue to pay the bills.

"What's up, joe?" Quick said to Lil' Garvin after speaking to everyone else.

"Ain't shit, joe. Where Lando at? He ain't tryin' to get none of this money?" Lil' Garvin asked.

Quick told him that Lando's girl had just got put out of her mother's house because she was pregnant by him and that he was staying in the house for the night. Short Dogg lit up a blunt of weed as he walked over and passed it to Quick. Quick took the blunt and leaned against the wall as he watched the Avenue like a moving snake that was sliding into striking distance.

Money had been coming through without a rest for the last half hour as Quick and everyone else got what was theirs. Running across the street to serve a pipehead, an older dude named Lip saw an old Dodge sitting in the alley down the hill from the Ave. Serving the pipehead quickly without taking his eyes off of the out of place Dodge, Lip ran back across the street to get his pistol. Grabbing his pistol form under the parked car, he put Quick and the rest of the younger dudes on point about the Dodge in the alley.

Just as everybody started walking toward Rittenhouse Street so they could see what was up with the Dodge that was in the alley, three niggas in ski masks dressed in all black bent the corner and opened fire on the mini mall parking lot. Lip started emptying his pistol at the gunmen. Quick and Lil' Garvin did the same while running behind a parked car. Short Dogg knew more than the rest about the gunmen, which drove him to run right in their direction fearlessly as he spit round after round out of the Mac-11 that he was carrying. The three gunmen came to do the shooting, not to get shot at. Short Dogg's rampage shooting caused them to run for their car. Followed by everyone else, Short Dogg ran behind the gunmen with the Mac-11 blazing causing the three gunmen to abandon their car and disappear into the darkness of the early morning hours.

As the night grew old, Nakia laid asleep on the extra bed in Tyesha's room dreaming about having Lando's baby. Waking up in the middle of the night, she couldn't stand being upstairs without him, knowing that they were in the same house. She got out of the bed and went downstairs with Lando, unnoticed as well as unheard. Looking at Lando lying asleep on his bed with the T.V. still on, Nakia laid down beside him and fell asleep as well.

Pamila woke up bright and early in the morning to get Tyesha ready for her first day of school. Pamila had been on Quick and Lando's back about getting into school, or at least taking a GED class like Mann had done. They gave her their word that they would do it when school started for everyone else, and Pamila was going to make sure they kept their word.

Going downstairs to wake Lando and Quick up so that they could go sign up for GED classes, Pamila saw that Quick wasn't in the house, but she was more surprised to see Nakia in the bed with Lando because she was asleep when Lando brought Nakia in the house last night. She never knew the girl was there. Walking over to Lando's bed, Pamila shook him. Lando and Nakia both woke up looking confused. Lando didn't even know Nakia had come downstairs the night before.

"What the hell is going on down here, Lando?" Pamila asked. She didn't like people in her house when she didn't know it. Wiping the sleep out of his eyes, Lando sat up on the bed and looked over at Nakia, who looked scared.

"Pamila," Lando said as he began to explain what was going on, "you know this my girl."

Pamila shook her head yes, and said, "And…" Lando told her that Nakia's mother had put her out and she had nowhere to go, so he let her stay over for the night.

"What did your mother put you out for?" Pamila asked Nakia. Full of fear and embarrassment, Nakia looked at Lando for help. "Cat gotcha tongue?" Pamila asked. Lando knew Pamila was too aggressive for Nakia.

Cutting in, Lando said, "Her mother put her out because she's pregnant by me." The whole room went silent. Pamila just stared at Nakia for a second, not saying anything.

Suddenly, Pamila looked over at Landom and said, "So, what you gon' do, mister?" Lando began to tell Pamila that he was going to take care of the baby.

"How you think you gon' do that?" Pamila asked. Lando knew he had enough money to do it, but he didn't know how to tell Pamila that he did.

"I'll find a way. You know that," Lando said. Knowing more than he thought, Pamila began to tell him that if he thought he was going to take care of Nakia and the baby by selling drugs all night, that he would be hurting all three of them more than he would be helping. She suggested that Lando get a job and get into a GED class like he said he was going to do. She told him that she would get Mann to give him a job if she had to, but she wanted him to get one somewhere.

"Okay, I'll work on that," Lando said.

"And, for you, miss hot drawers. You can stay here until everything works itself out, but you gon' have to let me talk to your mother. I can't have you in here without your family knowing where you are." Nakia was pleased that Pamila was so understanding and quickly agreed to giving Pamila her mother's number. Pamila told Lando that she would talk to him later on when she got home from work.

"Behave yourself," Pamila said to the two young people as she left to take Tyesha to school.

Wondering why Quick hadn't come home last night, Lando stood up and looked at Nakia, who seemed to be pleased by the way things went with Pamila.

"What's up?" Lando said with a smile as he stretched.

"I didn't know your peoples were going to be so understanding," Nakia said.

Laughing a little bit, Lando said, "Yeah, Pamila real peoples. She go hard, but she mean good." Lando began to explain to Nakia that she would grow to love her like a mother as time went on. Their relationship would be way more than rides down Oak Hill now.

"Shit gon' be cool, boo. Watch," Lando said as he leaned over and kissed Nakia.

After taking a shower, Lando was coming back downstairs when he heard the door open behind him. Mann was coming in the door wearing one of the sweatshirts with Jazmin's design on it.

"What's up, joe?" Lando said as he turned and walked over to Mann.

Giving Mann five, Lando said, "I got some shit to tell you, joe."

Mann walked over to the sofa and sat down, saying, "I got something to tell you, too. You want the good news or the bad news first?" Lando quickly became alert, wondering what the bad news could be.

"Fuck it," Lando said as he sat down beside Mann in his towel. "Give me the good news first, joe." Mann pulled a knot of money out of his pocket and gave Lando five hundred dollars, telling him that Jazmin's design was selling like hot cakes and that he wanted Lando to give her two hundred dollars for coming up with the design.

"For every shirt I sell, I'ma give her $15," Mann said.

Smiling, Lando said, "She gon' love this here, slim."

Bracing himself for whatever the bad news could be, Lando said, "So, what's the bad news?"

Growing up with all of the older dudes on Georgia Avenue where Lando and all of the young niggas sold coke, Mann knew Lip from back in the day. They were close. After the shooting on the Ave., Lip took Short Dogg, Quick, and Lil' Garvin to the hospital. Short Dogg had gotten shot in the leg as he ran toward the shooters. Coming back uptown, Lip beeped Pat-Pat to tell him what had happened and to see if he knew what was going on. Pat-Pat didn't know of anyone who would want to come up the Ave. shooting at the time, but did know that Quick and Lando were Mann's peoples, so he beeped Mann and put him on point with everything that Lip had told him.

"So, Short Dogg the only one that got hit last night?" Lando asked as his anger grew a little bit.

"Yeah shorty, the only one that got hit out there," Mann said. "But, I think shorty may know why them niggas came up the Ave. busting. When you catch up with 'em find out." Lando thought about what Mann said and was surely going to see if he could find out who shot his man.

"I got that, slim, don't worry about that," Lando said as he stood up with the money in his hand.

"So, what you got to tell me, joe?" Mann asked. Lando began telling Mann about how he was about to be a father and how Pamila was going to let Nakia stay over the house until he decided what he was going to do. Mann smiled. He could see that Lando was already looking forward to having the baby. But, Mann knew that he couldn't live in the basement with Nakia while Quick stayed down there.

"I'm happy for you, shorty," Mann said as he stood up. "But, now you gon have to think for three people. It ain't no more ride or die shit, you got a youngin' on the way." Mann told Lando that he felt that it would be best for him to get a little apartment for him and Nakia.

"I like that idea. I'ma need somebody to put their joint in their name for me, though," Lando said. Mann told him not to worry about it, and that he would have an apartment for Lando by the end of the week. Before leaving the house, Mann reminded Lando to find out if Short Dogg knew who had come up the Ave. shooting.

"I got that, joe. I'ma catch you later," Lando said.

Downstairs in the basement, Lando got dressed while he told Nakia that he was going to get them an apartment by the end of the week.

"So, if your mother still act like she don't want you to come back home, we'll go ahead and live together. I know you'll like that," Lando said, smiling at Nakia. She was excited by the sound of having Lando all to herself.

"What you think Pamila gon' say?" she asked.

Lando told her that he would make Pamila understand what he was doing. While they talked, the phone rang. Quick was calling from Short Dogg's aunt's house around the corner. Quick told Lando to come over as soon as he could. Lando hung up the phone and told Nakia that he would be back later.

"Where you going?" she asked as she stood up and hugged Lando.

"I gotta take care of something," Lando said. He kissed Nakia and hit the door.

Walking in the basement door of Short Dogg's aunt's house, Lando saw him lying on a pullout bed with his thigh wrapped up in bandages. Quick, Lil' Garvin, Baby-D, and Tank all sat around him, talking about what needed to be done about the three gunmen that had came up the Ave. shooting.

"Hold up! Hold up!" Lando said as he walked over and sat down beside Short Dogg. He just knew that he was missing too much of the story if they were already talking about what needed to be done. "Y'all already know who did the bustin'?" Lando asked the room as he looked around.

"Yeah, some niggas from around my mother's way out S.E. did it," Short Dogg said.

Two years ago, Short Dogg killed an older dude around his way along with an old partner of his who later testified on him in juvenile court which is how he got sent down Oak Hill and met Lando and Quick. The older dude that he killed had two little brothers that were Short Dogg's age. Short Dogg knew that they were looking for him along with an older cousin of theirs, but he thought he could take care of the beef himself without bringing Lando and everyone else into it.

"We in it now, joe!" Lando said as he looked around the room once again. "We ain't no fuck with you halfway niggas. If we fuck with you, we fuck with you, joe!" Lando made it clear that he was with whatever Short Dogg was trying to do and Short Dogg felt the realness in the room.

"So, where these niggas be at?" Lando asked. Short Dogg told him where the dudes could be found. Lando shook his head, and said, "We gon' see what them niggas really 'bout." Standing up, Lando told everybody to meet him at Pamila's house later on so they could take a ride out S.E..

"I gotta go sign up for dis GED class, I'm holla at Black on my way down there. We gon' get that K he got and tear shit up," Lando said as he left the house.

School was letting out as Lando was coming back from signing up for the GED class. He decided to stop in front of the High School to see if he could catch Jazmin.

Sitting in his car with Tupac blasting out of the speakers, Lando watched all of the young people go back and forth in all of their new school gear. Lando was surprised to see five sweatshirts with Jazmin's design on them, he felt good that he played a part of the whole thing. Seeing all of the high school kids getting on the bus, Lando thought back to when he was a regular kid. The fast lane had forced him to grow up and he was knee deep in it. There was no turning back for him.

Jazmin saw Lando's car as she walked up the hill on Georgia Avenue with a few friends. Breaking off from the crowd, she walked up and got in Lando's car.

"What's up, boy?" Jazmin said with an excited smile as she leaned over and kissed Lando on the cheek.

Starting the car up and whipping it into a U-turn across to the other side of Georgia Avenue through the traffic, Lando said, "I got a surprise for you," as he pulled out the money Mann had given him for Jazmin.

"My brother wants you to have this for your shirts. Them joints must be sellin'." With a bright smile on her face, Jazmin took the money and thanked Lando for getting her shirt made.

"I seen a rack of people at school with my shirt on," Jazmin said. She couldn't believe it. Not only had her respect for Lando grown, but her respect for Mann was starting to develop. Lando encouraged her to keep on working on her designs as he drove her home.

As the night grew dark, Lando made his way to Mann's old apartment out White Oak to pick up a few bricks. Walking in the door, he saw Black and Dre sitting on the sofa talking about some young dude that had disrespected Dre earlier.

Dre had given an old female friend a ride home after leaving Mann's World. When he dropped her off at her house, her baby's father was out front with a few other young dudes. Seeing his baby's mother get out of Dre's ZR1, the young dude smacked her and started talking shit to Dre. Dre got out of the car and stepped to the young dude, telling him that he wasn't messing with his baby's mother, but the young dude wasn't trying to hear anything. He pulled a pistol out on Dre and told him he better get to stepping.

"Who the fuck is this young nigga?" Black asked, not liking the way things had went down.

"Some lil' nigga name Shawn," Dre said.

Lando cut in, "You talking 'bout Lil' Mousy from around 21st Street."

Dre didn't know the young dude, but he knew he was from around 21st Street. Lando knew Lil' Mousy from junior high school. The young dude was known amongst Lando's generation for being a quick killer. Lando told Black and Dre about Lil' Mousy and how long he'd known him. Dre really wasn't even tripping off the young dude, but was fucked up that he pulled a gun on him.

"We should go around there and air that joint out!" Black said. Dre didn't agree. He felt that everybody would point the finger at him.

"Naa, let's let the shit ride for awhile, joe," Dre said.

Switching the subject, Lando told them about the dudes that had shot at Short Dogg and that he planned to go around S.E. with everybody else and catch the niggas slipping. One way or another, Black was going to get some gunplay.

"When y'all rollin'?" Black asked. Lando told him that everybody would be over Pamila's house in a little while. "I'll be over there in a half hour," Black said as he left.

Mann walked out into the living room after talking to Kelly for an hour.

"What's up, shorty?" Mann said as he handed Lando a Foot Locker bag with two bricks in it.

"Ain't shit, joe," Lando said before putting Mann down with who shot Short Dogg and why. Mann knew his little brother well. He knew Lando was going to roll with Short Dogg on the sole strength that he had love for the young dude. Not wanting Lando and the rest of the young dudes around the way to get into another long, drawn out beef, Mann asked Lando to take care of the situation as quick as he could and to leave no one that could tell on him.

"Watch yourself, shorty. Stick and move," Mann said. Lando took the advice his brother had given him and left. Mann thought about what the night would hold and didn't feel good about any of it, but knew that some things had to be done.

Heavily armed and sitting in Lil' Garvin's van at the top of 30th Street S.E., Black Lando, Short Dogg, Quick, Baby-D, and Lil' Garvin looked down the street and quietly watched the three dudes that they were after. Timing was everything and Lando wanted to get everything over with at one time.

"Let's roll up and jump out on them niggas!" Quick said as he sat on the floor spinning a chrome .45 on his finger.

"Naa, it ain't no telling what might go wrong like that,." Lando said as he explained that they only wanted the three dudes that had done the shooting. They all knew that they couldn't walk up on the crowd of dudes at the bottom of the hill as deep as they were.

"Fuck it!" Black said. "We gotta separate them niggas some how if we only want them three."

Fifteen minutes later, Lando gave up on waiting for the three dudes to leave the drug strip so they could follow them to their death spot.

"We gotta pull up on them niggas, joe," Lando said. "Let's roll." Lil Garvin wasted no time. He started up the van and started slowly rolling down the hill. "Clear everything out and then we gon' run the niggas down," Lando said to Black since he had an AK-47 that was just right for the job.

Creeping at a deadly pace twenty feet away from life or death, Black sat right in front of the sliding side door of the van with his hands wrapped tightly around his AK-47, just waiting for Baby-D to open the door so he could start spraying.

Behind Black on the floor talking to Short Dogg, Lando said, "You ready?" Short Dogg laughed, he wanted to get it over with more than anyone.

"Watch me work!" he said with a little smirk.

"Here we go!" Lil' Garvin said from behind the wheel, letting everybody know that it was game time.

Baby-D yanked the side door open and Black jumped out with the AK-47 firing murderously. Black went crazy waving the AK-47 from side to side, causing the crowd to run different ways. As automatic gunfire ripped through the late night air, Lando and Baby-D ran after two of the dudes that had done the shooting on the Ave. Quick and Short Dogg ran after the other one while shooting at everything moving. Waiting for everyone to get back to the van, Lil' Garvin sat behind the wheel firing his Glock in all directions out the window.

After Short Dogg and Quick had put slugs in one of the two dudes that they had went after, they had to shoot their way back to the van, allowing one of the dudes that had done the shooting on the Ave. to get away. Lando and Baby-D ran back to the van shooting back into the cut that they had just killed one of the 30th Street niggas in. He was one of the shooters that hit Short Dogg up the Ave. Allowing everybody to jump into the van, Black made sure no one would even think about running out into the street shooting by the way he backed into the van spraying in all directions. Still spraying, Black jumped backwards into the van as Lil' Garvin took them all flying out of sight with the tires screaming.

Mann woke up the next morning and looked at his radio clock. It was seven thirty a.m. and he had to be at the studio in thirty minutes. Wasting no time, Mann got up and jumped into the shower. In the shower, he could hear the local radio station playing all of the new music that was out at the time. A lot of West Coast music was playing.

Jumping out of the shower, Mann heard the DJ say, *"We got something new from a group of bad sistas outta D.C. called PASSION."* Mann couldn't help it; he was excited. He had waited for the day when he would hear PASSION on the radio. He sat on his bed drying off as he shook his head to *Destiny*, PASSION's soon to drop single.

"That was PASSION, their first single will be in stores September thirtieth. Go pick it up," the DJ said. Mann's morning was starting off on the right foot. After the next song went off, the DJ came back on with the morning news.

"There was a terrible shooting on 30th Street S.E. last night that left four dead and six wounded," the DJ said, *"Police said it was a gangland shooting."* Mann shook his head. He knew that Lando and the rest of the dudes from around the way were responsible. Mann got dressed and beeped Lando before leaving for the studio.

Mann had only been behind the track board for thirty minutes when Lando and Quick walked into the studio. Mann took his headphones off as they sat down behind him.

While PASSION kept going over their song, Mann turned around, and said, "So, what went down last night?" Lando began to tell Mann how they ended up spraying everything and one of the dudes still got away. Mann had a feeling that was going to happen.,Hhe never handled business like that, but he knew that he and his little brother were two different people.

In deep thought about the whole situation, Mann looked at Quick, and then back to Lando, and said, "So, what y'all gon do now?" Quick felt as though there was only one thing to do at the time.

"We gon' ride 'til this shit over. You know how we do it, Mann," Quick said, looking over at Lando to make sure that he shared his feelings.

"Yeah," Lando said, "We gon' ride the shit out. We ain't young and wild no more. We gon' be alright, joe." Mann thought about that for a second. They had slowed down a lot and they could hold their own in the streets. Mann told them to watch their steps and to try their best to get the beef over with as quick as they could.

Black didn't feel safe trying to make it all the way back to Georgetown late at night with an AK-47. He got Lil' Garvin to drop him off over his mother's house in N.E. D.C.. Black had given his mother hell his whole life, but she still loved him and kept a room for him all the time.

"Richard," Black's mother said. "Here, I got something for you to eat, boy." Black woke up smiling. His mother always had breakfast made at eight a.m. in the morning, her style never changed. The tall, dark skinned woman sat on the bed beside Black and tried to enjoy a minute with her only son.

"When you gon' slow down, boy? Them streets gon' kill you one of these days," she said. Black laughed as he bit into the egg and cheese sandwich that she had made for him.

"Ma, I'm chillin'. I got a job at Mann's store and everything," Black said as he tried to make his mother believe that he was leaving the streets alone.

"You can't fool me, boy. I been around too long. I'm hip to your lil' bad ass, you can tell that to the cops next time they get on ya ass, but I know betta," his mother said. Black sat back and listened to his mother talk about life and how things go, and then she popped up with some news.

"You know your friend Smoke called here from jail yesterday," she said. Black had just seen Smoke and Serge two days ago.

"Did you give him my number?" Black asked. His mother didn't give Smoke the number because she didn't know if Black wanted him to have it, so she told him to call back in a day or two. "Give 'em my number whenever he calls back," Black said as he got up to take a shower.

Tank and the rest of the young dudes on 5th and Rittenhouse all sat in the alley pushing coke in the late night darkness. Lil' Garvin had warned them that some dudes might come through looking for Short Dogg and everybody else, but Tank and his little men thought they were ready for whatever and went on with their everyday money making.

As the pipeheads started coming from every direction, the night began to move faster. The young dudes were making as much money as possible now that they had the 5th Street strip to themselves since Lando and everybody else were all getting money on the Ave. With every second that passed, death grew closer for the young dudes. Chip, one of the dudes from 30th Street S.E. that had gotten away, was on the move with payback on his mind. Not only had Short Dogg been responsible for the deaths of three of his cousins, but he was responsible for the death of one of his partners as well.

Rolling through Georgia Avenue along with two younger dudes from 30th Street, Chip could find no one. He had heard that some of the dudes that Short Dogg was now hanging with sold coke on 5th and Rittenhouse Street, so he decided to ride through and see what he could find because somebody had to pay for what happened.

Chip came rolling through Rittenhouse Street slowly and saw Dee-Dee getting out of a blue Pathfinder.

"What's up with the niggas in that Path?" one of the young dudes in the back seat of the old Chevy station wagon asked.

As the Pathfinder pulled off, Chip said, "We ain't looking for them niggas." Chip then pulled up to the corner of 5th Street ready to head back for S.E. when he saw Tank and the four other young dudes come out of the alley behind Dee-Dee's house. Chip had what he wanted. He didn't care if Short Dogg wasn't outside or not. He just wanted some kind of payback.

Chip circled the block and came back down the street slowly. Tank and everyone else spotted the car and posted up to see if trouble was on the horizon. Sure enough, Chip smashed on the gas and came flying down the street. The two younger dudes leaned out the window firing their automatic weapons at the group of young dudes in front of Old Tima's house. Tank and Lil' Moe were on the front line, they stood behind a parked car shooting at the speeding station wagon. Dee-Dee, Tank's little cousin, stood right behind Lil' Moe shooting at the car as well while everyone else with them did the same. As car windows broke and bullets slammed into bricks and metal, no one knew if they were hit or not, it was all or nothing.

Seconds later, the station wagon was bending the corner at the end of the block as the sound of gunfire died out. Tank ran into the street and spit a few more rounds as the station wagon bent the corner. When he looked back over to the sidewalk, he saw Lil' Moe standing over Dee-Dee. Tank knew he was dead. Tears began to gather in his eyes. Dee-Dee laid in Lil' Moe's arms with a chunk of his young head blown off. At only twelve years old, his young life was over before it even started in the fast lane.

Chapter Seventeen: It's on again

Every single night after Dee-Dee's funeral, Tank, Lil' Moe, and the rest of the 5th Street youngins made it their business to ride across town to 30th Street, get out, and spray anything that looked like it could be affiliated with the beef.

At first, Tank held a grudge against Short Dogg for Dee-Dee's death, but Lando explained to him that Short Dogg never meant for any of his beef to affect 5th Street. Tank had grown to respect Lando and tried to understand what he had said, but it was Short Dogg that eventually won Tank over by riding around 30th Street with him and killing one of the young dudes that had killed Dee-Dee after they had gotten word who they were.

The beef was in full swing with nightly shootings uptown and over S.E. Homicide Detectives were lost. They couldn't understand what had sparked such a war. Vice Cop Hall, on the other hand, knew everything about the beef, but kept it to himself so that he could crack the thing wide open as soon as someone left a loose end. Hall checked his traps on a regular basis and it was amazing how much information he got off the streets from pipeheads and dope fiends. Hall already knew that the whole beef was over a murder that Short Dogg committed two years ago. He also knew that Lando and the uptown dudes played a major part in the beef because of the first Georgia Avenue shooting. It was all a matter of time before Hall would have an arrest for someone's murder, and he didn't care who it was as long as they went to jail for the rest of their young life.

For Lando and the rest of his childhood partners, it was the first time they were involved in a beef with dudes that were bringing the heat back their way. Short Dogg, on the other hand, was used to it and really wasn't tripping one way or another. Now that he was hanging uptown, he still hung on the strip pushing coke when he wasn't riding with Lando and everyone else looking for Chip, who had been laying low until he could pop up and kill one of the uptown dudes or Short Dogg.

Now that Lando had moved into the apartment that Mann got for him and Nakia, he could really feel the strain that the beef was putting on his pockets. Most of his money came from selling weight to the young dudes on 5th and Rittenhouse, but with them going on nightly manhunts, they weren't moving as much coke as they used to, which caused Lando to hit the block more to cover the difference. The extra stress of wearing a bulletproof vest everywhere he went, having a baby on the way, and not knowing if he would see tomorrow had Lando and everyone else desperately trying to hit the head of the problem so that the body would fall, which in that case, the head was Chip and the body was the ruthless young killers of 30th Street.

At a rented mansion in Bowie, Maryland, Mann sat behind the director of PASSION's first video shoot talking to Black about how wild the beef was getting between 30th Street and the hood. Sipping on his drink in the cool fall wind, Black watched PASSION give the camera their best looks out back while the music of their first single blasted through the air.

"You gettin' too old for that beefin' shit," Mann said to Black. "You done done your dirt, you gotta get some money now." Mann knew that Black loved everything about the streets. He lived for it. But, Mann also felt the peace of mind that he got from not being on the block, and he wanted Black and everyone else to feel it as well. With Mann's World doing well business wise and PASSION's first single, which had been pushed back a month, looking promising, Mann was ready to give the game up all the way.

"I feel ya," Black said, "but I gotta ride with Lando and them. It's me, joe."

Mann could understand where Black was coming from. At the same time, Mann knew that Lando and the rest of the young dudes could hold their own. He wished that his cousin could see it that way, too. Instead of pulling himself back into the streets that he had worked so hard to get out of, Mann focused on making his business hustles work so that he could pull everyone else out of the fast lane. Black had to respect Mann's point of view.

As PASSION's video shoot came to a close, Black got ready to leave.

Giving Mann five as he hugged him, Black said, "I gotta go over the jail to see Smoke and Serge. They want me to take care of some BI for them about they case."

Mann smiled. As much dirt as Black did, he was real to his niggas. Mann respected that more than anything about his younger cousin, even though he didn't respect the dudes Black was fucking with. Mann knew Lil' Tim as well, and when he found out that Smoke and Serge had killed him, Mann just added that to his dislike and lack of trust for them.

"Come by the studio later on and holla at me," Mann said as Black left.

Despite all of the madness of the streets, Baby-D's love for boxing never went away. Fish Bone, his trainer, knew that Baby-D was deep into the streets, but he managed to get him in the gym a few nights a week. Even with Baby-D's lack of consistent training, his natural skills kept him above the rest, which was what placed him in the position to fight for the Golden Glove middle weight championship along with another D.C. boxer by the name of Robert Lane, who was going after the Golden Glove feather weight championship. The event had the whole city amped up at the possibility of the D.C. fighters bringing home the belts and being as though the fights were being held in the Howard University gym, it seemed as though the fights were world title fights. People from all parts of town flooded into the gym to see their homies fight. Lando and his whole mob came out. Ever mindful of the beef, Baby-D took three pistols in the gym for Lando to come get from his locker room once he and everybody else were inside.

Music was blasting inside the big gym as Lando and everyone else walked in. Lando told everybody that he was going to go get the pistols and that he would meet them back at their seats in about five minutes.

Lando made his way through the huge crowd and back to Baby-D's locker room. Fish Bone had Baby-D warming up for the fight while he gave him instructions.

"I'm tryin' to see a knock out, joe," Lando said as he walked over and grabbed the book bag with the pistols in it.

"Fuck that shit!" Fish Bone said as he held his mitted hands up for Baby-D to throw his combination into. "I want a smart fight, youngsta," Fish Bone said as he looked over at Lando with a look that told him to mind his business right now. Lando took the hint and made his way back out to his ringside seats.

Silk, Mann, and Black were already inside by the time Lando got back. Walking up and sitting down beside Mann with the book bag of guns, Lando began talking to Mann about how Short Dogg had gotten word where Chip was staying and that once they hit his head, the beef would eventually die down.

Through all of the noise, Mann managed to say, "When ya'll going to take care of that business?" Lando told him that they planned to put the work in that night if they could catch up with the dude. Mann told Lando that he really needed to get the beef over with because the longer he let it ride, the better his chances were to get himself killed.

While Lando and Mann talked, the ring announcer began to introduce Baby-D. You could tell that it was a D.C. thing by the way the gym went off as Baby-D and his entourage, led by Fish Bone, marched out to the sounds of Maze's *Back in Stride Again*. Baby-D could feel the love as he walked to the ring in a zone. As he walked by Mann and the rest of the dudes from the neighborhood, deep inside he told himself that he had to win. Just as he stepped into the ring, Baby-D looked up at the top seats and saw PASSION. Caramel was screaming his name out, which meant not only did he have to win, but he had to look good while he did it.

The Golden Glove middle weight champion was then announced as he and his Philadelphia entourage made their way to the ring with the sounds of NWA's *Niggaz 4 Life* playing.

Dre stood at the front door looking around for any sign of Mann or Lando. As the bell for the first round rung, Dre knew where to find his homies by the way they went off cheering Baby-D on. Walking down to the ringside seats, Dre looked on as the thicker champion slowly walked around Baby-D sizing him up. Dre could see that Baby-D was his same old self. Just as Dre was about to say something to Silk, the first punches exploded.

Baby-D stood with his chin safely tucked behind his shoulder, right hand waiting to fire, and his left hand dropped to the side as he weaved the champs six punch combination. Looking back up in the ring after hearing the sound of smacking leather, Dre saw Baby-D catch the last punch thrown by the champ as he quickly rocked away and slammed a punishing straight right hand hard down the pipe, splitting the champ's mouth wide open.

"Damn, young nigga!" Dre said as the whole gym flew to their feet screaming. The champ fell straight into Baby-D's chest, getting blood all on him as he went out. Hardly sweating, Baby-D turned and began walking to his corner as the champ fell hard to the canvas.

Caramel went crazy in the stands when she saw Baby-D smoothly step back to his corner. She felt herself getting wet in the pants as she screamed out Baby-D's name in the same way she did when they made love. She had a right to be excited. Her man was the Golden Glove champion and it only took him forty nine seconds to do it.

While Baby-D received his belt and was declared champ, Dre sat in between Mann and Lando telling them that he had just saw the 30th Street niggas at the front door. Lando wanted to head for the door so that he could catch them coming out. Quick,

Lil' Garvin, and Short Dogg felt the same way, but Mann thought different.

"Fuck that," Mann said, "Wait 'til this is over. If opportunity presents itself, follow 'em to a nice spot and air they ass out. Don't just run out into the streets shooting with no plan." Silk watched Mann at work, he liked how the younger dude passed the game on to his little brother, and was even more impressed by the respect they had for Mann's advice.

While Mann was somewhat schooling Lando and the rest of the younger dudes, the ring announcer began to introduce Robert Lane. The noise in the gym grew so loud that Mann had to wrap up what he was saying as him and his entourage flooded the gym floor on their way to the ring, led by the Golden Glove champion, Vernon Boykin, who had won his title in the same building. Local go-go band Rare Essence blasted through the speakers as Robert "Fighter" Lane climbed into the ring. By the time the announcer was introducing the champion, the gym was so loud you would have thought he was already the champion.

Two minutes into the first round, the taller and more experienced New York City Golden Glove Champion looked real good. He knew he had the belt and despite the D.C. crowd, he knew he was the champ. For the next round, the champ played it smart and stayed away from the lightening speed of 'Fighter'. Halfway through the 3rd round, Fighter knew he had to make something happen if he wanted to be champ. Fighter rushed the champ forcing him to throw jabs. Fighter put his speed to work and slipped under one of the taller fighter's jabs digging three sharp uppercuts to the body, one to the bottom of the gut and another two to the right side under the heart causing the champ to take a knee in the middle of the ring. It seemed as if the whole city came alive in the gym as the noise factor shot to a whole new level. Fighter could taste the championship. After the champ got up, Fighter rushed him throwing everything he had. A powerful overhand landed right on the champ's chin. As he began to fall, Fighter followed up with a quick uppercut. The referee stepped in waving his hands as the champ fell to the canvas. Fighter was disqualified. The whole gym went off while the champ's corner rushed the ring with smelling salt.

Quick and Black weren't pleased at all, they stood up and threw their large sodas in the ring. The police rushed the ring while most people tried to find the door. Lando reached for the pistol that he had in his waistband and began watching his back amongst all of the confusion. The angry mob grew so out-of-control that Mann had to get everybody's attention so that they could safely slide out of the locker room door.

Once outside in the darkness of the night, Lando and Short Dogg broke off and ran for Lando's Twin Turbo.

Running behind Lando in the middle of the street, Short Dogg said, "I just seen them niggas going down the street." As they ran up on the car, Lando looked back down the street to see if he could see the 30th Street dudes.

"It's too much shit going on out here slim. We gon' go ahead and slide out Maryland and lay on that nigga, Chip." Lando said, as they jumped in the car. What Mann had said to Lando about ending the beef as soon as he could, had hit Lando hard. Lando had his mind made up that he would be putting a stop to Chip tonight, even if it took all night.

The late night hours were hours only meant for those that worked the graveyard shift or those up to no good. Lando and Short Dogg laid in the dark woods across the street from Chip's apartment in Burtonsville, Maryland waiting for him to come home and walk into the arms of death.

At four forty five a.m., Lando and Short Dogg had been lying in the woods for over three hours. The sun would be up in about fifteen minutes and Lando was becoming impatient. Short Dogg had laid on niggas for nights on end and knew that it was all a matter of time.

"This nigga ain't comin' home tonight, joe. Let's roll, I'm tired as shit," Lando said.

Short Dogg smiled, and said, "I know for a fact he gon' be comin' home tonight. Just lay, joe."

Fate wasn't with Chip. He had made sure no one followed him home and had made it all the way there with no signs of trouble. As he pulled up in his building parking lot, he looked all around to make sure there was no one around. After checking out the scenery, Chip got out and began walking to the front door, which faced the woods that his young killers laid in, watching him unnoticed. Sliding his key into the front door, Chip heard slow moving footsteps behind him. Turning the key, he looked back and saw death coming his way. Quickly, he snatched the door open as the first sounds of automatic gunfire tore through the night air. Short Dogg and Lando ran up on Chip's body as it fell to the ground, and filled it full of lead before running back into the woods unseen.

A week later, Lando woke up to the sound of Nakia laughing in the living room. Walking out into the living room, Lando saw PASSION on BET talking about their video that had just went off.

Nakia, who was really beginning to look pregnant, said, "They was just on T.V. talking about Mann and his record label. Mann supposed to come on after this video go off." Still half sleep, Lando told Nakia to call him when Mann came on T.V. as he walked to the kitchen in his boxers to get something to eat.

Two minutes later, Lando came back into the living room and sat down on the soft black leather sofa with Nakia. Mann was just walking out to talk to Donnie Simpson about his record label. Lando put his arm around Nakia and watched as Mann did his thing.

Donnie Simpson asked Mann all about PASSION and what the world could expect from them and the city of D.C..

Looking into the camera, Mann smiled, and said, "Well, first the world can expect to see a whole new side of D.C. Fast Lane Records is going to be a way out of the streets for a lot of people, but right now it's going to be the way out for my family and friends, then we move on to the rest of the city and even the world."

Donnie Simpson was impressed by the way Mann carried himself, he wanted him to tell the viewers how a young man like himself was able to escape the fast lane. Being very careful, Mann told him about some of the things he faced coming up and how he worked for Pam at Mann's World store, and eventually bought it with money loaned from the bank.

"Overall," Mann said, "anybody can make it if they put they heart into it."

Lando watched as Mann finished his interview. He was always impressed with his bigger brother and he knew that one day he would be able to lay back and wash his hands of the streets as soon as he had enough money to do it. Now that Chip was dead, he could put his mind back on money making, even though Tank and the 5th Street youngins had their mind set on riding things out until there was no more 30th Street.

Laid back in the passenger seat of Quick's truck, Lando told Quick how Mann had carried things on BET.

Pulling up in front of Wilson High School to pick up Amber, who he had been seeing for a while, Quick said, "Mann always makin' something happen. I respect that about the nigga."

Looking out of the window at the school kids that were his age, Lando said, "That ain't all, slim." He began to tell Quick how Mann was going to wash his hands of the coke game and stick with his store and record label.

Not really believing what Lando had said, Quick responded, "So, Mann just gon' give up all that money on the streets?" Lando explained to him that Mann didn't care about the streets anymore now that he had made his way out. Mann was going to turn Lando on to his coke connect so that he wouldn't have to deal with someone he didn't know.

"So what, Mann gon' put you down with Silk?" Quick asked.

As Amber walked up to the truck with her books in hand, Lando said, "Yeah, we 'bout to be on for real, slim."

Feeding one hundred dollar bills into a money counter, Mann and Silk sat in the dining room of Mann's apartment.

"So, you out? No more hustlin', no more streets or nothing?" Silk asked Mann after he finished telling him that he was through with the coke game.

"I'm done, slim. I got what I came for," Mann said as he pulled one stack of money out of the machine and placed another into it. With nine hundred and fifty seven thousand dollars counted on the dining room table, Mann told Silk how he wanted him to deal with Lando so that he didn't have to deal with just anybody on the streets.

"We gon' see where Lando's head at," Silk said. "If shorty want to make some cash, I got 'em, but if he still wanna be some wild west gun slinger, I can't fuck with 'em." Mann had to respect where Silk was coming from and it was all on how Lando carried things when he arrived.

Lando walked into Mann's apartment minutes later and saw all the money that Mann was stacking into a big safe.

"What's up, shorty?" Mann said as he shut the safe and sat back down at the table. "Sit down, joe. We got to holla at you," Mann said. Lando walked over, gave Silk five, and sat down. Mann began telling Lando that Silk was willing to fuck with him as long as his mind was right. Lando understood just where everything was going.

"I feel y'all, slim," Lando said as he looked at Silk. "Man, I got a baby on the way now. I ain't trying to be stuck in the streets forever." Mann and Silk could see that Lando was serious about getting paper.

"Look here," Silk said, "I'ma make sure you get what you got comin', but you gotta understand a few things." As Silk told Lando that he would only be dealing with him and none of his little buddies, Lando listened and took everything to heart.

"Our business is our business," Silk said.

Mann looked at Lando, and said, "You dig what he sayin', shorty?" Lando understood very well. Standing up, Lando reached across the table and gave Silk five again before leaving to take Nakia out to eat.

Down Georgia Avenue on Morton Street, Black sat on top of his new Nissan Pathfinder talking to one of his old buddies about where to find a witness that was telling on Smoke and Serge. Will, a dark skinned, slick, young nigga that had been around a long time, began telling Black that he knew the witness, whose name was Kindle.

"That bitch ass nigga just asked me to drop him off down the court building to take a UA. That nigga probably goin' down the grand jury," Will said, becoming upset that he could have even indirectly played a role in some hot shit.

"So, when you think the nigga gon' be back around here?" Black asked as he watched the non-stop traffic of money and coke being exchanged from hand to hand.

Turning around to serve a pipehead, Will said, "That nigga should be back around here 'bout ten." Black jumped down off of the hood and told Will that he would be back later.

Tank and his little crew all stood on Rittenhouse Street pushing coke from hand to hand when Lil' Garvin came through in his 850.

Rolling down the window as he stopped in front of Old Tima's house, Tank walked up to the car, and said, "What's up, young?" as he jumped in. Backing into a parking space, Lil' Garvin handed Tank two bricks of coke while looking around to make sure no unwanted eyes looked on.

Tank tucked the bricks under his sweatshirt and handed Lil' Garvin a brown paper bag with nineteen thousand dollars in it, and said, "I'ma have the rest of that tonight."

Lil' Garvin had grown a lot of love for Tank and he knew that Dee-Dee's death was still bothering him deep down inside, but Lil' Garvin also knew that if Tank kept taking his little crew on murder moves over 30th Street almost every other night that shorty would eventually get them all killed or locked up. Lil' Garvin had to say something to Tank about the way he was carrying things.

"Look here, joe," Lil' Garvin said as he looked up the street through his rear view mirror, "I know you still fucked up about Dee-Dee, but the niggas that did that shit dead now. You can't keep ridin' to be ridin'. No matter how many niggas you kill, you can't bring shorty back." Tank could feel Lil' Garvin and he had felt a lot better when he found out that someone had killed Chip, but he just couldn't stop beefing with the dudes that were rolling with Chip when he was alive.

Tank looked at Lil' Garvin as he opened up the door, and said, "I gotta finish what they started, slim."

Pulling off, Lil' Garvin thought about how Tank might end up being one of the dudes that just never get out of the fast lane. Some people just couldn't think outside of the streets. Stopping at the stop sign, Lil' Garvin saw Baby-D flying around the corner in his red Twin Turbo. Baby-D started blowing his horn for Lil' Garvin to pull over as he passed by him and stopped in front of Dee-Dee's house.

Lil' Garvin parked and got out to talk to Baby-D, who was now sitting on Dee-Dee's porch. The nighttime fall air was blowing hard as Lil' Garvin walked up on the porch and sat down beside Dee-Dee, who had just came outside to see who was on her porch.

"Hey, boo," she said to Baby-D as she hugged him, she then turned around and hugged Lil' Garvin before going back in the house, swinging her behind from side to side.

"What's up, joe?" Lil' Garvin asked as he looked down at his beeper.

Baby-D began telling Lil' Garvin how some people had saw him fight for the Golden Glove title and that they got in touch with Fish Bone to tell him that they wanted to work with Baby-D to train him for pro fighting. Lil' Garvin couldn't understand what the problem could be.

Confused, he said, "So, what's the problem?" Baby-D told him that he would have to leave town and move up to Philadelphia for a while to stay at the camp of Bernard Hopkins so that he could start his training.

Lil' Garvin sighed, and said, "Man, you better jump on that shit. Ain't shit around here but the streets, joe. Fuck this shit! This shit gon' be here, young." Baby-D was glad his partner understood where he was coming from.

Smiling, Baby-D stood up excited, he gave Lil' Garvin five, and said, "You right, joe. I'ma try this boxing shit."

Black was twisting a silencer on to a 9mm in the front seat of Will's BMW as they pulled into an alley down the street from Morton Street.

"I'ma go get this nigga out his girl house and act like we 'bout to go get some smoke," Will said as he got out of the car and walked down the dark alley. Black was cool with the plan Will had given him. Will was supposed to lure Kindle out into the dark alley while Black was waiting in the darkness of the cool night.

Hiding behind a huge dumpster, Black waited to hear the back door of the old apartment building to open so he could get rid of another rat. As Black began to think how easy it was to kill a witness that really felt safe after coming home from the grand jury, the old wooden door opened. Black stood still and listened to the first footsteps that began to quickly move down the alley. While Black eased out behind Will and Kindle, he could hear Will telling Kindle how he had some bitches back at his house. Black smiled under the ski mask as he began to raise his 9mm in the air. Kindle heard someone behind him and Will as they walked. As soon as he turned to see what was behind them, Black placed two hollow point slugs into his forehead without a blink.

At noon on September 30th, people flooded Mann's World and many other record stores in the city and across the country to buy PASSION's first single. Dre couldn't believe how much business the single had brought Mann's World. Standing in the back of the store in front of a huge poster of the three beautiful young women known as PASSION, Dre smiled as three young girls left the store after buying three different color sweatshirts with Jazmin's design on it, along with a copy of the soon to be a hit single *Destiny*.

Dre walked by the counter and told Naomi and Dee-Dee that he had to go take care of some business, and that he had to leave early. Stepping out on to Georgia Avenue into the cool fall evening air, Dre thought of how Mann's plan worked not only with the store, but it looked as if the record label thing was going to work as well. Dre had his doubts at first, but Mann had made him and Black believers in no time.

Walking around the corner to his car, Dre zipped up his new Hugo Boss leather as he adjusted his .40 caliber that was in the inside pocket. Watching his back as he walked up Georgia Avenue, Dre saw an old blue Ford LTD at the corner with tinted windows. As the car slowly pulled up beside Dre, Dre made sure to get close to a parked car until he could tell what was going on. The LTD stopped and the passenger side window dropped. Dre saw the young dude, Lil' Mousy, in the passenger seat. Before Dre even thought about pulling his pistol, Lil' Mousy fired several rounds at him. Dre ducked behind the car as bullets crashed into the brick wall behind him. Dre pulled his pistol out quickly as he heard the car tires screaming down the street. Standing up to look over the car he was kneeling behind, Dre emptied his clip at the speeding LTD before running to his car.

"I told you to take that lil' nigga serious!" Black said to Dre as they sat in the stands inside of Coolidge High School gym watching Baby-D spar. Dre knew Black was right and by not taking Lil' Mousy serious, it could have cost him his life. Dre told Black how he had went looking for the young dude all night. He had even gone over his baby's mother's house, but he was nowhere to be found.

"I'ma catch his lil' ass. Believe that," Dre said.

Word was out that Baby-D was leaving town to go box in Philly. The whole neighborhood seemed to pop up at the gym to say their goodbyes. Lil' Garvin, Lando, Quick, and Tank walked in and sat down beside Black and Dre. While they watched Baby-D do his thing in the ring, Dre told the younger dudes about the situation with Lil' Mousy in hopes of being able to track him down. Lando sighed when he heard what had went down, if it wasn't one thing it was another. Quick knew that Lil' Mousy had a cousin that lived on 13th and Kennedy streets. Lil' Mousy used to live on 13th Street, too, when he went to junior high with Lando. Dre decided he would take a ride up 13th Street to see if he could find his man, and Black took the ride with him.

Waiting outside of the gym for Baby-D to come out so they all could hang out before he left for Philly, Lando and everybody else shot dice in the darkness behind Coolidge High School. Quick looked across the parking lot as he shot the dice and noticed a set of headlights coming in. Even though Chip was dead and the 30th Street beef was dying out, everybody was still on point and wearing bulletproof vests under their coats. As Quick stopped to see who was pulling up, Tank slowly pulled a .45 out of his big Eddie Bauer. As the money green 240 SX pulled up, they saw that it was Caramel in the car with Cherry. Everybody laughed as the two beautiful young women got out of the car looking like the up and coming recording artist that they were.

"Where Baby-D at?" Caramel asked as she and Cherry walked over to the crap game in their tight blue jeans and black leather jackets. Lil' Garvin, who had started liking Cherry, told Caramel that Baby-D was inside getting dressed. Smiling because she understood that Lil' Garvin wanted her to go inside by herself so that he could rap to Cherry, Caramel went on in after showing her love to the rest of her somewhat new extended family.

Baby-D was just getting out of the shower when Caramel walked into the locker room. Standing in only a towel, Baby-D laughed a little, and said, "I knew you was going to show up before I came over your house tonight." Caramel walked up and hugged her man.

"I was just in the neighborhood and I wanted to stop by before going out to the studio," she said as she kissed Baby-D in the mouth. Sitting down on the bench to put his clothes on, Baby-D asked Caramel what she thought about him going up to Philly to train.

"I'm all for you gettin' out the streets. We can both do something with our life. We 'bout to be on the road to promote our album, too. We still gon' see each other," Caramel said. She wanted to go after her dreams as well, so she understood where Baby-D's heart was. They talked for a while about how things would be and agreed to finish their conversation later at her house. Standing up to leave out with her, Baby-D kissed her as they headed for the door.

Mann and Silk sat in the office of Fast Lane Records talking about how Lil' Mousy had shot at Dre while Mann read over a copy of the contracts that Rick had drew up for PASSION, which would give them their first royalty checks for *Destiny* as soon as the first Sound Scan numbers came through.

"You gotta think ahead of this shit, Mann," Silk said, "Dre your man and all that, joe, but you got too much to lose now. Dre and them can take care of that shit. I'm sure they ain't gon' even want you to get caught up in nothin' that's gon' fuck all dis up." Mann shook his head in agreement; he knew that everyone knew that he was trying to make a way out of the streets for not only himself, but for everyone close to him.

Signing his name on the contracts, Mann leaned back in his chair, and said, "You right, slim. I'm not looking back at all."

Nakia was sitting on the living room of the apartment that she shared with Lando, getting her hair done by Trina when the doorbell rang. Trina went to answer the door and came back into the room with Pamila.

Nakia, now five months pregnant, stood up and hugged Pamila, saying, "Hi, how you doing?" Pamila had made it her business to come check on Nakia every now and then just to make sure that Lando was doing what he was supposed to do.

Sitting down on the sofa behind Nakia, Pamila asked her where Lando was. Like always, Lando was running the streets with his men at the time. Pamila shook her head. Lando just wasn't going to slow down at all.

"So, what you going to do about school, miss thing?" Pamila asked. Nakia told her that she was going to wait until she had the baby in March of 1993.

"I trust that you mean that because you can't do nothing in this world without an education. The little bit of money Lando call himself makin' up there on Georgia Avenue ain't gon' last forever," Pamila said. She had started to like Nakia and didn't want the young girl to mess her life up. As much as Pamila loved Lando, she knew that selling drugs only led to one of two things, either he was going to go to prison or someone would end up trying to kill him.

"Well, I just dropped by to see how you were doing. Tell Lando I came by," Pamila said as she left.

A few days later, Silk had Lando riding around with him in his new black Hummer. Silk had decided to give Lando the ropes just as he had done for Mann a few years back. Rolling through the city protected from the cold weather inside the truck, with PASSION's single playing, Silk said, "Shorty, this coke shit ain't meant to be something you do to pass time. You get in and get out. That's why I respect your brother so much. Slim got in and got out faster than most people get in and out of their pants." Silk could tell how much Lando looked up to Mann. He could see the drive to get money in his eyes, the same drive Mann had years ago.

"You gotta think bigger than your lil' block. Your brother made moves all over the city," Silk said, as he told Lando that he would be able to lock things down if he played his cards right, being as though almost every single young dude he went to school with when he was coming up was knee deep into the drug game now. Lando could see the picture that Silk was painting and it looked so good. He began to think of all the dudes he knew downtown, all he would have to do was talk to Quick and they both could talk to Wee-Wee about moving a lot of coke downtown.

Inspired and ready to take his shot at being the man, Lando said, "I dig what you sayin', joe. I'ma get that cash."

Mann had been on the highway for six hours on his way to see Kelley at the University of Ohio. He had so much time to think on the road by himself. It felt good to get out of the city and to leave all of the madness behind him. He had waited for the day when he no longer had to hustle this and that to get things he wanted in life, and it was now here. He knew it would be a while before Lando was ready to give up the streets, but as soon as he was ready, Mann was going to make sure he had a way for him to step into the corporate world.

Mann parked his truck outside of Kelley's dorm and got out to surprise her. Every female in sight seemed to be watching the dark skinned new man on campus as Mann walked into the dorm. Mann laughed to himself as he walked by a group of good-looking women sitting on the sofa in the front of the dorm.

"Y'all know where Kelley's room is?" Mann asked the girls.

A cute, brown skinned, tall young woman smiled and said, "You talkin' 'bout light skin Kelley?" Mann shook his head yes, trying to hurry up and get on his way. The young woman directed him straight to Kelley's room, and Mann was off with all eyes on him.

Kelley was sitting at the desk in her room when she heard a knock at the door. Letting out a deep sigh, she asked who it was. When she heard no one answer, she became frustrated because she had been studying all day and it was less than twenty four hours before she had to take a final exam in computer science.

"Who is it?" Kelley snapped as she walked to the door.

"Open the door and see," Mann said. Kelley knew his voice very well. She snatched the door open and jumped into Mann's arms.

"What you doing up here?" she asked as she led him into her room.

Mann sat down on her bed smiling. Sitting down on the bed with Mann, she said, "I heard your group on the radio up here. I got all my lil' buddies to go buy it." Mann laughed as he grabbed Kelley and rolled over on top of her.

"Things 'bout to get real big. By the time you come home for Christmas break, Fast Lane gon' be what everybody gon' be talking 'bout."

The first snowfall of the year hit the city as soon as November rolled in and everybody was in the back of Mann's World at Baby-D's going away get together. Mann had ordered drinks and all the fried chicken you could eat. With the music pumping through the speakers and everybody having fun, Mann sat behind his desk looking on at one of the few times when there was nothing to fear, no danger, and everyone was family, and it felt good to be a part of something that he could say that he put together from the floor up. As the phone rang, Mann snapped out of his moment of thought and answered it as he kicked his feet up on the desk.

While Lando and Lil' Garvin played football on Sega, Baby-D and Quick slap boxed in the middle of the room. Dee-Dee, Tina, Naomi, and Nakia sat on the sofa talking about girl stuff and who they thought had the most brains out of everybody in the hood.

"If you talkin' 'bout brains, you gotta count Black out," Naomi said as she laughed. Everyone else laughed, trying not to let Black and Dre hear what was being said being as though they were sitting only a few feet away talking about more serious things.

"My man gotta be the smartest," Tina said. "He ain't never into shit and his name don't be kickin' in the streets."

Dee-Dee cut right in, and said, "Shit, we all know without Mann, everybody around the way would be locked up or broke. Y'all know that."

"The lil' nigga can't hide forever," Black said to Dre. They had been hot on the trail of Lil' Mousy for about two weeks and had came up with nothing at all.

"We might have to snatch that bitch he gotta baby by," Black said. Dre felt that she had nothing to do with the whole thing and wanted to leave her out of it.

"We gon' have to do somethin', the lil' nigga fuck around and be looking for us now that he know we came by his people's house," Black said.

"One way or another, we gon' catch his lil' ass real soon," Dre said as he looked over at the door and saw PASSION walking in.

Mann was just getting off the phone with Cross Country Distribution when PASSION walked in the door. Mann waved his hand for them to come over to his desk.

"What's up, CEO?" Chocolate said as she and the other two girls walked over to talk to Mann. Mann smiled; he was too down to earth to separate himself from others that had came up in the streets.

"I just talked to our distribution company. They say that the single is selling well and that they gon' be sending us our first check next week," Mann said as he stood to walk over and talk to Black and Dre. Chocolate grabbed Mann as he tried to walk by and hugged him.

"I knew you was going to make shit happen," Chocolate said as she kissed him on the cheek.

Patting her on the back, Mann looked at Cherry and Caramel, and said, "We all made it happen and shit ain't even hit the fans yet."

Chapter Eighteen: Time is money

"I knew you was gon' take care of business," Smoke said to Black as he and Serge rode in Black's truck to PASSION's video shoot in downtown D.C. In no time, Smoke and Serge were back on the streets, thanks to Black killing their witness.

"We only been gon' four months and shit done changed like this, joe?" Serge asked. Black let them know that Mann had the drive of a speeding train when he had his mind set to do something.

"So, what's up with you, you getting some paper?" Smoke asked.

"I'm jive layin' on this Maryland nigga that supposed to be getting bricks from some down south nigga," Black said as he put his partners down with his upcoming caper.

As the New Year came in, Lando had more time to spend at home with Nakia since he and Quick had found a way to move all of the coke Lando was getting from Silk. Quick had worked out a move with Wee-Wee from V Street that had allowed him and Lando to flood downtown with coke and to help Wee-Wee fatten his own pockets. With not much to do on the block, Lando and Quick both spent a lot of time hanging out at the Fast Lane Studios or at Lando's apartment.

Laying in the bed with his soon to be baby's mother early in the morning, Lando reached over and rubbed Nakia on her round stomach.

Watching videos on BET, Nakia put her hand on top of Lando's, and said, "Can you feel her kickin'?"

Wanting a boy with all of his heart, Lando said, "Yeah, I feel him kickin'." Lando had grown more and more fonder of becoming a father while Nakia, at the same time, was thinking about becoming a mother and had started pressing Lando to get a job at Mann's record label so that he could get out of the streets.

Thinking about what Pamila had been putting into her ear every time she visited, Nakia turned to Lando and softly said, "We really got to think about what we gon' do when our baby get here. You not gon' be able to run the streets and shit like you want to." Lando assured her that he was ready to be a father and that he was going to slow down, but in the meantime, he had to stack his paper up so that they could be set in the long run.

Leaning over to kiss Nakia, Lando said, "We gon' be fine, boo. Don't worry."

An hour later, Quick let himself into Lando's apartment with Amber. Nakia came out of the bedroom and spoke to the couple as she walked up and hugged Amber, who she had began to grow close to since Quick would drop her off to hang out with Nakia when he wanted to run the streets with Lando.

While Nakia and Amber sat in the living room talking about their two men, Quick walked into Lando's room and dived into the bed with his big down coat on.

"What's up, nigga?" Quick said as he looked back at Lando, who was looking at his fresh cornrows in the mirror.

"Wee-Wee beeped me this morning. He got a move out VA for five bricks," Lando said.

"For how much?" Quick asked as he sat up on the bed to listen carefully. Wee-Wee wanted five bricks for eighty five thousand dollars, which he would sell and make forty thousand off of after he sold the bricks to the Virginia dudes for twenty five thousand dollars. Quick smiled, he loved how Lando had things going with Silk.

"We gon' lock the whole city down!" Quick said, excited about the whole idea of being one of the big niggas at last. Shaking his head in disagreement, Lando thought of all the things that Silk had been dropping in his ear for the last few months.

"Fuck the city, joe. We gon' do this shit for a hot second just like Mann did. Once we got enough to get outta this coke game, we gon', joe. Feel me?" Lando said. Quick thought about what Lando said, he didn't want to be trapped in the streets for the rest of his life, he wanted a way out as long as it left him well off.

Mann was hard at work trying his best to make Fast Lane Records a force to be reckoned with in the music world. Mann wanted Lando to witness how it was done, from start to finish. He told Lando to meet him at his apartment so they both could have dinner together with an executive from Priority Records. The whole dinner would be business, and a bigger distribution deal was what Mann was after.

Walking up to Mann's apartment, Lando had a lot on his mind. He was really starting to become a thinker. He had just left Quick at Pamila's house and ran into Pamila at the door. Pamila had been looking for Lando to scold him about not going to his GED classes. She had a way with words and when she was done talking to Lando, she really had him second guessing all the things that he thought meant so much to him as far as the streets were concerned.

Walking into Mann's apartment, Lando spoke to Dre and Black, who were smoking weed while they played video games on Mann's huge T.V. Walking into Mann's bedroom, Lando saw Mann on the phone. It was clear as day that Mann had something weighing heavy on his mind. Lando walked over and sat on the bed while he waited for Mann to get off of the phone. With all of the stuff that Mann had going on, Lando could understand why his brother would have a lot on his mind. After all, Mann was carrying a lot of people on his back and he wasn't even twenty years old yet.

Upset and not in a good mood at all, Mann got off the phone, and said, "Let's roll, shorty." Lando wasted no time as he walked with Mann out into the front room and out the door into the cold night time air.

Once inside the warmth of Mann's Range Rover, Mann finally opened up some as they cruised along the highway on their way to meet the executive in Georgetown.

"That nigga Black just won't grow up, shorty," Mann said. "He still doin' the same shit he was doing when we was growing up. I'm gettin' sick of that bullshit." Mann had just had a big argument with Black about the way he was carrying things in the streets these days. It was time to slow down and get some money without drawing too much attention, Mann was telling Black, but Black wanted to get his money the way he had been getting it all his life. Mann expressed his disgust with the way Black chose to live life all the way down Georgetown.

Houston's restaurant was packed. Mann and Lando walked in and saw a tall, white man sitting all the way in the back smiling at them, waving his hand for them to join him. Following behind Mann, Lando thought that the white man looked like he was eager to beat Mann out of something and it would be interesting to see how things went tonight.

After a little small talk, Mann ordered food for everyone and got down to business.

"So, Mr. Ferry," Mann said as he folded his hands on the table, "I really don't need a record deal as I told you on the phone earlier. What I need is nationwide distribution." Mann had no intention on throwing away what he had worked for just because Priority Records had ran across some sound scan information saying that Fast Lane Records had sold seventy five thousand copies of PASSION's single without a major distribution deal.

"Mr. Mills, you have to think about the future of your record label," Mr. Ferry said as he explained that with his label as a part of Priority Records, he would be sure to see money without worrying about anything but making music.

"Na, I ain't movin' that fast. I'ma maintain control of Fast Lane no matter what you can offer me. I know we gon' sell records," Mann said.

As Mann and Mr. Ferry went back and forth about what they could do together to help make each other money, Lando watched Mann handle himself as if he had been in the music business for years. Finally, Mann got what he wanted after breaking down a few numbers.

"This is all that I can give you, Mr. Ferry," Mann said, telling the man that he would only make an 85/15 deal or it was nothing in it for him. "It's about makin' money, not givin' it away. You can make some money with me, but you ain't gon' sit back and make no money off me," Mann said as he got up to leave.

As Lando stood up beside his brother, Mann turned, and said, "Holla at your peoples, tell 'em I'm tryin' to make some money with 'em, they'll understand. I'm sure I'll be hearing from you." Shaking Mr. Ferry's hand, Mann winked his eye at the man as he left the restaurant with Lando.

Broke and looking for some quick cash while they waited for Black to take them on a move with him, Smoke and Serge hid in the darkness of some bushes across the street from Lil' Garvin's house on Kennedy Street waiting for their chance to break into the basement.

"This our move right here," Smoke said as Lil' Garvin's older brother, Dex, walked out of his front door along with two other dudes. In the January nighttime air, Smoke and Serge jogged across the street and into Lil' Garvin's back yard. Looking around to make sure no one was around, Serge kicked the back door in as he and Smoke went inside with their pistols drawn. Once inside, they looked all around the basement room that Lil' Garvin shared with his brother.

"Damn!" Serge said after about ten minutes of searching.

"Let's get the fuck outta here, joe," Serge said as he began walking for the door.

"Na, hold on," Smoke said as he stared at the ceiling, "We might got somethin', slim." Grabbing a chair, Smoke stood up and stuck his hand into a hole in the ceiling that used to hold an old ceiling fan. The block of the ceiling that held that part of the ceiling fell down, making a lot of noise. Three plastic bags of coke fell on the floor as someone came to the top of the basement steps to see what the noise was. Smoke and Serge took the three bricks of coke and ran out of the door into the night.

Early the next morning, everybody from the neighborhood met up at Fast Lane Records to be a part of an interview for MTV about inner city independent record labels. While Mann, PASSION, and Lando were sitting on the sofa talking about how things seemed to happen overnight for Fast Lane, Lil' Garvin was telling Quick and Black how somebody had broken into his house last night.

"I'm fucked up 'bout this shit, joe," Lil' Garvin said as he expressed his anger. "I owe Dre some money for that shit, too." Lil' Garvin said. Quick told Lil' Garvin not to worry about owing Dre money because they all knew that Dre wouldn't be tripping off of some money that Lil' Garvin owed him.

"Who you think coulda did some shit like that?" Black asked as Dre walked up on the conversation. Lil' Garvin began to tell Dre how his house had gotten broken into. Dre told Lil' Garvin not to worry about the money that he owed him before asking Black to take him over his house so that he could get a bulletproof vest that Black had been trying to sell.

"So, what's up with the lil' nigga, Mousy?" Black asked as he and Dre pulled up at the gas station on Georgia Avenue just across the D.C. line. Dre hadn't seen the little dude since the night he had shot at Dre.

"I don't know where that lil' nigga hidin' at, I'ma catch his lil' ass sooner or later," Dre said as he got out to pump the gas.

While Dre walked over to pay for the gas, Black sat in the car thinking about how upset Mann was after their last conversation. Mann was right, Black thought, it was time to slow down. He knew he couldn't keep running wild nowadays.

"I gotta do something with myself," Black said to himself as he looked out the window into the clear winter day.

As car after car pulled into the gas station while Dre was caught up talking to a beautiful young woman that worked behind the glass at the gas station, Black noticed a big brown Cadillac pull up with dark tinted windows. Black watched the car carefully as Dre walked back to the car to pump the gas. The driver side door popped open and Black saw Mousy getting out of the car with a pistol in his hand.

In a flash, Black pulled his .40 caliber, jumped out of the car, and pushed Dre to the ground as he and Mousy opened fire at each other in broad daylight. Shocked and confused while the gunfire tore through the air right above his head, Dre covered his head as glass broke and car tires began screaming while people ran for their lives, crying out in fear. Mousy ran out of bullets and began to run across the street with bullets from Black's .40 caliber flying in his direction. Hearing only one set of gunshots going off, Dre uncovered his head and saw Black bleeding from the chest as he fired his pistol. Dre got up and saw everybody who was still around laying on the ground. When Black's pistol ran out of bullets, he turned around out of breath, and said, "Get me outta here, joe, I'm hit." Dre and Black jumped inside of Dre's Corvette and shot down Georgia Avenue just as the sound of police sirens hit the air.

"Time is money and I couldn't wait any longer, Mr. Ferry. Maybe next time," Mann said to Mr. Ferry when he finally called back willing to do business, but Mann had already made another deal with Cross Country Distribution for PASSION's album that would be out by the end of the week.

Hanging up the phone and spinning around in his chair to see who was winning the football game between Quick and Lando, he asked "Who winnin' over there?"

"I'm blowin' this nigga out, Mann." Quick said while he threw another touchdown with the Washington Redskins.

"Fuck this shit, let's start over," Lando said as he turned the game off. Mann laughed, and spun around to his desk to check on the numbers and locations of PASSION's sells from their single.

Cherry walked into the office and tapped Mann on the shoulder, saying, "Dre on line three." As Cherry went back down to the studio with the other girls, Mann picked the phone up.

"What's up?" Mann said as he picked the phone up.

Dre said, "I got some bad news, slim."

Letting out a deep sigh, Mann said, "What's up? Put me down." Dre told Mann that Black had been shot in the chest during the shoot out at the gas station with Lil' Mousy.

"Where he at now?" Mann asked, becoming frustrated with all of the madness.

"We both over his house with Mia," Dre said. "But I think we on the run, slim."

While Mousy was shooting at Black and Dre, he shot an old lady in the back that was sitting in the car across from Dre's. Eyewitnesses took Dre's tags down as he and Black went flying away. Dre had called Tina, whose father worked for the 4th District Police Station. She had told him that she thought he and Black were on the run because her father called her and asked her had Dre let someone drive his car because a Corvette like his was involved in a murder.

"Shit!" Mann said. Just when shit started to take off for him, things seemed to get worst. "I'm on my way over there!" Mann said as he hung up the phone.

Twenty minutes later, Mann walked into Black's apartment with Quick and Lando. Mia led them into the bedroom where Black was laying in the bed with towels wrapped around him soaked with blood. Mann saw that Black was sweating all over.

"How you feel, slim?" Mann asked. Black wasn't feeling good at all. He dug the .45 slug out of his chest himself with a knife, but he could tell that he was losing too much blood.

"I'm gettin' cold, slim," Black said to Mann. Looking back at Lando, Mann told him to go pull his truck up to the back door of the apartment complex. As Lando and Quick left, Mia asked Mann what he was going to do; she knew Black needed to see a doctor, but she couldn't get him to go to the hospital.

"I'ma get him to a doctor," Mann said. Dre and Black looked at each other with a worried look on their faces when Mann spoke of a doctor.

Knowing what they were thinking, Mann said, "I'ma take Black out my apartment and get a doctor to come over. I want you to come, too, y'all might be on the run."

The next morning, the news was out. Dre and Black's faces were flashed all over the news. They were wanted for murder once again. Dre had stayed with Black at Mann's apartment after the doctor that Mann got to come over had worked on Black. Not letting anything get in the way of his progress, Mann still went to the studio first thing in the morning, leaving Black and Dre in his apartment.

"We gotta get outta town," Dre said as he watched the news.

Black looked over at the TV and shook his head in agreement. "Yeah, joe, you right. We can't stay around here."

On 5th and Rittenhouse, Lando sat on the steps in front of Dee-Dee's house talking to Smoke and Serge while he waited for Dee-Dee to come out so he could give her a ride to Mann's World.

" I seen that shit on the news this morning, shorty," Serge said as he looked back and forth up and down the street, watching his back for the crud that lurked in his past.

Rubbing his hands together to warm them up, Smoke said, "Where do the lil' nigga that shot Black be at?" Lando told him that he knew Lil' Mousy and that he was from around 21st Street N.E., but he stayed on Kennedy Street.

"We gone see the lil' nigga. Don't worry 'bout that," Lando said as Dee-Dee came out the front door.

Later on, Pamila paged Mann and told him that she needed to see him as soon as he could find the time. Like always, Mann put everything on hold and went straight over to see what could be so important. When Mann got over Pamila's house, she was in the living room corn rowing Tyesha's hair with her thinking cap on. Mann could tell Pamila had seen the news, and knew that Black and Dre were wanted for murder.

Shaking her head in disgust, Pamila got straight to the point.

"Mann," she said in a very concerned voice, "you have come a long way. You have gotten your shit together and got out of the streets." Mann knew where the conversation was going and he felt as though he had to listen to what Pamila had to say, even though he had already had the conversation with himself. Pamila told Mann that she was convinced that Black was never going to do the right thing and that even though he was blood she didn't want Mann to let him or the madness that he stayed in cause him to lose focus of all the things he was doing.

Standing up to hug Pamila, Mann said, "You don't gotta worry about me, champ. I gave Black some money earlier so that him and Dre could go down Georgia to Dre's aunt's house." Mann had thought long and hard about what would come behind the latest heat, and he knew that the Feds would be looking all over for Dre and Black. Therefore, he couldn't have them around while he was trying to take care of business.

"My group's album drops in two days," Mann said as he gave Tyesha fifty dollars. "Ain't nothin' gon' get in the way of that."

After losing three bricks of coke, Lil' Garvin was back on the block serving rocks hand to hand. Lando had given him a brick to get back on his feet and Lil' Garvin had decided that he was going to push the whole thing, rock for rock, until he was done and in only a day, he was halfway finished.

Tank pulled up in Lil' Garvin's van and parked on Georgia Avenue. Jumping out in his huge coat, Tank walked up on Lil' Garvin and Short Dogg, who were both serving pipeheads with their backs turned to the street as they stood in the alley.

"What's up, shorty?" Short Dogg said as he stuffed some balled up cash into his coat pocket. Tank had just seen Lil' Mousy in Johnney's carry out on 5th and Kennedy Street, and he wanted to know what they were trying to do about him shooting Black.

"It ain't in the talk," Lil' Garvin said as he zipped up his coat. "Let's roll."

Lil' Mousy was still sitting in the carry out with two other dudes from around his way. Pulling a ski mask over his face, Lil' Garvin thought back to how Black always rolled with him about anything when he was coming up, which added to his drive to finish Lil' Mousy.

"Circle the block," Lil' Garvin said to Short Dogg as he and Tank jumped out in broad daylight with two .45 automatics.

Without a second guess, Lil' Garvin and Tank went inside the carryout and unloaded on the group of three, leaving no one breathing as they hit the door and ran to the van that was sitting right out front.

Once inside, Short Dogg said, "Did y'all get 'em?"

Laughing, Tank said "We smashed everything in that joint." Lil' Garvin wasn't as excited about the killing. He knew Lil' Mousy since they were eight years old, but he also knew that sometimes things went that way, and that was just one of those times. Black was like blood and in Lil' Garvin's world, blood was thicker than water.

Days later, the warrant squad was kicking in Mia's door looking for Black. Armed officers burst into her apartment at six a.m. and woke her out her sleep by slamming her to the floor. "Where is Mr. Mills?!" one officer yelled while he pointed a Glock at Mia. She swore that she didn't know where Black was and after tearing up the whole apartment, they left.

Drying the tears from her face while trying to calm her nerves, Mia began straightening up the place. The phone began to ring while she picked up a picture of her and Black ice-skating downtown. Tears flooded out of her eyes again as she looked at the picture. She didn't know if she would ever be able to enjoy life with the man she loved.

"Hello?" Mia said as she answered the phone. On the other end, a female sounded as if she was crying as well as she asked to speak to Mia.

"This is Mia. Who is this?" Mia asked. Tina's apartment had just been raided as well and she was calling to see if the same thing had happened to Mia. Both women sat and talked about how much trouble their men seemed to be in while they tried to come up with what they could do to help them, but the only thing they could come up with was to turn to Mann.

On a payphone just outside of D.C., Mann spoke to Black, who was also on a payphone down the road from Dre's aunt house at a local gas station.

"I can't stay down here, slim," Black said to Mann as he expressed his dislike of the country. "I gotta come back up top." Knowing how the Feds were looking for Black and Dre, Mann tried to talk Black into staying down south, but he had a feeling that he would be seeing him soon.

"What Dre gon' do?" Mann asked as he looked over his shoulder. Dre had no plans on going back home anytime soon. In fact, he was making plans to get Tina and his son to come down.

"Look here, Black," Mann said in a no nonsense voice, "you need to stay your ass down there with Dre, it's too much shit going on up here and I don't need you up here getting in no shit. I'ma send y'all some money down there in Dre's aunt name. Don't make no calls up here and don't tell nobody where y'all at." Mann hung up the phone and headed to the studio to put PASSION's album release party together for the up coming week now that their album was out and selling well, according to the Sound Scan.

When Mann got to the studio, Lando and Quick were in Studio D with PASSION, nodding their heads with the headphones on. Mann walked in and saw Silk sitting in the back smiling.

Sitting down beside Silk, Mann said, "What's up?" Silk pointed to Lando and gave Mann his headphones. PASSION's hit single was going off and only the beat that Short Dogg had made was playing, Lando began to rap something he had wrote while he was high the night before. It sounded good.

Looking over at Lando, Mann said "You think you could write some shit like that about what they talking 'bout in the song?" Lando laughed and told Mann he would try. Mann got a great idea, he would remix PASSION's hit single and if Lando could write something that went along with it, Mann was going to put him on the song.

Talking about how he might be on PASSION's remix, Lando told Nakia that if he could write something that was good enough for the song that Mann was going to put it out with him on it.

Nakia laughed as she and Amber went through a book of baby names. "Now you want to be a rapper. Boy, you too many things."

Quick walked into the room with Tank and Lil' Garvin saying, "That shit gon' work, joe. Watch." Tank already knew he could rap, as well as everybody else. When the news of Lando trying to write something for PASSION's remix was out, Tank asked if he could go back into the studio to record a song he wrote about Dee-Dee. Quick supported the idea and he had heard Tank rap the song outside the night before. He felt that the song was good.

Lando stood up, and said, "That's what we gon' do, slim. I'ma try to write this shit for the remix and if it work, we gon' get Mann to put out a rap group on his label." Everybody agreed with the idea. They only had to run it by Mann, and get Tank and Lil' Moe to stay out of trouble long enough to get into the studio.

"So, what you be doing with the money Mann be giving you for them sweatshirts with your design on 'em?" Lando asked Jazmin as he pulled up in front of Takoma Subway Station. Jazmin smiled as she grabbed her pocketbook and told Lando that she was saving all of her money for college.

"You need to think about something more than the streets, Lando. This shit ain't gon' last forever," Jazmin said as she got out of the car.

Rolling down the passenger window, Lando leaned over and looked Jazmin in the eyes as the cold evening wind blew into his face, and said, "I got something in the making now, you gon' be fucked up at this shit here, too." Blowing Jazmin a kiss, Lando took his Z flying up the street on his way to PASSION's album release party.

Lil' Garvin had been walking up and down Georgia Avenue all day exchanging crack rocks for money trying his best to recover from the three bricks that he had lost. After serving his last fifty rock, Lil' Garvin looked at his watch and saw that it was almost nine p.m. and PASSION's album release party was starting in thirty minutes. Sliding his hands inside the warm pockets of his huge coat, Lil' Garvin walked across the street to his BMW.

Just as Lil' Garvin stashed his pistol under the dashboard, Hall and the jump outs pulled up behind him, jumping out with their Glocks drawn.

"Freeze!" Hall said as he snatched the driver side door open, pulling Lil' Garvin out of the car slamming him to the ground.

"Get the fuck off me!" Lil' Garvin yelled as he tried to get up. Hall wrestled him back to the ground while the other officers tore the car up looking for anything that would give them the pleasure of locking someone up for the night.

"I know you killed the sorry sack of shit on 5th and Kennedy!" Hall said as he whispered into Lil' Garvin's ear, telling him that nothing went on uptown without him knowing it. Lil' Garvin felt his heart drop as Hall told him everything about Lil' Mousy's killing and why it happened. Things just weren't going Lil' Garvin's way that year at all, and a murder charge would just add to his troubles.

"You know what, though?" Hall said as his trained hounds told him that the BMW was clean. "I don't even want you. You are not the big dog. I want Black. This murder is on me this time." Hall got up and walked back to the car with the rest of the vice cops while Lil' Garvin dusted himself off, thinking about what Hall had just told him. Thinking about Black and Dre, Lil' Garvin shook his head and jumped into his car. He still could make it to the album release party in time.

Downtown on the 9th floor of a K Street office building that Mann had rented, PASSION's album release party was already in full swing with drinks, food, and a paid DJ. Lil' Garvin walked in the door smiling at the scene. Baby-D was the first person he ran into.

Standing against the wall with his arms wrapped around Caramel, Baby-D said, "What's up, slim?"

Lil' Garvin caught up on a few things with Baby-D, but he couldn't really say too much in front of Caramel, so he hugged his partner, and said, "I'll catch up with you before you leave, joe."

"Shorty got big as shit," Silk said as he and Lando talked about Baby-D.

"I hope slim do something with that boxing shit 'cause he got what it takes," Lando said as Lil' Garvin walked up on the scene. After showing his love, Lil' Garvin told Silk and Lando what had just took place between him and officer Hall on Georgia Avenue.

Silk shook his head in disgust, he had counted Black out long ago. "Slim stay in some shit," Silk said as he walked across the room to talk to Mann.

Alone with Lando, Lil' Garvin asked his man what he thought would come of the whole situation with Black and Dre.

Sipping a cup of soda, Lando said, "I really don't know, but the Feds know too much, so we gotta lay low. This music shit Mann got going look real good, I gotta feeling we can go along for the ride and say fuck them streets, so we ain't gotta worry 'bout what the Feds gon do." Quick walked up and sat down with Lando and Lil' Garvin.

Playfully punching Lando to the body, Quick said, "What's going on?" Lando told Quick what he and Lil' Garvin were just talking about with a serious look on his face.

"I'm with that, slim. I told you that already, it's on y'all," Quick said as he voiced his approval with the music idea.

Waving his hand for the DJ to kill the music, Mann got on the microphone, and said, "This next song is from Fast Lane Records first album, and I'd like to thank the three beautiful young women called PASSION for believing in the whole Fast Lane idea." As Mann spoke, the whole room began to clap in approval of his words.

"Second of all, I wanna thank all of you that came out to support this album. You can expect much more from us," Mann said as PASSION's single began to pump throughout the room.

Sitting back down with Silk and Supreme, Mann gave Silk five, and said, "I knew this shit would work, slim." Silk smiled as he began to tell Mann how he couldn't stop attacking the music business with all of his heart now that he had a group out with an album.

Looking from Supreme back to Mann, Silk said, "Supreme can tell you, now you gotta find some more talent to put out if this music shit gon' be how you make your livin'." Mann could feel where Silk was coming from, he was already thinking of how he was going to try to make something out of Lando and his desire to rap.

Supreme cut in, and said, "Son, you got a gold mine in all them young niggas your lil' brother be with, god. Just think, you can come right back at the music world with a group of real street niggas and they gon love 'em."

As Supreme told Mann how his rap group didn't work out because they were just rappers, Mann began to think about the idea Lando had been pushing him about letting him and the rest of the younger dudes record an album.

Shaking his head in agreement with Supreme, Mann said, "You might be right, slim."

Getting up to go use the phone, Supreme looked back at Mann, and said, "I know I'm right, god, don't miss your move, son."

Sunday night, just before Baby-D was supposed to leave to go back to Philly, he stopped by Lando's apartment on his way from Caramel's house. Sitting in Lando's empty second bedroom, Baby-D listened as he told him all about all of the stuff that was going on around the way while he was gone. Quick, being excited about Lando's plan to get Mann to put a rap group out with them as a part of it, had started writing raps in his free time and was thinking big already.

"Fuck this shit, joe," Quick said. "We gon' be able to make millions like them muthafuckas on TV."

Lando was thinking more realistic. He told Quick and Baby-D how they would still push coke while they tried the rap thing, but if it didn't work they would open up another Mann's World that they would run themselves. Baby-D had to respect how his men were thinking while he was gone and he felt that everybody just might turn out okay after all. As the night began to grow old, Baby-D had to be on his way.

Leaving his men with his love, he said, "I'ma be callin' from up Philly, joe. Stay on top of the rap shit. We all fuck around and get rich one way or another."

After a few days of thought, Mann got Lando to bring Tank, Lil' Moe, Quick, Short Dogg, and Lil' Garvin to the studio to sit them down while he gave them the run down on how things would go now that he was going to give them a shot at recording a record.

Sitting inside Studio C, Mann said, "This how shit gon' go. If y'all serious we can make some money. If y'all just gon' waste my time, we can go ahead and cut this shit right now." Everybody was in accord with Mann's request. "This how we gon' do this," Mann said as he put Lando in charge of the project.

"Y'all got studio time in Studio C for four hours in the morning and four hours after six at night." Mann told Short Dogg he didn't want anyone messing with the recording equipment but him and that if he needed anything other than what was in the room to let him know. After the plan was laid down, Mann left everything up to Lando and Short Dogg.

While Short Dogg was downstairs in the studio with everyone else working on their first track, Lando was upstairs talking to Mann about his chances of really being on PASSION's remix of their first single.

"Let me hear what you wrote for the song," Mann said. Lando stood up and beat on his chest as he began to rap his sixteen bars for the remix. Mann smiled as he leaned back in his thick leather chair with his feet kicked up on his desk. Lando sounded good.

"I'll tell you what, shorty," Mann said as he popped a track tape into the stereo that sat on the side of his desk. "Rap to this beat here." As the track began to pump through the speakers that surrounded the office, Lando rapped his verse again, sounding even better with the beat.

"We gon' start on the remix tonight," Mann said. Smiling, Lando gave his big brother five and went back downstairs with everyone else.

Mann picked up a book of dates that sat on his desk to see where he could book PASSION for a few shows to promote their album now that it had been out for two weeks and selling pretty well. On a Sound Scan listing, Mann saw that most of PASSION's album sells were along the east coast, New York, New Jersey, Philly, Virginia, and few in the south. Mann decided to build on the biggest crowd of fans and made a few calls to places in New York to book PASSION a few gigs. At the least, he would up their sales.

Caramel walked into Mann's office while he was at work trying to put his plan together. Walking up behind Mann and rubbing his shoulders, Caramel shook a set of car keys in Mann's ear. Mann turned around and saw Caramel in a black Mann's World sweatshirt and tight pair of blue jeans smiling at him with a set of BMW keys in her hand.

Mann stood up, put his hand out to see the keys, and said, "I thought we talked about all this spending money." Mann had to have a long talk with Caramel the last time he gave her a royalty check for their first single when she had spent over ten thousand dollars on clothes.

"You ain't made enough money to be out here just throwing money away," Mann said as he went into explaining to Caramel that she needed to save her money for other things just in case the album didn't do well. Mann knew that the music business was just like any other hustle. You had to stick and move because it was no telling when you would go broke. Mann put Caramel back on track, telling her to concentrate on making music and not on spending money. Once he felt that he had made his point, Mann gave Caramel the run down on how he wanted to work on the Destiny remix with Lando. All for the idea, Caramel went downstairs to get Chocolate and Cherry ready for their session.

A day after recording the first take of the Destiny remix, Lando was in the back office of Mann's World talking to Silk after getting ten bricks to move.

"Shit gon' be big, slim," Lando said to Silk as he gave him a book bag containing one hundred and sixty thousand dolalrs. Silk was pleased with the way Lando was putting his heart into the project that he was working on and he really wanted it to work for the young dude.

As Lando and Silk walked out into the store floor, Silk told Lando that he needed to start thinking about what he was going to do if the music thing paid off for him. "Hustlin' and rappin' ain't gon' mix. You should have you a nice stash by now, you been movin' ten joints a week. It might be time for you to throw your hand in." Silk gave Lando five as he left him with that thought on his mind, knowing that Lando would think about the statement for the rest of the night.

Leaning against the counter, still thinking about what Silk had dropped on him, Lando could see himself and the rest of his crew all over the TV making money, going here and going there, and he believed that he wanted to shoot for it. Dee-Dee, who was running Mann's World now that Dre wasn't around, came out of the storage room and gave Lando a copy of the inventory list to take to Mann. Seeing him in deep thought, Dee-Dee asked him what was on his mind. Lando simply told her, "Money," as he left the store with Naomi.

Making music wasn't as easy as everyone thought it was. Lil' Garvin had called it quits after two days; coming to the studio at eight in the morning was too much for him. Quick couldn't make it to the studio on time, either. He also lost interest in making music and decided to stick to the coke game. Tank and Lil' Moe would have fell off as well, but Lando knew that they were the only one's that could really rap, so he went to pick them up everyday for the last week and took them to the studio with him.

Lando had been working on the remix of the *Destiny* single for the last week and he was also starting to get tired of getting up to go to the studio. It was seven thirty a.m. when the phone rung in his bedroom. Nakia rolled over and answered it. Tank was on the phone wanting to know if Lando was going to the studio. Nakia woke Lando up and gave him the phone.

Half sleep, Lando said, "What's up?" Tank was up and ready to hit the studio.

"You comin' to the studio this morning?" Tank asked. Wiping the sleep out of his eyes, Lando rolled over and looked at the clock; it was too early for him to make it to the studio. Lando had been up all night smoking weed with Quick and couldn't find the energy to make it out of the bed.

"You talked to Short Dogg?" Lando asked. Tank said that he, Short Dogg, and Lil' Moe were all on Georgia Avenue catching the early morning crack sells. That was Lando's way out. He knew how much Short Dogg loved making music, so he told Tank to go ahead to the studio with him so that they could finish the song they were working on together. Tank went on to the studio after telling Lando that he would catch him later.

Lando hung up the phone and laid back down, staring at the ceiling.

"You ain't goin' to the studio this morning?" Nakia asked.

Lando rolled over, and said, "I'm tired of that shit, this rappin' shit ain't for me. It was good for a minute, but I got shit to do later on so I gotta get some rest." Lando didn't feel like he was giving up, he just felt that it was easier to move coke by the bricks than it was to get up early in the morning and go to the studio. Nakia took Lando's reasons for not going to the studio and went back to sleep herself.

Sitting behind the huge track board in Studio C, Mann listened to Tank and Lil' Moe rap a song about growing up in D.C. They had a sound that was real and everything they said went right along with the deep bass track that Short Dogg had made for them.

Shaking his head to the whole song, Mann turned to Chocolate, who was sitting right next to him, and said, "These three young niggas gon' be Fast Lane's first rap group." Feeling the rap song herself, Chocolate asked Mann what he was going to do about Lando. Mann had a feeling that the excitement of rapping would wear out for Lando, he was just glad that Lando laid down his verse for the *Destiny* remix before he lost interest.

"Lando doin' too much shit out there in the streets, this music shit take time, and he too used to fast money and getting everything when he want it," Mann said as he let Chocolate know that he was going to put it out after he gave the PASSION album a few more weeks to sale, but in the meantime, Fast Lane would be working on Tank, Lil' Moe, and Short Dogg.

Chapter Nineteen: Face off

Taking advantage of the warmer weather, Pamila was outside washing her car in a pair of gray sweatpants and a Mann's World T-shirt. PASSION's *Destiny* remix with Lando rapping on it was on the radio and pumping through the speakers of her Volvo 740. The sound of laughter and kids playing smoothly floated through the early spring air as Tyesha and a few other kids from the block ran back and forth playing hide and seek. Pamila had heard the Destiny remix over and over since it first hit the air waves two weeks ago, but every time Lando's part came on she would stop what she was doing and just smile.

Looking over her shoulder, Pamila saw Black's Pathfinder coming up the street. As he pulled up and parked behind her car, Pamila shook her head and wondered if Black really knew how much trouble he was in, or if he even cared.

Carefully looking around, Black got out and walked up to Pamila, saying, "What's up?" Black hugged Pamila and waited for her response, which he already knew would be about him being wanted by the police. Black and Dre had been on the run for two months, but despite Mann's advice, Black got tired of the country and went back to D.C. two weeks ago, and was roaming the streets like nothing had ever happened. After warning Black of how much trouble he was in, Pamila told him that he needed to be trying to find himself a lawyer while he was still on the streets so that he could work on clearing himself of a murder that he didn't commit.

"You right," Black said. "I'ma get on top of that."

As Black began to walk in the house to get Quick, Pamila said, "Pull your damn pants up before you take your black ass in my house." Black smiled and pulled his Mann's World jeans up as he went inside.

Downstairs in Pamila's basement, Quick and Wee-Wee were sitting on the sofa playing video games while Spice 1 blasted through the speakers on the wall. Wee-Wee looked up at Black with a smirk on his face. He knew Black was wanted by the Feds, he had also seen his face all over the news for weeks after the gas station shooting.

Reaching out his hand to give Black five, Wee-Wee said, "You bold as shit walking around town like you ain't wanted." Black flashed a Desert Eagle 50 and told Wee-Wee that he wasn't going back to jail alive as he walked over to the bed and got on the phone to call Lando's apartment. Ring after ring, Black didn't get an answer. Hanging up the phone, Black went and sat on the sofa to watch Quick and Wee-Wee play John Madden football.

A few hours later, Pamila sat on her front porch reading the paper as the sun began to set. She loved that time of the year. The cordless phone beside her began to ring. Pamila answered the phone finding out that it was Nakia. Breathing hard and out of breath, Nakia told Pamila that she was having back-to-back contractions and that she thought that she was about to have her baby.

Excited and on her feet, Pamila said, "Where is Lando?" Nakia had been beeping him for the last fifteen minutes and hadn't heard from him yet. Calling for Tyesha to come in the house, Pamila told Nakia that she would be right over.

Speeding around the beltway with Short Dogg, Lando made his way back to D.C. after spending a few hours at the gun range.

"Somethin' must be up with Nakia," Lando said as he looked down at his beeper.

Short Dogg puffed a blunt of weed as he slapped a Tupac CD into the disc player, saying, "You gon' stop and call her?" Lando looked down at his watch and told Short Dogg that he would just fly over to his apartment.

In less than ten minutes, Lando was pulling up in front of his apartment. Just as he parked his car his beeper went off again, that time it was Pamila's code followed by 911. Lando and Short Dogg got out the car, and quickly walked up to the apartment.

Once inside, they saw that Nakia wasn't in the apartment, but all of the lights and T.V. was still on. Short Dogg grew suspicious and pulled his .40 caliber from his waistband. Lando looked through all of the rooms, and then jumped on the phone to call Pamila back at the number she had paged him from.

"Where your little ass been?" Pamila snapped from the other end of the phone. Lando told her that he had been taking care of some business out Maryland.

"I'm at the hospital with Nakia. She's in labor right now. We're down Howard, so get your ass down here," Pamila said before hanging up the phone. Lando looked over at Short Dogg and told him what was going on.

"We gotta get down Howard Hospital, Nakia down that joint havin' my baby," Lando said as he and Short Dogg shot out the door.

Mann was the first person Lando saw as he and Short Dogg walked down the hall of the hospital. Dressed in a tan Armani linen outfit, Mann stood outside of Nakia's room playing with Dre's son.

"What's up?" Lando said as he walked up on Mann.

Mann smiled and shook his head, saying, "You five minutes too late shorty, you already a father."

At nine fifty seven p.m. on March 17th, Nakia gave birth to a ten pound eight ounce baby boy that already looked just like Lando.

"Where the baby at?" Lando asked.

Mann told him that the doctor had taken the baby down the hall to run some test on him and that he would be able to see him whenever the doctor was finished. Lando tried to walk by Mann and go in the room to see Nakia, but Mann put his hand out telling him that he had to get a hospital gown before he went in so that he didn't take any germs in the room with him. Lando looked down at his all black outfit and smiled, he could still smell gunpowder on himself. Looking over at Short Dogg, Lando told him that he was going to be staying at the hospital for awhile and that he could take his car and leave if he wanted to. Short Dogg gave Lando five and told him that he would ride back uptown with Mann.

"I'ma see you tomorrow or somethin', joe," Lando said as he went down the hall to get a gown.

Nakia was lying in the bed almost sleep when Lando walked in the room in the light green gown. Pamila turned and looked at him, placing her finger over her lips telling him to be quiet so that he wouldn't wake the exhausted girl. Lando sat down beside Pamila and smiled like the young fifteen year old that he truly was at heart.

"How does he look?" Lando asked. Pamila assured him that the baby looked just like him.

Nakia slowly turned her head over toward Pamila and Lando, opening her eyes halfway, she said in a tired voice, "I was waiting for you to come down here so that you could name our son."

Just the thought of a son some how made life a much bigger blessing in Lando's mind as he began to think of what he could name his son. Sliding up to the side of the bed, Lando softly grabbed Nakia's hand, looking her in the eyes, and said "Shit gon' be like it supposed to be."

Late night on Georgia Avenue, the talk of the town was that Lando had a son.

"I'ma uncle, nigga!" Quick said as he leaned against a fence in the darkness of the alley behind Sam's liquor store smoking weed with niggas from the hood.

"What Lando name shorty?" Black asked while lighting another blunt of weed.

Quick looked around for Short Dogg, and said, "You gotta ask Short Dogg. I think he said Eion, Eyone, or some shit like that."

Just as Black turned to see where Short Dogg had went, the short young teen came jogging down the alley looking over his shoulder, and said, "Black! You gotta get the fuck outta here! The warrant squad and a white van just parked across the street!" Black pulled his pistol and jumped the fence that led to 13th Street, leaving only the smell of weed smoke behind.

Fast Lane Records was quickly becoming a respected name by PASSION's aggressive climb of the Billboard charts, but Mann didn't let that go to his head. He saw something big in Tank, Lil' Moe, and Short Dogg. He named them 'The Youngins' and was devoting a lot of time to their soon to drop album, which Mann wanted out by the summer if he could get a good single out by May. That seemed very much in reach at the time. With the release of the PASSION album and the follow up remix featuring a young street nigga that sounded like a fifteen year old Q-Tip, Fast Lane Records was what everybody swore it could never be, a real record label.

Sitting behind a huge mixing board looking through the window at The Youngins, Mann talked to Tina about what he was trying to do for Dre and Black.

"I done been to see a good lawyer by the name of Mr. Williams, he's the best in the city," Mann said. "For twenty thousand dollars, he say he can clear Dre and Black, but they gotta turn they self in." Tina thought about what Mann had just told her. It was a little light upon what had become a dark nightmare for her and her son, but could it really work is what she wanted to know.

"Do both of them gotta turn themselves in?" she asked. Mann had never looked at it in a one or the other situation, he was trying to get both of them off of the hook.

"I never thought about it like that, but I'm sure that if Dre turned himself, in the lawyer dude could still work his magic." Mann knew what Tina was thinking and she was right. If anyone was going to turn themselves in, it wouldn't be Black in a hundred years.

Sitting on the edge of his bed, Lando watched Nakia breast feed their son, Eyone. Lando hadn't even left the house in the last two days since Nakia was able to leave the hospital. Everything that he needed or wanted was brought to him by someone.

"Don't that shit hurt?" Lando asked. Nakia laughed at him, Lando knew nothing about babies.

Reaching over to rub his son's head, Lando said, "Shorty ain't gon' ever want for shit." One thing Lando promised himself on the way home from the hospital was that his son would be protected from the fast lane and no matter what he grew up to be, he would know that the streets weren't a friendly place. Lando knew he had made a big mistake by forcing his way into the game when he never had to, but he was going to try with his heart and soul to keep Eyone away from the same fate.

At about four p.m., Quick and Lil' Garvin came over to see Lando's son for the first time. Sitting in the living room looking at Eyone like a new car, they all wondered how the little boy would grow up.

"Shorty ain't gon' be like us!" Lando said as he fed Eyone a bottle.

After Lando had finished showing off his son, Nakia came and got him, taking him back into the bedroom, and leaving Lando with his partners for awhile.

"Joe, I gotta sell for three bricks over S.E.!" Quick said. "I need you to get that for me from over Naomi's apartment, I ain't got no more stashed over Amber's house." Lando shook his head and laughed. When Quick met Amber, she was a quiet school girl and in only a few months he had her holding bricks of coke and automatic weapons in her mother's house in Rock Creek Park.

"I'ma slide over Naomi's house and get that sometime tonight, but it's gon' take a minute cause I'ma have to stroke her a lil' bit 'cause we gon' be beefin' about the news of me havin' a baby," Lando said. Quick and Lil' Garvin laughed. Lando always had to run some kind of game on Naomi to keep her holding his coke in her apartment, but he got the job done.

On the side of an old country road outside a gas station, Dre carefully watched his back as he spoke to Mann on the phone about the lawyer.

"I don't know about turning myself in, joe," Dre said. He was sick of the country, but would take it over a dirty cell in the D.C. jail any day of the week.

"You said something to Black 'bout that shit?" Dre asked.

"You know Black, he ain't tryin' to hear that shit," Mann said.

"Yeah, I know, but we gon' have to do something. I miss my son and I'm sick of being down here hiding out."

"Slim, I feel ya," Mann said. "Shit ain't the same up here without you, but it ain't too much I can do. It's your call, I'm down for whatever. You my nigga." Dre thought about his options for a minute and told Mann that he would get back with him after he gave the situation a little more thought.

"I'ma let you know something, but I need to hear from Black before I make up my mind," Dre said before hanging up the phone. He was truly stuck between a rock and hard space, shit was starting to hit home.

Since the Feds had kicked her door in looking for Black, Mia had moved back in with her father. She still loved Black and didn't care what her father thought about it. Even with Black wanted by the FBI, she still made sure she hooked up with him a few times a week in a spot that they would put together just to make sure that the Feds weren't watching her. Tonight, their spot was just outside of the National Airport where Black loved watching the huge planes take off with effortless grace and freedom.

Sitting in a rented black Ford Explorer, Black kept his eyes on the road with his hand on his pistol. He swore that the Feds wouldn't take him alive this time around and he meant it with all of his heart. Looking in his rear view mirror, Black saw a set of head lights at the end of the road. As the car got closer, he could see that it was a cab. Stopping a few feet behind him, he could see Mia's sexy, tall, and dark frame walking up on him. If Black had felt anything close to love for any woman in his whole life, it was her.

Kissing Black on the lips, Mia said, "I missed you, boo." Black let her know how much he had missed her as well while he pulled off. Mann had pitched the idea of Black and Dre turning themselves in to them both. As expected, Black wouldn't even think about it, but now once again, the idea came at him again from Mia.

"Black, you know how well I know the law and I've studied cases like yours everyday since the police came looking for you. I, along with the help of the lawyer that Mann spoke of, can beat this case for you and Dre, but y'all gotta turn y'all self in," Mia said. Black laughed as he pulled into a hotel parking lot in Falls Church, Virginia.

"Mia," Black said as he cut the truck off, "I ain't turning myself in. Fuck that. An old lady got killed that day. Somebody gon' pay for it and it ain't gon' be me. It ain't a lawyer around that can get me off this beef here."

The FBI knew that if you wanted to turn a neighborhood against a person, all you had to do was make it hard for the people in the neighborhood to make money, and that was just what the FBI and the U.S. Marshals were doing after they had gotten word that Black was back in the D.C. area. Lil' Garvin and the rest of the young dudes that used Georgia Avenue to make a living were having a bad week. The Feds were coming through four to five times a day flashing pictures of Black, and they said that they would be bringing the heat down everyday until they caught up with him or Dre.

Lil' Garvin had only made six hundred dollars before he got fed up with the heat the Feds were bringing down on the avenue. He followed his gut feeling and called it a day early. Jumping into his BMW, he decided to shoot out to Fast Lane Records and see what The Youngins were working on for the day.

Cherry was the first person Lil' Garvin ran into when he walked into the studio. Standing to the right of the front desk in front of a gold album of PASSION's first single, Cherry was conversing with the white boy that did all of the technical work for the record label. Lil' Garvin had tried his hand with Cherry a few times but she always played hard to get, and now that she was making more money than she had ever made before in her life, she was really caught up on herself.

With a black Mann's World baseball cap cocked to the side, Lil' Garvin cracked a smile and spit a little game at Cherry once again. As white boy Jimmy walked off, Cherry smiled at Lil' Garvin and said, "You don't give up, huh?"

"You gotta work hard for what you want and you just happen to be somethin' I want." Cherry was in the middle of recording a new song that PASSION was asked to do for Universal Studio's soundtrack.

Kissing Lil' Garvin on the cheek, she said, "We gon' get together," as she walked down the hallway in her skin tight black jeans.

Walking into studio C, Lil' Garvin saw Mann sitting behind the mixing board with white boy Todd while The

Youngins recorded a song for their upcoming album. Sitting in the back of the small room, Lando and Quick were shaking their heads to the thumping song. Lil' Garvin showed his love and grabbed a pair of headphones so that he could see what the song sounded like.

Turning around to the younger dudes, Mann said, "This the next big hustle, this rappin' shit. Anybody can do it. Y'all better think about this shit. Tank and them gon' get rich off this shit." Mann sounded as if there was no doubt about The Youngins becoming big in the music business, but Mann always sounded that way when his hand was involved in something.

In yet another hotel just outside of D.C., Black spoke to Dre on the phone for the first time since Mann had given them both the idea that the lawyer said would work. Black had no problem with Dre turning himself in and he would take care of any business for him from the outside, but he wasn't turning himself in for anyone, not even his pleading mother.

"Do what you feel is right, slim. I'ma try my hand out here on the run. I may find a way to leave the country or something, but I ain't turning myself in," Black said. After talking to Dre for a few more minutes, Dre told Black that he was going to turn himself in.

"Cool, slim. I'm here for you," Black said as he got off the phone and headed for the city.

Flying down Georgia Avenue, Black saw Mann's Range Rover sitting in front of Mann's World. Slowing down, Black pulled up and parked behind Mann's truck. Just as Black got out, Mann was walking out of the front door with Dee-Dee and Naomi. While they locked the store up for the night, Mann walked over and hugged Black.

"What's up, nigga?" Mann said. Black told him about the conversation that he and Dre had just had. Placing his hand on his chin, Mann thought that Tina must have talked Dre into turning himself in. "So, what you gon' do?" Mann asked. Black lit a Newport and smiled at Mann as if Mann should have known better than to ask him such a question.

Laughing, Mann said, "My bad, I shouldn't have even asked you no shit like that." Black explained to Mann that no matter how much people wanted him to turn himself in; that he was going to be Black, even if it cost him his life. That, Mann already knew, but he wished he could change it.

"Well, slim," Mann said with a sigh, "I guess you gon' be Black, but Black gotta come up with something to do about this mess. I done tried my hand and it wasn't good enough for you."

Walking up to Black and hugging him, Dee-Dee said, "Where you been hidin', boy?" Black laughed and told Dee-Dee that he was just laying low for a minute.

"Well, can I get a ride home with you?" Dee-Dee said with a look of seduction in her eyes. As much as Black wanted some pussy at the time, he turned her down on the offer.

"I jive got something to do tonight, but you think I could stop by your house later on to see how you doing?" Black said. Dee-Dee could read between the lines very well and told Black that he was always welcome to drop by. Kissing Black again, Dee-Dee and Naomi walked over to Mann's truck and got in to wait for Mann to drop them off at home.

"I'm 'bout to roll, joe," Mann said. "Watch your step out here. Life is short."

Black parked in the alley right behind Dee-Dee's house and walked around front to where everybody was. Smoke and Serge were sitting across the street on someone's front steps. Tank, Lil' Moe, and the rest of the 5th Street youngins were sitting on Old Tima's porch catching the few crack sells that were coming through. Nighttime was the time when Black could roam the streets and not feel too jumpy, so he made most of his moves at night.

"Y'all ready?" Black asked Smoke and Serge. They were supposed to go on a caper for seventy five thousand dollars. The move was sweet for the taking Black told them, all they had to do was snatch the dudes baby's mother and make her take them to the money. Smoke and Serge had been waiting for the move since Black had told them about it a week ago.

"We ready, slim," Smoke said as he stood up and dusted himself off.

Just as they began to cross the street, the moment of truth sprung itself upon Black. Hall and the vice cops slowly bent the corner in a dark green Buick. Hall knew Black's walk, talk, and anything else that could identify a man. Stopping in the middle of the street, Black looked Hall right in the eyes. Time seemed to stand still as the Buick slammed on the brakes. Mortal enemies were about to face off. Smoke and Serge had left their pistols in the alley and as the Buick's doors started to fly open, they both shot across the street and ran through Dee-Dee' yard into the alley. Black never moved. Just before the four vice cops stuck their feet outside of the door, Black sent two .50 caliber slugs flying through the windshield, one of which hit Hall right in the middle of his bullet proof vest and the other hitting him in the neck, snapping it. As the sound of gunshots hit the air, Black felt a bullet slam into his leg, then another into his back as he tried to jump behind a car. In minutes, gunfire had numbed his hearing. Falling to the ground on the sidewalk, Black thought he was dying, but at least he went out like he had planned.

Life had a way of doing what it wanted to do, and things didn't always go as planned. Black found himself waking up at Washington Hospital Center late the next day chained to the bed being watched by an armed police officer. Not only had he gotten arrested again, but he also succeeded in making his bed a lot harder to lie in. Hall died from the gunshots he suffered, which meant that Black was not only charged with one count of murder, but two, and one was the murder of a police officer.

Black was painfully sore when he woke up. He had been shot five times, the worst shot being the one he took in the chest. Even so, Black was alive and would have to face the music and that was far more painful than any gunshot wound when he began to think that he would never be free again.

When Black opened his eyes, the tall, white police officer that stood at the door broke the news to him.

"Well, Mr. Cop Killer, you finally woke up," the police said to him with a smirk on his face. Black listened as the officer told him what happened after the shooting stopped last night. Black would have been a dead man if Dee-Dee's mother and many other neighbors didn't come outside to see what was going on after Black fell to the ground.

"You might as well get ready to take your ride down Central Cell," the officer said. "You'll be in court in the morning."

Mann was hurt when he heard that Black had gotten shot on Rittenhouse Street, but some of his pain went away when Black's mother called to let Pamila know all that she had found out the next day. Mann had feared that the police would end up killing Black and sure enough, they ended up shooting it out, which was how Black said it would go. Now with the stakes higher and the situation much worse, Mann knew that he was the only person that could help Black in any way, so two days after Black was sent to the D.C. Jail to await trial, Mann made it his business to go see him.

Many times over the years Mann had sat in the D.C. Jail visiting area waiting to see his little cousin, but the stakes were never as high as they were now. Mann didn't know how Black would work his way out of this jam, or if he truly could work his way out of such a jam.

Walking into the visiting area with the look of a man with a lot on his mind, Black sat down behind the glass and picked up the phone.

"What's up, cuz?" Black said. Shaking his head in sorrow and pity, Mann asked Black how he felt.

"I'm cool, a little gunshot ain't the least of my worries," Black said. For the first time ever, Mann could see real fear in Black's eyes and he knew it wasn't a fear of being in jail or a fear of facing a dark situation, but a fear of the thought of spending the rest of his life in a tiny, dark, and dirty prison cell somewhere not even known at the time.

"Shit don't look good for the ole boy this time," Black said as he and Mann began talking about the case at hand.

"Slim, I'ma do all I can to get you out," Mann said, "Money ain't shit, you gon' have the best lawyer money can buy."

Smiling at Mann, Black shook his head, and said, "We both know money can't buy my way outta this one here, joe. I'm through. All you can do now is make sure I'm okay in here and make sure my mother is taken care of out there."

The stinging truth of the words that Black spoke with the utmost authority hit Mann right in the heart. Deep down inside, Mann felt the same way but would never allow himself to believe such a thing. Looking at reality from Black's point of view, Mann accepted the situation at hand in the way that Black gave it to him. As their visit came to an end, Mann felt his heart drop when he had to tell Black he would see him later. Mann knew that later would be behind a glass or in a prison visiting hall for a long time, but he had to wrestle with reality.

Black's present situation was weighing deeper on Mann's mind than he cared to admit, but nothing got by Pamila. As Mann dropped by to bring Tyesha a few outfits from his store, Pamila noticed a look of worry on his face.

"You still bothered about that situation with Black, ain't you?" Pamila asked from the dining room table. Sitting a brown Mann's World bag on the sofa, Mann walked over and sat down at the table with Pamila.

"Yeah, I been thinking about Black every single day since he got locked up," Mann said. "Life got away of taking a turn for the worse when you least expect it."

Stopping what she was doing, Pamila looked across the table at Mann, and said, "Life doesn't take a turn for the worse, people take their own turns. The Creator doesn't place a burden on a person that is too great for them to bear. We, as people, bring forth just about every single misfortune in our lives." Mann listened as Pamila spoke her words of wisdom. She told Mann that just as he worked hard to get out of the streets, Black had worked hard to stay in the streets.

"You both got what you worked for," Pamila said. "I love Black just as much as you, he's family, but he's also a grown man. We can't think for him as much as we would like to. If the Creator sees fit for him to come out of this situation without spending the rest of his life in jail, then that is what will happen. All we can do is stand by him at the time, but life goes on." Pamila had a way with putting things into the proper perspective, and she had surely done just that.

Smoke and Serge had been laying low as they could for three weeks after Black killed Hall, and they were desperately looking for a quick caper. Down to one thousand dollars between the two of them, it was time for another taking.

"We gotta find a move quick," Serge said as he and Smoke rode down Rittenhouse Street in Black's Pathfinder.

"One way or another, we gon' come off," Smoke said, "All these niggas getting all dis money out here, it's only right that we get some of it."

Tank and Lil' Moe were sitting on top of a sky blue 1990 300 ZX when Smoke and Serge pulled up and parked in front of Old Tima's house. Walking up on the two younger dudes, Smoke and Serge looked at the fresh paper tags on the car.

"Who joint is this?" Serge asked. Tank said that he had bought the car with the signing bonus that he got for signing a contract with Fast Lane Records.

"Mann just givin' money away like that, huh?" Serge asked.

"Naa, it ain't like that," Lil Moe said. "We be in the studio workin' hard as shit. Mann just gave us a lil' bit of money up front cause he think our album gon' sell." Smoke and Serge found it hard to believe that the two little young dudes were real artist on a record label.

"So, you mean to tell me that y'all gon' have a real album out in the stores and shit?" Serge asked. Tank told him that they would have much more than that if Mann was right about them being what the rap world was missing.

Quickly changing the subject, Tank pulled a bag of weed out of his shorts, and said, "Y'all tryin' to smoke with us?"

"Yeah, besides the situation with Black, shit goin' smooth down here. I'm just fucked up they got my man boxed up like that," Mann said to Kelley, who had just called him at the studio.

"So, what you gotta tell me?" Mann asked.

Kelley laughed, and said, "I told you that I would tell you when I came home this weekend. Just wait." Mann tried to talk Kelley into telling him what her surprise was, but she stuck to her guns and ended her conversation by telling Mann that she loved him and would see him Friday.

Lando sat in Naomi's living room with Silk and Quick, weighing bricks of coke while they talked about Black's situation. Lando was fucked up about Black getting locked up, and even more worried about the extra murder he picked up when he got locked up, but Black had always found a way to get out of fucked up situations. Lando truly thought that with Mann on Black's team that they would find a way for Black to beat yet another case. Silk, on the other hand, knew much better.

"Shorty, I hate to tell you this, but Black got his hands full this time around," Silk said. "He charged with killing a police. It's a whole new set of rules." Quick took in Silk's words. He had started to respect Silk in the same way as he had always respected Mann, and when Silk spoke, Quick tried to pay close attention.

"Black made a name for himself long ago," Silk said as he looked at the two younger dudes. "Even if he didn't kill that jump out, they still want him to go down for something because he done beat murder after murder since he was what, thirteen or fourteen?" Lando began to think of all the times Black had gotten away red handed with things from armed robbery all the way down to murder. As much as he didn't want Silk to be right, Lando started to see Black's situation for the big mess that it truly was.

Just as Silk was about to leave, he turned to Lando and Quick, and said, "Don't get me wrong. I don't want Black to go down on a beef like that, I just want y'all to look at the situation for what it's worth."

Mia was going to stick by Black for as long as he needed her. She not only put her education on hold to work on his case, but had talked her old law professor at Georgetown into taking Black's case for only ten thousand dollars, which Mann had put up without delay. Mia was sure that she would help Black and Dre both win their freedom.

Dre didn't find out about Black's murder charge for killing officer Hall until he came back to town to turn himself in. It didn't surprise him at all, it sounded like something Black would do.

Sitting in the NW-3 dayroom of the D.C. Jail playing chess, Dre and Black talked about their case and how they felt as though they could beat the murder charge for the old lady that Lil' Mousy had shot at the gas station.

"You ain't gotta worry 'bout that shit. You outta here." Black knew that they would beat the murder of the old lady, but deep down inside he knew that he had fucked up his chances of freedom when he killed Hall.

"All I can look for is some kind of cop," Black said about his murder charge for Hall. "They talking 'bout natural life for killin' that hot ass nigga, Hall."

"So, how you plan on going at that joint?" Dre asked.

"They ain't gon' give me a cop that I can do, so I'm have to wrestle with the natural life and hope that Mia can find a legal loop hole in the case somewhere down the line," Black said, sounding as if he had already given deep thought to his options.

"Whatever happen, I'ma be able to deal with it. Fuck it," Black said as he check mated Dre for the third time.

Kelley got out of the cab in front of Pamila's house at nine thirty Friday night. She couldn't wait to see the older woman so that she could be the first to hear the news that Kelley was pregnant with Mann's child. She just found out she was pregnant the week before and couldn't wait to see what Mann had to say. Kelley had a feeling that she would end up getting pregnant by Mann because when he came up Ohio to see her on his surprise visits, he would make love to her as if there was no tomorrow. All of his energy wasn't in vain.

Tyesha answered the door. Seeing it was Kelley, she opened the door and gave her a big hug. Tyesha had grown to love Kelley like a big sister over the years.

"What's up, big girl?" Kelley said to Tyesha as she picked the big child up. Tyesha said that she was just downstairs beating up on Quick in a race car video game.

"Where is mommy?" Kelley asked. Tyesha ran upstairs to get Pamila as Kelley closed the door and took a seat on the sofa. Quick walked upstairs to see who had just came in the house.

"What's up, girl?" Quick said as he walked over and hugged Kelley. "Mann know you in town?" Kelley told Quick that she was only going to be home for the weekend and that Mann knew she was coming over.

Looking down at his watch, Quick said, "I gotta move to make, so I'ma see you before you leave." Kelley laughed as Quick zoomed out the door. He was still Quick, Kelley thought.

"So, what's the big surprise?" Pamila said as she sat down across the room from Kelley. "You pregnant or something?" Kelley's mouth dropped to the floor when she heard Pamila's words, she couldn't believe how the woman hit it right on the nose. Kelley was only about five weeks pregnant and she knew she wasn't showing.

"How did you know that?" Kelley asked, no longer smiling.

"Come on now," Pamila said as she got up and went to sit down right beside Kelley. "I been around a long time. Not too many things would bring you all the way back home."

Pamila was right, Kelley only came home to see what Mann wanted her to do. She felt that he would want her to stay in school as long as she could, but she wanted to come back to D.C. and finish her education at Howard University.

"So, what you gon' do?" Pamila asked. "You gon' stay in school until you ready to have your baby, or you gon' come home?" Kelley had no plans on dropping out of school until she had her baby; in fact, she was going to stay in school as long as she could before she had to take some time out to have the baby.

"I want to move back down here for a minute and attend Howard until I have the baby," Kelley said.

Mann's timing had always been good. Just as Kelley was talking about what she was going to do about school, Mann walked right in the door with Lando. They both walked over and hugged Kelley.

"What's up, boo?" Mann said as he sat in a chair beside Pamila. "What y'all in here talking bout?"

Sensing that something was up with Pamila and Kelley, Lando said, "What's up with y'all? Y'all look like y'all up to something." Pamila stood up and asked Lando to go upstairs with her. Lando caught on quick and went with Pamila.

"What's up?" Mann said as he sat down beside Kelley.

Smiling at Mann, Kelley looked down at her shaking hand, and said, "I'm pregnant."

Mann looked down at her stomach, and said, "How long you known this?" Kelley told Mann that she was about five weeks pregnant and that she wanted to know what he thought about her coming back home until she had the baby.

"You gon' drop outta school?" Mann said with a look of disagreement.

"Naa," Kelley said with a laugh. "I wanna go to Howard until I have the baby." Mann told her that would be a good way to stay in school and still be close to home.

"I'm glad you understand," Kelley said.

Mann looked at her with a crazy look, and said, "How else was I supposed to act?"

Kelley leaned over and kissed Mann, saying, "I love you."

Kelley wanted to see Lando's son, so she got him to take her to see him after talking to Mann for awhile. Sitting in Lando's bedroom with Nakia and Eyone, Kelley could only think of how happy she would be to have Mann's baby.

"How you like being a mother?" Kelley asked the younger girl. She said that she loved having a child of her own, but it was a lot of work. She couldn't go out like she wanted to, but she did get to spend more time with Lando now that she had a baby by him because Eyone some how kept Lando in the house.

"So, it took a baby to slow Lando down," Kelley said as she held Eyone in her arms.

Nakia laughed, and said, "I don't know if you would say he done slowed down. You could say that he just be movin' fast around here. You know how Lando and Quick never take a minute to slow down." Both of the girls laughed at the thought of Lando or Quick ever slowing down.

"What the fuck is up with all this baby shit?" Lil' Garvin asked Lando as he sat beside Quick and Short Dogg on an old sofa in the alley behind Sam's Liquor store on Georgia Avenue.

Standing under the dim street light at the end of the alley, Lando said, "I can't call it, but I'm glad my son and Mann's baby gon' get to grow up together like me and Mann did."

Thinking down the road, Short Dogg said, "Now that you gotta son, you gon' have to lay low a lil' bit. You can't be hangin' out here like this all the time. Anything can happen out here." Quick shook his head in agreement.

"No bullshit," Quick said. "You don't even see niggas like Mann and Silk out here on the strip, joe. They know too much shit happen when a nigga runnin' da streets. You gon' have to start thinking like that, too, joe." Lando looked at Quick and smiled. Quick could tell everybody else how to slow down, but never thought that he should slow down, too.

"I guess that don't go for you, huh?" Lando said with a smile.

Tank and Lil' Moe came down the alley from the other end in Tank's new 300ZX, and pulled up right in front of the crowd.

"Shit look like it's going well at Fast Lane," Lil' Garvin said. "Why you ain't got no Z, Short Dogg?" Short Dogg told him that he put his signing bonus in the bank in his name so that if the rap shit ain't work, he would still have some legal money.

"That's smart," Quick said as Tank and Lil' Moe got out the car.

"What's up with y'all niggas?" Lando asked as the two younger dudes walked over.

Tank pulled some dice out of his pocket, and said, "What they hittin' for?" Everybody started pulling money out of their pockets.

"I guess you think your money long enough to chase mine now you a rapper and shit," Lando said as he grabbed the dice off of the ground and threw a fifty dollar bill under his Nikes.

Chapter Twenty: My Nigga!

The Youngins album dropped the first week of June and had already sold one hundred and fifty thousand copies by the middle of July, making Fast Lane Records stronger than it ever was as a record label. Mann took advantage of the strong underground support that The Youngins were getting and sent them on a small five city tour with PASSION starting in New York City. Mann started out the tour with them, but came back to D.C. after a week and left Chocolate in charge being as though she proved to have the balls and brains to keep everybody in order and what she couldn't handle, Mann had grown to know that Short Dogg would handle in a way that would not put the record label at any risk. At six thousand dollars a night, Fast Lane's small tour raked up a quick eighty thousand dollars and made hundreds of new fans up and down the east coast.

"I told y'all shit was gon' blow up," Mann said as he gave Tank and Lil' Moe their royalty checks from their July album sells. "All things take time. I tried to tell Lando and them this shit, but they couldn't wait it out." Tank and Lil' Moe understood exactly what Mann was saying. They both had just received a check for one hundred and fifty thousand dollars, and their royalty checks for last month were for fifty thousand dollars. Short Dogg had been paid a little more since he had been around longer and had not only made tracks for The Youngins album, but the PASSION album as well.

Tank folded his check up and slid it into the pocket of his shorts, saying, "I'm buyin' moms a house with this money here." Lil' Moe thought about what Tank had just said. He thought that he would like to do the same thing, but his mother was hooked on crack and all he could do was take her out the hood in the flesh. He knew that until she got her life together she would never get to enjoy any of his success.

"I guess I could buy my grandmother a house or something," Lil' Moe said, wanting to be able to share his blessing with someone close. Mann laughed, he felt good to have snatched two young souls out of the streets.

"Y'all got the right idea, but keep in mind that one hundred and fifty thousand don't make you rich. Put some of that money in the bank, at least until next month's royalty check. The way y'all shit is selling, y'all should be seeing checks like this for the next four or five months," Mann said.

On his way out Landover, Maryland to pick Eyone up from Mann's apartment, Lando and Quick smoked a blunt of weed while The Youngins CD blasted through the speakers of Lando's Twin Turbo.

Blowing a cloud of smoke out of the window into the cool summer air, Quick said, "I wish Dre and Black was around to see how shit goin' out here." Lando felt the same; they both went to see Dre and Black at least once a week with their fake IDs. Lando could see it in their face every time he went over the jail, Dre and Black both knew that they were missing out on all of the shit that Mann had worked for.

"They gon' beat that shit, joe," Lando said as he pulled into the parking lot. "I just don't know what's gon' happen to Black on that police joint."

Kelley was sitting in the living room playing with Eyone when Quick and Lando walked in the door.

"You gettin' used to being a mother, huh?" Lando asked as he laid on the floor beside Kelley.

Rubbing her stomach, Kelley said, "I can't wait to have my baby." Quick laughed as he walked to the phone to call Wee-Wee.

"Where Mann at?" Quick asked. As always, he was at the studio working with Short Dogg and PASSION for their second album, which Mann wanted out by the beginning of 1994.

"If you wanna catch Mann these days you gotta catch him at that damn studio," Kelley said.

"Mann got the *Source Magazine* coming to the studio Saturday," Lando said as he picked Eyone up. "They gon' have the whole Fast Lane Records family on their cover." Lando was going to make sure that he was around for that. He was starting to like the little spotlight he was getting hanging out at the studio.

"Shit comin' along like shit, joe," Mann said to Dre through the phone behind the glass at the D.C. Jail.

Looking over at Black, who was also in the visiting hall with Mia, Dre said, "I'm glad shit going the way you want it to, slim." he truly wanted Mann to succeed. Every time one of PASSION's songs would come on the radio at night, Dre would just think of how he would be a part of the glory if he could beat this murder, but then his loyalty to Black would snatch any feeling of hope away from him when he thought that Black might not be able to be a part of any of the Fast Lane Records era.

"So, how y'all case lookin' now?" Mann asked. Dre told him that he felt that he and Black could beat the case, but they had some people saying that they saw them both shooting, which was a lie. Even so, Dre felt confident that he and Black would beat the case.

"I guess it all comes down to what happens with Black's case on the police body, then," Mann said. Dre told him that Mia and the law professor that she knew were doing all that they could. As of right now, they were going at the case as if Black never knew there were police in the car that pulled up on him, being as though they were in an unmarked car, which would take away the government's felony murder intent as long as they could prove that Black thought he was being attacked by a car load of street thugs. The plan was one that would take a lot of time, energy, and knowledge of the law to pull off, but Mann knew that Mia would pull all the tricks out of the hat for Black.

"Well, I'm 'bout to roll, slim," Mann said as he stood up so that he could speak to Black before he left.

"You know where I am whenever you need me," Mann said as he hung up the phone.

Smoke and Serge were sitting on top of an old Cadillac in front of Dee-Dee's house in the baking sun trying to make a few dollars before the young dudes came back outside. Serge was upset that Lando wouldn't front him a half a brick of coke. hE really burned his bridge with Lando after getting a half a brick about a month ago and giving Lando a sad story about how he fucked the money up. Ever since then, Lando had told them both that they had nothing coming from him or Quick.

"These lil' bitch ass youngins get a lil' cash and start thinking they big shit!" Serge said as he vented his anger about Lando. Smoke lit a blunt of weed while his cousin went on about how if it wasn't for Black, he would have been robbed Lando.

"If you so fucked up about the shit why don't you do something 'bout it," Smoke said as he passed Serge the blunt of weed.

"I just might do that," Serge said, "but if I do I ain't goin' at the lil' one, I'm goin' for it all."

Smoke got up off the car to look Serge in the face, and said, "So what you sayin', you gon' rob Mann or somethin'?"

Serge looked Smoke straight in the eyes, and said, "Yeah, that's what I'm sayin'. You scared to snatch the nigga with me?" Smoke burst out laughing as he walked away, saying, "You trippin', I ain't tryin' to hear that snake ass shit!"

The Source staff had flooded Fast Lane Studios early Saturday morning trying to get all the information they could about how Fast Lane Records came about. A beautiful, tall, dark skinned woman in a pair of tight Guess jeans was in charge of the story and the photo shoot. She introduced herself as Grace and told everyone that she wanted them to be as real as they could, and to act like she was a part of the family while she got to know everyone.

Smooth as always, Mann had Grace feeling like she had known him for years in only thirty minutes, and yet, she would never have believed him if he told her the truth on how he built Fast Lane Records. Grace truly thought that Mann had worked hard as a teenager and had saved up to ten thousand dollars to start a little store called Mann's World, which gave birth to Fast Lane Records.

"So, you were never really a part of the madness that went on around you?" Grace asked. Mann told her that just because he grew up in the streets didn't mean that he had to be a part of them as he grew up.

"I was around, you know," Mann said as he cracked a slick smirk. "I'm not an angel, but I'm not what you would call a real street thug."

Pointing over at Lando and Quick, who were standing behind The Youngins while they took a picture, Mann said, "Them young niggas right there, they real street niggas. Ain't none of 'em over eighteen years old, and they done seen more and done more than most of these niggas out here rappin' 'bout the life they live. That's why I put them out on my record label. I put 'em out so they could tell their story and get rich off of it without worrying about going to jail or being shot dead on the streets." Grace was taken off guard by the power of Mann's realness. When she was done talking to him, she tried to think of any man she knew that was as strong-willed as Mann, and she could think of none as she walked over to talk to PASSION.

"So, tell me, girls," Grace said with a smile. "Which one of you thinks Mann is as fine as I do?" Grace's realness broke the ice well and got all three girls to open right up and tell her about how Mann ran Fast Lane Records so well. Chocolate was outspoken as always as she took Grace back to the days when they all worked at Bloomingdale's and were all broke.

"Mann pushed us, he inspired us to sing, he made us believe we could make it, and not even a year later we are here telling you how it all went down," Chocolate said. After Caramel and Cherry both gave Grace their outlook on how Mann made PASSION the album selling group that they had grown to be, she wished the girls well on their next album and went to see what she could learn about the new rap group called The Youngins.

"So, you not only rap with The Youngins and make all of the beats for the group, but you also make all the beats for Fast Lane Records as well?" Grace asked Short Dogg as she sat in between him and Lando on the leather sofa in Mann's office. Not wanting to steal the show, Short Dogg told her that he just did whatever he could to help out when he was around, and that he was just happy to be making clean money for once in his young life.

Turning to Tank and Lil' Moe, Grace said, "How old are you little guys?"

"I just turned fourteen last week," Lil' Moe said.

"You're just a baby," Grace said, meaning no harm.

Lil Moe snapped at her, "I'm a grown man! I take care of myself and I been doin that since I was nine." Grace some how just realized what Mann meant when he said that The Youngins were real street niggas.

"This what my man is tryin' to say, miss," Tank said. "We young, but we been on the streets all our life. It ain't just somethin' we rappin' 'bout."

Pointing his finger at everybody from Lando to Lil' Garvin and Quick, Tank said, "We all done did our dirt in them streets. While everybody getting rich off the life we live, we got the scars to show."

If Grace never understood the inner workings of real street niggas before, she did when she was done talking to The Youngins. Just as she was about to wrap up her story on Fast Lane Records, she asked if anyone had anything that they wanted to say.

Lando slowly raised his hand, and said, "Yeah, at the end of your story about us I want you to let the world know that Fast Lane Records got two members behind bars at the D.C. Jail and that we love 'em and can't wait for 'em to come home." Grace asked what their names were so that she could put them in the story.

"We call 'em Black and Dre, and shit ain't gon' be the same 'til they come home, and we got two other members of the family that ain't here that we call Silk and Baby-D," Lando said. "Make sure you put them in there, too."

Looking over at Mann, Grace said, "Anything else you wanna say?"

Mann looked around the room, and said, "What you see is what you get when you dealin' with us. Actions speak louder than words. You see how real Fast Lane Records is, let the world know what you seen while you was here with us. Ain't nobody like us, D.C. gon' bring a whole nother side of the game to the table with Fast Lane Records."

A month later, people all the way on the west coast were talking about the little D.C. record label called Fast Lane Records, thanks to the five page story in the *Source*'s August issue with Mann, PASSION, and The Youngins on the cover standing in front of an image of the White House. MTV decided that they wanted a piece of the pie and started playing The Youngins last video called *Masked Up*. Mann was on top of his game and it was no turning back.

Mann had spent all day at the studio today working on a single to PASSION's next album. From eight a.m. until one a.m.,

Mann, PASSION, and Short Dogg had been at work. Dead tired, they all called it a night.

"I'll see you in the morning," Cherry said as she walked out the door into the dark summer night with Caramel and Chocolate. Mann and Short Dogg followed right behind them and went their separate ways.

Thirty minutes later, Mann was pulling up in the parking lot outside of his apartment. Half sleep, he looked around and pulled his .40 caliber from under the dash board and got out of his truck walking down to his building. In the dead of the night, he could hear every living thing near by it seemed. Always on point, Mann heard something run across the parking lot and into the woods. Still walking, Mann went up to his building and let himself in the front door.

As Mann walked up the steps to his apartment, he got a strange feeling in his gut and he stopped dead in his tracks to look over his shoulder to see if he was alone in the hallway, no one was behind him. Mann began to think he was tripping as he turned back around and reached into his pockets for his door key. Out of nowhere, two dudes in ski masks popped out of the door to the stairway. Shocked and somewhat off guard, Mann froze as the dudes slowly walked toward him.

"Don't move, nigga!" the taller of the two dudes said as he pointed a .357 magnum at Mann. The other dude held a Tec-9, but he somewhat stood behind the taller one. Mann could tell that the two dudes were unsure how they wanted to come at him, so he tried to play his cards right.

"What y'all want, slim?" Mann said as he slowly raised his hands in the air. The taller dude began to walk closer and closer to Mann as if he was trying to grab him. Fed up with guessing, Mann rushed the taller dude with the .357. BOOM! The .357 went off, shaking the walls of the little hallway.

Hit in the chest, Mann wrestled the dude for the pistol while the other one tried to get a clear shot. The .357 went off again, going through Mann's hand and slamming into his thigh as he and the gunman fell to the ground. Mann managed to snatch the pistol away from the dude as they rolled over on the floor. With the masked man on top of him, Mann fired the pistol twice into his neck, killing him. Using the dead body as a shield, Mann fired the last two bullets at the short dude that had started to run down the hallway, but it did no good, he was gone down the stairs.

Coughing blood out of his mouth, Mann struggled to push the dead body off of him. Out of breath, Mann dropped the empty pistol and tried to stand up without success. He was too weak, so he did the only thing he had the strength to do; he pulled the mask off of the dead body beside him to see the face of the man that shot him. "Bitch ass nigga!" Mann managed to say when he saw his shooter. It was Serge.

Kelley heard the loud gunshots and ran to the door. She almost passed out when she saw Mann laying on the floor covered in blood.

"Ohmi God!" Kelley screamed as she ran over and tried to pick Mann up.

"Don't," he said. "Call an ambulance." Kelley ran inside to do just that as the hallway began to fill with people that wanted to see what was going on.

Mann and Serge were both dead by the time the paramedics and police got on the scene. Kelley broke down when she saw the police cover Mann with plastic.

She rushed the officer, screaming, "No! No! Don't put that on him take him to the hospital, he ain't dead!" The officer grabbed Kelley with both hands and tried to calm her down.

"Miss, we have to do this, that man is dead. Do you know what happened out here?" the officer asked. Kelley couldn't even think straight. She looked down and saw Serge's face for the first time and put everything together, he had to have been the one that shot Mann. Yelling and screaming, she began to kick Serge's dead body. The police grabbed her and took her inside of Mann's apartment to get her away from the dead bodies.

Pamila's phone rang at three a.m. Rolling over to see who in their right mind was calling her house at that time of night, she answered the phone and thought she heard Kelley's voice saying, "Pamila." She could tell that someone was crying, but she wasn't sure.

"Kelley?" Pamila asked.

"Yeah, it's me," Kelley said, still crying.

"What's wrong with you, girl?" Pamila asked.

"It's Mann."

"What about Mann?" Pamila said in a shaky voice.

"He's…"

"He's what?!"

"He's dead," Kelley said. Pamila sat on the phone for almost a minute before saying anything.

"What the fuck you mean he's dead!" Pamila snapped. Kelley exploded with sobs as she told Pamila how she opened up the door and saw Mann laying on the floor shot. Pamila almost broke down herself, but thought about how it was not the time. She asked Kelley where she was as she let the sting of painful news wear off. Kelley told Pamila that she was at the police station out Maryland and that they needed her to identify Mann's body. Pamila wiped tears out of her eyes, and got dressed in a state of shock and disbelief.

Pamila and Kelley both walked in the house an hour later with a piece of their souls lying in the morgue.

"I can't believe this shit!" Kelley said, still crying. "I know they was trying to rob Mann or somethin', that's the reason they would have shot him," Kelley said as she tried to make some sense of Serge and Mann both lying in the hallway. The police found a pistol on Mann, and told Kelley and Pamila that he had to have fought for his life and took the other man's pistol, which made Pamila and Kelley both understand what must have went on.

Sitting on the sofa with her face in her hands, Pamila thought of how much trouble was going to come with Mann's death. She knew that Lando and Quick were going to fall into a murderous rage.

"Shit is so fucked up," Pamila said as tears began to roll down her face.

Half sleep, Quick came upstairs to use the bathroom and saw Pamila and Kelley sitting in the living room crying. Walking over in his boxer shorts, he asked what was wrong. Kelley couldn't stand talking about the situation again, she looked over at Pamila, who looked as if her whole world had just came to an end.

"Quick," Pamila said with tears running down her face, "Mann is dead." Quick swore he heard her wrong.

"My Mann?" Quick asked in disbelief as he tried to make himself wake up.

"Yeah, your Mann is dead," Pamila said.

Quick could feel his whole body heat up as he sat down beside Pamila and tried to come to an understanding about what she had just told him. Looking over at Kelley, he asked what had happened. Kelley told him everything that she had seen when she opened the door. Quick knew exactly what had to have happened.

"Them bitch ass niggas!" Quick said as he got up and started walking toward the basement. He knew that if Serge was dead on the scene of the murder, then Smoke was still somewhere alive and knew all about what had just happened. For the first time ever, Pamila didn't try to stop what she knew was about to happen when she could see where Quick's mind was going.

"Hello!" Lando said as he answered the phone still sleep.

"Get over here, joe," Quick said in a deadly voice.

"What the fuck is up?" Lando asked. Quick simply told him the same thing and hung up the phone.

Pissed off and still sleep, Lando walked into Pamila's house ten minutes later and saw her and Kelley still sitting on the sofa in a state of depression. His heart began to beat faster and faster as he shut the door. Something was painfully wrong and he could feel it.

Fearing the answer, Lando looked at Pamila, and said, "What's up?" She looked up at him and just shook her head. She knew that Mann's death was going to shake Lando at his foundation and send him plunging back into the streets like he used to be.

"What's up!" Lando asked again, sounding more demanding that time.

"Mann is dead," Pamila said with tears running down her face.

No set of words ever said changed Lando's life as drastically as the words, 'Mann is dead'. Life, as Lando had known it for sixteen years, was changed in a matter of seconds. The one person that could make all things right as far as he was concerned was gone and would never be back. Lando couldn't believe it. Mann wasn't supposed to die like that. He deserved better, he meant too much to too many people. Someone was going to have to pay with their life and anyone in the way would have to pay as well, and Lando didn't care who it was.

"What happened?" Lando snapped. Kelley spoke up and told Lando that Serge was lying on the floor shot in the neck when she had opened the door to see where the gunshots came from. Lando immediately saw Serge being wrong and knew that if Serge was a part of Mann's murder, then Smoke had to be part of it as well.

"Smoke wasn't there?" Lando asked. Kelley told him that an old lady downstairs on the first floor told the police that a second man had fled the scene after the shooting.

Pamila watched Lando's body language change more and more as Kelley told him what she knew about Mann's murder. It seemed as if Lando could see everything Kelley was saying happening all over again in his mind. Quick came back upstairs dressed in all black as Kelley finished giving Lando the run down on the facts.

"Let's roll," Quick said as he walked toward the door.

Pamila stood up wiping tears from her eyes, and said, "I know y'all want to do something about Mann, but I can't deal with worrying about y'all two right now." As hard as it was at the time to disregard Pamila's wishes, Lando and Quick told her that they had to go and left to see if they could find out where Smoke may be hiding.

Pamila's heart began to pound as Lando and Quick left the house to somehow try to make a wrong situation right. Kelley knew that Lando and Quick were going to be out of control until they found Smoke, she knew that they were in a state of mind where nothing mattered and it scared her.

"I gotta do something," Pamila said as she tried to think. She knew that she was going to have to stay focused at this painful time in order to save Lando and Quick from their anger.

"Don't you know Mann's friend, Silk?" Pamila asked Kelley. Kelley told her she did, in fact, know him.

"Call 'em, I want to talk to him. He's going to have to help me calm them down," Pamila said.

By noon, Mann's death was the talk of the city from news to radio, everyone knew that the twenty year old CEO of Fast Lane Records had been shot to death in what police thought was a failed robbery attempt. Chocolate heard the news on the radio on her way to the studio the next morning. She felt as if she had just been shot herself when she heard Mann's name. Not believing what she had just heard, she continued on her way to the studio and just knew that Mann would be there when she got there.

Fast Lane Records was full of sorrow when Chocolate walked in the door. When she saw Cherry and Caramel sitting on the sofa in the lobby crying, she knew that what she heard was true.

"No!" Chocolate said as the truth hit her hard deep within her soul. "Mann ain't dead!"

Not used to seeing the stronger girl hurt, Caramel quickly got up and hugged her, saying, "It's okay, it's okay."

"It's not okay!" Chocolate said as she weeped on Caramel's shoulder. Short Dogg walked down the hall with Tank and saw the three girls all crying. He had just got off the phone with Pamila, who had told him all that had went down no longer than an hour after he had seen Mann. Short Dogg had grown up a lot after hanging around Mann at the studio and he knew that he had to do what Mann would have wanted done, which was hold everything together, so he did that. He calmly told PASSION that he had just talked to Pamila and that she wanted everybody to meet up over her house so that she could talk to them about the situation at hand. Knowing that he had done what Mann would have wanted him to do, Short Dogg still felt nothing but anger in his heart for Smoke and he couldn't wait until he caught up with Lando and Quick.

Dre was just coming out of his cell to get in the shower when he saw the news about Mann's murder on the twelve o' clock news. Walking into the dayroom in his towel, he listened as the news reporter gave bits and pieces of the story. Dre quickly jumped on the phone and called Pamila, who told him all that she knew. Dre felt truly helpless for the first time in his life when he got off the phone. He went to wake Black up with tears in his eyes.

Black took the news harder than Dre thought. Black began going crazy, throwing stuff all around his cell. The fact that Smoke and Serge were Mann's killers was something Black could not accept. He swore that it was his fault for not being on the streets. Dre thought that Black was going to end up taking his anger out on someone in the block by the way he had went off. Dre really didn't know how to calm Black down and if anyone could, it would only be Mann. The only thing Dre could come up with was getting Black to understand that it was nothing that either of them could do, but that they both knew Lando wasn't going to let anyone get away with killing Mann.

Mann's death had, no doubt, taken a piece of Pamila's soul with him. Even so, Pamila knew she was going to have to be the one person strong enough to pull things together before all that Mann had worked so hard for just went down the drain. Pamila had calmed down and was trying to think of the right words to say to the living room full of people that all some how had dealings with Mann's record label or his store.

Sitting on the sofa between Dee-Dee and Naomi, Pamila said, "I know that everyone here feels the same way about Mann's death as I do, but death is a very big part of life." Everyone listened as Pamila told them that they would miss Mann deeply, but that they had to keep alive all that Mann had started if they wanted Mann's efforts in life to live on. Seeing the look of agreement on the faces of the young people that Mann had helped get out of the streets, Pamila knew she was saying the right things.

"Like any other death," Pamila said as Dee-Dee rubbed her on the back, "we will mourn this great loss, but we will not give up on life."

When Pamila was finished talking, she could tell that everyone was in accord with her, and she really needed the support that she was feeling before she asked everyone to give her a little time to herself. As everyone began to leave, Short Dogg walked around Pamila with Tank and Lil' Moe. Pamila asked him if she could speak to him for a minute and pulled him to the side.

"I want to thank you for getting everybody together for me," Pamila said. Short Dogg could tell that the woman respected the way he didn't lose focus and go into a rage of anger like Quick and Lando and she let him know that.

"I only did what I thought would help the situation at hand," Short Dogg said. "It's no doubt that we all gon' feel the loss, but like you said, we gotta keep all that Mann worked for alive. What goes around comes around, so those that did slim wrong gon' get what they got comin'." Short Dogg hugged Pamila and followed everyone else out the door. He was sure he would be able to play a part in whatever was going to come back around for Smoke.

After explaining the whole situation to Tyesha, who really didn't understand how bad the situation was, Pamila went to lay down for a while. She needed some rest. She would have a lot of work to do in preparation for Mann's wake and funeral. Lying in the bed, she wondered what Lando and Quick could have done while they roamed the streets. She prayed that they hadn't gotten themselves into something that would bring her more stress at the time. Silk had assured her that he would find them both and talk to them, so Pamila waited to see what he would have to say.

Kelley laid in the bed trying to get some rest, but the thought of having to have her child without Mann wouldn't allow her to sleep. She tried to think like Pamila wanted everybody to think, but it wasn't that easy. The only thing that gave her any sense of peace was knowing that Lando and Quick had been searching the streets all night for the one other person involved in Mann's death. Even so, Kelley knew that the one man she loved was gone and things would never be the same.

Silk caught up with Lando and Quick after beeping them for hours. He told them to meet him at his barber shop so that he could talk to them before they made a bad situation worse. Knowing the love the two younger dudes had for Mann, Silk could only imagine what they could be doing out of anger. As he thought about Mann's death, he became very upset at the fact that the two dudes that Mann knew and had helped out in the past killed him. The good dudes in the game always got crossed by someone they knew. Silk was hurt, but he knew that Pamila would need his help to pull things together, and he was going to give it to her by all means.

Silk was in the back of the barber shop watching the news. Mann's murder was still the top story of the day. Silk shook his head in disgust, the media always found a way to paint a bad picture. Mann was now being portrayed as an ex-drug dealer that found a way to clean his money and open up a local record label called Fast Lane Records. Pissed off, Silk turned the T.V. off and turned around to see Lando and Quick dressed in all black coming through the front door.

Lando sat down on the sofa in Silk's back office telling him how he and Quick had roamed the streets looking for Smoke all night. Lando and Quick had checked every place they knew that Smoke could possibly be and had come up with nothing at the time. Looking at Lando and Quick, Silk told them that they were not using their heads by grabbing their pistols and looking for Smoke with no plan of where to find him or how they would get away with what they were going to do when they did find him.

"Y'all been around too long to go down out of anger," Silk said. "Y'all both know how Mann would deal with some shit like this. He gon' think, so y'all gotta think, too." Silk told them both that Smoke was going to get what he had coming and they would be the ones to give it to him, but for the time being, they needed to be there for Pamila and Kelley. Lando shook his head. He knew Silk was right and he was going to make sure he didn't cause Pamila any more stress.

For the next few days everyone mourned the death of one of the realest niggas the D.C. streets had ever seen. His presence would be missed far and wide without a doubt, and it would be awhile before things could get back to normal.

Lando had a lot on his mind. He wanted to say fuck everything and take his anger out on Smoke's family, but he knew Mann wouldn't approve of his actions. Black encouraged Lando to kill Serge's baby mother until he and Quick could catch Smoke. Quick was with the plan, but Lando let them both know that he was against it. Sitting next to Black in the visiting hall, Dre told Lando and Quick to check all through N.E. where Smoke and Serge had grew up. Lando decided that was the best course of action.

While those that had true love for Mann were preparing for his wake, Lando, Quick, Short Dogg, and Lil' Garvin were outside of an apartment on Maryland Avenue, just a few blocks from Black's mother's house. They had got word that Smoke was laying low over his cousin's apartment, who was Serge's bigger brother. Sliding on ski masks and checking their pistols, the four young killers jumped out of Lil' Garvin's old van and crept around to the back of the apartment with nothing but pay back on their mind.

In the safety of the nightfall, they got inside the back door of the apartment building unseen. Standing right outside of the apartment, they could hear people inside laughing and joking. Lando looked back at Quick, who had ran across the information of Smoke's whereabouts and asked him if he was sure that Smoke was inside.

With his pistol in hand, Quick said, "I been layin' on this nigga all day. I know he in here." With no further talking, Lando backed away from the door and told Lil' Garvin to kick it open since he was the biggest out of the four.

Lando was the first through the door firing his .45 automatic. Serge's older brother was standing in the middle of the living room with a drink in his hand. Lando hit him five quick times right in the head and stepped over his body as he chased Smoke into the back room with Short Dogg. Quick and Lil' Garvin opened fire on two dudes that were on the sofa smoking weed. With nowhere to run, the two dudes took slug after slug while Lil' Garvin and Quick unloaded.

Smoke ran into the bedroom and tried to get the window open with no success. Realizing that death was in town, Smoke turned around and tried to beg for his life.

"Please!" Smoke begged. "I didn't want anything to do with that shit." Balling up in the corner with his hands over his head, Smoke pleaded for his soon to be killers to understand him. Short Dogg slowly walked over to Smoke pointing his Mac-11 at him. Lando walked up behind Short Dogg and pulled out a straight razor.

Placing his .45 to Smoke's head, Lando said, "I should just get this shit over with, but it would be too quick." After slicing Smoke's throat, Lando watched for a few seconds before Lil' Garvin and Quick came in the room in a rush to hit the road.

"We ain't got no time for this shit," Quick said as he walked up and shot Smoke twice in the head. "Let's go!" Quick said as he led everyone swiftly back to the van.

An hour later, Lando walked into the funeral home on Kennedy Street followed by Short Dogg, Quick, and Lil' Garvin. Still dressed in all black jeans and sweat hoods, they leaned against the back wall and looked up front at all of the people that came to pay their respects to Mann. With visions of what had just took place still in his mind, Lando still felt incomplete. Watching people walk by him crying, Lando wondered if anyone felt the loss that he felt. Biting into his bottom lip and shaking his head out of anger, Lando looked down at the floor thinking of what was next. There was no one else to kill, nothing else to do about Mann's murder. All he could do now was deal with his brother's death and go on with life.

Caught up in his mixed feelings of hurt and anger, Lando felt someone tap him on his shoulder. Turning around with a look that could kill on his face, Lando saw Baby-D standing in the door way. Without saying a word, Lando hugged his man, patting him on the back. "Yeah, slim, niggas done killed my nigga," Lando said as he held back tears. Baby-D looked around and saw Lil' Garvin, Short Dogg, and Quick all leaning against the wall dressed in black. Being from the streets, Baby-D could tell that they all had been on the hunt for Mann's killer. Baby-D pulled Lando to the side and asked him what had happened.

Standing outside of the funeral home, Lando told Baby-D how Smoke and Serge had tried to rob Mann, and ended up killing him. Baby-D couldn't believe that they would try something like that.

"What Black got to say 'bout this shit?" Baby-D asked as he tried to come to an understanding about the whole situation.

"Black fucked up," Lando said as he looked up and down Kennedy Street. "Black wants me to kill them niggas mothers and some more shit, but I can't get down like that. Both of them niggas dead now. Leave it at that. No matter what I do, I can't bring Mann back." Baby-D felt Lando's pain. He had loved Mann like a brother as well, but he did agree with Lando about life going on.

Back inside, Lando sat down beside Nakia, who was holding his baby in her arms. Lando looked down at his son and began rubbing his little head.

"This what the future about," Lando said. He knew that he had to live for his son. Listening to Lando, Nakia was glad to hear him talk in such a way. She thought that Lando was going to go crazy about Mann's death, but he was taking it better than she thought he would.

Pamila spent less than five minutes at Mann's wake. She couldn't stand seeing him lying in a casket. His twenty years of life went so fast and just when he was starting to make something out of his life, it was snatched away. Pamila opened up an old box of pictures as she sat on the bed remembering all the good times and bad times that Mann had brought into her life. Pulling out an old picture of her deceased younger sister and Mann when he was first born, Pamila began to cry again. People took life for granted far too often, they didn't enjoy the times they were blessed with enough, Pamila thought as she looked through more pictures.

Lando walked into Pamila's room and saw her looking at an old picture of him and Mann coming back from the go-cart track.

Lando sat down beside Pamila, putting his arm around her shoulders, and said with a smile, "I remember that day. That's when Mann got his car."

Pamila looked over at Lando and cracked a slight smile, saying, "Y'all grew up overnight. I can still remember when y'all were babies." Pamila began to think about how hard her sister's death had hit everyone just over ten years ago.

She came across a picture of her sister and handed it to Lando, saying, "Do you remember how things were when your mother passed?" Lando looked down at the picture and began to think of the short time he was allowed to enjoy with his mother before death came her way.

Looking back up at Pamila, Lando said, "Yeah, I remember how things were back then. The whole family seemed to pull together." Pamila shook her head in agreement and began to tell Lando how they were going to do the same exact thing this time with Mann's death.

Hugging Lando, Pamila said, "I need you to work with me, though. You are going to have to do the right thing. You and Tyesha are all I really have left. I have to hold on to you both as long as the Lord allows me to." Lando felt Pamila's words deep in his heart and without even speaking a word, he gave her a look that said he would do all in his power to make things better in the up coming days that would follow Mann's funeral.

Quick knocked on Pamila's open bedroom door and asked if he could come in.

Pamila looked over smiling, and said, "You're family, you can always come in." Quick walked over and sat down on the floor in front of Pamila and Lando, and began looking at the old pictures. Pamila told Quick how everyone was going to have to work together to recover from Mann's death.

Quick looked up at her, and said, "I'ma team player, you know I'm down for whatever."

Pamila had truly grown to love Quick as a son. She leaned over and hugged him, saying, "Everything is going to be alright." They all shared one of their first moments of laughter since Mann's murder.

Kelley was lying in the bed with Tyesha, explaining to her where people went when they died. Kelley told Tyesha that Mann was in a better place now because he didn't have to worry about anybody doing anything to hurt him again.

Speaking from her young heart, Tyesha said, "If Mann is in a better place, why is everybody so upset?" Kelley looked at the young child in amazement. She had just asked her a question that put everything into perspective. Mann was in a better place. He really didn't have to worry about some broke niggas trying to rob him, he didn't have to worry about the police, or any other things that he had faced as he journeyed through the fast lane.

AFTERMATH

"Daddy! Daddy!" Lando's son said as he came into Lando's bedroom to wake him up so that they could get ready to go to the beach with Kelley and her daughter, Marcella, who looked just like Mann. Lando sat up on the bed and looked down at his son that was starting to act more like he used to everyday now. At five years old, Eyone thought he was the man of the house, and Lando allowed him to feel just that way.

"Where your mother at, shorty?" Lando asked Eyone as he stood up to get himself together. Nakia walked into the bedroom just as Lando asked about her.

"Kelley just called," Nakia said as she pulled a Mann's World T-Shirt over Eyone's head. "Pamila told her to tell you that everybody is waiting for us." Lando looked at Nakia and his son, and smiled. A lot had changed in the past five years since Mann passed away and Lando could feel it everyday he woke up, but instead of it bringing him down it made him feel good to know that he had picked up where his big brother had left off, and he was now the one that kept everything together.

"Is everything packed?" Lando asked as he walked to the bathroom. Nakia told him that everything was ready and waiting on him.

Ready for the trip to the beach, Lando walked down the hallway of the huge house that he had bought to raise his son and future children in. Walking by a huge picture of Mann that hung on the wall over the steps that led to the living room, Lando stopped to reflect on all that he had to be thankful for.

At twenty one years old, Lando was where Mann would have wanted him to be and doing what Mann would have wanted him to be doing. He was CEO of Fast Lane Records and had used everything he could get his hands on or hands in to make Fast Lane a name that would be around for years to come. Lando changed no rules, only followed the path that Mann had already laid down and success fell right into his hands as he learned the game as it came to him.

PASSION stayed true to Fast Lane Records and went on to sell millions of records in the five years that passed. Chocolate always paid close attention to every move Mann made when it came to the record label and thanks to her, Lando's job was easy when Pamila turned all of Mann's assets over to him two years after Mann's death. Now working on their third album and still attacking every song like their first, Chocolate, Cherry, and Caramel still gave all their credit to Mann. Chocolate had learned a lot from Mann. She used all she learned to open up hair salons all around the D.C. metropolitan area. Chocolate named her hair salons 'Styles of Passion' and it was a huge success. Cherry also became very business-minded and opened up a publishing company called Passion's Publishing. Caramel fell deep in love with Baby-D and had his baby, Louis Jr., two years after Mann died. PASSION was family.

The Youngins stuck with the rap game as well, even though it took them two albums to attract enough attention to sell a million records. Nevertheless, they had sold a million with their second album and made sure that Fast Lane Records had a heavy hitting rap group on the label as well.

Short Dogg became a sought after producer in the music business once the world found out who was behind the tracks that gave Fast Lane Records its one and only sound. Growing to love the success that was coming with the music, Short Dogg began to sell tracks for Fast Lane Records as he helped make Fast Lane everything it was growing to be.

Quick came a long way after Mann's death under Pamila's motherly direction and love. He owned a Mann's World store down the street from Silk's barbershop. He had a little boy by Amber and named the baby after Mann.

Baby-D was well established in the boxing world and was ranked number two on the WBC's top thirty welter-weight boxing list. He literally fought his way out of the streets and the fast lane. Baby-D, Caramel, and their son wanted for nothing. They lived in a huge house right outside of D.C. in Silver Spring, Maryland.

Silk left the drug game alone right after Mann died and opened several night clubs all over the metropolitan area. He stayed close to Lando and the rest of the youngins he watched grow up and they all still respected him and saw him as a wise big brother. He paid his respect to Mann by buying Pamila a house and paying for a lawyer to help get all of Mann's financial assets in order. He also paid the rest of Kelley's way through college after she had Marcella. Silk was real as it got.

Walking down the steps, Lando smiled as he thought about how things were going. Everybody that came along for the ride started out right in the hood, right on the same block. The dope game was over for Lando, Quick, Short Dogg, and Baby-D. Mann would be proud. Even so, Lando knew all too well that with the good came the bad.

Dre came home after being found not guilty of murder on the case that he had with Black. Once back in the streets without Mann by his side, Dre jumped back in the dope game and was moving bricks of coke in no time. As Lando started pulling out of the dope game along with Quick, Dre began to lock down everything that they once had. Lil' Garvin didn't see any sense in going along for the Fast Lane ride if he wasn't rapping, so he stayed in the dope game and hooked up with Dre. Two years after Dre hit the streets, the DEA raided five major drug areas and arrested thirty seven people who they accused of being in a drug ring. Dre was the so-called kingpin on the indictment of fifty seven counts of racketeering and gun running. Lil' Garvin was the so-called enforcer of the drug ring and was charged with murders as far back as 1989 when he was only thirteen. As the case grew bigger and bigger, making freedom look unreal for the many co-defendants that hardly knew each other, and Dre began to second guess his morals and principles. Sure enough, the government came at him with a deal for him to give up his drug connect and to point the finger at Lil' Garvin, and Dre broke. He got off with two years, leaving Lil' Garvin no option but to take a plea to ten years in prison along with many of their other co-defendants.

Lando never forgave Dre for becoming a rat and the only thing that stopped him from killing him was the fact that he had moved down south somewhere with Tina and his son. Out of all people to turn hot, Lando would have never guessed it to be Dre. After all, he was the same nigga that had stood strong on two murder charges with Black and had never cracked at all, but those were the ones that would get you every time. Grabbing the keys to his car, Lando wondered how Dre could give up all that he had ever been in life to be a witness for the government. Sure, things got hard sometimes in life, but that was never a reason to turn on your niggas. Black was a perfect example of standing strong through it all.

Black was doing fifteen to life in Lorton's Maximum Security Prison for killing Officer Hall. Mia and her law professor had attacked Black's case from every angle and made the judge and jury understand that he never intended to kill a police officer. Their whole case was that Black was under the impression that Officer Hall and the vice cops were stick up boys, and that Black began to shoot at the unmarked car trying to protect himself. By law, the judge had to drop the felony down to a second degree murder because it was no way to prove that Black planned to kill Hall nor did he know he was shooting at a police officer. In the end, Black still had light at the end of the tunnel, he had been locked up for five years and he only had six more years to do before he saw the parole board. Besides that, Lando was still paying his trial lawyer to handle his appeal, which was now in appeals court. If all went well, Black would get his case overturned and he would then fight to get his second degree murder turned into a manslaughter, which would get him back into the streets three years sooner. Black began to study Islam and became Muslim. Islam slowed him down and changed his outlook on life. Mia was so amazed at the change that she began to read the Holy Qur'an. Black came a long way as well.

Pamila had peace. She married Tyesha's father, Jimmy, and raised Tyesha well away from the streets. Pamila made sure Kelley, Lando, and Quick also kept their kids away from the streets. She never changed her lifestyle no matter how much money Lando and Quick made, she still worked hard five days a week.

Kelley graduated from Howard University with a degree in Psychology, but preferred to accept the position of vice president of Fast Lane Records. She lived with Pamila for three years after Mann died, but began seeing a dude she met at Howard. After slowly coming out of her shell, she opened up to the dude. Pamila encouraged Kelley to move on with her life, and she did just that after a long talk with Pamila. Kelley and Marcella moved in with Kelley's new boyfriend.

Dee-Dee and Naomi were also well off due to Mann. They ran the original Mann's World store. Lando let them run it as they pleased and it was damn near their store. Dee-Dee went back to school and got a degree in business management, which helped her run Mann's World better. Naomi got over Lando after awhile and fell for a dude across town named Antoine.

Jazmin also followed her dreams and went away to New York and later graduated from Parson's School of Design with a Bachelor's of Fine Arts. Mann also made a difference in her life.

"Come on, let's get outta here before Pamila call back," Nakia said as she and Eyone walked out of the kitchen with their bags. Lando looked down at Eyone and smiled. His son was holding Nakia's hand leading her to the door. At only five years old, Lando could see that Eyone wanted to be in control.

"You ready?" Nakia asked Lando as she opened the front door, letting the bright summer sun into the living room

"Yeah, let's go," Lando said as he rubbed his son on the head. Just as they were about to walk out of the door, the phone

Page
363

rang. Nakia gave Lando a look like don't answer it. Lando laughed and told her to go ahead to the car.

"I'm right behind you," Lando said as he picked the phone up, and watched Nakia and Eyone walk down the front steps to the driveway.

"Hello?" Lando said into the phone.

"Lando, is you comin' or what?" Kelley asked.

"Yeah, I'm on my way out the door right now. Where is Quick?" Lando asked.

Kelley told him that Quick was out front with Pamila putting her stuff into his truck.

"Everybody waitin' on y'all so hurry up!" Kelley said as she hung up the phone. Lando laughed as he hung up the phone and began walking out the door. Life in the fast lane wasn't always as smooth as it was now, but like Mann used to always tell Lando, life was what you made it.

About The Author

Eyone Williams was born and raised in Washington, D.C. He is a publisher (Fast Lane Entertainment), author, rapper and actor representing urban life in a way that is uniquely his. Known for hardcore, gritty novels, Eyone made the Don Diva best-seller list with his first novel, Fast Lane (Fast Lane Publications). He followed up his debut novel with Hell Razor Honeys 1 and 2 (Cartel Publications). He then delivered his readers a short story entitled The Cross (DC Bookdiva Publications). He's also a staff writer for Don Diva Magazine , his most notable work is featured in Don Diva's issue 30, *The Good, The Bad, and The Ugly*, where he outlined the rise and fall of D.C. street legends Michael "Fray" Salters and Wayne Perry. Eyone's first acting role was in the forthcoming movie *Dark City* (District Hustle). His latest mixtape, *A Killer'z Ambition*, is a sound track to the novel, A Killer'z Ambition (DC Bookdiva Publications) by Nathan Welch. His forthcoming novel Lorton Legends is soon to be released by DC Bookdiva Publications.

For more information about Eyone Williams visit his Facebook page: facebook.com/eyone.williams

Coming Soon!

Available Now On E-Readers!

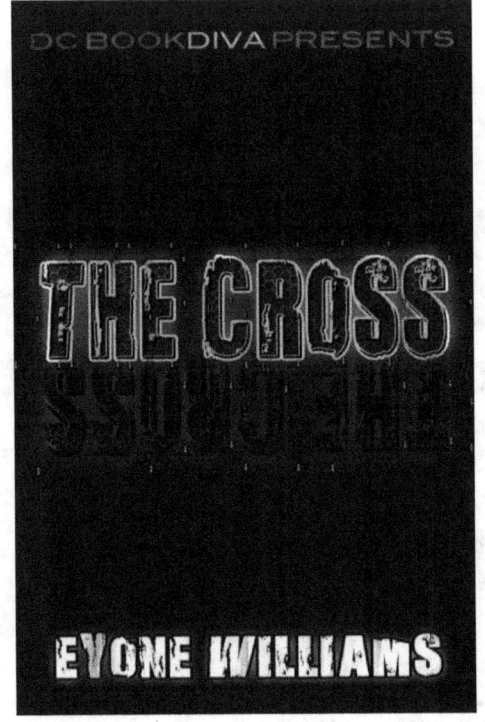

Fast Lane Entertainment
#245 4401-A Connecticut Avenue, NW
Washington, DC 20008

Name: _____

Inmate ID _____

Address: _____

City/State: _____ Zip: _____

QUANTITY	TITLES	PRICE	TOTAL
	Fast Lane	15.00	
	Hell Razor Honeys (The Cartel Publications)	15.00	
	Hell Razor Honeys 2 (The Cartel Publications)	15.00	
	COMING SOON!		
	Lorton Legends (DCBookdiva Publications)	15.00	
	Secrets Never Die (DC Bookdiva Publications)	15.00	
	Never Lay Down	15.00	
	Money Ain't Everything	15.00	

Sub Total $_____

Shipping/Handling (Via US Media Mail) $3.95 1-2 books, $7.95 1-3 books, 4 or more books-Free Shipping

Shipping $_____
Total Enclosed $_____

FORMS OF ACCEPTED PAYMENTS:
Certified or government issued checks and money orders, all mail in orders take 5-7 Business days to be delivered. Incarcerated readers receive 25% discount. Please pay $11.25 per book and apply the same shipping terms as stated above.